HOWLING STARS

Decker's War — Book 4

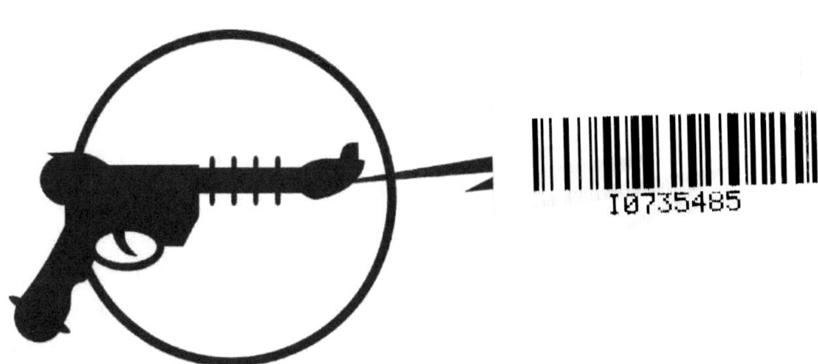

ERIC THOMSON

Sanddiver
Books

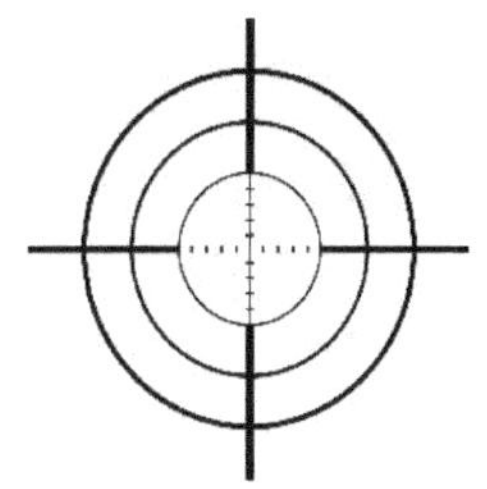

—ONE—

A fist like granite slammed into Decker's side with such force that he gasped in pain, wondering whether the thug had managed to crack his ribs. Another fist narrowly missed his head when he ducked, more by accident than design, thanks to the flare of agony spreading across his chest.

He dropped into a crouch and lashed out with his right leg, hoping to topple the hulking gangster. Larger than Decker, and much uglier with a bare scalp, beetling brows, and garish body art, the thug belonged to that interstellar group of smugglers, tax evaders, and starship aficionados known as the Confederacy of the Howling Stars. Nicknamed 'Star Wolves' by their admirers, Zack preferred to call them 'Howlers' or 'Jackals.'

A big man himself, with a height of almost two meters and carrying well over a hundred kilos, most of it muscle, Zack looked just as disreputable as his opponent did. He even sported a trickle of blood by the corner of his mouth, where an earlier punch had taken him unaware, although his body art, as well as his facial appearance, were temporary, courtesy of the Black Gang's disguise specialist.

His leg connected with the thug's knee, sending him off on a sideways stagger. But before Zack could follow up with a roundhouse kick to put him out of the fight permanently, another fist, this one not quite as dense, rearranged his left kidney. The second Jackal had come out of his Decker-induced stupor and rejoined the fight.

Zack turned to face this new threat, fingers folded over at the first joint, turning his hands into hard-edged tools of destruction, and aimed for the man's throat. He blocked the Marine's thrust with ease and lashed out with a jab at his solar plexus. Zack felt a brief twinge of relief as he managed to evade the strike, for it would have knocked him out of the fight, but he almost lost his balance again, saved only by dropping back into a crouch.

He lunged forward, grabbed the man's right ankle, and pulled, sending him tumbling ass over teakettle, right into his partner. Decker gained just enough breathing room to straighten and fall back into fighting stance, eyes going from one Jackal to the other, waiting for the signs that would tell him how they intended to bring him down.

Unlike some, Decker didn't make the mistake of thinking the Confederacy of the Howling Stars hired brainless brawn. They hadn't grown from a few disaffected veterans at the end of the last Shrehari war into the largest quasi-criminal organization on the Commonwealth Rim without a lot of sharp dealing, good planning, and an incredible ability to skirt the edges of the law.

The smaller of the two, who was almost Zack's size, shuffled to the left, while thug-mountain stepped to the right in an attempt to recreate the Battle of Cannae in a two-man version, but between them, they didn't have Hannibal's talent, nor did Decker have Gaius Varro's fecklessness.

With a sudden burst of strength, he charged at the smaller Jackal, but instead of unleashing a flurry of punches, he grabbed the man by his lapels, swung him around, and turned him into a shield, just as his bigger companion struck with all the might he could muster. A sickening crack filled the momentary silence, and the Jackal in Decker's arms turned into a limp rag, his spine severed. If the Confederacy didn't have access to advanced regen therapy, they'd be short an enforcer before the end of the day.

Major Zack Decker, Marine Pathfinder turned intelligence operative and his partner, Commander Hera Talyn, weren't supposed to inflict casualties during this mission, and the Jackals tried not to kill anyone unless it became an absolute necessity. They didn't want to give the law any reason to start ripping their operations apart. But when brawlers like the two who took exception to Zack met up with something they hadn't reckoned on, caution vanished like a fart in an ion storm.

He threw his temporary shield at thug-mountain and dodged to the left. His right hand snapped up and connected with the side of the man's head, slamming his skull into the sharp corner of a waste pumping module. Bone crunched, and the Jackal went down like a sack of jelly, leaving a smear of blood behind. When Zack reached down and pressed his fingers on the man's carotid artery, he couldn't feel a pulse.

Decker didn't care much about the death of a man who had likely maimed and killed his way through a successful career as a Confederacy enforcer, but it would be a lot harder now to keep the Jackals guessing. And if they became suspicious enough to wonder about outside intervention, their on-and-off patron and frequent employer, the *Sécurité Spéciale*, would become doubly so.

Naval Intelligence, and in particular the Special Operations Section, affectionately known as the Black Gang, didn't need to give the SecGen's civilian security service any additional reasons to spy on the uniformed branches of the Commonwealth government. The low-level guerrilla war between them had already cost too many lives, including those of people close to Decker.

The Marine took a few moments to catch his breath. He could feel every blow the two Jackals had dealt him, and they *hurt*. Confederacy enforcers were no choirboys, and they knew how to fight, but this pair seemed to have given him a heck of a beating. Thankfully, Decker had learned a few dirty tricks of his own during a long career mostly spent in special operations.

After a quarter century in and out of the Corps, fighting on planets scattered across the galaxy's Orion Arm, he had become good at the job of killing, be it fellow human beings or members of any number of alien species.

With a groan, he heaved up the larger man's corpse by the shoulders and dragged it behind some rusting, greasy machinery. He looked around for a way into the environmental recycling vats, where the body wouldn't be found until the next maintenance shutdown which, judging by the state of the Chisger Mining Corporation's Horus facility, could be years from now.

With none immediately identifiable, he settled for tucking him behind a pile of old parts still waiting for disposal long after they had been replaced. He wouldn't start to smell for a while, not in a place short on bacteria such as this artificial environment perched on the surface of an airless moon.

The other thug, however, presented Decker with a dilemma. Though severely injured, he still lived and could be treated. Zack had no qualms about killing a sentient being in the heat of battle, but cold-blooded murder clashed with his moral code, one of the many things that set him apart from most of the Black Gang.

Soft footsteps broke the silence, and he dragged the other man out of sight with as much gentleness as he could muster, then he ducked behind a block of machinery and pulled out his Shrehari-manufactured blaster. The original, taken as a trophy during a raid many years earlier, had long since vanished into the hands of pirates, never to be seen again. However, with time, this one had also become a natural extension of his right arm.

A woman with shoulder-length dark hair emerged from the gloom. Like Decker, she wore nondescript spacer clothing, but the blaster in her hand came from a human gunsmith.

She passed through a pool of light, and he saw a tired face, lined with age and worry. This wasn't one of Hera Talyn's more flattering disguises, but another worn-out middle-aged woman wouldn't seem out of place in a mining facility on the edge of nowhere. He stood and waved her over.

"Is everything good?" He asked when she came close enough for a soft whisper.

"All is good on my end." Then, she saw the thug with the severed spinal cord. "But obviously not on yours."

"No. Two Confederacy goons showed up without warning and decided they didn't like my looks." He jerked a thumb over his shoulder. "The big one is behind the pile of junk over there, dead. This one here is still alive, but he'll need a regen tank soon."

Talyn shook her head.

"I leave you alone for what, half an hour? And you start a new body trail." She sounded more amused than disgusted. "This was supposed to be a quick in-and-out mission. Now the Jackals might guess that someone with malicious intent came here and they'll start searching to find what we might have done. We can't have that, now can we?"

She knelt down beside the man and reached out to grasp his head in her hands. Then, with a quick motion, she snapped his neck, killing him.

"No witnesses. Have you found the environmental sludge vats yet? I'd rather we kept their bosses wondering. If nothing else, it'll give us more time to escape."

"I didn't see any way to access them."

"Let me take a look." She stood up and scanned the area, then indicated a catwalk near some large, circular constructs. "There, I think."

After a few minutes of heaving, followed by the bone cracking strain of prying open a hatch that hadn't been used in years, both bodies vanished without a trace.

Decker wiped a sheen of sweat from his forehead.

"Why do I always have to do the grunt work?"

"Because you're a grunt," she replied with a playful punch on his arm. "And because I still outrank you. Besides, those two were definitely out of my size range."

"And I'm not?" He leered at her.

"Later, big boy. Let's leave this dungeon and make our way off Horus, preferably before someone misses your two buddies and decides to call a lock-down."

Decker grimaced.

"The next shuttle to Kepri isn't for another ten hours, which gives the Jackals plenty of time to decide that Thug One and Thug Two are overdue."

"You should have thought of that before inviting them to play, honey."

"If I recall correctly, you told me to make sure your escape route remained clear. I did. It's a little late to regret not being more explicit with the rules of engagement." He shrugged. "Why don't we see if they have a hot-sheet pod available for a few hours? It'll keep us out of sight, and you can use the time to explain why the Jackals were too big for you, but I'm not."

*

The Nugget, a typical miner's bar which also rented sleeping pods, took up a fair chunk of the facility's second highest level, below the one where management schemed to keep the operation profitable through means fair or foul. And like the mine, it operated non-stop, and at a volume, both in noise and drinks served, that would have classed it among the highest performers on a typical colony. However, on Horus, one of the gas giant Amun's airless moons, it had no competition. That meant the industrial decoration, combined with some of the worst reconstituted food Decker had ever eaten, and high-priced, low-quality booze, didn't put a dent in the profits.

Vast and dark, it struck Zack as being a place where one could get lost for a few days, surviving on leftovers. Naturally, the Confederacy of the Howling Stars owned a controlling interest in the Horus Nugget and used its own enforcers to keep the peace, all with the tacit support of Chisger Mining's in-house security.

The Corporation didn't much care about what went on in the bar, as long as it received a share of the profits. It did care about the proper functioning of the ore extraction operations and happily employed the Jackals as unacknowledged auxiliaries.

Which, of course, meant that the only place on Horus where transients like Decker and Talyn could stay for a few hours without looking out of place would be heavily seeded with Thug One and Thug Two's friends. They rented a pod, because a man and a woman spending ten hours together in the bar, sipping drinks that seemed to last forever, would eventually attract the kind of attention they didn't need, especially as newcomers to the isolated mine.

Knowing that management had rigged all of the pods for sound and video because their primary use involved the bar's more specialized entertainers, they took turns napping, fully clothed, instead of scratching the itch that usually followed high adrenaline action. That would have to wait until they were on a ship headed back towards the more civilized parts of the Rim, from where they could make their way home again.

When they returned to the bar for a last meal before the flight off Horus, Decker nudged his companion.

"Is it me, or do I sense tension in the air?"

"Paranoid, are we?" She let her eyes roam over the patrons and the many enforcers recognizable by their watchful eyes and colorful body art. "You might be on to something, Zack. The Jackals seem edgier than before our nap."

"Which could mean a lot of things that probably have nothing to do us."

They bellied up to a dispenser and waited their turn.

"True," she said, still eying the Jackals sprinkled around the room. None seemed to take a greater notice of the pair than they did of anyone else.

They took their trays to an unoccupied table near the main door and sat, backs to the wall. Decker took a sip of his ale and made a face.

"I'm surprised the folks here don't revolt over this swill."

"A deep space miner's pay is so good, they'll put up with a lot of crap." She took a bite of her sandwich, eyes never resting on a single spot for more than a second or two. "Spend enough time in a place like Horus and you can afford to take several years off before the money runs out. Besides, they can have the good stuff shipped in on a personal consignment."

"I suppose." He ate in silence, then drained his bulb and belched softly. "There. Now I can last until we're on Kepri, where the catering's bound to be better."

"You hope." She finished her own food and was about to stand when something caught her attention. "I hate to say this, but your paranoia might have been right again. Three o'clock, near the main bar."

Decker glanced in the indicated direction without moving his head.

"I make three goons, one of them presumably female."

"Yep. They're going from table to table, checking faces."

"And the presumed female has a pad in her hand with a mugshot or two on it. Like I said, it could be unrelated."

"But why take chances. Let's pretend as if we're heading out for a stroll in the soft Amun light. We have an hour or so to kill before departure." Talyn stood in a fluid movement and headed for the nearby door.

Decker winced as he rose, the bruised parts of his anatomy still screaming outrage at their treatment by Thugs One and Two, and followed in her wake, glad to leave the Nugget's harsh sounds and rank odors behind. He resisted the urge to look behind him just before they walked around the corner, feeling a twinge of relief that they hadn't heard any shouted orders to stop.

Taking on a pair of Jackals in the bowels of the machinery compartment would seem like a short round of fisticuffs if they had to evade the whole pack up here.

They merged with the foot traffic, Decker slouching to reduce his apparent bulk until they peeled off the main passageway and headed down a less crowded corridor leading to the shuttle pad. The few people they met came from the recently landed shuttle and ignored the agents, preferring to stare at the anonymity of blank walls and scarred floor. Horus was that kind of place.

A Chisger Mining Corporation cop stepped out of an alcove and blocked their way.

"Leaving us so soon?"

"What's it to you?" Decker asked. "We did what we had to do, and now, we're getting out of your hair."

"Strangers passing through the Alpha Cephei system are interesting," the man replied. "Especially since visitors come in two flavors around here. Either you had business with the Corporation, or with the Confederacy."

"So?" Talyn shrugged. "We're leaving on the next shuttle. I'd say it's a little late for a customs and immigration interview."

"I know you didn't come to talk with management. They usually let us know about visitors." His hand hovered near the open hip holster holding a short-barreled scattergun.

"Again, what's it to you, since we're leaving?"

"Maybe the Confederacy would like a word with you."

"Not interested," Decker growled. He took a quick glance up and down the corridor, then gave the rent-a-cop the evil eye. "And you shouldn't be either if you want to enjoy the nightly entertainment at the Nugget once the shuttle has lifted off."

"Are you threatening me?" His hand grasped the scattergun's hilt, but he didn't quite draw it.

Decker fished a handful of cred chips from his trouser pocket.

"More like offering to bribe you so we can have some fond memories of Horus." He held out a stack thick enough to look a lot like the officer's monthly pay.

"You want to give me a bribe now? And why shouldn't I run you in for trying to corrupt a lawman?"

"Because we both know you're a greedy sonofabitch, not a lawman. Now you can take this and forget you saw us or..."

"Or what?"

"Ever tried doing EVA work without a pressure suit?" Decker asked in a conversational tone. His left hand reached down and seized the man's right wrist, preventing him from drawing the scattergun.

The security officer swallowed hard at the pain of Zack's vise-like grip. He shook his head.

"I can forget."

"Good man."

Decker released his wrist, then drew the gun and flipped it around to remove the power pack and ammunition case. He pocketed both and stuck the now harmless weapon back into the holster. Then, with a flourish, he tucked the cred chips in the guard's tunic pocket and patted him on the shoulder.

"Have a nice pitcher of swill on me, and try to forget you ever saw us."

Watching the security officer scurry away, Talyn chuckled. "For a moment, I thought we'd have to look for the nearest maintenance hatch, but well done."

"I do try to leave as few bodies as I can in our wake, sweetheart. I'm not a fucking sociopath."

"But you do like fucking sociopaths." Her innocent smile drew the expected bark of laughter, and she blew him a kiss.

"Not now. First, we get to Kepri, then aboard a ship out of this system."

Not long after, as they walked down the gangway tube to the spaceship sitting in the middle of the pad, they heard loud voices somewhere on the station side of the airlock, but the pressure hatch slammed shut and cut off the commotion before they could make out any words.

It was an even bet whether the Jackals had finally figured out they were connected to the disappearance of Thugs One and Two, or whether the Chisger Mining security officer had decided the bribe didn't quite salve his wounded dignity.

The gangway snaked back into its housing moments after Talyn and Decker had taken their seats and strapped in. This left the pilot free to lift off and escape Horus until the next scheduled flight, which he did with as little concern for his passengers' comfort as for his fuel consumption.

Decker leaned over and stared through the porthole at the rapidly dwindling mining operation perched on the edge of a dark canyon and grunted.

"If I never see that place again, it won't be too soon."

Talyn smiled at her partner.

"That's what you say every time we leave a place where they didn't have enough good booze and too many goons who couldn't find their ass with both hands."

"Well pardon me for having standards." He gave her a mock-wounded look. "In this outfit, one of us has to."

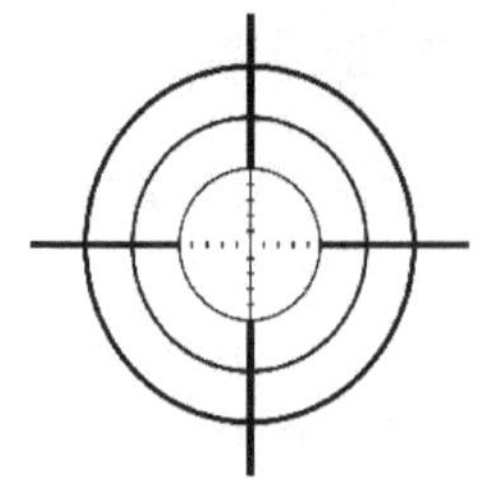

— TWO —

"Welcome home, Major Decker. I see that you're none the worse for wear."

Zack could hear a smirk in Commander Yang's tone, but the man's face remained as sphinxlike as ever. If Yang hadn't been Captain Ulrich's number two, the Marine would have found creative ways to express his opinion of the Special Operations Section's chief of staff.

"I haven't yet found the critter who could wear me down, sir." Decker tossed his beret on the desk he shared with agents currently out on their own missions. "Although I've found a commanding officer who tries really hard."

He winked at Yang and had the satisfaction of seeing a brief spark of disapproval in the latter's dark eyes.

"Speaking of which, where is Commander Talyn?"

"Search me." Decker shrugged. "We went our separate ways after landing. I assume she took a suite in the transient officers' quarters like I did, but I didn't see her in the mess hall this morning."

"I have a few questions concerning your after-action report, and it would be best to have both of you present."

"She's a big girl, Commander. She'll eventually show up. It's not like we have set working hours in this outfit."

He touched the screen sitting in the center of the desk and called up what he knew would be an extensive backlog of mail and other mundane messages deemed vital to the operations of a headquarters.

Decker could feel Yang's icy stare drilling through the back of his head. They held each other in mutual dislike. Yang believed Decker to be a dangerously loose cannon, an amateur in a business of stone-cold professionals, and Decker thought Yang represented everything he loathed about officers, notwithstanding the fact that he had been made one himself over Yang's strenuous objections if office gossip held even a smidgen of truth.

"Anything I can do for you, Commander?" He asked without turning around. "I can try to conjure up Hera, but she'll just get mad and take it out on you."

"That would be Commander Talyn to you, Major, at least within the confines of this headquarters."

Decker raised a mental rigid digit salute, but his partner's arrival stopped him from giving Yang a reply both of them might regret.

"Looking spiffy, Zack." She beamed at him. "The new rank insignia suit you. Is your arm sore from returning salutes yet, or are you still basking in the glow of being one of those rare majors with a bigger fruit salad and more qualification badges than the average HQ general?"

"Would you like me to salute you?" He growled, waggling his middle finger.

"No need. I've had enough of that from you lately." She finally deigned to notice Yang. "Hi, Manny. Is the boss still riding you hard and putting you away wet?"

"Nice of you to join us, Hera, and you know I prefer that people use Manfred, not Manny." Yang had repeatedly warned Captain Ulrich that Decker was rubbing off on his partner, and not in a good way. He used to get along just fine with Talyn before she decided to make the Marine her rescue project. However, since she started working with Decker, their relationship had deteriorated. "As I told Major Decker, I have some questions concerning your after-action report that I'd like answered before you meet with the captain."

"Did you find any multisyllabic words needing an explanation?" She managed to look perfectly innocent, but Decker saw the devilish gleam in her eyes.

Yang sighed. "I really must find a way to separate you two."

"Why?" Decker asked. "We're one of the most successful teams in the entire Black Gang."

"And yet we still have no definitive answer concerning the Coalition's involvement in the Garonne uprising."

"And yet," Decker parroted, "we no longer have a Garonne uprising. Give it some time, *sir*, the Coalition's reach will exceed its grasp soon enough and give us another way in."

"Be a good boy, Zack," Talyn chided.

"This *is* me being nice." He winked at her. "Shall we answer the commander's questions before I dig myself a hole so deep that I'll end my career reaming out sludge vats?"

"Or," he turned to look at Yang, "you could have me returned to a proper Marine Regiment."

"For some reason," the man replied, "Captain Ulrich seems inordinately fond of you, so that will not be an option in the near future."

"No accounting for taste, I suppose." Talyn sat on the corner of Zack's desk and blew him a kiss, something she knew would irk Yang.

"Taste has nothing to do with it," a voice boomed from the open door. "If you two are quite finished being unkind to my chief of staff, I'd like to hear you tell the tale. Perhaps you'll be able to fill in the blank spots Manfred found in your report."

The three officers stood and snapped to attention in unison.

"Aye, aye, sir."

"By the way, Zack, your mail stack contains a coded message that's been driving the analysts insane," Ulrich said while he ushered them into his office. "I'd like to hear about that as well once you've had a chance to read it."

He waved them towards a round table occupying one side of his office.

"You'll be glad to know," Ulrich continued, "that as a result of your work, the Horus operation is down, if not permanently, then for months or, more likely, years. They had time to evacuate everyone, but the facility itself is no longer usable, its systems destroyed. The other six mines around Amun fell within days of each other, and as of right now, Kepri is the only outpost still in operation, though its production has dwindled down to almost nothing."

"Chisger Mining Corporation's stock value dropped by seventy-five percent since the news filtered back from Alpha Cephei," Yang added, "and even the Honorable Commonwealth Trading Corporation, which owns a controlling interest in Chisger, took a fifteen percent hit. All of that will put a serious dent into profits, especially those not reported before they're diverted into numbered accounts."

"In other words," the head of the Fleet's black ops organization sat back with a gleam of satisfaction in his eyes, "another success. Well done. Since our analysts are of the opinion that the Amun mining constellation generated a lot of the Coalition's covert funding along the Rim before your sabotage, this will hurt them deeply. It may even force the leadership to overplay its hand. When that happens..."

"Then, the game of whack-a-mole continues, sir," Zack replied. "There are more of them than there are of us and they have better connections. Some days I wonder whether this is a game we can win."

"If we don't win," Ulrich replied, "then we'll have the unique chance of watching our democracy, deeply flawed as it is, morph inexorably into an empire run by the worst possible people. I'd rather that didn't happen on my watch."

"No arguments here." Decker held up both hands, palms outward.

"Perhaps you two need some leave. You've been going on mission after mission with a few days or at most a week's break between them for how long now?"

Talyn shrugged. "I can't say that I remember, sir."

"That settles it. Manfred, I believe you don't have anything urgent lined up for them."

"Well..." The chief of staff looked uneasy. "A few loose ends need tying up. Commander Talyn and Major Decker are the only ones available right now."

"Can these loose ends wait for a few weeks?"

"I suppose." He pressed his lips together, the only expression of disapproval he allowed himself in front of others.

"Then it's settled. You have the rest of the day to catch up on your personal administration, and then I want you on leave." He caught Zack's eyes. "Don't forget to let us know about that coded message you received. But first, let's go through Manfred's questions, so we can wrap up the Horus mission. Considering the results, I'd say manually planting a destructive virus directly in the core of a target's computer system is a tactic we might want to reuse."

"It certainly worked this time," Talyn replied. "But once the opposition figures out how we sabotaged them, the next time will be a lot harder. I only managed to penetrate the Horus computer core thanks to lazy security and poor maintenance, and because no one had considered the possibility."

She glanced at Yang. "Let's get your questions out of the way, Manfred."

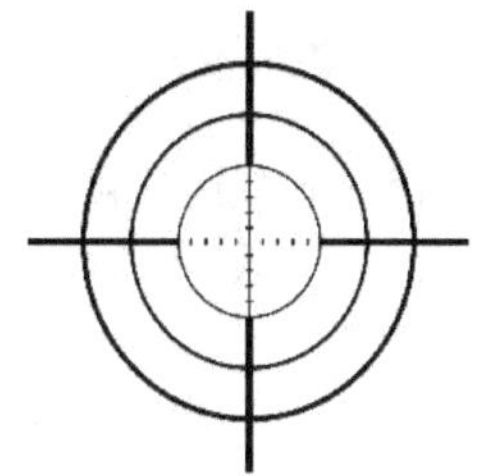

— THREE —

"Coded message?" Talyn asked once they had returned to the bullpen where agents temporarily on HQ assignments labored under Yang's gimlet eye.

He shrugged. "No idea, though it's nice of them to read my mail before I do."

"Standard procedure, Zack. I thought we went over the fact that you have no private life once you join the Black Gang."

"Hey," he put on a mock-angry expression, "I didn't volunteer for this, remember? You shanghaied me."

"And it earned you a major's billet."

"I was perfectly happy as a chief warrant officer. Heck, I was happy as a command sergeant."

"Sure." She winked at him. "But the day you come across one Captain Sarratt, late of the 9th Marines, and watch the sheer horror in his eyes when he's forced to salute *Major* Decker, you'll bless the day I took you on as my special rescue project."

Zack smiled beatifically. "I feel shivers just thinking about it. Perhaps I should dig into the system and figure out his current duty station. With any luck, it'll be in the basement of the main HQ complex, amending regulations. I could take a stroll across the road for an unannounced security inspection."

His air of joyful anticipation made her laugh.

"Let it happen naturally, Zack. It'll feel so much better."

"You heard the captain," Yang interjected. "Wrap things up and then scoot. The sooner you're out of my hair, and on some beach, the sooner I get your well-rested asses back here for the next round of Coalition hunting."

"Out of your hair?" Decker fought to suppress a sudden onset of the giggles. Yang, of course, had a scalp as smooth and shiny as a cue ball, without even the hint of a working follicle in sight.

Talyn smacked him on the arm. "Behave. I promised the boss you'd gained enough maturity to pass for a field grade officer. Don't turn me into a liar."

"You lie for a living, sweetheart."

"Never to the man who controls my destiny." She jerked a thumb over her shoulder at the now closed door to Ulrich's office. "Do as you're told. Even though the Corps finally saw the sense in giving you a commission, you're still the most junior officer in this room."

He stuck his tongue out at her.

"And the least mature," she added, amused by the disgusted expression on Yang's face.

"Fuck," Decker said after a few moments spent scanning his mail stack. The heartfelt emotion behind the curse drew Talyn's attention from her own perusal of accumulated mail and useless directives.

"What?"

"That coded message the boss kept referring to is from Hal Tarra, my old troop sergeant in the 902nd and one of the best friends I've ever had." He stared at his screen. "It's three damn months old."

"So Hal Tarra is a crypto genius?"

Zack snorted. "He's good at a lot of things, but coding? Never. This is a case of sclerotic analyst brains seeing something that isn't there. The message is in plain Anglic and in simple words any noncom, sober or otherwise, can understand."

"Let me guess," Talyn said, "any noncom provided he's called Decker, sober or otherwise."

"Well, yeah. Hal can pack a lot of meaning in a couple of words, but you have to know how he thinks to appreciate the full flavor."

"And what did your pal Hal say?"

Then she saw something in his eyes that gave her pause. "Are you all right, Zack?"

"Not particularly," he replied, the corners of his mouth drooping. "In fact, not at all," he added, feeling a sudden surge of anguish twist his guts. It must have shown on his face.

"Honey, you're scaring me. What's going on with my usually happy and frequently irreverent partner?" She jumped up and walked around his desk to stand behind him.

"She is alive," Talyn read. "A three-word message? You're going to have to lay this out for me."

A long, heartfelt sigh escaped the big Marine's lips.

"*She* can be only one woman, Elyce Sakal. Doctor Sakal, the one we couldn't rescue, Hal and me. We actually witnessed her abduction before she vanished somewhere beyond the Rim and couldn't do anything to stop it."

"Oh." Talyn laid a gentle hand on his shoulder. "I always thought the old saw that each Marine had a story like that was so much bull, but you really do have one of those."

"Yeah. Hal, me, and the rest of Third Troop, 902nd Pathfinder Squadron. And the crew of *Ruddigore*, the Q-ship we were assigned to, I suppose." He shrugged. "For the squids, it was just one more distress call that came in too late. Not for us. Hal took it especially hard for some reason. Truth be told, so did I. We weren't used to the idea of standing there helplessly while watching reivers kidnap civilians. Usually, when we arrive somewhere too late, we haven't had time to establish a personal relationship with any of the victims. That time, we spent hours speaking with Doctor Sakal offering what advice we could, while those damned mongrels pounded away at the research station's defenses. But no amount of praying would get us there any faster. The laws of physics didn't care. When we finally landed on Troy, that was the name of the airless hunk of rock where they'd built the station, we found nothing more than a lot of dead bodies, looted supply rooms, missing scientific equipment and three people unaccounted for. Doctor Sakal, whom we saw taken by the reivers, a Doctor Antoine Mazkow and a Sister Anca."

"*Sister* Anca? What would a monastic be doing on a research station?"

"I have no idea, and we had nothing to indicate which order she belonged to." Zack's grim expression matched his mood. "*Ruddigore* tracked the two reiver ships and we initiated pursuit while reporting back via subspace radio. After the first jump, we received a message from HQ. Abort, return to Troy and erase all traces of the research station, and then wipe all references to the incident from the ship's log. It never happened."

After a moment of silence, Yang asked, "Should you be discussing this, Major Decker? It sounds to me like your story is something that's been classified beyond top secret special access and buried in archives that won't be reopened before the heat death of the universe."

"No, and yes, Commander." Zack didn't sound contrite. "On the other hand, Hera asked, and I answered. If I can't trust either of you with this piece of my past, then life really has no meaning. Just take care to erase your organic memory banks before going home tonight."

Talyn returned to her console and touched the screen.

"Nothing about a Troy Research Station in the classified data banks," she said after almost a minute. "What system?"

"31 Aquilae. It has no habitable planets, nothing worth mining, nothing at all, really. The place is one of the Commonwealth's most useless possessions."

"Which makes it perfect for a secret facility. Did you say it was Fleet?"

"I didn't, but yeah, I guess the Navy owned the place, which means the order to erase it came from the rightful proprietor."

"Nothing," she said after a moment. "The database has all of the standard astrographic information and navigation data, but doesn't list any military installations, not even a refueling stop, even though 31 Aquilae has three gas giants.”

“As I said, we were ordered to forget that the incident ever happened and that Troy station ever existed. It wasn’t the first bit of sanitizing I’ve witnessed, but doing so when HQ knew reivers had taken at least one, if not three survivors really stank. So you’ll understand that we were damn mad. And it stuck with us.” Decker took a deep, calming breath, proof of his inner turmoil. “I can still see Doctor Sakal’s face the moment a pair of the scum seized her and dragged her out of the station’s commo room. Heck, I still have nightmares about the incident. If I never see that kind of fear and despair ever again, it won’t be too soon.”

“And now your buddy Hal Tarra thinks that Doctor Sakal is still alive. Are you certain that’s what he meant?”

“There’s only one ‘she’ that he and I will remember until our dying day. Yeah, I’m sure. Hal hasn’t been in touch since I left the 902nd, so for him to reach out to me now is pretty significant.” He paused, and then shook his head. “Not exactly right now, I guess. That message came in shortly after we left on our last mission, so it’s almost three months old.”

“If I have the right Hal Tarra,” Yang said, “the records show him retiring from the Marine Corps just about three months ago. He left no forwarding address.”

“What?” Decker sat up straight and turned to face the chief of staff. “Hal’s a lifer.”

“There’s more,” Yang continued. “I can’t find any record of a Sister Anca...”

“If she belonged to the Sisterhood of the Void, that wouldn’t be surprising. They’re notorious for avoiding the authorities,” Zack interjected.

“But Doctor Elyce Sakal is listed as having died in an accident while vacationing on Marengo six years ago, while Antoine Mazkow vanished at around the same time, steps ahead of an arrest for fraud. He’s presumed to have fled the Commonwealth to avoid facing up to his crimes.”

"Very convenient." Decker's words bathed in sarcasm. "It's a fine thing they can't erase what actually happened from my memory, or from Hal's. I wouldn't be surprised if they listed every single person killed on Troy as having left this life in a manner that can't be traced back to the raid. Unfortunately, those three names are the only ones that stuck in my memory, so we'll never know. Without a record of Troy in Fleet files, there won't be a trace of them anywhere."

"It's the way of these things, Major." Yang didn't quite sound sententious, but Zack had to suppress a surge of irritation nonetheless.

"You don't have to live with the memories, Commander."

"True."

"That's all nice and well, Zack." Hera gave her partner a sad half smile. "But I don't see where this is supposed to lead. Your buddy thinks Elyce Sakal is alive, turns in his uniform, and goes traipsing across the vast galaxy."

"Isn't it obvious?" He asked.

Uh-oh, Talyn thought, recognizing the mulish glint his eyes. "Not to me, no."

"We need to find Hal and figure out what's going on. If Doctor Sakal can be rescued, even after all this time, we have to try."

"I don't see where *we* have to do anything." She shook her head. "Command shut the file on Troy, Sakal, and the rest six years ago. It's not about to open a discussion of the incident without a direct order from the Grand Admiral herself, and short of the CNI taking up the matter, we're pretty much done."

"Then let's ask Captain Ulrich to speak with the CNI. He has coffee with him at least once a week."

Without waiting for a reply, he stood and, before either Yang or Talyn could stop him, knocked at Ulrich's door.

"Come."

Decker stepped across the threshold and came to attention.

"You wanted to know about that message in my stack, sir."

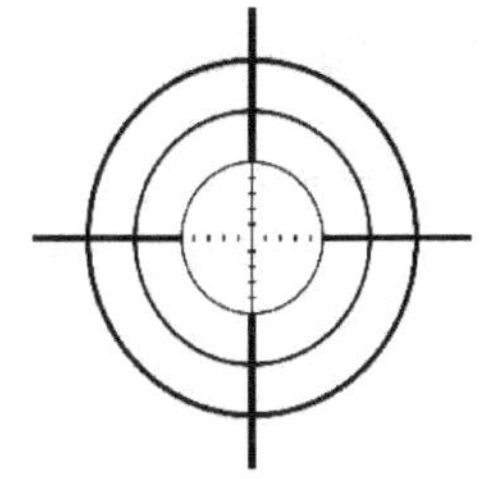

— FOUR —

"Interesting as your story might be," Ulrich said once Zack finished speaking, "I don't see how it concerns this section or even Naval Intelligence for that matter. The Troy Research Station never officially existed."

When he saw the Marine stare at him, one eye half-closed, the other radiating anger, Ulrich raised a placating hand.

"I do understand, Zack. We've all had missions that went sour and wish we could go back to fix things. But your friend Hal Tarra is no longer the Fleet's concern. If he's decided to go off on a quest because he believes Doctor Sakal might still be alive after all this time, that's his concern and his alone."

"So the cover-up continues," Decker growled. "What about the risk of Hal falling into unfriendly hands once he goes beyond the Rim and into the Protectorate badlands? He spent most of his career as a Pathfinder and has a lot of classified stuff locked up in his head."

Ulrich shrugged. "How much can a retired command sergeant know that affects Commonwealth security to the point where it becomes our problem? Not much if anything, I dare say. Pathfinders are tactical creatures, and the bad guys already know all about our tactics."

"So we let Hal risk his life to fix a mistake the Fleet made years ago, with no support, no backup, nothing," Decker paused just long to make it noticeable, before adding, *"Sir?"*

"We don't even know that he has something more concrete than a notion. You said the mission affected Tarra deeply. Why couldn't he have gone off the deep end? He'd hardly be the first special ops trooper to lose perspective after too much carnage."

"I've seen as much as him, if not more, and yet here I am, as sane as you or Commander Yang."

"And not Commander Talyn?" Ulrich asked with the hint of a smile.

"She wasn't sane when I met her, and it's been all downhill since then."

"Hey!" Hera smacked his upper arm with the back of her hand. "Show some respect."

"Sir, my point is that I think Hal Tarra's onto something and if it involves the survivor of a research facility so secret we were ordered to sterilize the site after the raid, then it should concern us."

"Sorry, Major." Ulrich shook his head. "It's not in our bailiwick. The best I can do is pass this along to the analysis section and let them surf the data streams to see if there's actually a threat somewhere along the line. I don't intend to bring this up with the CNI so he can petition the Grand Admiral to reopen the Troy file. Few missions tossed down the memory hole have ever resurfaced."

Decker sighed. Though a soft sound, it conveyed enough sentiment to alarm Talyn.

"Zack," she said, "tell me you're not about to do something all of us are going to regret."

"Me?" His face took on an injured expression. "Never. If that's your final word, sir, then I'll sign off and take those months of leave I'm owed after running my ass ragged for the Commonwealth over the last few years."

"By all means, Major. Try to enjoy yourself."

"Oh I will, sir, I will." He drew himself to his full height and saluted with the crisp, but almost mocking precision only a senior Marine noncom can carry off when he wants to convey his utter disappointment with a superior's decision. Then, without waiting for a word of dismissal, he marched out of Ulrich's office and through the special operations section's bullpen before vanishing into the hallway.

"He's about to go rogue on us," Talyn warned. "Marines have a thing about leaving someone behind. In this case, I'm convinced Zack sees two people left behind, Elyce Sakal and Hal Tarra."

"He's about to go on leave," Ulrich replied, straight-faced. "While he's on leave, we have no say over his actions, so long as they remain lawful and don't injure the Service."

"Hah!" Talyn's sharp bark of laughter overflowed with skepticism. "The man has a burr in his boot, and he's determined to do something about it, lawful or not."

"If that's the case, I hope he's prepared to face the consequences of his actions."

"Knowing Zack, consequences are the least of his worries, sir." A grimace of dismay twisted her lips. "My partner's far from dumb, but he's the most headstrong man I've ever met."

"I understand it's a requirement for members of the Marine Corps, Hera, but for the last time, Sakal and Tarra are none of our concern, nor is anything Zack does while on leave."

When he saw the glint in her eyes, he shook his head.

"No. As of right now, I'm dissolving your team. We can do without Zack for a few months. I'll need you back in fourteen days at most."

"That's hardly fair, sir."

Ulrich laughed with delight.

"My dear Hera, we've known each other for how long? Twenty years? And you still don't understand the word fair isn't part of my vocabulary? Major Zachary Thomas Decker is no longer your concern, understood?"

She held his eyes for several seconds before acquiescing.

"Aye, aye, sir."

*

The next morning, Talyn stormed into Ulrich's office, her face a mask of fury under a barely discernible veneer of worry.

"He's gone?"

"Who is gone?" Ulrich's expression didn't change, but she suspected him guilty gently mocking her.

"Zack, of course. He's ignored my calls since he left your office and when I went to his quarters this morning, they told me he'd checked out yesterday. It appears that he placed his personal effects in storage and vanished after signing out of the headquarters precinct. There's no trail of him since late last afternoon."

"He is on leave and not subject our control, Commander. And since you're no longer his commanding officer, Major Decker's movements aren't your concern." Ulrich shrugged. "Besides, I wouldn't be surprised if he's already left Caledonia, if not the system quite yet. And no, you do not have permission for a side trip to the orbital station to find him. If he has gone off on a fool's errand, I'd rather not lose one of my star agents on top of losing my most unusual and entertaining operative."

"Just like that?" She asked with flared nostrils. "You're going to let Zack go? After everything he's done for the Black Gang?"

"For the last time, Commander, Major Decker is on furlough and expected to report back once his leave runs out. Until then, he is his own man. Now if there's nothing else, I believe I told you to take a breather for fourteen days, but do stay on the planet." He locked eyes with her. "That would be what we in the Navy call a direct order."

Talyn snapped to attention.

"Aye, aye, sir. Is the commander dismissed, sir?"

"The commander is." He waved towards the door. "And please don't pick up too many of Zack's bad habits, will you."

Still furious, she took one of the desks in the bullpen and ran a trace on Decker's last use of the computer. Not unexpectedly, he'd searched for Tarra's whereabouts over the last three months, finding a very short trail leading towards the Rim before it vanished. First Sakal, then six years later Hal Tarra, and now Zack Decker. She'd give a lot to know what kind of research this Elyce Sakal had been doing on an airless planetoid orbiting 31 Aquilae.

Later that day, with Talyn long gone, Yang finally had a chance to ask the question that had been burning on his lips since the previous morning.

"Was that really a good idea, sir?"

"We won't know until it's over, Manfred." Ulrich took a sip of his tea and stared at the star map on the far wall. "Unfortunately, I couldn't think of anything else in the spur of the moment. This was before your time, but I had some involvement in the matter back then and disagreed with the decision to call off *Ruddigore*'s pursuit and make the Troy Project vanish. If Sakal and her research are still out there somewhere, it could pose a danger to the Commonwealth."

"May I ask what that research was, sir?"

Ulrich shook his head. "Sorry, Manfred, but that particular detail isn't coming out of the memory hole on my watch."

"Understood." Yang took no offense. After a long career in intelligence, he was acutely aware of the need to know principle. "Are you going to clear Decker's unacknowledged mission with the Chief?"

"No. Or at least not until I have to."

"And if Decker gets into trouble?"

"In that case, he'll have to find his own way out. Remember that the man is as resourceful as he is stubborn."

"A polite way of putting it, sir."

Ulrich smiled. "There's no need to be rude or crude, even about people who get up your nose. Enjoy not having to worry about our loose cannon for a few weeks or months. In fact, I'm going to make it an order that we do not refer to Major Decker and his story in any form or fashion unless it becomes absolutely necessary. That being said, please put out feelers to track whatever cover identity he took from the custodian. It wouldn't do to let him operate entirely without some sort of oversight."

"And Hera?"

"We should take advantage of the fact that she'll be solo for a while. Give her a few days to decompress, and then read her in on the matter of the Shrehari trade delegation's visit to Aquilonia Station. She'll be ideal for that one, though I'm afraid we'll have to tackle it with more overt force than we're used to, and we'll need the intervention of our friends from the Constabulary's Professional Compliance Bureau."

Yang made a face. "She's going to love that."

"She's a pro. Whatever the mission requires, in this case compromising herself, Hera's up to it."

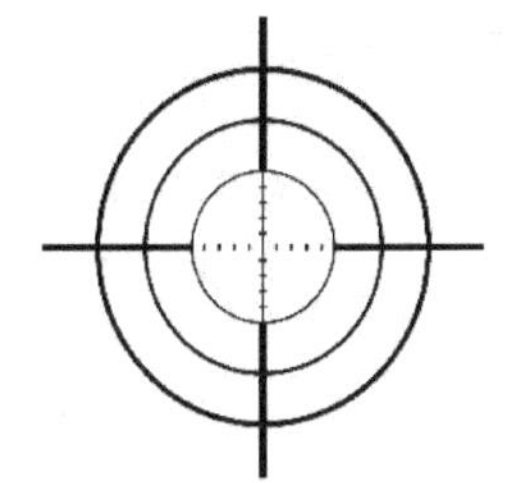

— FIVE —

Picking up Hal Tarra's trail didn't prove to be difficult for Decker. Like any good Pathfinder, Tarra knew how to arrange matters so the folks he trusted could reach out to him.

Zack hadn't told anyone about the second message he found on the Pathfinder community node, in the dark corners of the deep net, directing him to Kilia Station, where he and Talyn had spent a few hours not all that long ago.

He had checked the board shortly after leaving Ulrich's office, and there it sat, the next clue, written in a way only Zack and a few others could understand, addressed to someone whose name wasn't Decker, from someone whose mother didn't baptize Hal. Unfortunately, the indication that he had gone to Kilia dated from more than two months ago, a lifetime for someone planet hopping in pursuit of an elusive woman who vanished six years before.

After begging for a cover identity and the means to change his appearance from the section's custodian, on the pretext of an upcoming mission — wink, wink — he packed a light bag in which he could hide his blaster and ammo, along with his dagger. He then placed the rest of his belongings in the storage depot set aside for agents who spent most of their lives away on operations.

A few hours later, he sat on a shuttle headed for the orbital station and soon after it docked, he found himself at a terminal, looking for a berth on a starship headed towards the Rim. It would have to be something inexpensive where a rough-looking spacer might not seem out of place.

He knew there wouldn't be a direct connection to Kilia, a station built inside a hollowed-out asteroid. It lived in that gray zone between rogue colony and legitimate outpost. As long as it stayed sufficiently clean, the Navy didn't bother with more than the occasional patrol through the system, to remind everyone it still belonged to the Commonwealth.

He found a shared cabin on a mixed freighter headed for Marengo but grimaced at the price tag. This time, he didn't have access to the almost unlimited black fund and every single cred he spent came from his own savings. Yet, the ship would take him to the Rim sector well before any of the others, and he knew he could find something headed for Kilia at Valeux Station. He had seen enough sketchy operators docked there when he had passed through on a previous mission.

That thought, unbidden as it might have been, made him feel curiously empty and alone. Talyn had been his constant companion for long enough that her absence bothered him. It wasn't just the lack of someone to tease, talk to, or have fun with; it was not having someone he could trust at his side.

For a brief moment, a small voice emerged from his subconscious and asked him to reconsider this headlong rush to follow in Hal Tarra's footsteps. It was swiftly silenced by his resolve to have Hal's back, no matter what, and he paid for a berth on the ship in question, an old tramp by the name of *Giglio*.

It wasn't just because Hal was his oldest and best friend, a man who had fought at his side on more occasions than either of them cared to remember. He still recalled all too vividly the haunting image of marauders dragging Elyce Sakal away to suffer an unknown fate. The subsequent orders to erase her very existence had piled helpless rage on top of a sense of failure.

Though the incident still galled him whenever he thought about it, his work in the darkest corners of naval intelligence had made him appreciate that matters tossed down the memory hole sometimes came back unbidden and with disastrous consequences. That, as much as the chance to rescue Elyce Sakal and stay true to the Marine Corp's creed of 'no one left behind,' drove him now.

The station had no exit controls, leaving each shipper to ensure they didn't take aboard anyone they shouldn't, and he soon found himself facing *Giglio*'s middle-aged, plump purser after a short stroll down a gangway tube.

"Jack Lorenzo. I just booked myself a shared berth to Marengo."

He held out his ID chip.

The dark-haired woman took it and glanced down at her pad. When his particulars appeared on the screen, she gave the chip back and indicated the stairs to her right.

"Cabin ten, one deck down. Welcome aboard, Ser Lorenzo. I hope you enjoy the voyage."

He stepped past her and sniffed the air. Fresh, with no hint of overworked scrubbers or sludge vats past their empty before date. The passageway, though merely painted metal with conduits running along the ceiling, seemed clean enough to show him *Giglio*'s crew cared for the ship, or at least for its appearance to paying guests. Without a companion, he couldn't make his usual caustic comments about new surroundings and felt curiously unsatisfied.

Cabin ten's door opened at his touch, and he stepped into the kind of quarters he had expected. Bunk beds to one side, facilities behind a door to the other, a table, two chairs and not much else. The bed coverings, though worn, felt freshly washed to his touch. He tossed his pack on the lower bunk, figuring that any roommate would take one look at him and decide it would be preferable to sleep above and not beneath a hundred and ten kilos of hard muscle.

To his relief, *Giglio* undocked a few hours later without any befuddled latecomer stepping into his refuge to claim the top bunk. He spent the trip mostly in solitude, tearing through the ship's entertainment library, doing what physical exercise he could and missing Talyn's presence to a degree he hadn't expected. On more than one occasion, he caught himself having mental conversations with her, trying to explain why he had left so abruptly and why chasing down both Hal Tarra and Elyce Sakal was so important to him.

The Hera Talyn inhabiting his mind had never experienced the deep attachment that forms between Marines repeatedly sharing adversity and peril, and the sense of obligation that arose from it. Whether Hal had gone off on a futile quest or not didn't really matter. He had called for Zack's help to deal with unfinished business, and that's all there was to it.

You don't deny the man who had always stood by your side, whether it was in combat or when it came to dealing with the idiocies of the military bureaucracy. Hal had been one of his most vociferous defenders after the incident involving Captain Sarratt put an end to Decker's life as a Pathfinder, to the point where he was ready to risk his own career.

He found it harder to explain the rekindled obsession with Elyce Sakal, though the Hera in his imagination wondered whether he saw it at least in part as a way to get his own back on a Navy that had failed, in his eyes, to fulfill its obligations.

When they finally docked at Valeux Station, he took great joy in striding down the gangway tube and through the docking area to the customs and immigration barrier. Decker doubted he and Talyn had left enough of a trace during their last visit to Marengo that the local law would be looking more closely at middle-aged men of his stature.

After a cursory ID check, he found himself on the promenade deck, inhaling the aroma from a dozen restaurants. After selecting one where he could sit with his back against a wall, hidden in the shadows and with a perfect view of the passing parade, he enjoyed his first decent ale in a week.

Finding a ship bound for Kilia would be more complicated than walking up to a terminal and scanning the list of departing vessels. It would also take time, so he might as well settle in for a few days, until he could ferret out someone who might steer him in the right direction, such as a ship chandler, or someone living on the shadier side of the law.

Sadly, even the cheapest sleeping pod would chew up a fair chunk of his personal funds, as he found out later that day, when he tracked down the most anonymous transient hotel available.

It took him less than twenty-four hours to figure out none of the chandlery businesses were interested in steering an unknown visitor to a ship making the run into the wildest parts of the Rim, either out of choice or out of ignorance. So much for Talyn's notion that they could be informal intelligence hubs in these parts.

The evening of his second day on Valeux saw him in a booth by the back door of the most disreputable tavern on the promenade, which wasn't saying much, since Valeux's management enforced only minimum standards.

The clientele gave it that down-market feel and later on in the station's 'night' he began to see people with the distinct aura of membership in the largest unindicted organized crime group on the Rim.

He knew the Jackals had a steady hand in Kilia's affairs and likely controlled much of the shipping going in that direction, but from that to figuring out how he could approach one of them in the hopes of hitching a ride represented another order of difficulty.

They, more than any other group, personified some of his worst enemies, thanks to their sideline doing wet work on behalf of the *Sécurité Spéciale*, the SecGen's secret police and reputed action arm for the Coalition who had done so much to make his life a misery.

Decker studiously avoided looking at any of the men with the barely visible tattoos and yet, precisely that distinct lack of interest from a large, powerfully built man with the seedy look of a mercenary between jobs or a hired killer on the run, attracted their attention. One of them pulled up a chair and sat down across from Zack without so much as a by your leave.

"I've never seen you on Valeux before," he said, confirming the Marine's suspicions. A typical lowlife would have used something like 'here' or the name of the bar, but by using Valeux, the newcomer established that he had interests all over the station.

"I stepped off a ship yesterday," Decker replied, looking up to meet the man's eyes.

"Passing through? Or are you looking for work?"

"Mostly passing through, though I wouldn't say no to a short-term gig so I can replenish my stack of creds. This place ain't cheap."

"Orbital stations never are." The man stretched out his hand. "Gavin Bevaqua. I run a few of Valeux's business interests."

"Jack Lorenzo. I have no business interests at the moment." Though he'd rather grab Bevaqua by the throat and squeeze, Decker accepted the proffered handshake, unsurprised when he felt the grip harden, as if to test him.

The two men stared into each other's eyes as they sought to break bones, then Bevaqua relaxed, smiling.

"Pleasure, Jack Lorenzo. If you're passing through, mind me asking where to? Marengo's almost the ass end of the Commonwealth. Ain't much beyond this system other than places no human should visit."

Decker shrugged with disinterest. Playing the drifter came easily. He had been one for a time after the Corps tossed him out, in the days before he became Hera Talyn's rescue project and ended up doing Naval Intelligence's dirty work.

"I don't rightly know, to tell the truth. One planet is as good as the next. Maybe when I find somewhere that's has opportunities for a guy like me, I'll stop moving for a spell."

"And what's someone like you when he finds an opportunity? Muscle? Triggerman? Stevedore?"

The Marine let a slow, lazy grin spread across his craggy face. "I can be all of the above and then some if the pay's right and the chances of ending in a military prison are slim."

"You have something against stockades?"

"Only whatever anyone who's spent quality time on the inside has — a deep desire to never return." He sized Bevaqua up for a few seconds. "Have you ever been in one?"

"No." He laughed. "I've always avoided anything to do with uniforms."

"Probably smart. When you're being shot at, you figure out the pay's not worth the aggravation."

"What put you inside?"

"A stupid officer, what else?" Decker clenched a ham-sized fist until his knuckles turned white. "Damn near cost me and my buddies our lives. He didn't like me telling him about it, and I lost my cool. I did a quick stint in a disciplinary battalion to find it again, and now I have a lifetime on a crap pension to regret it."

Bevaqua smiled. "I figured you for ex-Fleet the moment I saw you walk in. Any combat experience?"

"Plenty. What's your interest?" Decker raised his glass and drained it, to hide the fact that he was more interested than he let on.

"Business and some of it can always use a man who's good with his hands. Tell me, Jack Lorenzo, if I query the Fleet's personnel archives, what would I find?"

Decker snorted. "Nothing. They don't talk to civilians."

"Humor me. Assume they decide I'm a nice guy looking to do a solid for a Fleet veteran down on his luck."

"You'll find what I told you, and a lot of other fun details besides, like how I did during boot camp, what I shot on my last annual qualification, that kind of crap."

And he would. The Lorenzo identity, like all those doled out by the special operations section custodian, had a complete and verifiable legend backing it up.

"But like I said," Decker continued, "they don't do reference checks. The Fleet gives us a copy of our service record to carry around for when we're looking for our next job, which I'm not, thanks just the same."

"Okay, Jack." Bevaqua stood. "You can't blame a guy for checking out the newcomers, right?"

"No harm no foul. I'll even buy you a drink for your trouble." He held up his glass and caught the human bartender's attention, then raised two fingers.

"Very kind of you." The man nodded with approval. But when the waiter delivered their beers, he took one and walked off to rejoin his friends by the bar.

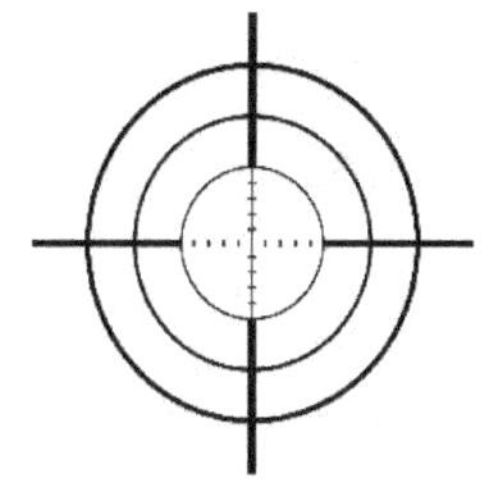

— SIX —

"What's his story?" A slim, hard-faced woman asked Gavin Bevaqua, pointing at Zack over her shoulder with an extended thumb.

"Ex-Fleet jailbird, he says. Moving around until he finds something to keep him amused." Bevaqua shrugged. "Claims he's not looking for a job."

"Too bad. Big, rough-looking guy like him could be fun." She pouted for a moment before continuing. "And useful."

"Down girl."

"Variety's the spice of life, Gavin, and I've pretty much run out of new playmates on Valeux."

"You want to try him on, be my guest. Just lay off the pillow talk, in case he's not actually taken his retirement papers, or still has scruples about violating his oath."

"The only thing he'll ever hear from Ros is gimme more," one of the men joked.

"How would you know, Piet?" She asked. "You can't even give a little without falling down on the job."

When the gales of laughter had died down, Ros asked, "You want me to try, Gavin? The bosses have asked us to keep an eye out for folks with military experience and no ties to hold them back. Big boy over there looks like he's right on the money."

"Fill your boots, Ros, and whatever else needs filling." Bevaqua grinned at her. "And if he's not biting after you've taken your all, let it go. Another prospect will drift through soon enough. Fresh meat for your appetites, so to speak.”

She gave him the rigid digit salute, then walked over to where Zack sat, staring into his glass.

“Like I told your buddy,” he said, without glancing up, “I’m not looking for a job.”

“And I’m not recruiting for work,” she purred. “Buy a lady a drink?”

This time, he lifted his head and met her eyes.

“Sure.” He raised his hand to signal the bartender. “Aren’t you going to ask me if I come here often?”

“A comedian! How delightful. Ros Skillen, by the way. Gavin tells me you’re a man who thinks he’s good with his hands.”

Decker smiled. “You have no idea, Ros Skillen. And it’s Jack Lorenzo, in case your buddy forgot to say.”

She gave him the once-over, a faint smile on her thin lips and Zack returned the favor. Short hair dyed red, brown eyes that didn’t open into her soul, olive skin toughened by radiation and hard living, and the edge of a tattoo peeking from her lavender shirt’s collar — a typical star lanes rat who lived for the day and had no cares about tomorrow. He could guess what she saw by the lascivious expression on her face.

“Are you an ex-Marine? There’s that look about you...”

“You’re obviously not,” he replied. “Otherwise, you’d know there’s no such thing as an ex-Marine.”

“Right. Once a Marine, always a Marine. But that still doesn’t answer my question.”

“Do I look like a squid or an army puke?”

The bartender dropped off two glasses, picking up Zack’s empty.

“You don’t want to hear what I think you look like to me.” She pushed an errant strand of hair behind her ear before picking up her glass. “Skoal, Jack Lorenzo, of no fixed address and a retirement certificate in his pocket.”

“Are you asking to see my retirement certificate or find out what else is in my pocket?” He asked after taking a healthy gulp.

“Buy me supper, and we can discuss it.”

"Discuss what?" Zack cocked an eyebrow at her

"Variety, also known as the spice of life."

"I had plenty of that during my time in the Corps, honey."

"But nothing like me, I'll bet."

"Plenty like you." He grinned. "Only I had to watch out. A lot of them tried to bite me if they weren't after something worse. Although you're prettier than most recruiting sergeants I've known, I suppose."

He jerked his chin at her neck. "Got more of that ink under the shirt?"

"Yep. And elsewhere. Like I said, buy me supper, and we can discuss it."

"Any place in particular?"

"Of course and it's not here. C'mon."

She stood and waited for him to drink up. He hadn't noticed at first, but Ros Skillen was a tall lady, taller than Hera. He swallowed the last of it and pushed himself to his feet, eyes darting towards the cluster by the bar.

Bevaqua and the other men were openly staring, and Ros blew them a kiss before slipping her arm into Zack's. Then she guided him towards the door and out onto the promenade, where they merged with the rest of the pedestrian traffic.

"Piet." Bevaqua nudged his right-hand man. "Go get the big guy's glass and take down the biometrics. Then get on the subspace net and do your magic with our friends. I have no doubt Ros will wrap Lorenzo around her finger, and I'd rather know if he's who he says before we send him along."

"On it, boss." Piet Noone drained his glass, and then ambled over to Decker's table while pulling a hand-held sensor from his pocket. Moments later, he had the fingerprints and DNA signature of one Jack Lorenzo, Commonwealth Marine Corps, retired on administrative grounds. Fifteen minutes after that, a query went out via a coded message that left the Marengo system on the back of the hourly subspace packet, boosted along its way by an automated relay buoy just beyond the outermost planet's orbit.

*

"So," Ros Skillen swirled the wine in her glass, smiling at Zack, "you ride the star lanes for kicks, with no goal in mind?"

"Pretty much." He took a sip of his ordinary Shrehari ale, ordinary in everything but the price, that is. "My pension, though small, still pays my way. If I need more, I'll pick up the odd job for a few days or weeks. There's a lot out there for a man to explore and only one lifetime in which to do it. I've already seen most of the colonies, so now my goal is to push out beyond the usual, maybe visit parts of the Rim and the badlands that I've never seen, or those I've only ever visited to do a bit of heavily armed ass-kicking."

"It's not easy finding ships that'll sail through the badlands."

"Tell me about it." Decker grimaced. "During my time in the Corps, I've seen top secret files more openly shared than non-standard shipping routes."

"It would probably be easier to find someone who's hiring rather than digging up a passenger berth."

"I might have mentioned this before, but I'm not looking for a job."

He finished his drink and signaled the waiter for a refill, cost be damned. If he seemed to be flush with money, the courtship might continue until it would appear as if he was signing on with reluctance, and not give them the idea he could be an eager infiltrator from the Fleet or the Constabulary.

The Confederacy had many faults, but they didn't include being stupid. And right now, taking them up on their recruiting effort looked like his best way to find a ship bound for Kilia, their headquarters in this part of the Rim.

"But," he continued, spearing another piece of vat steak, "I'll listen to any proposals that include a recruiting bonus."

"Recruiting bonus?" Skillen purred, a knowing smile revealing sharp white teeth. "How about a close look at my complete body art gallery?"

Decker cocked an eyebrow and smiled as he settled back in his chair. "Okay, I'll bite. Why are you guys so interested in me?"

"The people with whom I work are on the lookout for ex-military personnel. Folks who are good with their hands, with whatever guns those hands might be holding and who don't mind a good payday for work that could be skirting some government regulations. Not that the government says much about what happens along the Rim and beyond." She took a sip of her wine, eyes on Decker, trying to gauge his reaction. When she saw nothing other than the sardonic expression he had worn all evening, Skillen shrugged. "You've been asking around for transport into the badlands, you have the look of someone able to take on three longshoremen single-handed, and you have that military bad boy aura. That hits our target demographic pretty much dead center."

"Really?" The waiter swapped his empty glass for a full one, and Zack took a long sip to wash down the last of his meal. "So you're mainly looking for mercenary wannabes. I'm pretty much done with soldiering. It's a life of no strings attached adventure for this bad boy."

"We can offer as much adventure as you can handle." The seductive purr began to feel overdone, but he wasn't about to tell her. "As you found out, there aren't all that many ways to get into the badlands from here, but my colleagues enjoy frequent visits to some of the more exotic ports of call. And when it comes to strings, think of it along the lines of joining a club."

"Oh? What kind of club? Role-playing furry chess enthusiasts?"

"Ever heard of the Confederacy of the Howling Stars?"

"Sure. It's a social club for psychopaths, isn't it?"

"Something like that." Skillen seemed untouched by his choice of words. Quite the contrary. A predatory expression hardened her features. "We have a lot of fun in the Wolves, Jack. Real money when you need it, too."

"An ancient philosopher once said that he wouldn't join a club that would have him as a member. I'm pretty much of his opinion."

"There's still the recruiting bonus." She gave him a smoldering glance that promised something more raw and primitive than mere money.

"I can't quite reciprocate since I don't have any body art. Had some at one point but it didn't suit my mood."

"I'll bet you have quite a few stories etched into your skin, however," she countered. "A career Marine such as you with plenty of trigger time."

"We prefer to call it combat experience, honey. Trigger time is for low IQ, high testosterone cretins, and yeah, I have a few souvenirs. You interested in a tour?"

"I was going to ask whether it should be my place or yours," she replied, "then it occurred to me that you're probably bunking in a hotel pod and I like a bit more space to play."

"You know damn well that I've booked a pod, seeing as how you know I've been asking around for a berth. But I've had plenty of practice at playing in tight spots, so I don't particularly mind if it's my place."

She finished her wine, and then jerked her chin towards the door. "I have a tolerable single malt in my quarters. Shall we?"

"Sure." He raised his hand to signal the human waiter, but she reached over and laid long fingers on his forearm. "The meal's paid for, courtesy of the social club for psychopaths."

He barked a laugh, feeling pleased that he'd been wined and dined at the expense of people he loathed.

"Part of the recruitment drive, right? A deductible on the old tax return as a business expense?"

"Something of the sort."

When he stood, she slipped her arm back into his, led him out of the restaurant and away from the promenade.

For some reason, Decker felt like he was being taken into the lair of a praying mantis.

*

"Ros and Lorenzo have settled in for the night," Piet reported as he slid into a chair across from Gavin Bevaqua, "and I have an answer on our boy."

"Impressive turnaround."

"The price we're paying, it better be. But in this case, I was lucky with both the timing of the subspace message packet and our girl being at work." He pushed a data wafer across the table. "Jack Lorenzo, former sergeant first class, combat engineers, 11th Marines. He did a few months in a disciplinary battalion for decking his company commander in a combat zone. Less than honorable discharge, but since he had his twenty-five years in, he's drawing a pension. The biometrics we picked up match what's in his file at the other end."

"Combat engineers, eh?" Bevaqua rubbed his chin. "That could be useful."

"Career man tossed out on his ear like that, could be he's not that fond of his oath anymore either."

"Let's see if Ros gets him interested in anything more than her charms before we get excited, Piet. In the meantime, I'm going to turn in. Remember we have that meeting with the station's maintenance manager tomorrow, to discuss the new waste disposal contract."

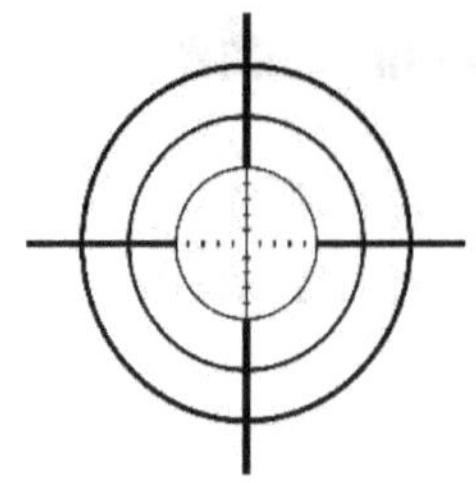

— SEVEN —

"You're quite the work of art." Zack ran his fingertips over Ros Skillen's bare skin, tracing the outline of a purplish vine crossing her chest.

"Some people are addicted to tats, honey," she murmured, gasping when he brushed her nipples, "me among them."

"Not my cup of tea, but on you, it works."

She tensed up with a sharp intake of breath. His hand had wandered below her navel, sending shivers up her spine.

"Why do I have the feeling you're the one enjoying a bonus," he said, nibbling on her ear lobe, "and not me?"

"Because I am." She smiled lazily at him, leaning over for a kiss.

Later, while exploring the network of scars covering his body, she said, "I didn't know Marines saw that much combat. You look like you've been put through a thresher."

"You must not have met many. I'm hardly alone in looking like a human version of a star map."

A soft laugh escaped her lips.

"You're right, we don't see too many veterans of the Corps come through here, at least not the kind who'd hang out at Wolves bar, and definitely no active service other than Marengo militia, and they're useless swine."

"Hence your interest."

"Honey, I'd have been interested even if we weren't looking for a few good men." She reached down to grab him. "I don't get to play like this every day. Now, less talking and more doing."

"Slave driver."

She laughed with delight. "You have no idea."

After that, conversation became impossible once more.

Decker couldn't tell how much time had elapsed when Skillen climbed out of bed and vanished into the bathroom. He had believed his partner, Hera Talyn, to be enthusiastic, but Ros beat her easily when it came to tiring him out.

Hopefully, he would be able to travel on one of the Confederacy's ships, or one controlled by them, and escape to Kilia Station before he turned into a mere shadow of his former self.

"What did you do in the Marines?" She asked to the sound of running water.

"Combat Engineer. I was a platoon sergeant before they turfed my ass."

"So you know about blowing things up."

"Among others, yeah. I'm a bit of an artist with explosives."

"Anything else?"

She reappeared, pausing in the doorway to stretch and give Zack another eyeful.

"The recruiting sergeant's back on duty, I see." He smirked. "If you want to read my service record, it's in my jacket's inner pocket."

"Later." She climbed back into bed and straddled him. "I already know you have a quick tongue and delicate motor control of your fingers."

"Good control is a job requirement for a sapper, sweetheart. You wouldn't want to set anything off before its time."

"Or set yourself off before I'm done."

"Cruel woman." He pulled her down and then took it like a proper Marine.

*

"Quite the recruiter you have there," Decker nodded towards Skillen.

A knowing smile tugged at Bevaqua's lips. "She puts her appetites to work for the cause." He took a sip of coffee. "We checked you out, Jack Lorenzo. Want to know what came back?"

"A big fat nothing?"

"Cute. If you want a job, we can really use someone with your background. We don't see Marine combat engineers coming through on a quest for adventure all that often."

"I keep saying I don't need a job, but Ros convinced me that visiting the more exotic places out there is better done as a member of the crew rather than as a passenger."

"She didn't lie. You know who we are, right?"

"The Sociopaths' Social Club. Sure. Your hungry she-wolf gave me a full song and dance number," a nasty smile appeared on his face, "along with a detailed inspection of her howling mad body art."

"You know who we are and joke about it?" Bevaqua's eyebrows shot up. "They have a word for that back where I come from."

"Chutzpah?"

"Insanity," the Confederacy boss replied. "People have been known to receive an attitude adjustment for less than that."

"Not quite the way you want to entice recruits into whatever scheme that has you hitting up unknown veterans." He drained his cup and carefully placed it on the table. "Besides, I'm the one usually adjusting attitudes. Ask that dumb ass captain who thought he could just crap all over me in front of the troops. They took his testimony for the court-martial from his hospital bedside."

"You seem to think pretty highly of yourself." The smile returned. "There's nothing wrong with that, as long as you can back it up."

"Try me." Decker shrugged. "Or not. But if it'll keep me from turning into a faint copy of myself through too much Ros, I'll listen to your pitch."

Bevaqua slapped the tabletop and said, "Good man."

"A hard man too," Skillen added, "one of those who's good to find."

"Friends of ours have put together an outfit made up of ex-military out beyond the Rim."

"And beyond the Adjudicating Authority's reach," Decker said, smiling with understanding. "Understood. What's the purpose?"

"I can't quite say, but the pay's good and the strings short, meaning once the job's done, you can be on your way, or stick around and work with us some more."

"What's the pay?"

Bevaqua quoted a figure that caused Zack to whistle.

"Generous. Are we expected to take on a Marine Regiment with our bare hands for that much cash?"

"Nothing quite so spectacular, Jack. They'll give you more details when you arrive at Kilia, and if you decide it's not your kind of gig, then fair enough."

"Just like that?"

"Yep. Your passage to Kilia will have been payment for showing interest. Walk away, and you owe nothing."

"What's the catch?"

"There isn't any." A mysterious smile suddenly appeared and then vanished just as quickly. "Let's just say that it's all part of the vetting process."

"So I'm a prospect now. You guys certainly move fast."

"Maybe not a prospect to become a full member of the Confederacy," Bevaqua shrugged. "At least not yet. But we're branching out into other lines of business where we'll need members who can bring in profits."

"I seem to keep repeating myself that I don't need a job." Decker's face took on a dismissive expression. "But I'll consider it in exchange for a ride to Kilia. If nothing else, it gets me off the dull commercial star lanes and into adventure territory."

He thrust his open hand at Bevaqua. "I believe we have ourselves a deal."

And just like that, he had found transport.

*

With little to do for the rest of the day, Decker wandered through those parts of the station open to ordinary civilians.

He had just dropped onto a bench facing one of the two plazas connected by the circular promenade when a nondescript, middle-aged man sat beside him.

"You should really be more careful about your choice of associates, Mister Lorenzo. Or is that Sergeant Lorenzo?" The man kept staring at the passing parade, seemingly uninterested in Zack's reaction.

"I prefer mister these days, and I don't take anyone's advice about who my friends should be, especially rude fucks who don't bother introducing themselves."

"Inspector Hallan, Constabulary." He sounded amused at Decker's use of expletives.

"Since when do the gray-legs have a branch office on an orbital station in the ass-end of the Rim?"

"Since that brief fracas surrounding the violent regime change on Garonne. The Commonwealth government decided it didn't want any more of those happening without warning. Or at all, for that matter."

"And they sent the plod. Typical." Decker sneered. "What'll you do when a rebel walks up and goes boo? Die of fright? Ask him to surrender nicely, or you'll quote the law until he gives up out of sheer boredom?"

Hallan shrugged. "I don't make policy, Mister Lorenzo. I just enforce the law."

"And you play busybody when there are no law-breakers to cuff, right?"

"I'm sure a veteran of the Corps like you knows who he's been hanging out with, so I have to wonder why. Marines aren't known for going over to the mob."

"You mean that innocent little social club for psychopaths, also known as the Confederacy of the

Howling Stars? They play pinochle and sip tea, with nary a mobbing in sight.”

“Laugh all you want, Mister Lorenzo, but you’re heading down a path that leads to nothing but tears if you join their pinochle games, to use your expression.”

“Thanks for your concern, Inspector.” Decker stood and looked down at Hallan, who kept sitting on the bench like a man without a care in the world. “But I don’t see what business it is of yours.”

The inspector raised his hands, palms facing outwards. “I’m merely looking out for a veteran, Mister Lorenzo. And curious as to why the Confederacy is interested in men like you.”

“Not a clue and none of my business.” Then, Hallan’s words sank in. “Are you saying I’m not the first they’ve befriended?”

“Oh, so you are interested in what I’m saying.” He smiled. “No, Mister Lorenzo, you’re not the first ex-military man to hear the full recruiting spiel from Gavin Bevaqua and his accomplices. I hope Ros Skillen was worth your while, by the way.”

“Aren’t you the pervert with a badge?”

“Intelligence gathering will have one peer into the darkest corners, where some sights can never be unseen, don’t you agree?” Hallan examined Zack with renewed interest, sensing that he had piqued the latter’s curiosity.

“I wouldn’t know about the Constabulary’s voyeuristic impulses, but if watching Skillen and me get it on helps you get it off, then I’ll consider it as my part in entertaining our beloved police force.”

“Cute. What if I tell you that they’ve pulled this recruiting stunt on almost a dozen vets over the last six months?” The policeman asked

“And you’ve had this very same conversation with each of them, I suppose?”

“Of course.”

“And like me, none of them took a bite of what you’re offering.”

“I haven’t offered you anything yet.”

"But you will, and I'll say no."

"Funny, Mister Lorenzo, but I could swear that I saw a spark of interest in your eyes when I mentioned other Armed Services veterans just now. Maybe a quid pro quo could satisfy that spark."

"Here's my quid, inspector — I'm off to Kilia Station in a day or two. That's all I can tell you because that's all I know. What happens on Kilia, I'll find out when I show up there. The Confederacy might be a bunch of gangsters to the plod, but that doesn't make them stupid. They're businesspeople."

"Sure." Hallan made a dismissive gesture. "I heard that from the others too, but if you're in mind to remember your oath to the Commonwealth, maybe we can find a way to talk after you have a better idea of what's going on. Heck, we might even be able to help if ever things go sour and you need an out."

Decker crossed his arms and peered down the bridge of his nose at the inspector.

"If you know my name and rank, you also figured out my serial number and disciplinary record. Do I look like someone who still gives a shit about his oath?"

"I guess not, but you can't blame a guy for trying." Hallan stood and pulled a tiny data wafer from his pocket. "If ever you change your mind, the contact information is on here."

When Zack made no move to accept the chip, he shrugged and tucked it away again. "In that case, I'll wish you a good day, Mister Lorenzo."

The Marine watched Hallan walk away until the crowd swallowed him.

"Making friends with the law?"

He turned to find Piet Noone staring at him, a suspicious frown creasing his forehead.

"The law tried to make friends with me. I told him my interest had kind of taken a hit during my stay in the disciplinary battalion." He raised an eyebrow. "You make it a habit of sneaking up on people?"

"When I see them having a cozy chat with the gray-legs, sure." He indicated a nearby staircase. "Gavin wants to see you."

"Now?"

"No, next week, genius," he sneered. "You ex-military pukes are so fucking literal, it makes me want to hurl. Come on."

Decker indulged in a brief fantasy involving Noone, his fists and a lot of sprayed blood. Noone's blood, of course. With a nod, he fell into step beside the Star Wolf and followed him off the promenade deck down to the cargo hangars.

"Get a lot of us coming through?"

"None of your business."

"I thought I might know some of them. The Fleet's a small family, compared to the rest of humanity."

"Is that what Hallan told you? That we sign up a lot of veterans who pass through Valeux?"

"He might have mentioned something like that." Decker paused. "The guy's interested in what's going on to the point where he tried to recruit me as a snitch."

"The Constabulary's a pain in the ass, but he doesn't have any jurisdiction here, so he can't reach out and nab someone. I can't see the local cops being all that keen on helping him, either."

"It sounded to me like he works the criminal intelligence angle."

Noone made a face. "Fancies himself a specialist on organizations like ours, but since we're not breaking any Commonwealth laws, let alone local ones..."

"Nothing that he can pin on you, at the very least."

"It'll take someone smarter than Inspector Hallan to do that, mark my words."

Though the Jackal sounded dismissive of Hallan, Decker couldn't help wonder whether the policeman's approach had been a test set up by Bevaqua. Hallan wouldn't be the first Constabulary officer to take a stroll on the wrong side of the law in return for a bribe or two.

They emerged in a wide corridor very different from the promenade two decks up. Here, cargo shifted from dock to dock. Some of it was outbound for the Commonwealth core or elsewhere along the Rim or inbound for transshipment to the surface. The decor reflected that practical nature, as did the scent of metal, lubricants, and sweat. They dodged automated pallets in silence for a few minutes until Noone stopped in front of a door leading, by all appearances, to just another loading bay.

"After you." He touched a pad in the frame, and it slid open with a tired sigh.

Zack stepped into what must have once been a storeroom but which now looked more like a clubhouse for overgrown delinquents. Bevaqua sat at a round table in the far corner, Zack's pack and its contents neatly lined up before him. Ros stood against a metal cabinet nearby, arms crossed. Two other men occupied chairs at a wooden bar, dominated by the image of a garishly lit wolf's head, its teeth bared as it howled at a supernova.

"I can't recall giving you permission to dig through my stuff," Zack said, taking a chair opposite from the local boss.

"You signed up with us, we take care of you. In this case, we moved you out of that pod hotel and down here. Otto thought there was something strange about your bag, so just in case the cops had tried something funny, I checked." Bevaqua held up his blaster and the black-hilted pathfinder dagger. "Nice. Well-hidden too. Did you forget to share some stuff about your time in the Corps?"

"Like how they taught me it's not polite to snoop?" Decker made a disgusted face. "Those are simply souvenirs that come in real handy sometimes. The blaster I took off a dead Shrehari marauder. He didn't have any use for it and I did."

"And the fancy super-trooper blade?"

A cruel smile split Decker's features. "I didn't take it off a dead Pathfinder if that's what you're asking. But it's been blooded. More than once."

"I thought you were a simple combat engineer."

"Who saved a pathfinder's life once upon a time. He gave me the toothpick as a way of saying thanks."

"Nice." Bevaqua put both weapons down. "You had a chat with our resident organized crime honcho?"

"Yep. He told me that he likes chatting up veterans who pass through Valeux on their way to fun times in bad spots. I guess he doesn't get many dates."

"He doesn't get any," Ros said. "Man's a regular monk. I never could understand that stupid celibacy thing myself."

"No doubt." Decker snorted.

Bevaqua indicated the personal effects littering the table.

"Go ahead and pack that away, Jack. Don't carry on the station. The cops will tolerate a lot, but no guns. They have enough problems down on the surface. The stuff that happened on Garonne scared government folks in the sector."

I'll bet, Decker thought. He wondered how Bevaqua would feel if he knew the catalyst for regime change on Garonne sat across from him.

"The gray-legs said a dozen or so vets came through here in the last few months and signed up with you. Could be I know some of them."

"Then you can look forward to tearful reunions once you get where you're going."

He stood. "You leave in two days. Try to avoid trouble."

"I can help with that." Skillen blew Zack a kiss.

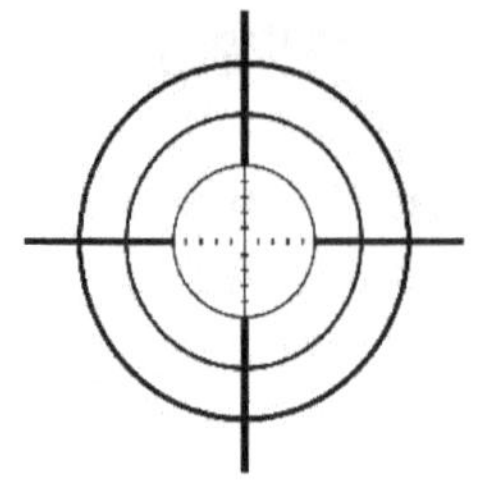

— EIGHT —

Decker felt no regrets at finally leaving Valeux far in his ship's hyperspace wake. Ros Skillen had turned out to be a one-trick pony and the rest of Bevaqua's gang mostly kept him at arm's length. Not that he had been overly keen to socialize with sociopaths, but time spent studying the opposition was rarely wasted.

Captain Ulrich would probably chew him a new one when he returned home. Taking a cover identity and disguise on false pretenses to carry out a private, unauthorized mission violated any number of rules, but it might reduce the pain if he had some fresh data for the analysts. Besides, it wouldn't be his first time to go beyond orders since the day Talyn had made him an involuntary member of the Black Gang, and Ulrich had never argued with the results.

The ship taking him on the leg to Kilia could have been one of the two that chased them to Garonne, for all he knew. Smaller than a sloop, cleaner than he expected and, up close, less well armed, its crew quickly made it clear that he sailed with them on sufferance and only because of orders.

By comparison, the trip to Valeux on *Giglio* had been a whirlwind of social events, but at least he didn't have to pay for his berth. Since this quest would quickly drain his bank account, he would gladly take all the freebies he could, scowling crew included. Docking at Kilia Station came as a relief.

Zack blew the bosun, who had been the least friendly of all, a kiss before stepping through the airlock and into the arms of a two-man reception committee. One of them examined his face, and then glanced down at the pad in his hand.

"Lorenzo, first name Jack?"

"The one and only." He gave the dour Wolves an overly broad smile. "But I also answer to 'hey you,' 'asshole,' and the sound of a Shrehari ale popping open."

"Great. Bevaqua sent us another comedian." The man shook his head. "Is that something they teach you in the Fleet?"

"Teach us what?" Decker fell into step beside the smaller of the two.

"Low-brow comedy."

"It's one of the performance objectives during basic training. Make the instructor groan. Followed immediately by extra physical training. All good stuff." Then, he decided to take a chance. "Got many ex-Fleet comedians coming through?"

"Enough to make it old hat."

"I remember this one guy," the other Wolf said, "six, eight weeks ago. Ex-Fleet but no sense of humor whatsoever. Man on a mission, with a streak of sarcasm like you wouldn't believe."

"Let me guess, a guy my age, tall, wiry, dark hair shot with silver strands, mustache bushy enough for a nest of squirrels, brown eyes to make you weep, kind of permanently tanned?"

"Yeah." The small guy nodded. "What was his name again? Terra, Luna, something like that."

"Tarra. Hal Tarra."

The Wolf snapped his fingers and pointed at Zack. "Just the man. Buddy of yours?"

"We got in trouble together a few times back when the universe was still young."

"I hope he doesn't owe you money."

"Why?"

"Because we haven't paid him yet." He laughed uproariously at his joke.

"Speaking of comedians," Decker grumbled. "Don't give up your day job."

They spent the remainder of the long trek up the docking arm in silence.

Built inside a spinning, hollowed-out asteroid, Kilia seemed unchanged from the day he had docked there with Hera. That visit had turned out to be brief after the station's administration, no doubt prodded by the Star Wolves' local boss, had shown too much interest in their ship, the late Harmon Amali's yacht, suitably reconfigured by the Navy after events on Nabhka.

Decker hoped no one would pull out old security recordings and compare Jack Lorenzo to his cover identity at the time. Disguises, even those dreamed up by Naval Intelligence, couldn't do much to change his height and bulk. Or his more ingrained mannerisms.

He thought they would lead him into the main habitat cavern, but other than skirting its outer edge, between the airlock leading to the docks and the entrance to a warren dug into the rock, his guides avoided it. The reason soon became apparent when his eyes lit on the image of a wolf baying at a supernova painted on a wall just beyond the door. This had to be the Confederacy's domain on Kilia, a place that few outsiders ever entered.

They shoved him through a side opening and into what looked like a typical middle management office. An older man with a salt-and-pepper beard, wearing black leather clothing, sat behind the desk. He examined Zack with emotionless eyes for almost a minute.

"Jack Lorenzo, former sergeant first class, combat engineers, 11th Marines, I presume," the man finally said. He held out his hand. "Service record, if you please."

Zack fished the wafer from his pocket and leaned forward to drop it in his palm.

"Gavin Bevaqua says you were a hard sell, even for Ros Skillen, but that you check out." He placed the wafer against a matte screen. "However, when it comes to prospects checking out, I'm like Saint Thomas. You know that service records can be faked, right?"

"Pretty much anything can." Decker gave a half shrug, seeming unconcerned. Naval intelligence cover identities were the best in the business, and even though he had obtained this one on false pretenses, it remained just as potent. Unless, of course, Yang had found out and wiped Jack Lorenzo from every database in the Fleet, just for shits and giggles.

"I'm glad to see," the man looked up at him after a few seconds of uncomfortable silence, "that your service record matches what's in the Fleet archive. Of course, Jack Lorenzo could still be a fake but have a very well-constructed legend to bolster his claims, the type of legend given to undercover agents."

Another penetrating stare, looking for a reaction.

"I'm not even a legend in my own mind, let alone playing an agent under covers, unless Ros has been telling tales out of school," Zack replied, sounding miffed. "Bevaqua convinced me that if I wanted to bounce around parts less traveled, taking a job with you guys would be the way to go. If you don't want me, I can find my way to an outbound ship and no hard feelings."

The Star Wolf raised a placating hand.

"Easy there, Jack Lorenzo." He smiled. "Don't let your temper take the upper hand. We don't bother with penal battalions here. A short step through an open airlock usually takes care of guys too quick with their fists."

"I'm Kyrell Stokke," the man continued. "You could say I'm the Confederacy's human resources officer around here. Various government organizations have tried to infiltrate our business before, on the pretense that we're involved in organized crime. It never works, of course. We're neither criminals nor stupid. And before you say it, Bevaqua shared your joke about the social club for sociopaths. It might play in a place like Valeux, but I suggest you keep that kind of humor to yourself if you intend to have a pleasant time working for us."

"I'll consider it, but no promises. If we're done posturing, can we discuss the gig?"

Stokke contemplated him for a moment while a faint smile played on his lips.

"The gig? Security work, well beyond the Rim and deep in the Protectorate badlands. You'll have a chance to see places the Fleet never visits and where no regular commercial traffic ever goes. Bevaqua told you about the pay. I think it's generous, even for the risks one is expected to assume in that part of the galaxy."

"Sure." A dismissive expression momentarily creased Decker's features. "Like I told your man on Valeux, I don't need a job, but I'd like to see more of the universe. Is that all you're going to tell me?"

"Of course. Someone of your experience can understand why."

"A man of my experience is always leery of buying a pig in a poke."

"And I understand that," Stokke replied. "All we know about you is your record. You might be useless for the kind of security work we have. Fortunately, we do have ways of satisfying our concerns."

A mean smile split Decker's face.

"I wouldn't have expected anything less, Mister Stokke. If I pass your test, are you going to tell me more? Or do I have to sign up for the job to find out what it is?"

"Let's see what you have first, Lorenzo. Then we'll talk some more."

*

"You have to be kidding me." Decker groaned the moment he stepped into a large chamber burned out of the asteroid's metal-rich core. "A fucking cage match?"

"Do Marines get scared? Who knew?" The smaller of the two Wolves who'd met him at the docks cackled.

"Just tired of beating up guys to prove a point." He raised his shoulders in a weary shrug. "But if you insist."

"We hire fighters," Stokke said. "If you're no good at hand-to-hand, there's no point in seeing if you can shoot straight. Your call."

He jerked his chin towards the far side of the room.

"That's Orlov, our head enforcer, and martial arts trainer. You'll have protective gear, so it's not bare knuckle and to the blood."

As big as Zack, with a shaven head and a bare torso covered in body art, Orlov looked like someone who didn't have to get physical very often in his job, not with an ugly mug that made the Marine look like a beefcake in a romance novel by comparison. He grinned, revealing a mouth guard.

Decker stripped down to his skivvies and the bantam with the cackle help him slip pads over his hands and feet, protective gear on his head and a mouth guard over his teeth. Finally, he stepped into a harness that drew a hard cup over his genitals. The blows would still hurt, but unless Orlov lets his inner berserker out for a bit of fun, there wouldn't be any permanent damage.

Decker entered the cage, followed by Orlov, and the two men took up a stance one pace apart in the middle of the mat. Then Orlov raised both fists for the traditional bump before the match.

"Good luck, probie," he growled, "I'll try not to make you scream like a little girl."

"I won't," Decker replied, blowing him a kiss. The enforcer roared with laughter, then launched himself at Zack.

He managed to fend off the initial flurry of fists and feet coming at him but seemed unable to get a riposte going. Orlov knew his stuff, that became apparent within the first ten seconds of the fight, and he had better-honed reflexes. Decker called up every dirty technique he could remember and finally managed to land some blows of his own, although he knew that if the bout went on for very long, he'd lose and lose badly.

If he hadn't been wearing even the little protective gear provided, and if Orlov had been going at him with bare hands and feet, the chances of walking out of the cage unaided would have been nil. The likelihood of needing medical attention, however, would have approached one hundred percent.

He heard what sounded like a defective environmental recycler puffing in great gusts and realized it was his increasingly labored breathing. He had more problems than merely encroaching middle age. The lifestyle of a spy had eroded his physical edge to a greater degree than he thought possible.

A hard kick caught him on the side of the head, and he spun around while bright points of light flashed in front of his eyes. He grunted once before collapsing to the mat. Expecting Orlov to continue battering his bruised body, he curled into a protective ball, but nothing came.

Instead, he felt a nudge. When he looked up, the enforcer stretched out a hand to help him stand.

"Not bad for an old guy," he rasped. "You lasted longer than I expected."

When Decker didn't respond, Orlov laughed.

"I'm the undisputed mixed martial arts champion here on Kilia and many other places on the Rim. If you'd beaten me, I'd have been out of a job."

Zack took the hand and hauled himself to his feet, feeling every blow that Orlov had landed.

"Remind me to never piss you off," he replied.

"I'm going to guess you've been living too soft, buddy." Orlov led the way out of the cage. "I saw good muscles and reflexes, but you've not done a lot of sparring in the last while. You might want to put yourself on a training regimen and improve your diet." He nodded at Stokke. "Your man's a better fighter than most who've come through here. He's a dirty sonofabitch too. Just out of practice. He'll do."

"Better than most?" Decker's chuckle sounded like the deep rumble of a volcano about to erupt. "Shit. Orlov there beat the snot out of me in one round. I'd hate to see what he does to those who're even more out of practice than I am."

"It's usually over a lot faster," Stokke replied, tossing him a towel. "You almost lasted the full round."

"And I can feel it." Zack grimaced, stripping off the protective gear. "Brutal interview technique."

"But necessary. A strong man will survive beyond the Rim. A weak man quickly becomes a liability we can't afford."

"Your buddy Tarra lasted as long," Bantam interjected. "Wiry bugger had Orlov chasing him up and down the cage walls."

Stokke's right eyebrow shot up.

"Tarra? Yes, I remember him. About two months ago it was. A friend of yours, Lorenzo?"

"A buddy from the Corps. I haven't seen him in years."

"If you pass the weapons and tactics test, and then sign on with us, you'll see him again in a few weeks. He's already out in the badlands."

"Excellent." Decker stepped into his boots and shrugged his jacket on. "Nice to know there will be at least one other guy who can find his ass with one hand. I had a vision of being surrounded by ex-guard pukes who never heard a shot fired in anger."

"We don't lack for professionals," Stokke replied.

He led the way to an armory and watched Decker field strip a weapon of every type they had in inventory, many of which should never have ended up in civilian hands, let alone in those of Confederacy gangsters.

A session in a surprisingly sophisticated battle simulator confirmed that the new prospect couldn't just shoot but think on the move, and the scenarios they put him through were a few notches above average difficulty.

"Okay, Lorenzo," Stokke said, leading him back to his office. "Your skills match your record, and you can fight. I'll say the same as Orlov, you're better than most who've come through here."

"If those sims had been for real, I'd have left an awesome body trail."

"I seem to recall your buddy Tarra did even better."

"Heck of a scrapper, Hal. A good man to have at your back in a fight, too. Or a bar for that matter."

Stokke slid into his chair and motioned at Zack to sit.

"It's time to talk specifics." He hauled a thin pad from one of the drawers and slid it across the desk. "The standard contract is on there. Read it. Ask any questions you want. I may or may not answer them. If you're happy with what it says, thumb it and welcome aboard. If not, it'll have been nice to watch Orlov work you over but talking to anyone about what you saw or heard here will have you wishing you were back in the cage."

Decker read the contract, taking his own sweet time, so he could memorize as much of it as possible.

"Seems to me like you've set up a private military corporation beyond the reach of the Adjudicating Authority," he said when he came to the last page.

"We prefer the term security contractor. It's both more accurate and less burdened by regulation. And our pay rates are better than a PMC's."

"I'll say. What if after the initial six months, I decide I'm done, will you guys ship me back here on your dime?"

"Yes."

"That's mighty generous. Most merc outfits pay up then tell you not to let the doorknob hit you in the ass on the way out."

"I didn't know you had experience with the private sector." Stokke frowned.

"Buddies of mine went private after their hitch. They didn't much like the smaller outfits," Decker replied without missing a beat. He pressed his thumb on the screen and said, "There. I'm all yours."

Stokke took the pad back and smiled.

"Welcome, Jack Lorenzo. You have six hours to go shopping for whatever you think you'll need out there. Weapons and uniforms will be provided at the destination. Your ship leaves in eight hours."

"You guys don't screw around, do you?"

"It's nothing out of the ordinary. You made it to Kilia in time for the weekly run. Twenty hours later and you'd have had seven days of liberty, spending your signing bonus on overpriced booze and cheap companions."

"Lucky me."

Stokke dropped a pile of cred chips beside the pad.

"I'd advise you to stock up on your favorite booze and delicacies. It's vat meat and rotgut out there, and you need the rotgut to digest everything else."

"Sounds like fun." Decker pocketed the money.

"Hence the rates of pay. Docking arm fourteen, at twenty-one hundred hours, station time. Don't be late. Orlov has a thing about punctuality."

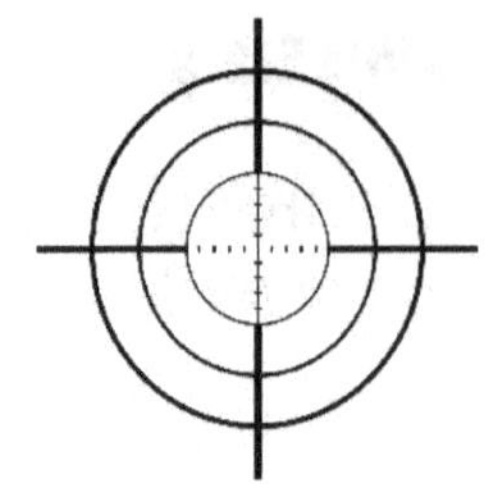

— NINE —

The sentry at the docking arm didn't even blink when Decker showed up carrying an extra pack filled with goodies, at the appointed time, sober and without a station security escort. He merely scanned the Marine and waved him through the airlock.

This ship hadn't come from the same architect or yard as the one that had brought Decker to Kilia. In fact, it reminded him more of the mercenary ships he had fired on while covering the rebel convoy making its final approach to Garonne.

He wondered whether the Avalon Corporation still had a marker out for an over-sized space yacht called *Phoenix* with a rigid digit ensign instead of the skull and crossbones. That bout must have cost them a pretty penny and hopefully cost at least one Avalon captain his command. Decker smiled fondly at the memory, earning a curious frown from the rating who led him to his quarters.

"You're sharing," he said, waving Decker into a cabin with four bunks, "in case you were wondering. Stay on this deck but feel free to use the saloon at the end of the passage."

The man vanished, leaving Zack to stare at the familiar shape occupying one of the lower beds. A woman with short hair, a muscular build, and a scar running down her cheek examined him with that cynical smile he remembered all too well.

"As I live and breathe," she said, "look what the rat dragged in. It doesn't look quite like I remember, but what the heck."

Decker stuck out his hand and quickly said, "Jack Lorenzo, formerly of the 11th Marines, in case you'd forgotten my name."

"And I'm still Miko Steiger." She jumped to her feet and hugged Zack with surprising strength. When she let go, her eyes searched his face. "Got an itch that needs scratching?"

"Not right now, no." He gave her a crooked leer to prove that he still had fond memories of their one encounter on top of a missile launcher.

"What happened to your sidekick, Pru Pasek, also known as Hera once she's on the ground?" Steiger stepped back, smiling at the way his eyes ran over her from head to toe.

"We're taking separate vacations this year. And how about you? What brings you aboard this ship of the damned?"

"Boredom, mostly. After you had left without saying goodbye," she scowled at him, "I stuck around for a while, to help Verrill settle things down, but then the wanderlust returned, and I left. Word on the merc grapevine spoke of a contract beyond the Rim for top pay, apply to your nearest Confederacy clubhouse, so I did, and here I am."

"Funny," he said, "you don't look like you've been through Orlov's tender mercies."

"Who's Orlov?"

"A one-man wrecking machine, champion of the cage match on Kilia. The man who evaluated my fighting skills and almost kicked my middle-aged ass back into the dark ages."

Steiger giggled.

"Oh, honey. That's why you look so stiff in places where you shouldn't be. I signed up elsewhere after a quick bout on the mats with their local sensei."

She dropped back down on the bunk and patted the space beside her.

"Sit your middle-aged ass down and tell me how you ended up here. Last I heard, you left with Pru for greener pastures after telling Verrill to watch his step."

"The pastures turned out to be artificial turf, so we kept moving." He tugged his earlobe, giving her a meaningful look.

"Ah yes, some contracts you don't discuss once they're over. So what inspired you to sign up for this one?"

"Same as you, boredom. I've been bumming around the Rim for the last few weeks, looking for fun. The Confederacy boss on Valeux figured I'd be a potential recruit and sent his succubus to work her charms on me."

The mercenary laughed with unfeigned delight.

"And you fell for it. Next thing you knew, you'd thumbed the contract."

"Meh." Zack shrugged. "The succubus turned out to have a single-minded obsession with self-gratification, and after a few times with her, the wanderlust came back. They offered me a free ride to Kilia, where I wanted to go anyway. I thumbed the contract there, after meeting Orlov the bone-smasher. Like you said, the pay's top notch for security work."

He could see skepticism in her dark brown eyes, and the desire to ask the question she really wanted him to answer. Why was Decker bumming around the Rim?

"After my bout in the disciplinary battalion, I wanted to see parts of the galaxy that I couldn't when the Corps still owned me," he said.

"I see we have some catching up to do, Jack Lorenzo, formerly of the 11th Marines." The twinkle in her smile promised more than just words and he winked.

Miko Steiger had enough smarts to go along with the Jack Lorenzo legend and not ask awkward questions where anyone could overhear, but he knew she would be whispering more than sweet nothings in his ear after lights out.

Before they could start comparing notes, a wiry, rat-faced man walked into the compartment with a swagger that seemed to imply that he owned the place.

"So this is where soldiers of fortune hang out." The smile on his thin, almost non-existent lips radiated insincerity. "The name's Langton, Alex Langton, at your service." He sketched a short bow, waving his right hand near his eyebrow as if in salute. "It looks like I'm going to be part of this band of brothers and sisters."

Decker stood and unfolded his body to its full height. Langton took a step back, tilted this head up, and whistled.

"You're a big man, brother."

"The name's Lorenzo, Jack Lorenzo." The Marine stuck out his hand. "My sister here goes by the name Miko Steiger."

"Pleasure." Langton inclined his head in a quick bow. Then he asked, "You two aren't really brother and sister, are you?"

"More in the way of kissing cousins," she replied. "And the big man is an excellent kisser."

"Gotcha. You two ex-Commonwealth military?"

"Maybe." Decker shrugged.

The newcomer's eyebrows shot up.

"Sure. No names, no pack drill." He dropped his duffel bag on an empty bunk on the far side from Steiger's and sat down. "Does either one of you know where we're going?"

"Somewhere with work that pays well." Steiger shrugged. "Other than that, your guess is as good as mine."

She nudged Decker.

"Let's go check out the saloon, big boy."

"Don't mind if I do." Langton jumped up and, with an exaggerated motion, waved Steiger towards the door.

Miko glanced at Zack with a spark of annoyance in her eyes, but the Marine merely shrugged.

"You go on first, friend Langton," he said. "I'm a big fan of always sending reconnaissance ahead of the main body. If you can dig up a trail that leads to decent ale, I might just spot you a drink."

Langton made a doubtful face. "I'd be surprised to find anything decent on a ship of this sort, but I'm willing to try."

He vanished down the passageway, leaving Zack and Miko to grimace at each other.

"It's going to be a long trip without privacy," she muttered.

"You had indecent designs on someone?" He smirked at her.

"Yeah. I decided tonight was the night I'd make love to myself." She jabbed her elbow into his bruised ribs. "Middle-aged asshole."

"Still a witch with those pickup lines, aren't you." Decker blew her a kiss, and then followed Langton to the saloon.

The lone human male occupying the lounge took up plenty of space by himself. He glanced up at Langton, then Decker, without a single glimmer of interest in his eyes, before staring down into his bulb again.

"Remember that Orlov character I told you about?" Zack whispered in Steiger's ear when she stepped through the door. "The one who kicked my ass? Well, buddy over there could be his brother from another mother."

Then in a louder tone, he asked, "Is the booze any good?"

The man looked up again, this time with a pained expression on his face.

"No, and I'm not interested in small talk, so fuck off."

Decker's eyebrows shot up. He turned towards Steiger and smiled.

"I like a man who doesn't beat around the bush, especially if he looks like he can beat up said bush and the Celestan mammoth hiding behind it."

"Hangovers are a bitch when you're out of meds," Langton commented.

"A fist in the kidney is even worse," the man growled.

"So much for no small talk." Langton took a bulb from the dispenser and grimaced at the label. "Getting hung over on this stuff would be painful."

He took a table far from the hulking giant with the ham-sized fists and slouched back in his chair with an air of expectancy as if waiting for Zack and Miko to join him.

"Did man-mountain there come with the ship?" Decker asked in a low tone, his eyes on the menu.

"Not that I know. I've never seen him before. Maybe he boarded here and made straight for the saloon in search of a little hair of the dog."

"Probably." He grimaced at the selection. "Another sad display of Pacifican horse piss. How I miss those days aboard *Phoenix*, where I could tap into a stash of the good Shrehari stuff at will."

Steiger smiled at the memory. "You did have some of the finest vintages I ever tasted. Speaking of which, whatever happened to your ship?"

"My partner parked it with some acquaintances while we're off on our separate vacations."

A sudden glint of understanding lit up Miko's eyes. "Right."

Decker was about to order when a twinge of pain from Orlov's beating reminded him of the man's words. He grimaced and changed his choice. The dispenser spat out a bulb of purple liquid.

"Are you feeling alright?" Steiger asked. "I've never seen you drink grape juice before."

"I'm fine. The booze isn't. Let's leave it at that."

He studied her intently, wondering how much to share with the mercenary. She had proved to be trustworthy and professional during the Garonne affair, but he still had reservations concerning her past and her motivations. And it seemed all too convenient that she would appear now, headed in the same direction as he was.

Steiger must have read his thoughts because she gave him a wry smile.

"Like our new friend over there said, no names, no pack drill, but you give me the impression that you're no more on a vacation than I am. I won't pry, but if you ask, I will help. For old time's sake and for whatever's driving you right now, okay?"

He considered her for a few more moments in silence before nodding.

"Okay. Without Hera to watch my back, I'll take the best deal on offer, which around here doesn't mean much."

"Bastard." She playfully slapped his arm.

"Didn't we already have the conversation about my parents being married?"

"You mean the one where you won't confirm whether it was to each other? Yeah." Steiger's eyes speared Langton for a split second before returning to Zack. "If you feel the urge to share, we'll have to do it lips to ear, and that means slipping in a bunk together, so it doesn't seem like we're trying to hide."

"That's what I really need right now," he replied with a snort, "a bit of exhibitionism to entertain our cabin mates."

"But you have to admit that as misdirection, it'll be ideal." She nudged him with her hip. "And I get to see if you stayed in shape since we last scratched an itch together."

*

"I figured there had to be more than just vacation wanderlust behind your signing up with the Confederacy," she murmured into his ear once Decker finished telling her about Hal Tarra and Elyce Sakal.

He had suitably edited the story to avoid any mention of Troy Station, of the Fleet making the incident vanish and anything concerning his real job. In this version, Tarra had reached out to a retired buddy who might want to help him fix the one failure that had haunted them for years.

The fact that he told her anything at all could cost him his security clearance and maybe even his career, if Captain Ulrich ever found out. The trick was to make sure he didn't. Besides, if Ulrich hadn't wanted Decker to go rogue, he shouldn't have granted him an extended furlough in the first place or denied him permission to go after Hal with his regular partner. Field agents need someone to watch their backs, and he had to adapt to his circumstances.

The bunks had turned out to have a privacy curtain that cut off sound as well as sight, but he'd still told the tale in a tone so low it could have passed for the whisper of a breeze, though not without the constant distraction of her earthy scent and roving hands.

"Trust me," he replied, "the Jackals are still on my list of vermin most likely to need a good stomping, but they're the best way I have to catch up with Hal."

"So you said. Any idea what you'll do once we get where this tub is going?"

"Not a clue. I'm hoping Hal will have some ideas when I finally speak with him in person."

"When *we* speak with him. Your caper sounds like it might be right up my alley."

"I know something else that's right up your alley," he replied.

After that, neither of them spoke for a while.

The cabin was empty when Decker emerged from behind the privacy screen, wearing nothing but his shorts. Sometime during their itch scratching the ship had left Kilia far behind, accelerating towards the hyperlimit where it could safely transition to FTL without straining its hull.

Steiger climbed out behind him, wearing nothing at all. If Langton had witnessed the sight, he might well have felt rather inadequate. Though marked by the odd scar from old combat injuries, her musculature and skin tone would have been the envy of most women and not a few men.

"Try to keep from frightening the children," Decker remarked, tossing a pair of trousers at her. "It's time to find some grub after that very long debriefing."

"I did squeeze you dry, didn't I?" She leered at him. "A good thing your keeper with the biting sarcasm isn't aboard. Old Pru or whatever she calls herself these days didn't really like me much."

"Nope." Decker pulled on his pants and stepped into his boots.

"Too bad. I thought she was kind of cute." Another smirk. "You two did make a lovely couple."

"And right now, we don't, hence separate vacations. Put your clothes on, succubus. Our roommates might show up at any time."

"Are you afraid that I'll ruin your reputation?" She mimed biting him.

"There's nothing to ruin, honey." Decker shrugged on his jacket and checked that he could draw his blaster without hitting a snag. "But I am hungry."

A dozen men and women had joined Langton and Hangover Guy, the sexes split almost equally, but with little difference when it came to looks and surly attitude. Zack and Miko received a once over from most of them the moment they stepped into the saloon. Alex Langton graced them with a knowing smile.

One of the men stood and gestured at them to take a seat. Hard-faced, with flinty eyes, he bore none of the usual signs marking full members of the Confederacy, yet he exuded an aura of authority at odds with his mostly unremarkable appearance.

"Now that the last two of the group have graced us with their presence," he said, "perhaps we can sort ourselves out."

"Old friends having a tearful reunion," Decker smiled. "You know how it is."

"In future, try not to let it interfere with the job you signed on to do." He glanced around the room. "For those who don't know me, I'm Magnus Roby, and until we're at our destination, I'm your beloved commanding officer."

Zack and Miko glanced at each other.

"Commanding officer?" She mouthed, mischief dancing in her eyes.

"Is there a problem? Steiger, is it?" Roby turned his hard stare on her.

"No problems. I just didn't expect a job like this to sound like it's going to be run on regular military lines."

"Surprise." He cocked an eyebrow, the first sign of emotion he'd shown so far. "Now that you're aboard this ship consider yourselves under military discipline and my word to be law."

"Fair enough." She smiled pleasantly. "Sir."

"Roby will do just fine. Now, if there's nothing else on your mind, Steiger, can I continue?"

She made a go-ahead gesture winking at Decker.

"Perhaps a round of introductions is in order. Since this is Steiger, first name Miko, it means her old friend must therefore be Jack Lorenzo. Welcome."

Decker dipped his head once by way of acknowledgment.

"A ten-second bio, folks?"

"Sure," Zack replied. "Like Roby said, the name's Lorenzo. I retired as a sergeant first class from the 11th Marines after twenty-five years. My branch was combat engineers."

"Steiger?"

"I used to be an infantry command sergeant in the Commonwealth Army. I did twenty."

Hangover Guy turned out to be one Atli Tiktin, a former corporal in the Celeste National Guard, also infantry, while Alex Langton claimed a past as staff sergeant in the Army's military police branch. The remainder was evenly divided between former National Guard, from half a dozen planets, and ex-Commonwealth Services, including two more Marines whose shifty looks might well mean they were real penal battalion veterans, unlike Zack.

When everyone had spoken his or her piece, Decker asked Roby, "What about your background? I'm sure we'd all like to know about the man giving us orders."

"Me? I've been freelancing for more than twenty-five years and can turn my hand at pretty much all of the combat arms specialties, though I'm infantry first and foremost. Good enough?"

The Marine shrugged. "You're the organ grinder, which means it's good enough. Now that we've done the intros, I wouldn't mind finding out which planetary government we're going to overthrow with this much talent in one room."

Roby raised his right hand, palm outward.

"All in good time. As I said, you're now under discipline, and that means whatever rank you had before, it doesn't exist anymore. I'm the boss, manager, den father, whatever suits friend Steiger better than commanding officer." This time, he cracked a faint smile. "And that means whatever I say, goes. You signed a contract, and I sincerely hope you took the time to read it beforehand. Where we're heading, there's no Adjudicating Authority to lay down the law on mercenary outfits, nor is there a Fleet to enforce those laws. As you're all former professionals, I don't expect that I'll need to invoke any of the disciplinary articles in your contracts, but if necessary, I won't hesitate to knock heads. Understood?"

He locked eyes with each of them in turn, waiting for a sign of understanding, but before he could speak again, the jump klaxon sounded, followed by a human voice giving them a thirty-second warning before the universe shifted and caused their stomachs to attempt a mass escape. Roby wisely sat down and waited until the transition nausea had abated before moving again.

"Okay," he finally said, climbing to his feet again. "That'll do for introductions. We'll join up with more recruits at our destination, and like you, they're all experienced and have been vetted, so you needn't concern yourself."

"I wasn't about to," one of the ex-Marines grumbled.

"Excellent." Roby indicated the dispenser. "Grab yourselves a drink and stick around. The galley will be serving soon. I'll speak with each of you individually over the next day or so, to gauge how we can best use your skills and experience."

He sauntered over to Zack and Miko's table and pulled out a chair. Sitting down with a friendly smile, he asked, "Am I going to have problems with you two?"

"Why?" Decker put on a puzzled expression.

"Bond pairs can be trouble in a small outfit, for one thing."

Steiger laughed. "We're old friends who scratch an occasional itch. He already has a full-time partner somewhere else in this big galaxy, and trust me she's one mean bitch. I wouldn't dare muscle in on her."

"You said for one thing." Decker tilted his head to one side, eyes narrowed.

Roby seemed to chew on his words for a long time before he spoke.

"There's something that makes me think you're a cut above the rest of the former Marines we've recruited, and definitely above the Army or Guard guys, no offense, Steiger."

"None was taken," she replied with a sweet smile. "Jack is a cut above everyone else in this room, present company included."

The man's eyebrows shot up. "It's like that, is it?"

"Try him."

Roby laughed softly as he stood. "And you tell me you're not a bond pair. We'll have a long talk later, my friends. Right now, I could use a good beer, and since they don't have any aboard, I'll make do with whatever's on offer."

"Pretty tragic, isn't it?" Zack grimaced. He glanced at Steiger. "You want something, honey?"

"Rotgut is fine, big boy. It'll help rinse out my mouth after our alone time together."

"Not a bond pair." Roby walked away, shaking his head.

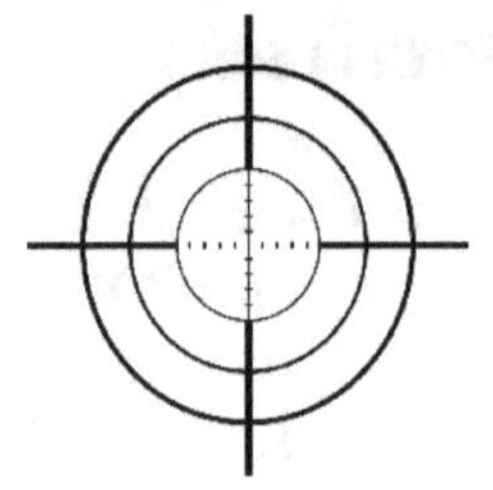

— TEN —

Decker saw movement out of the corner of his eyes, just beyond the door to the compartment set aside as a gym, but he and Steiger finished their kata sequence undisturbed, moving gracefully around each other in choreographed unison.

With the ship in hyperspace, they had nothing to do, other than shoot the breeze, drink, or sleep. However, he still felt the aches from his encounters with Confederacy thugs, both on Horus and on Kilia and thus spent several hours a day exercising, sparring with Steiger and generally working more suppleness into his forty-something body. None of the others spent as much time in the gym, and that fact hadn't escaped Magnus Roby's notice.

Once they finished, after bowing to each other, he picked up a towel to wipe the sweat off his face and only then acknowledged Roby's presence. The mercenary commander gave them a brief, if ironic round of applause.

"Nicely done. It would have been even better if the others showed your dedication to the martial arts."

"I guess it's our turn to play fifty questions. You've gone through the rest of the bunch. Who do you want first, Miko or me?"

"Does it matter? You two seem to be joined at the hip."

"Only in polite company." Zack leered at her. "In private..."

"It's a good thing I can see through your act, Lorenzo. Someone else might think you're the type who uses his balls for brains."

"Nah. That would be Langton. You know how those former meatheads are. So, what'll it be? Miko or me?"

Roby gestured at Steiger. "Miko. I'll save you for last, funny guy."

Alone on the mats and not particularly interested in mingling with what he had begun to privately call the Band of Losers, Decker went through a new kata sequence, determined to make all of his muscles scream for surrender. After three hours of hard physical exercise with Miko, it didn't take long.

When he stepped out of the shower, Steiger still hadn't returned from Roby's interview, so he threw himself on his bunk after grunting a brief greeting at Atli Tiktin, the former Celeste Guardsman. He preferred to be called Atty, but inevitably, everyone ended up calling him Tiny.

Without the hangover, Tiktin was much friendlier and could even tell a joke or two that might amuse the Marine, but the big guy was no genius, a term that could also describe the two retired Marines who reeked of the stockade. For some reason, they kept well out of Decker's way, as if they could smell the former command sergeant in him and feared that their less than stellar pasts might be exposed.

Steiger shared Zack's opinion of their merry bunch being on the wrong side of par, except for one or two, Roby and, surprisingly, Langton among them. They had both come to that conclusion after noticing how the man watched everyone else with keen eyes that missed nothing. The oily demeanor had to be an act, designed to lull people into classifying him as annoying but harmless.

About ten minutes later, Steiger reappeared and stripped off her sweat-soaked training singlet.

"Boss man says it's your turn." She leaned down as if to kiss him whispering, "We had a thing going when I served on Cimmeria, where my regiment worked with the 11ᵗʰ Marines, six or seven years ago. Then, I cashed in my retirement, and we never did the nasty again until meeting up here.”

“Thanks for the warning, Miko. Is he going to ask me for details of our whirlwind romance?”

She laughed, straightening up again. “No worries. Apparently, I’m not his type, so he isn’t exactly interested in details.”

“Figures.”   Decker climbed out of his bunk and stretched muscles that had begun to seize up. “If that means I’m his type, I hope you made it clear that the two of us are an item.”

“May I use those words the next time we see your friend Pru Pasek, also known as Hera the avenging Fury?”

“Sure, provided she’s not armed. I figure you can outrun her, fury and all, as long as she doesn’t have a gun. Or a knife.”

He pulled on his pants and shirt before stepping into his boots. Since he saw no reason for being armed, the dagger and blaster stayed in his locked duffel bag.

“Where’s the boss hiding?” He asked.

“In his cabin, at the end of the corridor.”

“It must be nice.”

“Small as heck, though.” With that, she walked to the heads, Tiny’s eyes glued to her muscular gluteus.

Decker, who noticed the man’s keen interest, tapped him on the shoulder.

“Don’t let Miko catch you doing that, buddy. She can be one mean bitch if she smells the slightest whiff of disrespect. And big as you are, you’ll only fall harder.”

Tiktin grunted. “I’d like to see her try. It could be fun.”

“No, you wouldn’t, and no it wouldn’t be fun. Words of wisdom, Tiny. Heed them.”

He grinned at the man’s puzzled expression, and then left him to wonder about Steiger’s reputation.

The door to Roby’s cabin was open, so he tapped on the frame with his knuckles.

“Come on in, Lorenzo and grab a seat on the bunk.”

Roby examined him for a few moments, a vague smile on his lips.

"You puzzle me."

"Why?"

"I've been watching everyone for the last few days, and you don't fit in. There's something hardcore about the way you spend hours in the gym when you're not tearing through the ship's library or playing doctor with Steiger."

"So? I like to stay sharp, and at my age, I need all the physical training I can get so that some young punk can't come around and hand me my ass. What Miko and I do behind my bunk's privacy curtain is our business, but you should be glad about it. Like a wise man once said, a soldier who won't fuck won't fight."

"George Patton. Early to mid-twentieth century. Are you a student of history, Jack Lorenzo?"

"Yup. If discussing my sexual habits was the only thing on your mind, then I guess we're done."

"Stay right there, Jack. We're done when I say we're done." Again that vague smile. "You're not a man who's overly impressed with those in authority, eh?"

"If those in authority waste my time, I tend to cut my losses. Life is too short for dumb shit."

"Was your time in the disciplinary battalion worth it?"

"Captain Slatten had it coming. It was just a matter of luck that no one had been killed by his stupidity up to then." Decker shrugged. "My career might have ended, but I had enough time in for a pension. Slatten's career ended too, but he has to stick around doing crap staff jobs for a few more years while I'm swanning around the Rim having a grand old time. Advantage, Jack Lorenzo."

"If I give an order you disagree with, am I going to have trouble?"

"It depends." A slow, lazy smile spread across Zack's face. "If the order's going to get me or my troops killed for no good reason, you're going to have a brief moment of trouble with me. Then, you'll never have problems again. If the order's just dumb but not life threatening..." He shrugged.

"I do believe, Jack Lorenzo," Roby said, an unexpected twinkle in his dark eyes, "that you mean every word you just said. I've met your kind before."

"Oh? And what kind is that?"

"Deadly. Professional. Guys whose entire lives are spent soldiering and who are very, very good at it." That inquisitive look returned. "As I said, you puzzle me. A man like you doesn't really fit in with the average mercenary outfit."

"The National Guard warriors out there do?"

"Yes and so do the Commonwealth Armed Services veterans, Steiger included. You strike me as being the odd man out."

"Because I spend time keeping my body and brain fit?" Decker raised a sardonic eyebrow.

"That's part of it. You know how some people have an aura of violence around them?"

"Sure."

"You exude a variation of that aura." Roby's smile broadened. "You exude controlled violence, the kind that stays leashed until it's necessary, and when that happens, whoever pissed you off is a dead man walking. I won't ask how many you've killed in your career, but I can guess you probably have a higher body count than everyone else here put together."

"Higher than you?"

"Definitely." The smile vanished as if vaporized by a disruptor. "I know you didn't sign on because you wanted a job. The Confederacy folks who recruited you at Valeux provided us with a very detailed report, so I'm curious as to what your real motives might be. By the way, you'll have to tell me one day how a hard bitch like Ros Skillen was able to seduce you into volunteering."

Zack snorted. "I like 'em tough as leather, and all tatted up. It's one of my little perversions. No, I didn't sign on because I wanted a job. The pension plus my savings are enough for the life of a star lane hobo. I'm here because I want to see more of the galaxy and the Jackals on Valeux made me understand that the best way of doing so would be by signing up."

"Jackals?" Roby's eyebrows shot up. "Risky calling Confederacy members by that name within earshot of anyone who might be an associate, if not a full patch Star Wolf."

"You're not one of them, not even a hanger-on, so why would you care?"

"How do you know I don't belong?"

The Marine winked at Roby. "You don't have that aura of dumb-ass violence."

This time, the mercenary laughed aloud.

"Okay, funny guy. You got me there. No, I'm not a fan of the Confederacy, but they have their uses on the Rim and beyond. You may think of them as dumb-ass, violent misfits, but plenty is going on out there where a Star Wolf's fearlessness comes in handy."

"Maybe." Decker gave a half shrug, his eyes meeting Roby's without a hint of self-consciousness.

"You know, there's something about you that reminds me of a retired Marine sergeant who joined up seven or eight weeks ago. He was with the batch I brought out of Kilia before this one. He also had that controlled violence aura, and like you, he spent a lot of time in the gym, but his humor was pretty damn dry, not like yours."

"There are plenty of them in the Corps. What's his name?"

"Tarra. Hal Tarra. He gave me the impression of being a man on a mission, just like you."

"I know Tarra from way back. He's a strange bird but a heck of a fighter."

"He didn't fit in with the other mercs either." Roby's eyes narrowed, and he took on a thoughtful look. "Are we just being lucky here, with two Marine veterans, hardcore professionals both, showing up one after the other or is it too much of a coincidence."

"You have the two jailbait clowns in the saloon," Zack pointed out.

"Sure. A pair of corporals who couldn't make sergeant to save their lives, hence their exit from the Corps after twelve years. Parker and Barrow have a bit of that violence aura all right, but they don't come across as hardened pros. Not like you and Tarra. Not even close."

"I'm not going to argue with you on that point. Parker and Barrow are the kind of Marines who take up a lot of a sergeant's time, to keep them out of trouble when they're not on operations."

"You can tell that quickly?"

A guffaw escaped Decker's lips. "They have the kind of dumb-ass aura an old sergeant like me can spot from ten parsecs away. They're probably useful in a fight, but not over-endowed with brains."

"Want to give me your impression of the others?"

"Not particularly, but I'm hoping that you intend to use most of them as rank fillers. Other than you, Langton, Steiger, and me, there's not much going on. Maybe one or two of them will prove me wrong once we're working, but I doubt it."

"You know the old joke that the true measure of a man's intelligence is how much he agrees with you?"

"Yep."

"I figure there's plenty of intelligence under that rough exterior, Jack Lorenzo. And that's why you puzzle me, returning to where this conversation started."

"Meh." Decker shrugged, a tired look relaxing his features. "I'm really a very simple, easy to understand guy. I like fighting and fucking, and if pressed, I can do both at once. The Corps encouraged me to retire after I took great exception to Captain Slatten, so now I'm looking at the galaxy to see if there's something else I'd like to do."

"And yet, here you are, fucking and preparing to fight."

"I guess I'm set in my ways." Another indifferent shrug. "When we get where we're going, I'll give it six months, as per contract. If I'm having fun, maybe I'll extend. If not..."

"Fair enough. We can use someone like you, needless to say. Since the others in this batch are mostly rank fillers, we're going to be looking for particular people to provide leadership, and you strike me as having the right temperament and background. There's more pay in it, of course."

"And more headaches."

"Nothing you can't handle, I'm sure. Anyways, that conversation is a bit academic until we get to our destination and my superiors measure up this new draft of recruits based on my evaluation." He tapped the pad on his desk. "Anything not in your official file I should know about?"

Decker winked knowingly at him. "Nothing that I'll admit to."

"Okay, funny guy." Roby stood up. "Do me a favor, keep an eye on the others, and if you sense any more auras that I should know about, be a pal. You don't want a dumbass watching your back any more than I do."

"I will."

The mercenary stretched out his hand for a shake.

"Welcome to our ragtag band, Lorenzo. It's good to find out the Confederacy can snag decent recruits once in a while."

*

Tiktin glowered at Zack when he came back to the cabin he and Steiger shared with Langton and the big Celestan. A harsh laugh escaped the Marine's lips upon seeing the anger and humiliation in Tiny's eyes.

"You pissed her off, didn't you?" He asked. "Why is it that no one ever listens to me when I warn them about women?"

Tiny looked away and shrugged.

"She doesn't play fair," he muttered.

"Fairness is for children, Tiny. Miko's all grown up, as you might have noticed. And she learned how to fight dirty. In fact," Decker winked at Tiny, "you have no idea how dirty she can be. Where is she, by the way?"

"Saloon."

"C'mon, big guy. I'll buy you a beer."

Tiny looked at Zack with undisguised suspicion, but he nodded once before climbing out of his bunk. Everyone had a weak spot. Booze seemed to be Tiktin's.

Most of their crew of would-be mercenaries sat in the saloon, drinking and talking. On the way to the dispenser, Tiktin gave Miko an angry stare, and Zack laughed.

"Let it go, Tiny. She has. We still have to live together for a while." He held out a bulb. "Here you go. Finest Pacifican piss, but have enough of it and you won't care."

"Thanks." The Celestan's reply sounded grudging. He jerked his chin towards the far end of the saloon. "I'll see what Parker and Barrow are up to, okay?"

"No strings attached, buddy. Have fun."

He took his juice over to where Langton and Steiger sat and pulled out a chair.

"You're going to have to tell me what you did to the poor guy. He has a major case of butt hurt."

"Maybe later." She glanced over at where Tiktin sat with the two ex-Marines. "He's not a bad guy. Just not a very smart guy."

"And he won't gain any IQ points by hanging around with them," Langton remarked. "Not the Corps' better bargains."

Decker grunted. "There's a lot of that around here."

"Tell Jack what you said to me, Alex," Steiger said.

Alex, is it? The Marine threw her a questioning glance.

"When I'm bored," Langton replied, "I tend to feel the urge to investigate whatever tickles my fancy and I'm bored stiff right now. You may have noticed that our employers have been careful to ensure we don't know what ship we're on and who operates it."

"Not unexpected," Zack replied, "considering the wording of the contracts they had us thumb."

"I think this tub belongs to Avalon. You've heard of them right, the private military corporation?"

"Yep. One of the bigger outfits. Decent grunts, so-so officers, but Avalon's ultimate owners aren't friendly people."

"Just so." A sly smile played on Langton's thin lips. "Well done, Jack Lorenzo."

"What makes you think this is an Avalon ship?"

"Let's say I've been able to bypass some of the safeguards and leave it at that. My time in the military police has taught me a thing or two."

"Fair enough." Decker took a sip and grimaced. "Why tell us?"

"Why not? We're all children of the Commonwealth Services and seem to have more brainpower between us than the rest of them put together."

"Other than Roby," the Marine pointed out.

"Other than Roby, yes."

"Funny, I just had my welcome aboard interview with good old Magnus, and we had a similar discussion concerning the intellectual heft of this bunch of rank fillers."

"I'm not surprised." Langton nodded. "Roby's no dummy. He watched us for a few days before holding his one-on-ones, so he could see what kind of meat the recruiters had signed up. I'd say talking to you last was no accident."

"Why?" Zack examined the ex-MP through narrowed eyes.

"You already know the answer to that, Jack." Langton drained his bulb. "Some people just have that aura around them. Refills, anyone?"

Before he could stand, the remainder of the mercenaries streamed into the saloon, with Magus Roby entering last.

He waited until they were seated, then cleared his throat to get their attention.

"Now that I've had a chance to speak with everyone, and to see how you choose to spend your time, I'm going to lay down a few rules. As your commanding officer," he inclined his head towards Steiger, "I want to ensure you don't lose your edge by lollygagging around for the whole trip. First of all, everyone will spend at least three hours a day in the gym, exercising. No exceptions.

Although he doesn't know it yet, Jack Lorenzo has been appointed training officer for this purpose, seeing as how he spends most of his waking hours trying to stay in shape."

"And the rest doing the horizontal tango with Steiger," one of the others muttered to a smattering of laughter.

Ignoring the heckler, Roby turned to Zack and said, "You have full control of the training plan, but I want to see them sweat."

"Second," Roby continued, "You're going to be given access to the kind of weapons we use at the other end. You'll spend at least an hour a day working with them, including marksmanship simulations. Third, you can have as much booze as you want, but if you show up for training hung over or in anything that smacks of less than peak condition, I'm cutting you off for the rest of the trip. In fact, you might want to emulate your new trainer here and stick with non-alcoholic drinks."

"May I make a suggestion?" Decker asked.

"Go ahead."

"Sparring. Everyone goes through a few rounds of sparring over and above the gym time. Folks can use whatever fighting style they wish. I'll do the first demo tomorrow morning." Decker turned to look at the other corner of the saloon. "Tiny's going to be my partner for the occasion."

"That sounds like an excellent idea. I'll be joining you in all those activities, of course."

"Of course, as any good commanding officer would." Decker's grin spread across a few parsecs. It widened even more when he saw several of the others look less than enthusiastic.

On a long trip going FTL, you had to make your own entertainment, and Zack had become an expert at that. It was a shame that they didn't have access to the rest of the ship. Running a tough parkour trail once a day would keep the troops sharp.

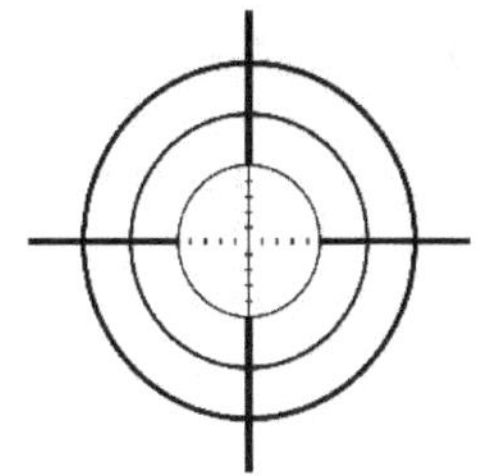

— ELEVEN —

"I think you're officially the most hated person aboard," Steiger murmured after the last class of wannabe martial artists left the gym, egos, and bodies bruised in equal measure. Only 'Tiny' Tiktin remained, still dazed at the ease with which Decker had demonstrated how to use an opponent's size against him.

"And I should give a flying fuck why?" Zack wiped the sweat from his face with an already soaked towel. "Tiny might not be the biggest brain of the bunch, but at least he showed some heart. I'm actually embarrassed at Parker and Barrow. Marines shouldn't be that incompetent at hand-to-hand combat, but they managed to make some of the National Guard pukes look like Special Forces operators."

"What I like about you, honey, is your naiveté," she replied. "Don't try to hold mercenaries to professional standards. If they were able to meet them, the buggers wouldn't be freelancing. About one in ten of us know how to fight. The other nine are in it because of excess testosterone, insufficient brain cells, and a general inability to keep a steady job."

"So you admit to being an inferior form of life." Decker nudged his companion.

"More like a big fish in a small pond, as opposed to a small fish in a big pond, which is what you and I were back in our salad days with the regulars."

"Fish, big or small, won't do much to cover my ass when the plasma's flying." He grabbed a water bulb and emptied it in a single gulp. "And I don't have the feeling most of them will be able to do that either. I had no idea the National Guard standards had gone downhill that fast."

She put a hand on his arm and caught his gaze.

"Kind of unfair to compare, considering where you came from, *Jack*, and with the combat experience you've accumulated."

After a few moments, during which she reminded him wordlessly that he was a former Pathfinder, one of the Corps' elite, he said, "Got it."

"And now you have a captive audience to bore with your war stories and beat up until they show some signs of sentience. Try to enjoy it."

With that, she walked out of the gym, tracked by Decker's admiring eyes. Good thing Hera was light years away.

"C'mon, Tiny. Time for a shower and then lunch. You've earned an extra helping."

"Will you teach me how to do what you did?" The Celestan asked, lumbering down the passageway behind Decker.

"That's part of the idea with these classes," he replied over his shoulder. "It's not only about keeping everyone busy, tired, and on edge."

"Oh."

They entered the cabin, where Steiger sat on her bunk, stripped naked. She indicated the door to the heads.

"Alex is using the shower right now. If you don't mind it being tight, you can join me, Jack."

Decker almost laughed at the look of pure envy in Tiny's eyes. Envy tinged with more than a little respect. He winked at the big man and said, "As long as you're not expecting to play pick up the soap, darling. I'm too hungry for games."

"I don't think there's enough room to play."

"You'd be surprised." He waggled his eyebrows.

*

One of the former guardsmen sneered wordlessly at Decker when the latter entered the saloon.

"Trying to look prettier, Hobai?" Zack asked with a smile. "I'm sorry to say it's not working. You have the kind of face only a mother could love. A blind mother."

"Fuck you, Lorenzo," he replied, the sneer hardening.

"Nope. Not pretty enough for that either. Besides, Miko might object to me slumming."

"Yeah, yeah," one of Cezek Hobai's buddies said, "you Commonwealth Services pukes are too good for us ex-guard critters."

Decker leered at her.

"You, on the other hand, *are* pretty enough, but as you may have heard, I already have a playmate."

Steiger took Zack by the arm and pulled him away.

"Stop flirting with Mona and grab some food. We're going to raid the weapons locker for some afternoon fun in an hour, and you promised Tiny he could eat a double ration."

When they had their trays, Langton waved them over.

"I'm guessing," he said, "that I don't need to warn you about all the friends you made this morning."

"Nope." Decker shook his head as he took a seat. "I don't intend to have any of these beautiful specimens in my fire team anyway, so it's a moot point."

He glanced at Steiger for a brief moment, thinking that he probably wouldn't be around long enough to get a fire team. Once he met up with Hal, that is.

"It might have been more palatable if you hadn't taken such evident pleasure in showing them how out of shape they were," Langton said with a faint grimace.

"Can I help it if my face is an open book?" He took a forkful of food and shoved it in his mouth.

"Something tells me that you only open that book when you feel like it," Langton replied with a half shrug. "It's your business, and you strike me as someone who can handle it without my help."

"That's a fact," Zack replied after he had swallowed.

Tiny walked up to their table, a tray in hand and asked, "Can I join you guys?"

"Sure." Decker waved at the remaining empty chair then examined the food piled high on a couple of plates. "You think that's enough for a growing boy?"

"He can always go back for seconds," Langton said with a dry smile. "Or thirds for that matter."

"Yep," Tiktin confirmed with an enthusiastic bob of the head.

"Have you ever pondered," the former MP said, leaning back in his chair, looking oddly contented, "the curiosities of the human temperament? Here we are, a dozen freelancers, four to a cabin and in the saloon, we congregate with our cabin mates rather than mingle. Instant tribalism writ small."

"Or not so little in our case, considering Tiny and Jack." Steiger indicated the two larger men.

"Would that be a complaint?" Zack asked, mischief dancing in his eyes.

"Just a statement of fact, my dear." She patted his thickly corded forearm. "If I have a complaint, you'll know about it."

"Something tells me that we'll all know about it," Langton said before taking a sip of his coffee.

Steiger made a face at him, but the corners of her eyes crinkled with suppressed merriment.

Magnus Roby showed up and headed directly for their table. He pulled a chair from a neighboring one and sat down without so much as a by your leave.

"Interesting session, Lorenzo. I don't think you made many friends."

Decker groaned. "You're the third or fourth person to point that out. Can we put a paragraph in the routine orders, one that says Jack Lorenzo is well aware he's the least liked person on board? I'd like to hear an original line every so often. Otherwise, I become really cranky, and then me not making friends is going to be the least of your worries."

"Touchy, touchy." Roby smiled.

"He can be that." Steiger winked at Zack.

"Too touchy for a stroll down to the cargo hold so we can take a look at the ordnance we're bringing with us?"

"Everyone's a comedian," Decker grumbled before spearing the last bit of food on his plate.

"There," he said a few moments later. "Let's see what kind of crap the Jackals managed to round up."

Roby's eyebrows shot up. "Crap?"

"Maybe, maybe not." The Marine shrugged. "Why take me?"

"Because I've read your service record. I want to see how good you really are with weapons."

"Can we join you?" Steiger asked.

The mercenary shook his head. "Not this time. Right now, it's just Lorenzo and me."

Roby took Decker through a part of the ship forbidden to the passengers and into a cargo hold that seemed too small for a commercial sloop, further confirming Langton's suspicions.

There they found stacks of unmarked containers, each sealed with an elaborate lock that nonetheless opened soundlessly at the mercenary's touch. He took a plasma rifle from the first one and tossed it at Zack, who caught it with one hand, then went through the approved procedure to ensure it had been rendered safe. Roby dipped his head in approval.

"Not bad." Zack expertly field stripped the weapon. "It must have fallen off some National Guard transport skimmer seeing as how this is one generation behind what the Corps and the Army are using. By the looks of it, this thing spent most of its life sitting in the strategic reserve stocks. I'm not going to ask how that ended up in your hands, by the way. There are plenty of quartermaster sergeants in the galaxy, whatever the species, who'll name their price. I might have had occasion to corrupt one or two myself back in the day. Can I assume the rest of them are in equally good shape?"

"Yes." Roby held out his hand, and Decker gave him the reassembled weapon. "Everyone who's been in a regular uniform sometime in the last twenty years should be able to operate this, right?"

"Yup. Even the dumbest of the bunch. Of course, the universe is always winning the stupidity war and producing better idiots, so that's not one hundred percent guaranteed."

"How about this one?" Roby unlocked another container and nodded at a metal case with familiar markings.

"Portable missile launchers. Nice." The Marine picked it up and removed the lid. "Still current with some Commonwealth units. This definitely shouldn't have fallen off an armory transport. Kudos to your procurement officer."

He turned on the launcher's power pack and watched it run through the test cycle. When the indicator on the control screen turned to a steady green, he looked up at Roby.

"Another piece from the strategic stocks, I'd say. This one has never been used."

Fleet Security would have a collective heart attack once he told them the Confederacy of the Howling Stars had been helping itself to the war reserve.

"How about the missiles themselves?"

Roby indicated another container. "Ten per launcher."

"Adequate, but I wouldn't waste any on live training. The built-in simulator is good enough to make the smarter dumbasses proficient."

And so it went, container after container. Mortars, heavy automatic weapons, battle armor, drones, all seemingly drawn from the reserve. They had enough to start a small war and Decker commented to that effect.

Roby chuckled.

"You're not far off, Lorenzo, but all in due course. Answer me this, however. How does a combat engineer sergeant first class, even one from the Commonwealth Marine Corps, get so good with weapons? You handled each one of them like an extension of your own arm. Are there some skills you might have picked up on the sly, or some particular assignments that might not be on your record?"

Decker gave a half-hearted shrug, annoyed with himself more than anything else. When it came to ordnance, he just couldn't keep his inner master gunner under control, and that represented a significant failing for an intelligence field agent, especially one from the Black Gang.

"I prepared for the command sergeant examinations before my run-in with the code of discipline, and part of that meant taking training in preparation for the master gunner's entrance test."

"I see." Roby examined him with slightly narrowed eyes as if weighing his answer. "As I said yesterday, you puzzle me, Jack Lorenzo. But I think you'll be more useful than the rest of this draft put together, and then some."

"Depends on the mission," Decker replied, meeting Roby's eyes. "Some types of operation, I do better than others. Some, I don't do at all."

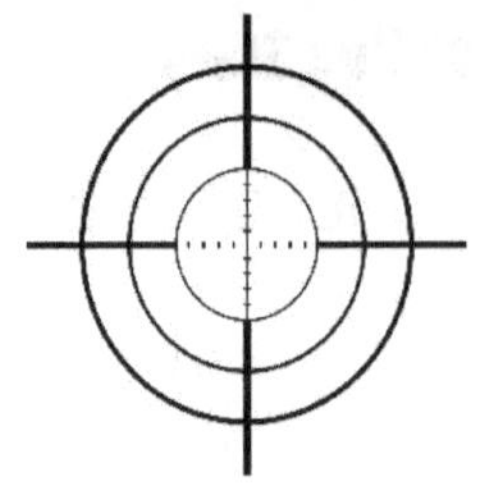

— TWELVE —

"So this is our destination," Decker said when the image of a rapidly growing orb swam into focus on the saloon's main screen. "It looks pretty wild."

And to human eyes, it did. Its greens seemed too deep, its blues too blue and its clouds too shredded. The planet struck him as being a world of violent colors, large oceans, and long, sinuous continents, dotted here and there by browns that seemed perfectly reasonable for arid deserts. He could make out at least three cyclones raging over the open seas, not much above the equator, each looking like a giant eye staring back at him, threatening death for anyone so foolish as to challenge it.

"I don't suppose," he continued, "that you're going to bother sharing the location of this star system with us lowly grunts."

"Of course not." Roby shook his head. "It's need to know, even though I doubt lowly grunts would make heads or tails of galactic coordinates, or even the star's catalog designation. This one's deep inside the Protectorate Zone and pretty much on everyone's ignore list. Our employers call this planet Asgard."

"Why choose a name out of Norse mythology?" Decker asked. "The theme's been overdone for so long it's beyond cliché."

"Why? Why not?" The mercenary shrugged. "I didn't name it. They could have called it New Earth and I still wouldn't care. This is where the Confederacy wants us, and they pay us well to be here."

"Cool with me. I joined up because I wanted to see more of the galaxy and here I am, seeing more of the galaxy."

Steiger joined him and draped her arm over his shoulder.

"End of the line?"

"They call it Asgard, would you believe."

She snorted. "Oh dear, how highly unoriginal and done to death. But as a wise man once said, what's in a name?"

"A crap hole by any other name would still stink to high heaven." Zack wrinkled his nose in mock disgust. "Something tells me we won't find a nice, quiet place to retire down there."

"Between the weather and the wildlife," Roby said, "the government won't be paying out your pension for very long."

"So why are we still tripping around in orbit?"

"See that lovely cyclone to the far left? It's almost over our base of operations. Landing in two hundred kilometers an hour winds isn't advisable."

"Ah." Decker's eyebrows shot up. "I see. That means we have time to relax while we wait. How about a round?"

Roby and Steiger exchanged looks, then the latter shrugged. "Jack has a point."

"He also has a capacity for reconstituted fruit juice no one else can match around here." Roby's elbow nudged Zack in the ribs. "However, you're right. He does have a point. Let me buy you the paint thinner of your choice, with or without ethanol. I'm afraid what's available on Asgard isn't any better. Worse, in some cases."

Several hours passed, during which the passengers either fidgeted or mellowed out, depending on their disposition. In Decker's case, the mellowness was owed mostly to his phlegmatic outlook on things he couldn't possibly affect one way or another. Finally, the storm veered away, opening a window of calm sufficient for their unnamed starship's captain.

A loud voice on hidden speakers ordered them to strap into their bunks, no exceptions tolerated, and ensure they had secured all loose objects. Most, if not all of them were veterans of large ship landings and knew the score. It didn't make the wait, in a horizontal position beneath security netting, any easier. History was replete with stories of crash landings that turned humans into a pink paste.

To Steiger's annoyance, Decker quickly fell asleep, a soft snore escaping his lips. She narrowly suppressed the temptation to toss something hard at his bunk, a bare meter below hers, just to keep him awake like the rest of them, wondering whether that cyclonic storm had actually left the designated landing area.

Then, the ship's artificial gravity vanished as it began to spiral downward into Asgard's atmosphere, replaced by a natural pull that played havoc with the other human senses until a new normal replaced the old one. Fortunately, none in their cabin felt the urge to let their latest meal roam free. As they discovered after landing, not all were that lucky.

*

A stench thicker than a drunken Shrehari's breath momentarily stopped Decker's measured pace down the grounded starship's ramp. Fetid odors of alien decomposition, overlaid by the miasma of a nearby brackish swamp swirled around him, punctuated here and there by the more familiar aromas of cooling metal, old lubricants, and soot from thrusters used with more enthusiasm than skill.

The tarmac seemed to be rammed earth solidified by hundreds of starship landings into something resembling concrete. Numerous fluid spills had created a patchwork of darker stains on the human-made gash violating an otherwise pristine jungle.

A lazy breeze, the one that wafted the unpleasant scents up Decker's nostrils, gave movement to vegetation that might have been at home on Earth a hundred million years earlier, including huge plants that by all rights should not have been able to grow to something several times the Marine's not inconsiderable height.

Here, at ground level, the violent green he had seen from orbit seemed even more implacably hostile to any advanced species. Small *things* flitted about, singly and in swarms, generating a background buzz that would give Zack a headache in short order. Fortunately, none approached the new arrivals, as if they had already determined these beings from a world far away provided nothing more worthwhile than indigestion, if not instant death. Nonetheless, he felt his level of irritation rise rapidly and with force.

Human soldiers, wearing light chameleon armor, stepped out of the tree line and advanced towards them, carbines slung low, their barrels pointing at the ground.

"The welcoming committee is right on cue," Decker grumbled just loud enough for Steiger to hear. "And an ugly bunch too."

He swatted away a critter that had come too close to his squinting eyes. The cloud cover, still thick after the cyclone's glancing hit, failed to stop some of the primary's harsher rays, making him wish for a visored helmet like those worn by the troops who would escort them away from the jungle tarmac.

"Cheer up," Langton said. "At least we're off the ship and able to stretch our legs."

"Glass half full kind of guy, aren't you," Decker replied with a half-hearted sneer. "I always thought you meatheads were more the glass totally empty sort."

"Scurrilous rumors, Mister Lorenzo. I assure you. We've been known to find glasses with all kinds of fillings."

The Marine snorted. "I'll bet. And yet they'd still have been handed to the evidence sergeant perfectly empty."

Beads of sweat began to sprout from Decker's hairline and beneath the furry appendage covering his upper lip.

"Join up and see the galaxy, they said." He slung his duffel over one shoulder. "They just didn't mention side trips into the armpits of the universe, and this one hasn't been washed in a couple of million years."

"You know what they say." Steiger nudged him. "If you can't take a joke, you shouldn't have signed on."

"Is he always this cheerful?" Langton asked her.

"He just hates walking, I think. It's something about crossing the stars at FTL speed and then making the last bit of the trip on his own little legs."

"So you've witnessed this behavior before."

"Sadly, yes." Her tone rang with disappointment, but she winked at a mock-outraged Decker.

"Phew, it stinks." Tiny Tiktin had finally taken a full whiff of the turgid air, and his broad face twisted into a grimace of disgust. "Someone forgot to cap off the latrine pit."

"Welcome to the ass end of the galaxy," Decker replied.

The troops in the chameleon armor waved them down a broad path between towering plants, and the stench of putrefaction increased to the point where Tiny retched noisily.

"Keep it in, buddy," Decker slapped the big Celestan's shoulder. "Consider this a test of your gutsiness."

"Or his ability to keep his guts where they belong," Steiger said, nose wrinkled against the pungent odor.

They emerged from the forested strip and came face to face with a sprawling, fenced-in base set up hard against the deep blue waters of a broad bay where the white-topped waves still bore witness to the recently departed cyclone. The buildings looked like re-purposed containers of the type used to drop material from orbit.

Decker grunted at the sight.

"Someone with a lot of money bought themselves an instant base. Nice."

"Sure," Steiger agreed. "But why?"

"Ours not to reason why," Langton remarked with a philosophical air. "Ours but to do and die."

"Cheerful bugger, aren't you?" Zack snorted with derision. "But I'm impressed that a meathead can quote Tennyson."

"And I'm impressed that a jarhead knows who Tennyson was," Langton retorted with a chuckle.

Tiny Tiktin shook his head, grimacing. "I never know what you guys are talking about."

"You're not missing much," Steiger told him. "Jack has a weird fetish for pre-spaceflight history and as for Alex? Who knows what meatheads consider entertainment."

"Not this," Langton replied. "But maybe it'll grow on me."

"So will fungus." Decker jerked his chin at the defensive rings enclosing the base. "Not bad. Any unwanted guest looking to break in via the surface is going to find it painful."

"And if someone wants to come in by air?"

"Look at that cluster of containers in the center," he replied. "If that's not an air defense array masquerading as a pile of junk, I'll buy a round of whatever they distil around here, sight unseen."

They passed through a complex set of barriers designed to discourage any head-on assault, watched by armored troops with clear helmet visors.

"Welcome to Midgard Base," Roby called out from the head of the column. "Your new home for now."

"Midgard?" Decker rolled his eyes. "Next thing you know they'll tell us the commanding officer is called Heimdall."

"Now, now," Steiger said, "don't let the theatricality of it all get to you. They had to name this place and a crap pile by any other name..."

"Is still a crap pile. I think I've heard that one recently." He took a deep breath of sea air and sighed with satisfaction. "At least they were smart enough to build where the jungle stink can't reach."

The rammed earth streets between the converted containers seemed clean and well maintained. The buildings, however, showed signs of hard use, not least from their last drop, which had decorated them with black streaks, pitting and dents. Troops in battledress moved around with apparent purpose, all of them armed, if not armored.

"It looks like a heck of a forward operating base," Langton commented. "Though forward of what and operating where I couldn't even begin to guess."

Decker's eyes never rested on a single spot for very long, though he did examine every human in sight, hoping to see Hal Tarra or someone in a visored helmet who moved like him.

Hal might not recognize Decker in his current disguise so the Marine knew he might have to make the opening move, provided, of course, that Tarra hadn't shipped out to somewhere even less appealing.

Roby halted them in front of a building facing an open square where a platoon of soldiers moved through some elaborate battle drill, their helmets projecting a virtual reality combat environment for the wearer's eyes and ears.

"This," he waved at the former container, "will be your temporary barracks, until you've been assigned to a unit. Grab a bunk and relax. Stay inside until you're told otherwise, or you hear a bell announcing chow time. The large complex on the other side of the parade ground is the mess hall. You go eat there and come back here right after. Someone will be by in the next few hours for your in-processing."

"Typical," Decker murmured. "Hurry up and wait, the motto of every armed service ever invented. Glad to see the merc world isn't any different."

Roby turned his hard eyes on Zack. "Any problems, Lorenzo?"

"No. I was just remarking on humanity's ability to be consistent over the centuries and across the light years."

The mercenary held Decker's eyes for a few moments before looking away.

"Dismissed."

*

Chow time came and went, along with Zack's hunger, but without a glimpse of Hal Tarra. The platoon training on the parade ground had vanished, leaving the broad expanse empty save for a few native avians brave enough to venture into the intruders' den.

By mid-afternoon, a stocky, square-faced woman with a face like thunder and an attitude to match chased Decker off the container's front steps and through the open door. With all twelve of the new arrivals assembled in a half circle between the bunks, she slowly examined them with eyes oozing dismissive contempt.

"My name is Barzee, and I'm the officer tasked with your in-processing. To ensure this happens in an orderly manner, you will only speak when spoken to, and obey every order without question."

"If we can't speak without permission, we can hardly question orders, right?" Decker muttered for Steiger's ears only. This earned him a dirty look from Barzee, but the woman didn't single the Marine out for an immediate dressing-down.

In Zack's estimation, the chicken had arrived, ready to defecate all over the place. He hadn't figured a mercenary outfit would be this uptight, but then, his only experience with freelance soldiering had been as a janissary, a slave soldier on the far side of the Orion Arm.

The administrivia turned out to be as painfully trivial as he expected. Relief came when Barzee led them to the quartermaster's hangar to draw their basic issue of clothing, armor, and weapons. No ammunition, however, even though they received power packs for their guns. It all seemed smooth enough to pass for a regular operation and before the sun dipped towards the horizon, they'd been turned into proper private military contractors.

"Welcome to the Frontier Solutions PMC," Barzee announced once they'd formed up in two uniformed ranks in front of the barracks, along with everything they owned split between a duffel bag and a backpack.

"Yippee kay yay," Decker whispered to Miko Steiger in a theatrical aside.

Barzee glared at him with unfeigned exasperation once again.

"Magnus Roby did mention you'd be trouble, Mister Lorenzo. For the last time, pray keep your lips zipped until we're done."

Zack's smile, as he nodded, failed to reach his eyes. She held his gaze for a few more seconds before continuing.

"We've seen copies of your various service records, and you've all been evaluated by Roby during the transit from Kilia. As a result, we've determined your assignments within the unit. These are not negotiable." She pointed at Zack, Langton, and Steiger. "You three are going to the Special Assignments Company. For some reason, the boss decided it needs a new smart ass along with his grown-up escort."

Decker's smile turned into a broad grin. Barzee did have a sense of humor somewhere behind the mean eyes.

"The rest of you are going to the General Duties Battalion, for employment within your prior military specialties. With the exception of Lorenzo, Langton, and Steiger, you'll stay in these barracks until further notice." She turned her basilisk stare on Decker again and then pointed at a building on the other side of the parade ground. "You three report over there. They'll tell you where you're to bunk."

Decker cocked a questioning eyebrow at Barzee.

"Yes, you may go," she said.

"It's been a pleasure," he replied before walking off without a backward glance.

Chances were good that Hal Tarra had also ended up with Special Assignments. After all, what better use could Frontier Solutions find for a retired Pathfinder?

They dropped their kit by the building's front door and entered, Decker in the lead.

A familiar face looked up from a field desk and smiled.

"I see Flora has you all sorted out," Roby said.

"Flora? You mean Barzee. Yeah. If you ask me, I think she could use a personality transplant, preferably from a human, but she has the chickenshit down pat," Decker replied. "Let me guess. You're our CO?"

"I am." The smile widened. "I try to pick the cream of the crop for Special Assignments. Rank fillers need not apply."

"And yet you chose us. Go figure." Decker looked around but saw very little beyond the usual camp furniture one would expect in a company orderly room on a forward operating base. "So what does this Special Assignments Company do for a living?"

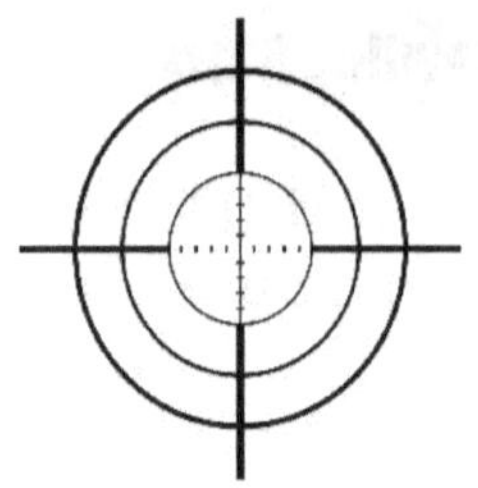

— THIRTEEN —

"You definitely puzzle me," Roby muttered in a voice so faint only Decker's helmet audio pickups could detect it.

The two men, wearing chameleon armor and full fighting rig, had tucked themselves beneath a rocky ledge that masked what few emissions they gave off. Around them, the sounds of the Asgard night variously chirped, crackled, and whispered with wildlife that had decided the human invaders were no threat.

Somewhere to their left, an infantry company slowly approached what Decker hoped would be a spectacular ambush. A few dozen meters to their right, Langton and Steiger also lay in wait, four of them against eighty troops. The operation would test the Special Assignment Company's most recent recruits as well as the newly formed company that included the rank fillers who'd traveled to Asgard with them. No doubt they had given Tiny Tiktin the unenviable task of humping his platoon's heavy plasma gun.

They had been training non-stop for the last seven days, every minute designed to show Roby how good they were. Of course, Decker already knew Steiger was no slouch when it came to combat, but Langton's quiet competence had come as a pleasant surprise, hinting at a past that included more than directing traffic and running stockades.

The only fly in his personal ointment came from finding out that Hal had been shipped off to an unknown destination weeks earlier, after a period spent training with Special Assignments. As a result, Decker had been letting some of his inner Pathfinder shine through so he could demonstrate the kind of competence that might see him sent to the same place as Tarra. He knew it was a dangerous game and might attract the kind of attention he couldn't afford, but saw no other choice.

"Why?" Decker asked, eyes not shifting from the sensor readout projected on the inside of his helmet visor.

"You're a better operator than I would have expected from a mere combat engineer, even one from the Marine Corps."

"So? Langton's a better operator than I expected and he's an ex-Army meathead."

"Sure, but I'm talking about you, not Langton."

"The Corps trains its senior noncoms really well, Magnus. You must not have had much exposure to members of my tribe." He paused. "Mind you, I'm puzzled as to what Frontier Solutions is and who it works for. But you don't see me asking while we're supposed to be sitting in the dark like bumps on a log so that the rank fillers don't detect the surprise we prepared for them."

"Touché," the mercenary replied. "But I have met other members of your tribe. And yet, here we are."

"Here we are." Decker agreed. "And our targets will be here soon as well. Might I suggest we both keep our curiosity confined to the current mission?"

"Of course."

For some reason, the Marine could picture Roby's sardonic smile beneath the visor, and he repressed the urge to snort.

They waited in companionable silence for another half hour before the first signs of non-native life appeared on Decker's sensor.

"Look sharp," he murmured. "They're here."

He dialed up the visual projection and saw two point men stalk silently down the animal track below their observation post. Barrow and Parker, the two misfit Marines. Decker would have recognized them anywhere thanks to the way they moved — one like a spastic monkey and the other like a wooden doll. Zack couldn't fathom how they ever made it through a hitch in the Corps, let alone earn corporal's stripes.

They passed the entrance to the ambush zone without detecting the remote-controlled gun that would close off any retreat. Another, set to cut off the way forward, sat a hundred meters further up the trail, within sight of Steiger and Langton's position.

In theory, four operators who knew their stuff could fuck up three full platoons of light infantry without breaking a sweat, provided they kept the element of surprise. So far, so good.

The first platoon came hard on Barrow and Parker's heels, too tightly bunched together. Good for the ambushers but bad for the platoon. At least their noise discipline met Decker's uncompromising standards.

He raised his automatic rifle, its plasma-spewing barrel replaced by a low-power laser that would count coup on the opposition's battle suit sensors, and began to track the column's shadows beneath the silvery light of Asgard's largest moon.

A gap appeared, then a small cluster of troops: the company commander's party, right where they expected it. Steiger would have the pleasure of taking him and his wingers down. When the second platoon entered the ambush zone, Decker looked for and quickly found the platoon leader.

He was the one looking around without pause, while the other troopers kept their eyes on the ground ahead of them or to the side they'd been assigned. It wasn't a bad mistake, but anything that singled out a unit's leadership could help the enemy in a day and age where no one wore rank insignia in the field, and everyone carried the same basic equipment.

Decker flicked on his system's active targeting, and a red pip appeared on the inside of his visor, glued to the dark shape of the platoon leader. Beside him, Roby waited for the third and last platoon to pass the remote-controlled gun, his rifle ready to lock onto that one's leader.

When Langton triggered the ambush once Barrow and Parker reached the far cutoff, it came as an utter surprise. The infantry company never stood a chance. Lasers struck armor, and under the weight of fire from the special ops team, battle suits began to register casualties and lock up.

Decker quickly took down his intended target, as did the others, leaving the three platoon leaders and their company commander helpless bystanders to a patrol suddenly gone very wrong.

Some of the section and squad leaders kept their heads and tried to force the troops into a broken line facing the oncoming fire, in preparation for a mad rush at their tormentors.

They knew without having to give it much conscious thought that their only way out was charging the enemy. The remote guns were hammering both ends of the company and the underbrush on the far side of the trail would have been booby-trapped, not to mention that running away would expose them to shots in the back.

One big soldier, carrying a heavy automatic weapon at the hip, stood up and began spraying simulated plasma at the slight rise where the four operators had found secure firing positions. Heartened by the sight, the remainder of the company, those whose battle suits hadn't locked up yet, rose, and, under the impetus of the remaining junior leaders, pushed their way through the lighter undergrowth and towards where they thought the enemy still lay in wait.

But it would prove to be in vain.

With the company's senior leadership taken out, the four operators had skedaddled, abandoning the remote controlled guns which still did sterling service in keeping the trail shut at either end. Decker just had time to see Tiny Tiktin rally the 'surviving' troops for a charge at the ambushers before following Roby into the dense woods on the far side of the rise.

They met Steiger and Langton fifteen minutes later, by a shallow ford across a rapidly moving river.

"That was amusing," Miko murmured when the four operators knelt in a tight circle on the soft ground. "It's been ages since my last time on the fun side of an ambush."

"We'll hear the casualty report when the company commander calls in, which should be any moment now," Roby said. "Their suits will have unlocked once the remote guns stopped firing, but I think we managed to render them ineffective for some time, or would have if this had been for real."

"And now we get to hump out. At least, we won't have to carry the remotes." Decker sounded just a tad weary. "Or make that I won't have to carry the remotes."

"You're the biggest and strongest," Steiger said. "Don't forget the rest of us hauled crap too."

"Transport is coming," Roby quickly said before the discussion went any further. "Though we will have to swing by and pick up those guns you seem to love so much, Jack. They can be disposable on a real mission if necessary, but not during training."

"Will there be a debrief?" Langton asked. "I don't mean us, but the grunts? They could probably profit by hearing about the ambush from our end."

Roby shook his head. "Not an immediate after-action. They still have a raid to carry out. We'll arrange something when they're back at Midgard. Excellent set-up, by the way. I doubt anyone could have done it better."

*

A meaty hand slapped Decker's shoulder as he waited in line at the chow hall three days later. He turned and came face-to-face with Atli 'Tiny' Tiktin's smiling face.

"Hey, Jack! How are they hanging? I hear you and the other special squirrels pulled that number on us the other night."

"Tiny, my friend." Decker grinned at the big man. "One still hanging lower than the other and yes that would have been us. I saw you have a moment of glory yourself with the heavy gun just before we high-tailed it out."

"I figured if we wanted to get the ambush drill going right, somebody needed to deliver covering fire and let everyone see him doing it, so they'd push their asses in gear. A lot of the guys were pissed when we found out you'd left."

Decker picked up a loaded tray. "Come and sit with us, Tiny. A little cabin mate reunion."

The Celestan shook his head. "I'd better not. There are still a few folks sore at you guys."

"Sure. I understand. Talk to you later."

When he sat down, Steiger asked, "How's man-mountain?"

"In a good mood." Decker took a bit of his stew and frowned. "Someone needs to adjust the damn protein vats, so they stop producing leather. Tiny told me we didn't make any friends in his company with our ambush. They're kind of miffed that we didn't stay to fight it out."

"Par for the course, where you're concerned, buddy," Langton pointed at him with his fork. "The not making friends, I mean. Not staying to fight it out is just good sense, though not everyone will see it that way. There are plenty of puffed chests around here if you take my meaning."

Roby dropped down beside the former MP, face like thunder.

"Someone stole your bag of dirty tricks?" Steiger asked when she saw his expression.

"Almost." He dug an angry spoon into his stew and shoved a heaping into his mouth. After the first chew, a frown similar to Zack's replaced the anger. "The damned idiots have the vats running too warm again."

"Yep." Decker nodded. "My thoughts exactly. Maybe some informal counseling would help."

"I'll talk to the CO about it."

"Not until you've lost that look of eternal damnation," Langton suggested. "We might be able to help with that if you're so inclined."

"I'm not going with you," Roby replied. "The CO is sending me back into the Commonwealth for reasons you don't need to know. I had hoped to take this team to Naraka where most of the Special Assignments Company is plying its trade, but that plan just flew out the door."

"Naraka?" Decker raised a questioning eyebrow.

"Next star system, about four light years. It's our primary contract with plenty of special ops. You'll receive the full briefing later because you're still going."

"Who takes over?"

Roby jerked his chin at the Marine. "You do, of course. For some reason, you're the best operator I've seen go through here, myself included. Combat engineer, eh?"

Decker didn't take the bait.

"We're short one in that case since teams shouldn't be less than four," he said instead. "If you want me to take over, we need to find a fourth, vetted by me."

"Vetted by you?"

"If I'm the best operator you've seen, including the one in the mirror, then yeah, by me." He glanced around the rapidly filling chow hall. "I'm going to go out on a limb here and venture that the pool of potential candidates is pretty shallow."

"Shallow is right." Roby grimaced. "All of the ones who might be good operators are already on Naraka or at this table. You'll have to pick through what's left."

"Oh joy," Decker muttered. He seemed disheartened, but for the first time since arriving on Asgard, he knew where they had sent Hal Tarra. A sudden feeling of impatience came over him, and it took all of his restraint to finish the meal at a reasonable pace.

"When do we leave?" He asked, after swallowing the last bit of gravy soaked bread.

"Five days, maybe seven." Roby shrugged. "We don't exactly have regular starship service out here."

"Then you'd better lead me to the personnel files of everyone available, so I can find my fourth. Five days isn't much to integrate a newbie into an existing team, especially someone who didn't pass your own selection process."

*

"The gods wept." Decker tossed Roby's tablet back on the desk and sighed. "I don't see anyone with the right background or aptitudes, if your vetting methods are anywhere near accurate."

"They work well enough," Roby replied slumping in his chair, feeling unaccountably tired.

"People with the stuff to become operators are rare in the regular services, let alone the freelance business," Steiger reminded them.

They had been reading files for hours and outside, night had fallen. Muted thrashing in the undergrowth beyond the defensive perimeter had replaced the avian buzz as larger predators came out to feed. It reminded Zack that his stomach would soon be clamoring for an evening snack.

"Then we'll have to find someone we can teach enough to be useful, even if it's only as a beast of burden. We don't all have to be skilled assassins."

"Beast of burden, eh?" A sly smile pulled at Langton's lips. "And teachable too. What about Tiny?"

A derisive laugh escaped Roby's lips but then he saw Decker's thoughtful expression.

"No." The mercenary officer shook his head. "You can't be serious. Tiny?"

"Of the bunch on our ship, he was the only one who showed a genuine willingness to train and learn. And he did pick up a few tricks." Decker related what he'd witnessed as they were evacuating the ambush site. "Plus I kind of like the big lug. I'd rather take a man I've already seen in action than an unknown with no better qualifications, and when it comes to our kind of job, none of them have qualifications."

"Agreed." Steiger gave him thumbs up.

"I guess that makes it unanimous. Tiny it is." Decker pushed back his chair and stretched. "If all he does is carry the heavy ordnance, we'll still be a few steps ahead of the game."

"On your head be it." Roby stood. "And if you'll buy me a beer, I might even wish you good luck."

"Sure. When can I have the lad?"

"If you can track Tiktin down tonight, you can have him shift to our barracks right away. I'll let Flora Barzee know about the change of assignment tomorrow."

Decker made a face. "Better you than me."

Before Roby could reply, the Marine made it out the door and halfway across the parade ground, headed for the most likely place he might find Tiktin at this hour of the evening.

Fortunately, it happened to be the same place he wanted to visit now that their work for the day had come to a grinding halt. With a shrug, the mercenary officer followed at a more sedate pace, Steiger and Langton in his wake.

Decker found Tiny leaning against the improvised bar, built from large ammunition crates topped by a shiny piece of metal. It had no purpose other than to provide atmosphere. Drinks came from a dispenser, not a robotic or human bartender.

The big Celestan seemed to be nursing a bulb in solitude even though a crowd of rank fillers surrounded him with loud, often incoherent conversation desperately trying to drown out the latest in human music booming overhead.

Decker winced at the noise but plowed through the semi-inebriated crowd nonetheless. An infantry company set loose after a frustrating week or two in the jungle needed to party as hard as it could with what little means Midgard offered.

Along the way, he received a few angry stares from troopers sober enough and plugged in enough to recognize him as one of the Special Assignments assholes who ruined a perfectly good patrol three days earlier.

Decker shoved an indignant trooper aside and bellied up to the bar beside Tiny. When the former made to protest, he gave the man a full-on view of his snarling face. It sufficed.

"Staring into that witches' brew won't make it taste any better," Decker shouted into Tiktin's ear.

Steiger appeared before his eyes, on the other side of the bar.

"Nothing could make it taste better," she said before producing a new bulb that landed right in front of Tiny. "But I suppose where we're going in a few days, it won't matter."

Tiktin looked up for the first time and did an almost comical double take at seeing not only Decker but also Steiger and Langton, with Roby hovering in the background.

"Finish what you have, buddy." Zack shoved a hard elbow into the Celestan's ribs. "Because as of right now, your ass is mine."

"Huh?" Tiny turned a puzzled frown on the Marine, then his two companions.

"Very eloquent," Miko said. "You'll fit right in."

"Right into what?"

Decker laid his arm across the big man's shoulders.

"The team, Tiny. You've been transferred. As of right now, you belong to the Special Assignments Company, and more specifically, to my team."

Tiktin stared at Decker, stunned.

"He's at a loss for words," Langton remarked. "A good trait when stalking the enemy. Can we finish this elsewhere? The noise is degrading my hearing to the point where I fear permanent damage."

"Right." Zack indicated at the machine. "Grab a few bulbs of hooch for yourselves and a fruit juice for me. We'll continue this in the barracks."

He leaned in towards Tiny.

"Swallow what you have, then grab all of your kit and haul it to the Special Assignments hut. Your ass is bunking with us tonight."

"No shit, Jack?"

"Have I ever crapped on you? When you didn't deserve it, I mean?"

"Never."

"Then go."

Tiny drained his bulb and hurried out, oblivious to the quizzical looks from his former platoon mates. He was a man on a mission.

When the Celestan showed up at the Special Assignments barracks ten minutes later, burdened with everything he owned, the others were lounging on their bunks, bulbs in hand. Decker nodded towards an empty cot.

"Set yourself up over there."

When Tiktin had stowed his gear, the Marine tossed him a fresh drink.

"You're probably wondering if this is a dream, a nightmare or some kind of hallucination stemming from bad booze and worse food, right?"

"A bit of all three," the big man confessed. He twisted open the bulb and took a big gulp. "So why did you guys decide to pull me out of grunt central and into the lap of luxury?"

"Spec Ops teams are usually a minimum of four. We always work in pairs. Roby just received new orders, leaving us one short and me in charge," Decker replied. "And since we're leaving on a mission within the next week, I didn't have time to screw around with folks I don't know. Congratulations, you're the least objectionable pick of the entire lot in grunt central."

"How's that?"

"You're willing to learn, and you're big enough to haul a lot of gear. Plus you have a brain somewhere in that thick skull, one that hasn't been thoroughly pickled yet."

"Coming from him," Steiger chimed in, "that's a heck of a compliment."

Tiktin smiled with pride. "That's what I figured. Thanks for taking me on, Jack. I'm really close to strangling a few guys who think they're hot shit but can't find their asses with both hands and a Mark Nine battlefield sensor.”

“Don’t thank me yet. The three of us are going to ride you hard until we ship out because our lives depend on having a fourth man in the team who can find his ass with both hands. If it turns out you can’t, I’ll go into action one man short, capisce?”

“Capisce. I won’t let you down. Where’s this mission going to take us?”

“Does it matter?”

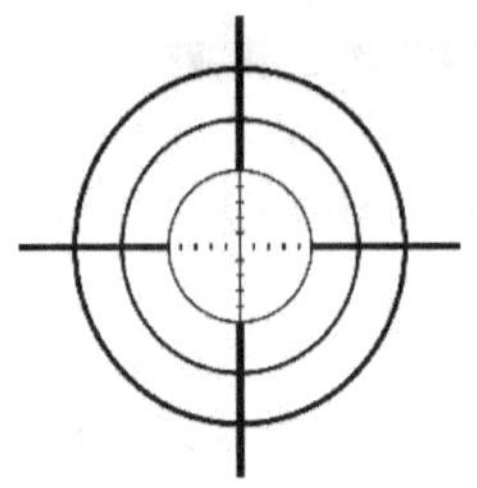

— FOURTEEN —

In the end, Decker had six days to ride Tiny Tiktin's ass ragged. The Celestan would never make the grade for a Marine Pathfinder billet, let alone a Special Forces team, but he did have enough of a brain to learn a few basics, and he had a lot of heart.

At the end of four days alternating between the simulators, the ranges, and the stinking jungle, he felt reasonably comfortable having Tiny as his wingman on simple operations. Besides, mercenary special ops couldn't be anywhere near as challenging as the real — read regular services — thing, although dead was dead no matter whose uniform you wore.

After a bit of good-natured ribbing, Tiny's former buddies began to ignore him, other than Parker and Barrow, who stared at the big guy with venom in their eyes every time they crossed paths in the chow hall or bar. Decker heard from Roby that the two former Marines had complained about the job going to an ex-Guard puke.

Late in the afternoon of the seventh day since Roby had handed the team over to Zack, while they sat outside their hut cleaning weapons, they heard the beginnings of a loud rumble far above, one that increased rapidly. A sleek starship eventually broke through the low cloud cover, riding hard on its thrusters, headed for the improvised strip where they'd landed a few weeks earlier.

"Confederacy tub," Decker shouted to cut through the din. "It must be our ride to Naraka."

They watched the ship's descent slow until it merely hovered, then most of its hull vanished behind the dense tree line.

Moments later, the noise evaporated, leaving a stunningly silent void in its stead. None of them spoke for a few seconds. Then Decker slammed the power pack back into his blaster and stood, wiping the dust from the seat of his pants.

"I don't think it'll be staying for the night, kids. We might as well finish packing before someone shows up to hustle us aboard."

"Indeed." Langton followed suit. "I won't be overly sad to see the last of this place. It always scares me when I get used to a stench."

"For some reason, I have the feeling we might remember Asgard with fondness once we're on Naraka," Steiger replied. "There's a rationale as to why Frontier Solutions set up their FOB here and not closer to the action, even if it's only a couple of light years away, and it isn't because of the recreational facilities."

"I'm afraid you might be correct." The former MP checked his carbine one last time. "Come on, Tiny."

Magnus Roby showed up twenty minutes later with their orders and found Decker's team sitting on stripped down bunks, their bulging duffel bags, and backpacks at their feet. A slow smile spread across his face.

"Now I'm really annoyed that the boss has put me on a different task. Leading folks who can actually anticipate orders is a rare treat around here."

"Blame Jack." Steiger jerked her thumb at the Marine. "He has Asgard's equivalent of ants in his pants and can't wait to be off."

Which wasn't far from the truth. Decker's impatience at finally catching up with Hal Tarra and finding out what had driven him this far beyond the Rim had become almost unmanageable.

"You'll be well served then." He handed Zack a tablet. "Everything you need to know for the moment is on there. It'll unlock automatically once you're in space, for obvious security reasons. Draw a basic load of ammo so that you don't land on Naraka looking like damned tourists, then head off for the landing strip."

"Tough place, is it?" Langton inquired.

"Let's just say that I wouldn't set foot there without some basic precautions." Roby stuck out his hand. "You'll be fine, Lorenzo. Good luck and remember to duck. We'll likely meet up again soon enough."

I wouldn't necessarily bet on that, Decker thought but accepted the handshake nonetheless.

"The round that'll take me down for good hasn't been minted yet, Magnus."

"Though you've caught enough non-fatal ones in your day," Steiger pointed out with more than a hint of mischief, "if I recall the number of scars crisscrossing every part of your anatomy."

"You should remember them correctly." Langton bestowed a mildly vulgar leer on her. "Considering all the close-up study time you've put in over the last few weeks."

"Children." Decker held up both hands to stop the conversation before it went further downhill. "Let's go pick up our ammo and pack it away properly. We can continue maligning each other's chastity once we're aboard."

As if driven by an unspoken signal the three of them snapped to attention in unison.

"Your wish is our command," Langton said, tossing off a mock salute.

*

Conspicuously unmarked, the Confederacy of the Howling Stars vessel sat on the tarmac like a giant, well-worn metal wasp sporting the signs of too many atmospheric re-entries and too few stints in dry-dock.

Smaller than the sloop that had brought them to Asgard, it also seemed more menacing, though it wouldn't provide much of a challenge to even the Fleet's smallest FTL-capable warships.

Decker figured that this one could outrun what it couldn't outfight, and that suited him. He'd seen more deep space combat in the last few years than was decent for an honest Marine, even one who'd been shanghaied into the darkest of Naval Intelligence's black ops.

Besides, he'd already shown too much knowledge and experience for a mere combat engineer sergeant, enough to trigger Magnus Roby's bullshit detectors, though it seemed like the mercenary officer wasn't inclined to look a gift Marine in the mouth.

A bored looking woman with the usual Howler body art stood at the foot of the ship's belly ramp and watched them approach with about as much interest as Decker had shown for last night's meal.

"I'm Jack Lorenzo," Decker called out once they were within speaking range. "Since this place is about as much fun as listening to Shrehari opera, my team and I are looking to hitch a ride for Naraka. You guys have some space for us?"

Without even cracking the hint of a smile, she jerked a thumb over her shoulder, pointing up the ramp. "Get on, funny guy. The skipper wants to be off the ground an hour ago, and we still have some crap to load. There'll be a crewman at the top to show you to your bunks."

"Thank you."

The passageways, once out of the small cargo hold, seemed claustrophobic and if Zack felt the oppression of bulkheads closing in, he could only imagine the effect on Tiny, but when he turned back to glance at the Celestan, he saw nothing but unfeigned interest on his face.

This being Decker's first time aboard a Confederacy ship, he resolved to memorize every detail, even though some other agent had probably infiltrated the group already and reported back to HQ. Their guide, an equally dour member of the Howlers, stopped at an open door and turned to wave them across the threshold.

"Your palace, brave warriors," he said without a trace of irony on his pockmarked face. "Stay there until we've lifted. After that, don't leave this deck. The saloon is four doors down."

Once they'd stepped into the tiny compartment, barely big enough for four stacked bunks, arrayed in two pairs facing each other, and an equal number of lockers, the door slammed shut with finality. Decker and Tiktin took the two lower bunks, with Langton settling in above Tiny rather than argue with Steiger.

After stowing her gear, the latter inspected the heads and reported back to the team with a grim expression.

"There's barely enough room in there to change your mind. Playing with the soap is entirely out of the question."

"Not that anyone had the intention of doing so," Langton commented with a wry smile. "I assume the door is locked?"

Decker touched the control panel without success.

"Of course. I'd do the same thing in their shoes."

"So you would." Steiger winked at him, a reminder of how he'd treated her aboard his and Hera Talyn's ship *Phoenix* the previous year, during the Garonne uprising.

"Our Jack has a suspicious mind?" Langton asked.

"Dirty mind, more like," she replied.

"I'm here if you don't mind." Decker pulled out his blaster and tossed it on the bunk. "And I have first dibs on the heads right now."

"Aren't commanding officers supposed to let the troops go ahead of them?"

Zack gave Langton the rigid digit salute before vanishing into the narrow compartment.

"I guess not." The latter sighed theatrically and dropped down onto Tiny's bunk, there being no other seating available.

An hour later, the take-off warning sounded over the ship's public address system, ordering them to strap into their bunks until they reached orbit and artificial gravity came on.

*

The same voice over the PA system released them once they felt a regular one gee pull instead of the wildly fluctuating pressure stemming from a thunderous takeoff.

Tiny had barely managed to keep his last meal down during the moments of weightlessness before the artificial gravity kicked in, emitting a loud burp instead, but his appetite seemed to recover quickly.

"I think I'll check out the saloon," he said, climbing to his feet. "We didn't have supper before leaving, and my stomach tells me it's time."

"I'd rather find out what's on that tablet Magnus gave Jack," Steiger replied, jumping down from her upper-level berth.

"How about we grab a table in the saloon and then check it out together?" Decker suggested. "I'm with Tiny. My stomach is about to make an announcement and no one wants to hear that."

"Indeed."

Decker cocked an amused eyebrow at Langton's dry tone and smiled.

"How you manage to sound like a former CO of mine is a mystery I'd rather not explore."

The saloon proved to be minuscule compared to the one aboard the sloop that brought them to Asgard. It had a few tables, chairs and a counter where they presumably served food at mealtimes. A pair of Confederacy crewmembers sitting in one corner looked up at them and, upon seeing the drab uniforms, went back to their quiet conversation. Each had a bulb in his hand, though Decker could see no visible dispenser. He approached the men.

"Hi there." When they looked up again, annoyance visible in their eyes, the Marine gave them his best aw-shucks grin. "Sorry to disturb you gentlemen, but my teammates and I were wondering where we could find something to wet our whistles."

One of them, the older of the two, indicated the counter, and then went back to whatever he'd been discussing with his friend.

"Thank you."

Upon closer examination, Decker found a recessed handle to one side that opened a fridge set into the bulkhead. Within, he found mostly non-alcoholic drinks, but it did contain beer of a brand he'd never seen before. After grabbing four bulbs, water for himself and booze for the others, he joined them at a table on the opposite side of the saloon from the Howlers.

"I don't know if this stuff is any good, but it's the only potent potable I saw."

Langton uncapped his and took a tentative sniff. "It's not equine urine if that's what you feared. I can sense a hint of hops and malted barley."

"Just as long as you can detect booze," Tiny said before taking an enthusiastic swig of his.

"Whoa there, young bronco. Pace yourself." Decker patted the big man on the shoulder. "I don't think we should abuse our hosts' hospitality by going through their stash at full speed on the first night out. They don't seem too enthusiastic at seeing us in the first place."

He pulled out the tablet and set it on the table, then touched a control surface, summoning a vertical holographic screen half a meter square, its virtual surface visible only from a given angle. Steiger and Langton had to crowd in on the bigger men so they could see and hear.

Less than ten minutes later, the holo vanished, and Decker sat back, shaking his head.

"If anyone thought Asgard was bad," he said, "may I present the planet that beats it hands down? At least Asgard isn't overrun by gigantic creatures the size of tanks."

"For the Confederacy and its partners to throw that much money and effort at Naraka, it must have something much more worthwhile than what Asgard offers," Langton noted, "even if it seems to take its name from what I believe is Sanskrit for a place of torment."

"Agreed. But seems like a nasty place to turn a profit." Steiger emptied her bulb in one sip and grimaced. "Just watching all that volcanic activity made me thirsty."

Decker grunted. "Wait until we're on the ground. You might end up remembering this horse piss with more fondness than you've ever shown me."

"So what do they need special ops teams for?" Tiny asked.

"That would be the question, wouldn't it? I think we can safely assume the Confederacy is trying to either take something valuable away from someone else or protect said valuable something from someone else.   The briefing makes no note of native sentient life, so it has to be another invader. Around here, your guess is as good as mine when it comes to the possible players."

"If there had been native sentient life, it would have become a taboo planet," Tiny interjected.

Decker's derisive laugh sounded like a predator's bark.

"Since when do folks like the Confederacy," he replied, "or even Frontier Solutions for that matter, worry about taboos that can only be enforced by the Fleet? Sadly, the Fleet can't officially intervene in the Protectorate Zone. Otherwise, the Shrehari Empire will want to do the same and the next thing you know, we have another war no one wants. Ergo, shady outfits, reivers, and the like can pretty much screw over native life forms any way they want. You can't enforce a law if you can't put a gun in the lawbreaker's face."

It wasn't entirely accurate, but Decker couldn't very well discuss covert Q-ship patrols, some carrying Pathfinder squadrons, that allowed the Navy limited means to intervene without provoking the Empire. He'd been deeper inside the Protectorate with the 902nd than the official records would ever show.

"Remarkably   cynical,   but   accurate,"   Langton commented

"That would be me in two words, Alex," the Marine replied with a wink. "Cynically accurate or accurately cynical. Take your choice. I've seen too much crap in my time to have any illusions about how the universe works."

"Ditto.."

Zack nudged Tiktin. "Why don't you grab us another round, Tiny. Suddenly, I'm as thirsty as Miko."

"And why do *you* think they need operators?" Langton asked. "To pick up on the young lad's question."

Decker shrugged. "Why does anyone need dirty tricks troopers? To fuck with the enemy in a way regular infantry can't manage. Not knowing what the opposition on Naraka looks like, we can flap our lips forever and still come short of a reasonable answer. The only sure thing is that we'll find action. You don't bother with special teams if the job is only to guard a moneymaking operation against wildlife, despite the fact that Naraka seems to have more than its share of nasty critters. You use basic garrison grunts to do that, or rent-a-cops, something inexpensive and disposable. Based on the gear we've been given, we're not the cheap ones."

"Fact," Tiny said, passing out fresh bulbs. "The stuff I have now is light years ahead of my initial issue."

"From the mouth of babes." Decker smiled at the big Celestan. "Our armor is Fleet grade. Current Fleet grade, including the sensor suite and not war stock from a generation ago. The weapons are war stock, but there haven't been many advancements in the last fifty or sixty years. You can only shoot plasma in so many ways before you settle on a design that'll last until someone comes up with a different kind of ammunition."

"So we know we're headed for somewhere nasty, to do the kind of dangerous jobs regular infantry can't do. Does that about cover it?" Langton cocked an eyebrow in question.

"That's pretty much the extent of our data." Decker twisted the cap off his bulb and took a sip before asking, "Would this be the first time any of you go into a situation with a less than complete mission briefing, perchance?"

"Well..." Tiny's voice trailed off when he saw the others shake their heads.

Something rattled behind them, and the aroma of food wafted through the saloon. Decker patted Tiktin on the shoulder.

"We'll see what we'll see, buddy. Right now, I'd say we should go look at what this tub considers edible food."

"Besides," Steiger added as she stood up, "like we used to say in the Army, you shouldn't have joined up if you can't take a joke."

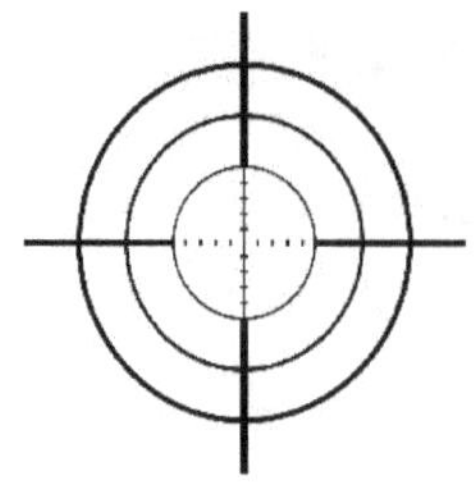

— FIFTEEN —

"What's with those weird clouds all over the place?" Tiny jerked his chin at a screen taking up most of the saloon's aft bulkhead. Their ship had entered orbit around Naraka an hour earlier, after a quiet and relatively short trip.

"What you're seeing, young Atli," Langton said, "are volcanic ash plumes, lots of them."

"Lovely." Steiger made a face. "Here's to hoping none of our missions will bring us close enough to see an eruption in person."

"Agreed," Decker replied, eyes on the screen but thoughts on finding Hal the moment they touched down. After all these light years, he would finally catch up with him and utter those three immortal words — what the fuck?

A voice sounded throughout the ship, telling them to strap in for re-entry, so he led the team back to their cabin.

They wore battle armor this time around, on the general principle that any place where one landed with a basic load of ammo deserved the full protection package. Besides, Naraka seemed nasty enough that wearing the suit on arrival showed common sense.

Landing appeared to take a long time, but eventually, the rumbling and vibrations ceased, the gravity stabilized at something that felt just a tad more than one gee, and a voice called the all-clear. A few minutes later, their cabin door opened, and a crewmember stuck his head inside.

"End of the line for all grunts. Grab your luggage and follow me."

"Helmets on?" Tiny asked.

"Helmets on," Zack replied. "But you can leave the visors up. There's nothing like a good whiff of the local air to feel like you've arrived."

"How about the weapons?"

"Lock and load." The Marine pulled out his Shrehari blaster and worked the action, then did the same with his carbine, imitated by the others. The crewman watched them with tired eyes, and when he figured they'd done their weapons worship, he headed aft without a further word.

Decker's team, Zack in the lead, trudged down the belly ramp and into hot, humid air.

An eddy of sulfurous emissions swirled beneath his flared nostrils, and he sneezed.

"Charming," Decker muttered, just loud enough for Steiger to hear. "This mission is going to be a laugh a minute."

She snorted softly. "You went after this one, lover boy. You get to wear it."

Tiny seemed to catch the same rotten eggs aroma because he let loose a few choice words in Celestan Anglic.

A man in the same type of battledress they wore beneath the armor stepped out of a rusty container building at the edge of the landing strip and walked towards them with a vigorous stride. From somewhere to the left, a transport skimmer burst from the dense vegetation and headed for the ship at a leisurely pace. The man reached them first.

"Welcome to hell, folks." A grim smile temporarily relaxed his hard features. "I'm Jon Gerin, the Special Assignments Company CO here on Naraka. I assume you're the Lorenzo team, formerly Roby's."

Gerin seemed to be Zack's age, with a short, silver-flecked beard framing a wide jaw and dark hair cut short enough to show plenty of shiny scalp. His height matched the Marine's, though he carried his muscle on a leaner frame. The brown eyes beneath thick brows seemed like the kind that missed little.

"We are." Decker stuck out his hand. "Jack Lorenzo at your service. She's Miko Steiger; the big guy is Atli Tiktin and tail-end charlie's Alex Langton."

"Glad you're here. We're always short of spec ops teams, and although Magnus keeps promising more, the recruiting system just doesn't seem to catch enough folks with the right experience."

"Quality like us is always hard to come by," Decker replied with a confident smile.

Gerin snorted. "You four are quality?"

"Give us a try."

"Oh, I will. You can bet on that." He motioned towards the edge of the landing field. "Follow me. The main compound is on the other side of that ridge."

"No skimmer ride?"

"Why? Are you afraid of a short walk?"

Decker shrugged. "It seems that my life is devoted to crossing light years at FTL speed only to spend the last few kilometers walking. There's something wrong about that if you ask me."

"Don't mind Lorenzo," Steiger said. "It's his ritual to complain whenever he sets foot on a new world."

*

The landing strip sat at the bottom of a shallow depression. When they reached the crest of the rise, a savage panorama greeted their eyes. In the distance, a purplish mountain range seemed to span the horizon from one end to the other. Plumes of smoke and ash lit by frequent bursts of lightning, crowned many of the jagged peaks.

Multicolored fuzz carpeted the foothills and mountain slopes, the distance transforming dense vegetation into a mere hint of texture. Closer in, a low cliff loomed over a riot of pre-fabricated buildings, containers, and other assorted human constructs, scattered along the banks of a lazy, gray river and surrounded by a tall rammed earth berm topped with glass wire that could slice through anything organic foolish enough to touch it.

Individual purplish plants, twice Decker's height, dotted the open prairie, their feather-like tops swaying in the sulfurous breeze, seemingly out of sync with trunks that appeared to have little rigidity. Tiny life forms skittered about, communicating with high-pitched yips.

As he examined the vista with greater care, Decker noticed the cluster of oversized rectangular shapes stacked hard up against the cliff side, their configuration reminiscent of every frontier mining operation he'd ever seen.

Gerin motioned towards the town. "Welcome to Moria. Or as we like to call it among ourselves, the Confederacy's Folly."

Decker glanced at the mercenary with a quizzical expression in his eyes.

"Isn't Moria the name of a mine from some pre-spaceflight legend?"

"Sure, that's why the Star Wolves chose it for their wholly-owned colony. But another among its many definitions is an archaic medical term denoting foolishness or dullness of comprehension."

"Ah." The Marine guffawed. "That's cute. Did anyone tell the Howlers?"

"Why? We're the hired help. They pay us well to protect their business interests, not to criticize their choice of literary allusions."

"Those business interests being that mine I spy?"

"Among others. Moria is largest of their outposts on Naraka." They resumed walking down the gentle slope towards a separate compound with its own perimeter berm sitting to one side of the settlement. "It's also Frontier Solution's HQ, although we have detachments at every settlement."

"It's a funny thing to think about the Howlers as rock moles," Decker remarked.

Gerin laughed. "Heavens, no. That job belongs to the subsidiary of a large Commonwealth mining company. The Confederacy takes care of shipping and sales. And security, though they've outsourced most of it to us. Call it a three-way contract if you like. The Wolves are the majority share owners with us and the mining outfit as minority partners."

"Nice setup."

As they got closer, Decker's appreciation for the thoroughness of Frontier Solution's defenses rose. A comprehensive fixed sensor net as well as properly sited automatic weapons that could cover every angle gave the wire-topped berm some added punch.

He recognized the dome in the middle as an aerospace defense array, equipped with surface-to-air guns and missile launchers capable of sending ordnance into orbit. A Marine FOB on a hostile, rebellious colony couldn't be any more heavily fortified than this place.

"What's the threat?" He asked.

"That would be the competition. You're an ex-regular, so you probably know how it is beyond the Rim. Without a Fleet to keep things non-violent, wildcat mining tends to be heavy on the wild part. There are a lot of outfits who want to make a profit, both from the rare elements that are abundant and easy to extract from Naraka's crust and the native plant life that can be distilled into some heavy duty pharmaceuticals."

"You mean drugs?" A dangerous edge had crept unbidden into Decker's tone.

"The Confederacy stays away from narcotics."

"Really?" Skepticism oozed from every pore.

"Really." Gerin stopped a few steps from the base's main gate and waited for it to open. "There's enough legal stuff coming out of here that the Wolves leave the illegal shit to reiver clans. It doesn't stop the buggers from trying to evict our clients, however. Of course, exporting the local wildlife probably falls into a gray zone where Commonwealth authorities are concerned, but that's apparently good money too."

"This place is a regular Treasure Planet, eh?"

"It is, provided you're willing to work hard and take risks. Ask the miners how much fun it is to be underground when one of the frequent earthquakes rumbles through. However, the pay is good. It's better than ours, in fact."

"But we're here because there's competition from lowlifes. Does it mean this planet is so blessed with natural riches that lazy reiver mongrels are willing to put in some sweat equity?"

"Of course not," Gerin replied. The outer gate opened, and he waved them in. Then, it closed again before the inner gate slid aside. "Reivers use indentured labor."

"You mean slaves."

"If you like."

"I don't," Decker growled.

"We're beyond the Rim, Lorenzo. No laws here, other than that of the gun." He led them between orderly rows of single-story, pre-fabricated buildings, each with a sign that identified its occupants or its function, before stopping in front of one labeled 'Special Assignments Company.'

"This is home, at least for those times you'll be in Moria, which won't be all that often." Gerin led them inside and through a relatively standard company office to a barracks with four bunk team rooms on either side of a narrow corridor. He pointed through an open door. "This one's yours. Drop the kit and lose the armor, but keep a loaded side arm. You have five minutes. After that, I'll take you around the base."

"Guns at all times, is that it?" Decker asked, tossing his pack on a lower bunk.

"Yep. We've had the occasional attempt at a raid. You never know when one of the reiver clan leaders gets his dander up and orders a fresh attempt to dislodge the Confederacy."

"Dander? Is that what they're calling getting drunk or stoned, or both on Naraka?"

Gerin grinned. "You got it, Lorenzo."

In addition to four bunks, the room had four lockers, a table, and four chairs, all of which had seen hard use, probably all the way back to the last Shrehari war. A set of standing orders taped to the scarred plastic wall passed for the sole decoration. Decker had seen worse quarters on FOBs in his career, but this place seemed pretty austere, even though they had a hard roof over their heads.

"Are we the only team on base?" He asked, buckling a gun belt over his dun-colored battledress, now that the armor hung inside one of the lockers.

"You are, and not for long. I have five teams in the field right now, making reiver lives miserable, the goal being to convince them that ignoring us is better than constantly trying to see who has the biggest set of balls on the planet. The planet has enough room for everyone to make real money."

"Though I suspect easily mined lodes aren't overly abundant," Langton said. "Having slave labor doesn't make one immune to the lure of quick results."

"Is any of the slave labor human?" Steiger asked.

"None that we've seen." Gerin shook his head. "A mix of whatever they could capture or buy in the Protectorate Zone."

"Can I assume that we're authorized to free any captive humans we come across?" Decker asked.

"Of course." Gerin, seeing that all four were ready, turned on his heel and led them back through the company office and out into the dusty street. "There's one battalion — three companies — guarding Moria. They're garrisoned here. Generally, one company is doing close-in protection of the settlement and mine, one company is patrolling the countryside, and the third is on rest and retraining. We also have a separate heavy weapons company here on the base, to man the surface-to-air defenses and provide fire support on demand to the infantry. Finally, we have an aviation and a service support company. On this continent, there are four other Confederacy operations, each with a company group guarding them. If needed, we can fly in reinforcements with our armed shuttles, which I also use to insert and extract my teams."

He led them to a central square and began pointing at various structures.

"That's the HQ building. Over there is the mess hall, which we'll visit after the orientation tour. The armory is near the airfield on the other side of that barracks cluster, where the Moria battalion lives. And that one with the prominent markings is the medical facility."

"Does it see much use?" Decker asked.

"Some. We're fighting what's essentially a low-level guerrilla war between several opposing commercial interests. Most of the injuries we can treat here. The ones we can't handle are evacuated back to Asgard or even Kilia, in stasis chambers if necessary."

"Good to know."

Gerin took them on a long hike around Moria base before returning to the central plaza.

"Anyone have questions?"

"Yeah," Decker said, unable to contain his impatience anymore. "I heard that a guy I knew back in the Corps, Hal Tarra, is working for you. He's not around right now, is he?"

"No." The mercenary officer shook his head. "He's taken his team to harass some reivers who've begun interfering with the Kastell operation south of here. They won't be back for a few days unless they incur casualties. Anything else?"

When no one spoke, he said, "Supper's on."

Tiktin rubbed his hands together with glee. "The best part of the tour."

But just as they were about to enter the sprawling structure, he caught sight of someone leaving the HQ building out of the corner of his eyes. A lean, rather petite, if muscular woman with a narrow face framed by dark hair in a pixie cut. He caught Steiger's arm, to hold her back while the others went through the open door.

"Don't turn around. Just look sideways at the woman on the other side of the parade ground and tell me we're not in trouble."

She did as told and a low growl escaped her lips.

"We're in trouble."

They ducked through the doorway, then went to a dirty, scratched side window and stared out. The woman, thankfully, seemed to be heading for the main gate.

"How in God's name did Rika Kozlev end up working for Frontier Solutions," Decker murmured. "I thought her bosses in the Celeste National Guard were going to have her shot for screwing up on Garonne after Verrill shipped all the Celestans home."

"Interesting as that story might be," Steiger replied in a hushed voice, "the more important issue is that she'll recognize me as the one who handed Tianjin over to the rebels, and I doubt a psychopath like her is big on forgiveness."

"Worse than that," he said. "She knows who I am, the real me. I told her former boss, ex-Colonel Harend, in the prisoner stockade after we took Iskellian just so I could metaphorically shove my blade in deeper, and he'll have passed that tidbit on to her. If Kozlev finds out you and I are here, we're dead meat, especially if she's plying her old trade."

"If she is, we'll take a few days dying." Steiger shivered theatrically at the memory of Kozlev's interrogation techniques. "Do you really think she'll recognize you? After all Jack Lorenzo doesn't look like the man she might remember from back then."

"She will. People like her never forget those who wronged them, and she's an intelligence specialist, a decent one. The moment Kozlev lays eyes on me, she'll see the guy she had naked in her dungeon, the one who took out half of her staff while escaping with the best lead into the rebellion they had. Count on it."

"Are you guys coming?" Tiny shouted from the main hall.

"You know there's only one way to make sure she doesn't tell our current employers, right?" Steiger waved back at Tiktin.

"Do to her now what I should have done on Garonne, if I hadn't been trying to make a point about the rule of law with newly minted, acting President Verrill." A grim expression hardened the Marine's features.

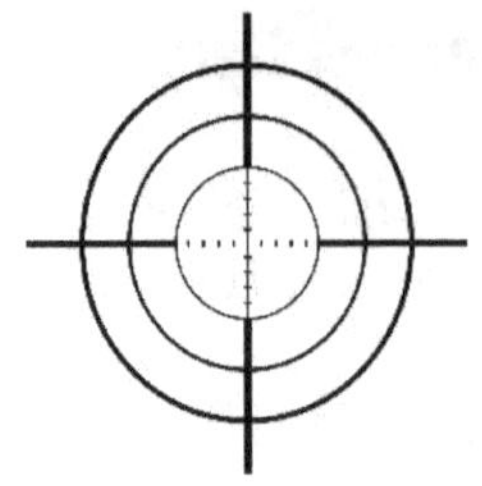

— SIXTEEN —

"Is there a problem?" Gerin looked from Zack to Miko, a slight frown creasing his forehead when they rejoined the others in the main hall.

"No." Decker shook his head. "Just catching some 'us' time, but we're good now."

"In that case," the mercenary waved towards the food line, "grab a tray, and sample our cuisine. You'll probably be eating your next supper from a ration pack."

"That quick, eh?"

"I believe I did mention that we need more teams in the field. Besides, former pros like you would rather be out there chasing reivers than sit around here watching fungus grow on the walls, right?" Gerin helped himself to utensils and joined Tiny in contemplating the day's offerings.

Steiger leaned over and whispered in Zack's ear, "That might delay the need to solve our problem."

"Until she looks at the nominal roll, honey," he replied in the same tone. "I'm the man of a thousand faces and ten thousand names. You're still Miko Steiger, betrayer of the Garonne militia and perpetrator of other vile, disloyal crimes. For all we know, she's already hatching a plan to turn you into her newest plaything."

"Thanks for that thought, asshole. I hope you choke on whatever vat grown crap you're about to eat."

"You're a tad touchy for a woman who's going to watch me solve our problem before it gets out of hand." He blew her a kiss, then took a tray and some utensils, and joined the others in picking out something unlikely to give him digestive regrets.

"Why should you be the one solving our problem?" Steiger asked when she caught up with him.

"Because I know you're not a cold-blooded killer."

"And you are?"

Decker didn't answer. Instead, he took a bowl of stew and went to join the others, already seated at a table. Behind them, noisy troops began to pour in, looking for relief from their hunger and the boredom of guard duty.

When Steiger finally sat down, Langton examined her and Decker in turn with emotionless eyes, though the latter could sense curiosity if not obvious puzzlement.

"What I think we'll do," Gerin said once everyone had begun eating, "is have the intelligence section give you a full briefing tomorrow morning, and then we can discuss your first deployment."

Decker nodded once, his attention focused on a tough chunk of vat meat. Gerin glanced at Tiktin.

"By the way, Tiny, our intelligence officer is a former Celeste National Guard lifer. You might know her. She goes by the name Rika Kozlev and used to be a captain."

Tiktin shook his head and replied, around a mouthful of bread, "Nope. Guard's a big outfit, and I didn't have much to do with folks outside my battalion."

"Mind you," Gerin continued, "I doubt she'll conduct the briefing. If this is one of her nights out, we won't see her back on base before noon."

Something in the mercenary officer's tone caught Decker's attention.

"Wildcatting, is she?" He asked.

"Kozlev's very close to the guy running the mining operation if you get my drift. I don't know if it's just sex, or if there's more involved, but it seems to take a lot of her time. Just as well, in my opinion. Some people take too much pleasure in their work." A brief flash of revulsion passed across his face.

Bingo, Decker thought. Gerin's not a fan. Rika must have begun plying her trade in earnest.

"Is she one of those intelligence officers who like hands-on interrogation techniques?" Zack asked as innocently as he could manage.

"Yes." Something in Gerin's tone made it clear he wasn't inclined to pursue that line of conversation. "Her head analyst is a good man. I'll have him set up something for you guys after breakfast tomorrow."

Decker forced himself not to glance at Miko. However, she didn't have the same degree of self-control, and Langton noticed that something bothered her. The former MP studied both of them with unfeigned curiosity.

Once they had eaten, Gerin took them to the bar next door and bought the first round by way of welcome, then excused himself for a moment when he spotted someone across the room. He returned a few minutes later.

"There. It's all arranged. Raj Lisk will give you guys a full run-down at oh-eight-hundred. As I suspected, Kozlev's out in town for the night."

Zack could sense Steiger's relief at the news. If Gerin really wanted them out in the field tomorrow, they might just avoid crossing paths with Kozlev. However, that would merely delay things, not solve the problem. Eventually, they'd have to come back to Moria for a few days rest and replenishment, and by then, she would certainly have come across Miko's name on some roster or other.

*

After the second round of drinks, Gerin wandered off to take care of some administrative matters, leaving Decker and his team to fend for themselves. As newcomers to Moria, they received the usual side-glances and frank appraisals from the other Frontier Solutions mercenaries, although socializing with the CO of Special Assignments had marked them as operators, and therefore folks who lived apart from the rest.

When things became loud enough that they could only converse in shouts and hand signals, Decker suggested they grab a few bulbs and return to their quarters. Stepping out into the relative silence of the Naraka night came as a relief for their ears, if not their noses.

Langton shook his head. "I'm too old for that kind of atmosphere."

"Ditto," Steiger said. "Whatever happened to taking a quiet drink?"

"Life happened." The Marine shrugged before trudging off across the central square. "We're all a bit older than the kids in there, except for Tiny, of course. Think back at when you were full of piss and vinegar all the time."

"True." Langton fell into step beside Zack. "Some days I wonder why I'm still playing the soldier game after putting in my twenty-five years."

"You're a glutton for punishment?"

"Addict is probably more accurate." Langton chuckled. "Speaking of punishment, care to tell me why I have the impression that the name of Frontier Solutions' intelligence officer isn't exactly unknown to Miko and you?"

Something in Langton's tone told Decker he'd be better off telling the truth, or at least a sanitized version of it. They'd be busy watching each other's backs soon enough, and trust was a big part of getting the job done.

"We know her, and not in a good way. If she recognizes either of us, there could be blood on the ground. Scratch that. *When* she recognizes us, there will be blood."

"That bad, eh?"

They entered the Special Assignments building and headed through the empty office for their team room. Decker shut the door once all four were inside, and then pulled out his personal sensor to check for listening devices. After a few moments, he tucked it away with a satisfied nod.

"Miko and I have a little problem called Rika Kozlev, as Alex has figured out," he said. "We were both involved in the Garonne uprising, on the rebel side and got to know Kozlev up close. She was on loan to the Garonne Militia, doing some truly disgusting stuff. As a matter of fact, I spent time in her interrogation room before busting out. Kozlev is one sick puppy, a pure psycho. I'm not convinced that we ever found out how many rebels or suspected rebels she murdered during or after interrogation. Miko infiltrated the militia and worked for Kozlev, worming her way into the bitch's confidence to the point where she could hand over one of the key district capitals to the rebellion with barely a shot fired."

"Ouch." Langton winced. "Some things, you just never forgive."

"It gets better." Decker dropped into a chair and sighed. "After the rebellion took control, they rounded up the Militia, including those on loan from the Celeste National Guard like Kozlev and put them in a prisoner stockade. I took some time to visit dear Rika and give her my best slice of the knife across the throat. I know I should have resisted the urge, but since she threatened to geld me while she had me strapped naked to an interrogation chair a few weeks earlier, I felt this irrational urge to extract a measure of revenge."

He pulled out his Pathfinder dagger and mimed the gesture.

"Mind you, it was a mere nick to count coup rather than inflict the death she deserved. She probably still has a scar from that right here." He touched his own throat with the tip of the blade. "I wasn't going by my real name at the time, and look different now, but she'll recognize me, if not right away, then eventually. As for Miko, she only has to take one look at the updated personnel roster tomorrow."

"How she ended up here is a mystery," Steiger chimed in. "Jack left Garonne shortly after the independence movement took over, but I stuck around for a while, so I witnessed the provisional government shipping all of the National Guard personnel back to Celeste in chains, to face a government that wouldn't show them much mercy for losing a colony in such a spectacular fashion."

"I heard about that," Langton said. "A superbly executed decapitation that ended what would likely have become a long, drawn-out, and bloody colonial war."

"And yet, Kozlev is here on Naraka, a freelancer, instead of rotting in a Celeste Guard stockade, where she belongs."

"Intelligence officers know where the skeletons are buried," Langton reminded them. "She probably had a failsafe hidden away for just such an occasion. What are you going to do?"

He looked at Decker and Miko in turn.

"Do?" Zack shrugged wearily. "We don't have many options. Kozlev will find a way to get us in her clutches, where we'll die by exquisitely painful degrees, and there would be nothing Gerin could do about it. I have no doubt she's wormed her way into Frontier Solutions' inner command group and made herself indispensable for operations on Naraka. Against that, a pair of low-level newcomers, even those hired as special operators, don't stand a chance."

Especially once she reveals that Jack Lorenzo is actually Zack Decker, Commonwealth Marine Corps, definitely not retired, he thought with a mental grimace.

"Our new CO doesn't seem fond of this Kozlev," Langton said.

"And that speaks well of him," Steiger replied. "But where Rika's concerned, what she wants, she gets. I've seen her in action with the Garonne militia commander. He basically gave her license to fulfil her every desire, war crimes included. Why should it be different with the Frontier Solutions boss? Especially since there's no need out here to check the Rules of War every time you feel like torturing a captive."

"At least we have a bit of breathing room, with her off doing the horizontal rumba in town." Decker downed the rest of his mineral water and belched softly. "And we might escape Moria before she returns, but that only defers the problem."

"Do you think she's going to take past events seriously enough to wish you harm? No water under the bridge with her?"

"I've stared into her eyes and seen pure evil stare back at me, Alex. She'll have her revenge, especially after I publicly counted coup on her. Psychos never forgive, and they never forget."

And she'll be pleased to out a Fleet spy, he mentally added.

"Then, as I see it, there's only one solution," the former military policeman said.

"Yeah. We pretty much figured that."

"Do you need any help?"

*

The next morning, Gerin ushered them into a sparsely furnished briefing room in one wing of the HQ building where a slender man with a face darkened and seamed by the radiation of a thousand suns waited. His sparse hair had long ago turned to gray, but his deep-set eyes held a gleam of barely suppressed energy.

"Raj Lisk, meet my newest spec ops team, Jack Lorenzo, Miko Steiger, Alex Langton, and Atli Tiktin, also known as Tiny for obvious reasons. Team, in Rika Kozlev's absence, Raj will take care of you."

"On behalf of Frontier Solutions' intelligence staff, welcome," Lisk smiled at them, waving towards the rectangular table. "Grab a seat, and I'll tell you all you need to know about Naraka and our employer's numerous and violent competitors. I gather that Jon is anxious to send you out into the field, so we'll focus on the particular area that's about to become your responsibility."

The briefing took just under an hour, covering not only the opposition but also some of the larger or more toxic lifeforms that called Naraka home, and Decker felt relief at leaving the building without any unfortunate encounters. Gerin took them back to the Special Assignments office and had them cluster around a three-dimensional map projection.

"We'll start you off easy on this one. The Qhazd clan has been a minor thorn in our side for a few months now, but need a reminder to avoid disrupting our operations on the Mahar peninsula. As Raj said, they've tried their hand at sabotaging the Mahar digs, killing one miner and injuring three of our guards, one of which we had to evacuate back to Asgard. The Qhazd are nasty shits, but we've had to deal with worse than them." He lit up the peninsula and icons representing friendly as well as Qhazd positions winked into existence.

"Why not simply bomb them back into their version of the stone age?" Decker asked.

"Other than leaving them guessing about the identity of their attackers, we can't afford to lose our aircraft to their defenses. This is a six-sided guerrilla war, and the opposition will sniff out and exploit any weakness. Our policy, for now, is to encourage the other parties to either leave Naraka or at least leave us alone. Once we have enough military strength, we'll hit the buggers one at a time and clean up, but we're not there yet. We're not even close. Shipping troops and material out here is expensive."

Decker grimaced. "Understood."

"We'll fly you to the Mahar settlement, which will be your forward operating base on the peninsula. From there, it's up to you. The garrison has a pair of thopters you can commandeer for insertions and extractions, and it will provide you with logistical support, but you remain answerable only to me. The aim is to make the Qhazd operation unprofitable. Painfully so. And to remind them that causing casualties will attract casualties."

"No rules, then? I can go medieval on their asses as much as I want?"

"Within reason." A faint smile twisted Gerin's lips at Decker's choice of words. "Don't risk your team unduly and don't do anything that'll put the Mahar operation in greater danger. I'll leave you out there for a few weeks to see how things go. The only caveat is that I might need to temporarily join two or three teams together for specific operations, so don't be surprised if you receive last minute orders to fly out to one of the other FOBs.

And yes, if you see humans used as indentured labor, you can try your hand at liberating them. Humans only, mind."

They discussed various details for another half hour or so, then Gerin led them to the company's storeroom and told them to stock up on whatever they needed and could carry in one go. Then, suited up, armed, and heavily laden, they trudged across the base to the airstrip and climbed aboard a waiting thopter. The ungainly craft lurched into the air, giving them a bird's eye view of Moria, the base, and the mine, and of a small, uniformed figure approaching the main gate.

Their escape to the wilds of Naraka's Mahar peninsula had come just in time. The last thing Decker spotted before the thopter swung away was Kozlev's pale face turned up to watch them leave. She couldn't see their faces, of course, not with helmet visors down, and he couldn't make out those soulless eyes at this distance, but he felt a chill run down his spine nonetheless.

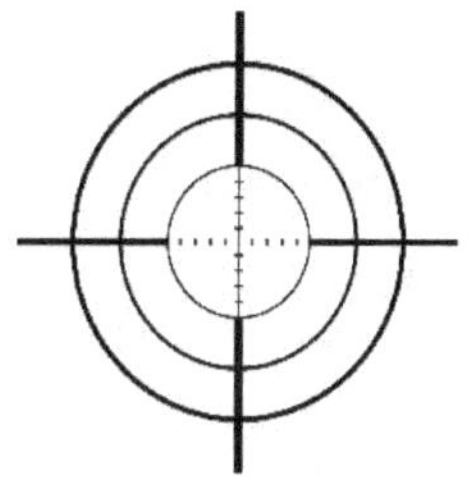

— SEVENTEEN —

"Was that the new team heading out to Mahar, just now?" Rika Kozlev asked Raj Lisk by way of greeting when she entered the intelligence section's office suite.

"It was." The older man replied, not bothering to look up at her. Since she didn't care about the finer points of courtesy, he kept working on his analysis. "Gerin has been sent three former Commonwealth Services noncoms and a kid from your old mob. They seem like a smart bunch. The leader, Jack Lorenzo knew just what questions to ask. He reminded me of the other ex-Marine who came through here a few weeks back — Hal Tarra. I do believe they'll make enough noise around Mahar to give the Qhazd a fright or two."

"Lorenzo, eh?" She sat down at her desk and picked up a tablet. "I trust you have pictures of the newbies?"

"Of course. I took them this morning during the briefing. They're in the database, along with their service records. By the way, our latest customer has asked to speak with you. I think he's ready to give up his clan leader in exchange for a clean death."

"Really?" A tinge of disappointment colored Kozlev's tone. "I'd hoped he would last a bit longer, but these non-humans are still hit or miss for me."

She dropped the tablet, her urge to become better acquainted with the newcomers replaced by an even greater urge to hear what their prisoner had to say. If he indeed intended to betray his leader, this would be a minor victory for her. All the previous non-humans had died before revealing anything useful. That fact that hadn't gone unnoticed by her commanding officer, a career mercenary who wasn't used to the more refined interrogation techniques she liked to practice.

"Shall we visit the dungeon?" She asked, a cruel smile of anticipation revealing small, white teeth.

"If you don't mind," Lisk replied. "I'd like to finish this while I'm on a roll. You go ahead and have fun."

"Ta." She waggled her fingers at her deputy and sauntered off, the anticipation of pleasure putting an extra spring in her stride.

*

The thopter, another item that had likely come from the Army's war stocks, courtesy of a corrupt senior quartermaster officer, could only manage subsonic speeds and the flight to the Mahar peninsula took several hours.

Decker and his companions spent the time either sleeping, reading or staring out the window at the monotonously purplish, broken landscape, punctuated here and there by plumes coming off distant and not so distant volcanoes.

Dark lines eventually appeared on the horizon where the dense forest abruptly stopped. These soon grew to become the black waters of an alien sea washing up against a long tongue of land. The thopter lost altitude, and for a moment, the treetops seemed about to engulf them, but they kept flying without feeling so much as a shiver of contact.

"Nearing hostile territory?" He asked the woman in the cockpit.

"Yep. Every so often, a few of them, maybe after too much partying, try their hand at shooting us down."

"And this low, they'd have to be immediately beneath our flight path to even see us."

"Right. You can't shoot at what you can't see. We're almost there anyway."

Soon enough, Decker spied a break in the forest canopy equidistant from either shore, exposing a cliff wall like the one at Moria, another result of massive tectonic upheavals that exposed layer upon layer of rock to the open air. At its base, near a narrow, winding river, a miniature version of the main settlement shimmered in the red afternoon sun, snug within a double ring of rammed earth topped by wire.

The thopter lost all forward momentum the moment it passed the tree line and dropped further until it hovered a few meters above the rocky, lichen-covered ground. Then, as if obeying an unheard and unseen signal, the pilot nudged her craft forward and over the defensive ring, then down on a marked square.

The soft whine of the engines died away, replaced by a muffled sound of machinery somewhere beneath the surface.

"Welcome to Mahar," the pilot said. "Not quite the ass end of the universe but somewhere close to it. I'll see you again in a few weeks. Or at least, you'd better hope I'll only see you in a few weeks."

"Thanks." Decker thumped her on the shoulder. "We'll remember to duck, so you won't have to bother yourself with a casevac mission."

"That's the spirit." She gave him thumbs up and then pointed at the door. "Now get off my craft."

They emerged from the thopter, looking like armored beasts of burden and headed towards a man in battledress standing by the edge of the landing field, arms crossed.

A trio of miners in well-worn coveralls appeared around the corner of a prefabricated hangar, bags slung over their shoulders and jogged towards the aircraft as if they couldn't escape Mahar fast enough.

Decker stopped in front of the waiting mercenary, dropped his bags, and raised his helmet visor.

"Jack Lorenzo, Special Assignments, and three are reporting in."

"Alun Howe, the garrison CO." He thrust out his hand. "Welcome. I've been busting Jon Gerin's balls about getting a team of operators out here to give the Qhazd a thorough reaming out."

"You have one now." Decker grinned. "We're ready to play cowboys and aliens."

He jerked his thumb at the others. "Say hello to Miko Steiger, Alex Langton, and Tiny Tiktin."

"Welcome," Howe repeated. "Let me take you to your barracks, then on an orientation tour around the base. I know you'll be spending a lot of time on the other side of the fence, but we do suffer the occasional raid, and if you're around, I'd be glad to have some extra firepower."

"Sure." Decker picked up his bags again and fell into step beside Howe, the others following close behind. "How often do the buggers try you on?"

"Whenever the Qhazd's local chief feels like throwing a tantrum, which, lately, has been every three to four weeks."

"Could it be that their operation's not producing too well?" Langton asked.

"We're sitting on the best site for a thousand kilometers, so that stands to reason. Plus, they're lazy fucks, even with slave labor, so digging up the poorer lodes isn't as much fun. They'd rather take from us, except they're not organized enough, or strong enough to overrun this place."

"And our job is to go out and make their operation even less profitable so that they pack up and leave. Understood."

Howe led them away from the landing strip towards a cluster of the ubiquitous space-dropped containers turned into habitation modules.

"My company is eighty-strong," he said, "but there's room for a full complement of a hundred and twenty, so you'll have your own team hut."

"Is eighty enough to guard this place?" Decker asked.

"The way we've set up the perimeter, plus the air-defense module," he indicated a dome sitting in the center of the settlement, "they'd have to come at us in battalion strength, and they don't have that many bodies to waste."

"Unless all five of our employer's competitors band together," Langton replied. "Which is, admittedly, improbable."

"But not impossible. Still, the cost would be too high for beings without the discipline or training to take casualties and keep moving."

"True."

"Personally, I worry more about some of the mega-fauna deciding to see if we're tasty," Howe added. "A herd of the larger ones could really ruin our day before we manage to put them down. They're not exactly well endowed with brains. Fortunately, they've been giving this place a wide berth."

They stopped in front of an unmarked container that had been pierced with a door and half a dozen windows.

"Home, sweet home," Howe announced. "Just drop your bags inside, and I'll give you the grand tour."

Unlike the orientation they'd had at Moria, this tour included the mostly automated mining operation, with its enrichment plant, tended by three dozen civilians working in shifts to keep the things running around the clock.

"How do you send the product upstairs?" Decker asked the mine manager while jerking a thumb skywards.

"When a ship comes in for a pickup, it'll send down robotic haulers. We fill 'em up and send 'em back."

"Has the opposition tried hijacking them?"

"When pickup days roll around, we're on full alert everywhere," Howe said. "All thopters are in the air and the AD systems are live. Besides, the ore freighters have their own escorts which provide overhead cover from orbit."

"Very slick," Decker replied. Then, a sign on the side of the enrichment block caught his eye.

"I see Chisger Mining Corporation is involved. They're a top-notch operation," he said, figuring some soft soap might earn him useful intelligence, the kind that would have Captain Ulrich contemplate a measure of forgiveness.

If Chisger was running the mines on Naraka, the Coalition had to be somewhere in the background, taking its cut to finance various schemes. The money they had plowed into stoking the Garonne rebellion could well have come from Naraka profits.

"We're actually an extra-territorial subsidiary of Chisger," the manager replied. "All of us have been recruited from the mother company to work here for a year."

"Good pay?"

"You have no idea. After deducting the cost of this," he patted the side of the block, smiling, "our salaries and of course shipping, the rest is pure profit. There are no royalties to pay out, no expensive and useless regulations to enforce, and no bribes to pay, well, nearly none anyway."

And no taxes on their profits either, Decker thought. Very slick indeed.

"That takes care of showing you guys around," Howe said. "The kitchen is about to open, so if you want to drop your armor now and head on over..."

"Side arms at all times?" Decker asked.

"Oh yeah." He patted his holstered weapon. "You never know when the Qhazd assholes are going to decide that today's the day. Take the evening to settle in and sort yourselves out. Tomorrow after breakfast, we can talk about where you might give the competition their first taste of payback. Say oh-seven-thirty in the company office?"

"Works for me." Decker stuck out his hand. "Thanks for the walk-around, Alun."

*

"Not going out tonight?" Lisk asked when he walked into the intelligence office after supper and saw his boss sitting at her desk, forehead creased in thought.

"No." She shook her head without looking up. "By the way, our late guest didn't really want to talk. He just wanted to die, and I eventually lost my patience with him. Have his body tossed into the river. At least he can give the critters a meal."

"I doubt the local fauna would find Itrulan protein to their taste," Lisk replied. "You seem preoccupied."

"I'm checking up on our newest Special Assignments team. One of them, Miko Steiger, has crossed my path before. She crossed me, as a matter of fact."

Lisk shrugged.

"That would have been at a different time, in a different place. We don't carry grudges in the freelance business, Rika. Otherwise, there would be no way of pulling together new outfits. There are a few guys in Frontier Solutions whom I once saw through a targeting sensor when I worked for another corporation. These days, I don't mind hanging out with them. It's a way of life in the private sector."

"Perhaps." She glanced up at her deputy. "However, Steiger's the kind of snake you want to keep an eye on. I don't know about Langton or this ex-Celestan Guardsman, Tiktin, but Jack Lorenzo looks disturbingly familiar, and not in a let bygones be bygones way. I'll eventually figure it out, but I know I've seen him up close before, with a different name and face. My gut instinct tells me he could be a real danger to us. He looks like a pro, and the questions he asked during your briefing sounded like those of a pro. And the last pro I came across ended my career with the Guard. He damn near ended my life."

Her hand went up to her throat by its own volition when she remembered the razor sharp slice of the dagger and the almost overwhelming fear that she would die. Kozlev stared at Lorenzo again, feeling the nagging sense of familiarity turn into an irritating mental itch.

"Who are you?" She murmured, loud enough for Lisk to hear.

"Why don't you take the Mahar liaison visit next time around," he suggested. "Then you could meet Lorenzo face to face and see if he really is a ghost from your past. At the same time, you can renew your acquaintance with Steiger, but as comrades fighting for the same employer."

"What a fantastic idea."

For some reason, Lisk felt a cold lump of dread in the pit of his stomach at her tone. Something about Kozlev had rubbed him, and many others, the wrong way from the outset, but she'd proved to be an excellent intelligence officer, with a sharp, incisive mind, though some of her methods remained questionable.

The Frontier Solutions commander on Naraka thought highly of her and so she had a reasonably free hand to get the job done in her own way. Lisk would have felt better if he'd been able to find out why a Celeste National Guard lifer like her had ended up in a mercenary outfit beyond the Rim, though looking at those dark, soulless eyes, he could think of a few reasons.

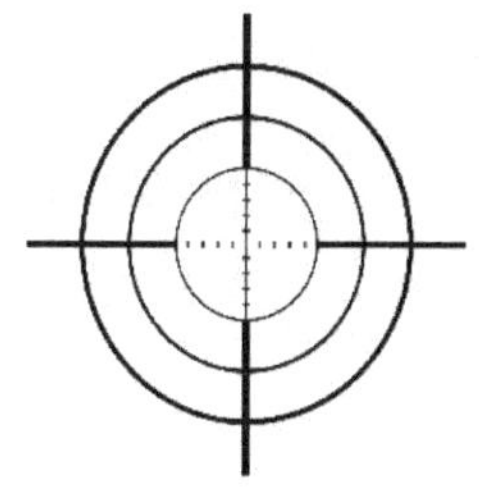

— EIGHTEEN —

"What the hell?"

Steiger stepped out of the underbrush and came face to face with a bleached skull easily bigger than Tiny. She was walking point on their approach to the Qhazd settlement, leading them parallel to the peninsula's southern shore. The animal path they shadowed ran a few dozen meters inland from the water's edge, where the purplish dancing trees grew in more widely spaced clumps but still gave enough cover from watching eyes and sensors.

"It looks like a hexadragon," Decker said when he saw the massive skeleton taking up most of the clearing. "I'd hate to see the critter than killed it."

"Perhaps one of the aquatic species." Langton pointed at fractured and crushed bones near the first of its three pairs of legs. "The thing must have tried to feed in the shallows and forgot to pay attention. There are things in the water that make this one look cuddly. It must have dragged itself here to die."

"Yeah, but imagine the steaks you could from that critter."

Decker turned towards Tiktin with a grim smile.

"You must have been snoozing during Lisk's rundown of the local wildlife. A bite or two of their meat and you get killer indigestion. Fortunately, it only lasts a few agonizing minutes before your system shuts down permanently. It's a damn fine thing that our flesh will kill them as well."

"I'll try to keep that in mind when a hexadragon bites me in half." Langton's tone was as dry as the bones in front of them. "It'll be a consolation to my grieving friends and family, if not quite to me."

"It certainly doesn't keep its tiny cousins from trying." Steiger shooed away a dozen insect-sized flying versions of Naraka's dominant, six-limbed phylum.

"Let 'em bite you," Tiny suggested. "They'll die, and you'll have some peace and quiet."

"Not a good idea." Decker shook his head. "Bites will inject toxic proteins into your bloodstream, and you'll wish this big boy had bitten you in half. You'll survive, of course, but for a few horrible hours, death will seem preferable."

He tapped the back of Tiny's helmet.

"Try to pay attention the next time someone talks to you about nature's beauty on an alien planet, even an intelligence puke who sounds like he's pulling facts out of his ass. Someone's life may depend on it, maybe even your own."

Tiktin bowed his head in contrition. "I will, Jack."

"This is as good a place as any to stop," the Marine said. "There's no point in rushing, and I'd rather not stumble over the Qhazd in the darkness, which is what'll happen if we keep going. The sun's going to set in an hour or so, and there's about six klicks left. Miko and Alex, go set the perimeter sensors. Put an extra one where the wood line meets the beach, just in case. Tiny, get supper going."

"And what will you be doing, oh great leader?" Steiger asked.

"I'll be figuring out how to banish the smart-ass attitude from my beloved team. That and taking an accurate fix of our position, just in case a herd of hexadragons creeps up on us, and we need air support. Without a proper satellite constellation in orbit, it gets complicated."

"I'm not convinced that the armed skimmers from Mahar are going to make much of an impression on something with a skull this thick." Langton tapped the dead creature's head. "Not when the brain box is so damn small by comparison. We might need a whole fleet to save our butts if we're ever caught between a herd of them and whatever lives out in the water."

As if on cue, they heard a distant roar, followed by a loud splash.

"If anyone is thinking about doing a bit of fishing," Langton said, sensors in hand as he stalked off to place them around the clearing, "count me out. The rations will be fine."

"Water critters are just as dangerous for humans as this kind." Tiny nodded towards the skeleton, mostly to show Zack that he hadn't completely ignored the fauna and flora portion of Lisk's briefing. "So it would be kind of dumb to go fishing anyway."

Langton laughed.

"Greater truth was never spoken on this day. Well done, friend Atli."

Later, as they sat in the shelter of a humongous ribcage overgrown with vines, eating their meal from warmed up pouches, Steiger sighed.

"Spending twenty-four hours a day for four or five days at a stretch in this tin suit is going to be one of my least favorite memories of this contract."

"More like twenty-one hours a day," Langton said by way of correction. "Naraka has a faster rotation. It also means Friday comes around a day faster, compared to universal time."

"Be that as it may," she replied, "I can't wait to sample the stench when we strip down, back in our team barracks, after this one."

"Keep your helmet on, visor down, until we've had our first run under the showers," Decker suggested.

"I might just do that." She rolled up her meal pouch and tucked it back into her pack. They operated on orders to leave no traces because in a six-sided fight, keeping an enemy guessing as to who hit him almost became a principle of war. She stood and stretched. "I'll go make my round of the perimeter now. Jack and Tiny, you two might as well take your first bit of shut-eye even though there's still some daylight left."

"Roger that." Decker finished his meal, slammed down his helmet visor and rolled over on his side, head comfortably wedged between his pack's external pouches.

With a shrug, Tiny followed suit, but unlike the Marine, he didn't have the ability to fall asleep at a moment's notice. That left Langton to man the long distance radio set, necessary on Naraka in the absence of communications satellites, and the tablet-sized console tied into the perimeter sensors.

Soon, the daytime sounds of things thrashing in the underbrush faded away, replaced by the more ominous howls of smaller, nocturnal predators and the screams of their prey. A few even ventured to the very edge of the clearing, as witnessed by the sensors, but after sniffing the air cautiously, they turned tail. Humans wrapped in metal and polymers must not have appeared particularly appealing, or nourishing.

After what seemed like only minutes since he'd fallen asleep, Decker felt a gentle hand shake him. His eyes snapped open, and he was instantly awake, senses probing into night as dark as the bottom of a mineshaft, thanks to a thick blanket of cloud hiding the moons and stars.

"Is it our turn already?" He whispered when he felt a helmet touch his, so they could speak without using their communicators.

"Nearly, but that's not why I've given you a premature call," Langton replied. "Something is moving up the beach, from the general direction of the Qhazd compound, and it's humanoid, not Narakan. The sensor makes out twelve individuals. They're about a kilometer away right now, and closing slowly."

"Huh," Decker grunted as he sat up, one arm reaching out to shake Tiny. "Just our luck the buggers have sent out a patrol."

"What are you thinking?" Langton asked.

"That depends. What are the chances they'll walk by without noticing us?"

"In the dark? With the kind of crap gear reivers usually have? Pretty good."

"What's up," a sleepy voice whispered.

"Bad guys coming up the beach. Could be Qhazd from our target area."

"Oh." Tiny turned over onto his knees and levered himself up. He immediately grabbed the team's heavy chain gun and checked both the power pack and the ammo box almost as if by instinct.

Steiger dropped down on one knee beside the others. "Ambush?"

"Four against twelve? The odds are excellent, but if it goes sideways on us, we might have problems completing our mission," Decker said. "My first instinct is to let them pass. We'll radio back to Mahar and advise them that a dozen Qhazd are on the loose. Let's slip into the tree line where we can watch. No one shoots without my say so, understood."

"Understood," Langton said. "Do we shift camp after that?"

"If they don't find us, why should we? I'd rather not risk walking into a second group if it's a larger patrol moving by echelons."

Steiger picked up the sensor readout and glanced at it.

"We'd better get into position now. Otherwise, it'll be too late."

"Right," Decker replied. "Miko, you're on the left, closest to their approach. Alex, to her right, five meters away, I'll be another five meters down and then Tiny with the big gun as our anchor."

A few minutes later, after a lot of quiet slithering on ground by turns soggy and sandy, they lay in an extended line beneath the low brush, facing dark water that crept up and down the beach with the metronomic regularity of the waves driving it.

Decker dialed up his visor's magnification and quickly found shadows walking on the harder, more compacted sand at the top of the beach. Armed and armored, they moved like fighters who weren't expecting to encounter an enemy patrol so close to their home base.

The lead humanoids didn't seem to be taking the usual scouting precautions. He saw no handheld sensors in use, nor did their helmeted heads swivel left and right.

As they came closer, he could make out armor that seemed to come from many sources, pieced together here and there so it fit, which meant minimal systems integration. Also, the long arms they carried probably came from a dozen different worlds, with widely varying levels of quality. In his opinion, the humanoids on the beach were ripe for the picking and the temptation to take them down became irresistible.

Somewhere in the back of his mind, a very tiny, very irritating Hera Talyn tried to remind him that the mission came before his enjoyment. He struggled to ignore this new and disturbingly bizarre manifestation of his conscience, telling himself that blooding his team *was* part of the mission.

However, in combat, the enemy also gets a vote.

"Shit." Steiger's soft curse broke their radio silence. "The point critters have slowed down and started paying attention to their surroundings. One of them now looks like he has a sensor in his hand."

"Let's see this through," Decker replied. "No one fires unless I give the order."

The humanoids along the beach began to spread out in a broken line as if they expected trouble but had no idea from what direction. Try as he might, the Marine couldn't figure out what had triggered the patrol's instincts. Maybe the local wildlife. Hopefully the local wildlife. If they had picked up his team, or even just the sensor they'd placed by the beach, the buggers had better gear than he expected.

"Two of them just slipped into the tree line," Steiger reported moments later. "They smell something, even if it isn't us."

"Pull back level with Alex and go deeper," Decker ordered. "We're turning into this into a ninety-degree ell formation. Tiny, you have eyes on them?"

"Yep," the Celestan replied.

A minute passed, then another. Decker thought he heard the soft slithering sounds of Steiger pulling back into the woods to cover their left flank, but couldn't be sure.

Then, a shout in an alien tongue shattered the silence. Ten shadows dropped to one knee, weapons at the shoulder, nervously scanning the dark underbrush. The two who'd vanished a few minutes earlier burst through the tree line, yelling and gesticulating at something behind them. After a brief moment of incomprehension, the patrol coalesced in a tight clump, weapon barrels pointing outward like the quills on a porcupine.

"What the f..."

Langton's voice trailed away when a low-slung, massive, six-legged creature exploded from the undergrowth and charged at the humanoids. The size of an overgrown saltwater crocodile, it had a smooth hide and a jaw that seemed to take up half of its length. It opened its mouth, revealing fangs the size of fighting knives that seemed preternaturally white in the darkness, and an unearthly roar washed over them.

The Qhazd opened fire without discipline, pouring out as much plasma as possible to stop the animal's charge. Decker could almost sense their panic, and he came to a snap decision, ignoring his inner Hera in favor of seizing the opportunity fate, or rather the patrol's mistake in disturbing the reptile, had placed before him.

"We attack. Fire at will. Leave no survivors."

The thump of Tiny's heavy gun almost drowned out the creature's roars.

At first, the Qhazd seemed not to notice they'd come under enemy fire, thanks to their focus on the animal, now thrashing on the sand in pain. Then, their cluster began to crumble at the edges.

Caught between the dying beast and unknown assailants, a few of them broke and ran towards the water, hoping for a way out. That sufficed to destroy any remaining cohesion. Two or three managed to keep their heads and fired back at Zack's team, but he, Steiger and Langton picked them off one by one, while Tiny hosed down those who'd chosen to run.

It took no more than half a minute to wipe out a patrol of twelve armed humanoids. The Narakan hexacroc kept flailing about, spraying sand and blood over dead and dying humanoids. Something splashed near the waterline, where Tiny had mowed down the runners, and a giant creature emerged from the darkened bay, its open jaws snapping up one dead Qhazd after the other.

"Doesn't it know alien flesh isn't good?" Tiny asked, watching the bodies disappear.

"Not your problem," Decker replied. "Put the other critter out of its misery. Then, we'll take advantage of the local clean-up service and toss the rest of them in the water. Maybe life on Naraka can digest non-humans sentient species, maybe it can't. So long as it takes the dead buggers out to sea, I'm happy."

"I think that went well," Langton commented, climbing to his feet. "Twelve for twelve. Let's just hope they didn't have a chance to call home."

"If they did, it would have been because of the hexacroc, not us. We didn't leave them enough time."

A ripping plasma burst nearly tore the animal's body in two, and it stopped moving altogether.

"You still want to camp around here?" Steiger asked once they'd disposed of the humanoids.

Decker snorted. "Of course not. This place is going to be rife with scavengers in the next while, and if the whoresons did call home, some of those scavengers might show up in a skimmer. We move back to the last waypoint before the skeleton clearing."

"And take care we don't step on another one of those." Steiger jerked her chin at the dead hexacroc.

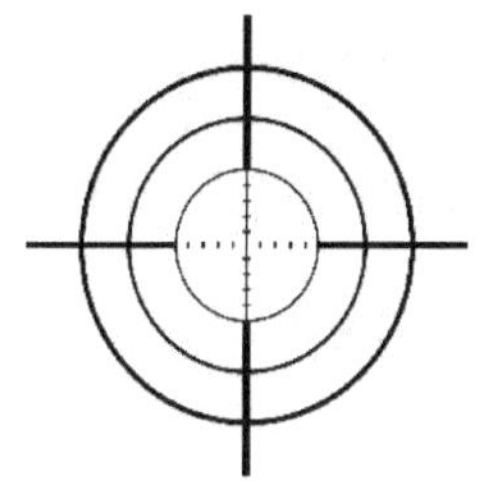

— NINETEEN —

"A real who's who of species that should never have been allowed off their home worlds," Langton said, watching the Qhazd settlement clustered at the base of a striated bluff torn from the Mahar peninsula's surface by some ancient spasm.

"Slave labor's all Itrulan, though," Decker replied, naming a bipedal reptilian species from a technobarbarian planet deep inside the Protectorate Zone.

The two men had found an observation post on a rise opposite the encampment, about a kilometer and a half away. Tiny and Miko were behind them, watching for anything, native or imported, that might cause trouble.

"So are some of the guys with the prods. Have you ever been on Itrul?"

"I visited it a couple of years ago."

The reply came out before Zack could think it through and he silently cursed himself. He had visited the primitive planet while working as a gunner aboard the civilian merchant vessel *Shokoten* after the Corps pensioned him off for slugging his temporary squadron commander, well before his recruitment into Naval Intelligence.

Jack Lorenzo, on the other hand, would have had no occasion to see Itrula during his twenty-five-year career. However, the damage was done, so he might as well keep being brazen about it. At least he no longer felt any pain at the thought of his long gone lover Raisa, with whom he had enjoyed a night on Itrula he would remember forever.

"The place isn't as nasty as you'd think, based on the Itrulans one meets over open gun sights along the Rim," he continued. "But the ones down there won't be the kind of model citizens preferred by Itrul's ruler, the Akmin of Tanira."

"You're a well-traveled man," Langton said, without a trace of irony in his voice. "Any other species you know close up?"

"Plenty." Decker's eyes narrowed as something struck him. "I think the labor, and its overseers, are on contract to the Qhazd. Probably guys who are used to mining back home."

"What makes you say that?"

"The way everyone moves down there. Reivers sometimes sub out work they're too lazy to do themselves. Besides, Itrulans might make decent thugs, but they don't run their own clans."

He fell silent for a few heartbeats, and then a distant figure stepped out of a container hut, one whose appearance under magnification triggered those old memories of his time aboard *Shokoten* again.

"Well isn't that special," he muttered. "See the pale biped with the red hair that just showed up?"

"Sure."

"That, Alex, is an Arkanna. They're a highly predatory mammalian species very close to us, physically. Excellent fighters, with built-in advantages that you don't want to face first hand."

"You *are* well traveled. I've heard of them. Apparently, they don't leave their home world much. Did you visit Arkanna?"

"No. But I did come to know one of their exiles."

I came to know her very well, he mentally added. This time, his mind's eye presented an image of Raisa that stirred a feeling of loss he had thought to be long gone.

"I'm starting to understand why Magnus Roby finds you so puzzling, Jack."

This time, Decker could hear the irony loud and clear.

"I had a seriously misspent youth. You know how it is. But seeing an Arkanna down there changes the math."

When Langton didn't reply, Decker turned to glance at him.

"What?" He asked when he saw the man staring back.

"You're no combat engineer sergeant first class, buddy. That's what."

"Isn't the mercenary rule, don't ask, don't tell?"

"That only applies to sexual matters, and you're not my type. Now tell me why an Arkanna changes the math."

Decker held his eyes a few seconds longer, before turning them back on the encampment.

"He has to be running the place. One of the reasons you don't see many Arkanna on the star lanes is because of the way their society works, and the way they see other species. That would be mainly as prey, by the way. If he's working for the Qhazd clan, he's in charge of that operation, with his one up boss somewhere else. His kind doesn't make good subordinates for non-Arkanna, at least not the males. And he has to be another exile." Decker paused for a few heartbeats. "Actually, it wouldn't surprise me if the Qhazd clan is a front for Shrehari corsairs. The one species an Arkanna would respect enough to work for are the boneheads."

"How does this change things?"

"Arkanna don't like to lose, especially if this one has sworn fealty to a Shrehari. He'll have that place sewn up tight, and the beings under his control terrified of making a mistake. There won't be a single one capable of standing up to him."

"Could you?"

"In hand-to-hand combat? I'd rather not try, thank you very much," he replied, remembering Raisa in full fury, then trying to imagine a male version. "The one thing we will not do is underestimate the defenses down there. What happened to the patrol doesn't matter. They didn't have an Arkanna at their head. Heck, they might have been from another operation altogether."

"Then we take him out first."

"What is it with you guys," Decker growled, "always wanting to leave a body trail? You're like a lady friend of mine who has an unfortunate fixation on death."

"I seem to recall you had a burst of enthusiasm last night on the beach."

"A saint wouldn't have been able to resist that kind of target-rich environment. Besides, by now the patrol would be officially listed as vanished without a trace. It'll make the rest nervous when they leave camp, and nervous rental soldiers are quicker to run away. We go in and whack the Arkanna, they'll know who did it, or at least that something with four limbs instead of six did it. I'm sure you see the difference. Our mission is to disrupt their operations while making them wonder, not cause all-out war."

"Easy, there. I was just making a suggestion."

Decker turned to scowl at Langton but then saw his sly smile.

"What?"

"Who are you really? Most of the mid-level grunt noncoms I've met don't think the way you do. Nor do they have that kind of knowledge."

The Marine snorted. "You're not going to give up, are you?"

"Forgive me for wanting to know who the guy covering my ass really is, Jack. You're not as secretive with Miko."

"That's because we've worked together before."

"So you don't trust me."

"I don't know who you really are either, Alex." Decker put a slight but unmistakable emphasis on Langton's name.

The sly smile broadened. "Touché."

"Can we focus on the job at hand now? I think we'll spend the rest of the day and overnight watching. We're bound to see something that'll give us ideas on what we could do next."

"And here I thought you already had a master plan."

"You're a pain in the ass, Langton, like every fucking meathead I've ever met."

Movement in the camp cut off Decker's follow-on comment, and he grunted.

"Skimmer. Maybe they finally decided to look for their lost patrol."

The low-slung ground effect car, a civilian cargo hauler with armor plates and a pedestal-mounted heavy gun, emerged from a pop-up hangar, fans howling to wake the dead. An Itrulan stuck his leathery head out the driver's compartment and shouted something at the Arkanna, who waved him towards the wire-topped earth berm protecting their mining operation.

Dust blew in all directions when the driver gunned his engines, and the skimmer bounced over the defenses, before heading down a narrow lane cut through the trees. It slowed almost to a walk before reaching the beach, to avoid overshooting the narrow strip of sand while doing a ninety-degree turn. After seeing a specimen of the wildlife inhabiting the bay, Decker couldn't blame them, but he did have an idea.

He nudged Langton.

"What do you say I take Tiny down there and wait for the thing to come back? If they slow down again to make the turn away from shore, maybe I can toss one of our magnetic mines at it, set to blow once it's back in camp."

"Sounds like fun. What if they spot you while you're doing it?"

"A mounted patrol on the way back to camp over a known route? Their minds will be on returning inside the wire, especially if they figure that the ones from last night fell victim to a large critter. Chances are they're not going to be scanning every meter of ground. Stay here and keep watching. I'll send Miko to join you."

Decker slipped out of their observation post and slithered through the undergrowth to where the other two were relaxing under a rocky overhang. He quickly explained his findings and idea to Tiktin and Steiger.

"Don't stumble over any sensors, Jack," the latter warned. "If that operation is owned by Shrehari corsairs, they might have better gear than the average reiver clan."

"That's why I'm taking Tiny. Between the two of us, we're big enough to register as a hexacroc and the buggers won't bother sending out a pair of eyeballs."

"That's real funny, big boy. Anything you'd like me to do while I'm up there with Alex?"

"Come up with some ideas of your own."

He turned to the Celestan. "We're taking everything, Tiny, just in case we can't come back here afterward."

"Wise move." Steiger patted his shoulder. "Stay in touch."

Then, she vanished up the path Decker had used.

The walk through dense forest took longer than Zack had expected and he began to fear the skimmer would return before they could get into position.

What critters lurked in the undergrowth let the two large, armored men pass, making him wonder whether the hapless Qhazd troopers of the previous evening had accidentally bumped into the hexacroc while it slept. If so, they'd have been better off to stay on the beach and ignore whatever their sensors had shown. Without the animal attack, Decker would probably have held his fire.

Sweating, their chameleon battle suits covered in muck and debris, they finally reached the edge of the gap, where it met the sandy beach and the bay beyond. The waters seemed calm, with a few wind-blown ruffles, but showed no evidence of the giant life forms that lurked beneath the surface.

Leaving Tiny to watch for the skimmer, Decker scanned the area to find any detection devices the Qhazd might have placed around the gap. Had he been in their shoes, this is where he would have concentrated his resources. Then, he looked for a place to hide the explosive device where it wouldn't be seen, but still be close enough to the passing skimmer's underside for the magnet to lock on.

"Shit." Tiny's voice crackled over the short-range radio. "They're coming back."

Decker cursed under his breath, knowing he'd run out of options. He dropped his pack inside the tree line, then took the two explosive devices, one in each hand, and jumped into a crack behind a fallen log near the center of the gap. With any luck, the skimmer would run over him. It would suck, but he didn't have time to find anything better.

A few minutes passed, but then he began to hear the roar of badly ducted fans in the distance. He checked the devices one last time and braced himself.

The skimmer slowed down in preparation for its turn and Decker tensed his muscles. Then, a wall of air slammed down his spider hole, and daylight vanished. Though his helmet tried to filter out most of the sound, the vibrations felt like ten thousand tiny hammers pounding him at hypersonic speed. He flicked on the magnets and tossed both mines up towards the skimmer's keel, then tried to make himself as small as possible. A second or two later, the vibrations stopped, and daylight returned while the roar of the fans began to abate.

Decker stayed still until he could no longer hear the vehicle, then he cautiously peered over the rim of his hole. There, in all its glory lay one of the mines. It had failed to connect. Thankfully, he couldn't see the other, which meant it had successfully hitched a ride. He crawled out, picked up the device and disarmed it, then scuttled back into the undergrowth where he'd left his pack and his wingman.

"I think that went well," he muttered to himself.

With a tap on the shoulder, he signaled to Tiny that they were heading back to the observation post. Decker wanted to witness the device going off, if not for its own sake then to see how the beings in that encampment would react.

Their actions would tell him a lot about how quickly he could disrupt operations without unduly risking his own team. After all, he had come to Naraka for something completely unrelated to the Confederacy of the Howling Stars' corporate guerilla war.

*

"Hey Tarra, how are they hanging." Jon Gerin looked up from his tablet and smiled at the tall, wiry man who'd stepped into the company office as if he owned it.

"Evenly for once." He jerked his head to one side. "Her Nibs away again?"

"If she's not in the office, then yeah."

Open contempt shone from dark eyes set beneath brows that bristled as much as the silver-shot black mustache on his upper lip.

"She should be spending time on her fucking work instead of the other way around." Tarra dropped into a chair across from Gerin and sketched a mocking salute. "Hal Tarra, leading the Kastell team, reporting to the company commander as ordered. Four special assignments operators back from the beyond. I'd have loved to get the debrief out of the way now, but with her Nibs away and Lisk off at one of the remote sites, I sent the team to the shacks for a hot shower and a cold beer."

"Fair enough."

Tarra pulled a data wafer from his battledress pocket.

"Here's my report. Do you mind passing it on for me? I don't particularly want to see Kozlev's crazy eyes tomorrow when I'm supposed to be on four days of intercourse and intoxication before we head back into the muck. Long story short, the enemy operations in the Kastell hills are down by fifty percent, and they still don't know if we did it or if another group hit them." Tarra shook his head. "You have to love six-sided wars. You can't tell who's screwing whom even with a program. It makes a refreshing change from watching Kozlev walk across Moria every second afternoon. Did any fresh meat come in while we were chasing shitheads?"

"Yup. Magnus sent us a new team. They're on the Mahar peninsula as we speak. Alun Howe's been screaming for some operators to keep the Qhazd busy."

"Are they any good?"

"You tell me." Gerin touched his tablet and then pushed it across the table. "One ex-Marine, two ex-Army and one Guard."

"There's no such thing as an ex-Marine."

Tarra picked up the reader and examined the pictures in silence. Of the four, only the Marine, one Jack Lorenzo, caught his eye. He'd have identified Zack Decker, former command sergeant, 902nd Pathfinder Squadron and one of his best friends, under any disguise.

You don't forget the man who watched your back during some of the hairiest missions, and you definitely don't forget the man who lived through the crap at 31 Aquilae with you. They shared a failure and the nightmares that came with it.

"I think I know the Marine," he finally said, mentally adding, it's about time you showed up, buddy. Elyce Sakal isn't going to find her way back home by herself.

"I figured that. He said he knew you. Is the guy any good?"

"Sure," Tarra shrugged, "provided you keep an eye on your booze. The man's always thirsty and knows all the ways in which he can quench it. Other than that, he's a heck of a good gun to have at your back."

He looked up at his commanding officer.

"Is there any chance of me speaking with Lorenzo?"

"For a trip down memory lane?" Gerin cocked an amused eyebrow at Tarra.

"The jerk owes me money."

"His team is tackling the Qhazd operation at the base of the peninsula right now. He'll be out of contact from Moria for two or three days until he gets back to Howe's garrison."

Tarra nodded once, climbing to his feet.

"Well, whenever I can speak with Jack, that'd be nice. If you ever need to combine teams for a mission, I'll volunteer to work under Lorenzo. At least I know he's not going to step on any tripwires or piss on an electric fence. If you have nothing else, I hear the shower calling. Make sure you give Kozlev my report because I won't hear *her* calling for as long as we're in Moria."

"See you at the bar, Hal," Gerin said, returning his mock salute with a wave of the hand. "Try not to empty out the fridge before I show up."

"No promises."

Back in his team room, Tarra stripped down and tossed his bits of armor and uniform aside. Living alongside one of the satellite mine operations wasn't precisely a hardship posting, but at least here in Moria, he didn't have to worry about any of the filth trying a stealth attack while he was busy soaping up and singing Wagner.

The main settlement not only had good defenses, including the better part of a battalion that didn't need transient special ops teams to stiffen them during an attack, it also had unlimited hot water, cold beer, and so-so entertainment. Unfortunately, it also had Frontier Solutions' HQ, including Rika Kozlev. What it didn't have was Zack Decker.

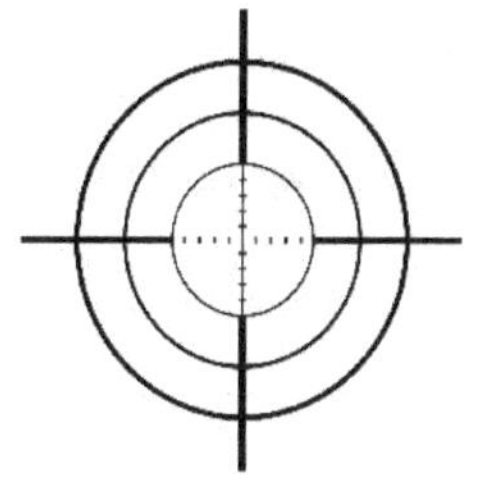

— TWENTY —

"Did anything happen while I was gone?" Decker slipped into the observation post between Langton and Steiger after a hard march back from the beach.

"Your target went over the berm and into the pop-up shelter. Two Itrulans came out. The End," the latter recited.

"Other than the driver having a long conversation with his Arkanna boss critter," Langton added. "Since then, it's been quiet."

Decker pulled a pad from his utility harness and checked its screen.

"The device is still active."

"Are you sure it's the one on the skimmer and not the one in your pack?" Langton asked. "Being run over might have screwed with your brain. It looked like a lot of fun from up here."

Decker gave him the rigid digit salute. "Unlike some, we Marines actually receive proper explosives training."

"Especially combat engineers, right?"

"Sure. If you like, I could demonstrate how I'd stick an IED up your ass without anyone noticing."

Before Langton could reply, a loud rumble, like that of a starship preparing to land, rolled over them and they felt the ground sway from side to side, tossing them into each other.

"What fresh hell is this?" Steiger dug her fingers into the long grass.

"That was a seismic tremor. Welcome to Naraka, where it's like Earth, only three hundred million years ago," Langton said.

Down below, beings streamed from the various buildings and milled about, like ants whose nest had been kicked over.

"I'd hate to be in a mine shaft right now."

"Is it time to blow up the skimmer?" Tiny asked from below them.

"Not yet. We'll wait until this is over and they're ready to breathe a sigh of relief."

"That's cruel."

"Yeah, but it's also fun. For me, that is."

The tremors subsided without causing any visible damage, and someone organized the Itrulan workforce in orderly ranks. They saw the Arkanna emerge from the large box that presumably held the headframe and join the formation.

"Um, Jack." Steiger nudged Decker.

"What?" The Marine kept his eyes on the camp, his pad in one hand.

"Is that what I think it is?" She pointed at the mountain ridge that ran down the peninsula's spine, its foothills only a few kilometers from their position. In the minutes since the tremor's onset, it had spouted a growing plume of ash with a fierce glow at its base.

"That would explain the earthquake. One of those mountains blew its top," Langton said.

"Are we in any danger?" Tiny asked.

"Maybe. Pyroclastic flows can travel for long distances, and at speeds you wouldn't believe possible. Ash goes even further."

"That thing's pretty far away, Alex," Steiger said, sounding unconvinced.

"It's still uncomfortably close if it wants to spew hard."

"The buggers down below have noticed." Decker nudged Langton.

Dozens of heads had turned in the volcano's direction, including the Arkanna's.

"Speaking of pyroclastic flow," the former MP said, "I do believe that ground-hugging plume coming down the mountainside is headed in our general direction."

"Crap." Decker spat out a few more choice words. "We need to figure out where it's headed and then go in the other direction. If that thing rolls over us, we're dead. Instantly."

He looked down at the camp again, wondering whether they were doing the same math, then back at the volcanic eruption.

"I think we need that skimmer I planned to blow up," he said. "The pyroclastic flow is probably going to cut us off from Mahar if it doesn't take us out completely."

"And you intend to do that how, exactly? I doubt walking up to their fence and asking for a ride is going to work."

He called their attention back to the mine. "The buggers are shutting down operations and preparing to evacuate. We'll hitch a ride by the gap where I planted my bomb. It's time to run, folks."

With Decker in the lead, they raced down the path he and Tiny had taken, urged on by rumblings from the eruption, and the increasingly alarmed shouts in Itrulan from the encampment. Nature would be doing the job of disrupting Qhazd clan operations. Their priority had become a quick getaway.

Decker and his team were almost at the gap when the first skimmers, fans roaring, raced down towards the beach before turning left, where the base of the peninsula met the mainland, away from the pyroclastic flow's probable path. Then, a tidal wave of native wildlife crashed through the undergrowth, instinctively fleeing the onrush of volcanic death.

A hexadragon the size of a large shuttlecraft stomped out into the gap and almost collided with the last of the skimmers. The craft slewed sideways when its driver tried to avoid the saurian and came to a halt, fans howling through bent ductwork, its cab facing away from the team.

The covered transport had hand and foot holds on both sides and the back, but no windows other than at the front. It didn't even have a remote weapons station on the roof, unlike the one carrying the still unexploded device on its underside.

"Come on," Decker shouted before bursting into a sprint over the uneven ground, carbine at the high port to help push thorny branches out of the way.

They jumped on, two per side, moments before the driver regained control over his craft and had to hang on for dear life when he gunned his fans to catch up with the others.

The afternoon sky had darkened beneath the spreading ash plume, and now a roiling cloud, the approaching pyroclastic flow, turned the northern horizon black. The skimmers dodged animals left and right as they sped down the beach towards the mainland.

Once their vehicle stabilized, Decker turned back to look at the where the mine sat, abandoned and just had time to see it, and the hill they had used as an observation post, disappear beneath a thick carpet of hot gasses and rock particles.

Moments later, the flow met the dark waters of the bay, creating a massive steam column that reached for the heavens. Then, a wall of heat slammed into his armor, accompanied by a choking stench of sulfur and he feared they wouldn't make it when the flow began to widen as if it wanted to run them down.

The animals, slower than their vehicle, were engulfed by the cloud and killed instantaneously. Out in the bay, massive carcasses bobbed to the surface, the aquatic creatures boiled alive within moments. To Decker, it seemed like the end of the world. For Naraka, a planet much younger than Earth, it was merely Tuesday.

Dropping off the skimmer while it was going at full speed would mean death, if not from the fall, then from the pyroclastic cloud. Decker shuddered at the thought, feeling a kind of fear he hadn't experienced in a long time — the fear of nature unleashed and unreasonable. He hung on tighter and watched, praying they'd escape, while daylight turned to early night.

After a while, it seemed like they were gaining on the cloud and the crushing heat began to abate, then they crossed over a shallow river and left Mahar for the mainland. Their vehicle, having caught up with its mates, began to slow, which meant that someone ahead might notice four armored soldiers hanging onto the last truck like carbuncles on an ocean-going ship's hull, and realize they didn't belong to their own guard detail.

The skimmer's speed still precluded a drop and roll, even for an old pathfinder like Zack, never mind the other three, especially with heavy packs. The convoy curved along the beach, and he had his first real glimpse at the other skimmers. A cruel smile pulled up the corners of his lips and, still hanging on for dear life, he pulled his pad from a leg pocket.

A flick of the wrist turned it on and set it to search for the explosive device's signal. He had a lock almost immediately.

The lead vehicle came to another shallow inlet, this time, a salt-water swamp bordered by Naraka mangrove analogs. It launched across, giving birth to a rooster tail of water. The next skimmer slowed down to give itself breathing space before sprouting its own tail.

When it reached the midpoint of the inlet, Decker touched his pad, blowing the vehicle apart in a bright orange ball that sent debris flying in all directions. The explosion's shockwave reached them a fraction of a second later, but the next trucks didn't start braking until the third in line had committed to crossing the water, its driver desperate to change course, in case the one ahead had hit an IED.

It slewed sideways, unfortunately pointing out into the bay and shot forward for almost a hundred meters, roiling up the dark surface in a doomed attempt to return to shore. A six-limbed sea creature rose from the shallows, dwarfing the craft, then crashed down to take it under.

All semblance of convoy discipline vanished.

Skimmers skittered over the beach, desperate to shed forward momentum without crashing into one another or venturing out over the inlet. The one carrying Zack and his team bounced a few times when the driver re-oriented his fan ducts to avoid joining the clusterfuck ahead of them.

That slowed it down enough for a safe dismount, but the Marine knew they still had problems. Their wild ride away from the eruption had taken them in the opposite direction of the Mahar mine, with the volcano cutting off any way of returning on foot, at least on this side of the peninsula.

None of the parties exploiting Naraka had bothered to put up satellites, for fear of a competitor taking them over or shooting them down, which meant everyone used good old radio waves to communicate with home base. Unfortunately, the spreading ash cloud, with its highly charged particles would limit, if not shut down their ability to use even their powerful long-range set.

In other words, they couldn't walk back and couldn't call for a ride. And they were stuck in the middle of the Qhazd clan survivors, at least a third of whom were armed guards, hailing from a species not reputed for mercy or gentleness, under the command of an Arkanna, one of the most predatory humanoids in the known galaxy.

The skimmer came to a shuddering halt where the inlet met the wood line, and Decker jumped off, yelling, "We need this one for ourselves."

He ran up to the cab, yanked the door aside, and reached in. Grabbing the Itrulan driver by his harness, he tossed the reptilian humanoid out onto the sand and took his seat. On the opposite side, Tiny had done the same with the crew commander while Steiger and Langton opened the doors to the truck's bed and climbed in.

Decker studied the controls before deciding they weren't much different from those he'd used before.

Four-limbed, bipedal humanoids tended to build along similar lines.

"You'll be happy to know," Langton said, "there are no workers back here, but plenty of crates."

"Cool. Now buckle up." He gunned all fans, lifting the large craft off the beach in a cloud of sand. Something in an alien tongue crackled over the radio, distorted by the eruption.

"I think that may have been a question along the lines of what the hell do you think you're doing," Langton said.

"Thanks. That would never have occurred to me," Decker's reply dripped with sarcasm. "How about everyone look sharp to see if the buggers turn their guns on us."

"And if they do?"

"Use your imagination. Perform an interpretive dance, write a haiku, or paint a picture. Or better yet, open the fucking windows and shoot back," he snarled. "Goddamn army amateurs."

"Is he always this touchy?" Langton asked Steiger.

"Not now, Alex."

A burst of plasma streaked past the skimmer.

"Shit. The jackasses decided we weren't playing on the same team. Hey Tiny," Steiger indicated a closed hatch above the Celestan's head. "Want to see if you can stick your big gun out and give 'em hell?"

"Wilco." Tiktin reached up to push the metal plate out of the way, swaying when Decker slewed around to aim them at the bay, their only way out.

"As a bonus," he said between clenched teeth, "you can tickle the sea monsters once we're over the water."

"We're going where?" Langton's voice rose by an octave.

"If you have any better ideas, spit 'em out or shut up and shoot back."

Gun first, Tiny squeezed through the opening, then dropped the heavy barrel down on its bipod, facing aft. Another burst of plasma streamed by, still a warning and not an attempt to disable them.

The skimmer sprouted a rooster tail of water the moment it left the beach and Decker poured on everything their wheezing, ancient power plant could muster.

Somewhere above him, Tiny fired measured, controlled bursts, more to keep the Qhazd's heads down than with any hope of scoring a hit. He turned the vehicle parallel to the shore, a few hundred meters out, hoping to bypass the worst of the eruption's flow and put them back on a trail leading to the Mahar mine.

More shots came at them, and some managed to burn neat holes in the rear of the bed cover, but, as most beings tended to do, the Qhazd shot high, missing the most vulnerable part of the vehicle. Then, as they sped further away from the inlet, the enemy fire lost what little accuracy it might have had.

Something made a hump beneath the choppy surface ahead, and Decker swerved out to sea.

"Look sharp, critter to starboard," he shouted up at Tiny.

A dark body rose from the water, met almost instantaneously by a stream of large caliber plasma. They heard an agonized roar and the massive, six-limbed aquatic reptile fell back, mortally wounded.

"Find or make yourselves an opening up top," Decker yelled at Steiger and Langton. "Tiny can't cover three hundred and sixty degrees, and buddy out there wasn't alone."

The volcanic ash plume lit up with one lightning bolt after the other, the jagged streaks looking like white flowers emerging from the fiery orange glow that crowned the shattered mountaintop, adding to that end of the world feeling.

Decker began to wonder whether their own home base would be immune, but the winds seemed to be pushing the plume across the mountainous spine and not towards the Mahar mine further down the elongated finger of land. However, that could change.

They passed the area where the pyroclastic flow had almost overwhelmed them. Nothing had escaped. The

Qhazd mine had vanished, likely forever, as had their observation post, the gap leading to the beach and every tree, bush or blade of grass along a wide swath of destruction.

Decker heard the high volume cough of Tiny's gun, firing at yet another dark hump lurking beneath the water's dark surface. Between volcanic action and over-sized, stupidly aggressive wildlife, Naraka was a heck of a vacation spot.

The zone of destruction soon faded in the distance, smothered by the gloom of premature twilight, though a sulfurous stench trailed them for a while longer. Decker aimed the skimmer towards the beach at a shallow angle, anxious to get away from the water without losing an iota of speed, in case the Qhazd had launched a pursuit.

He called up a map projection of the peninsula and, after finding their approximate position based on where the reiver mine used to be, he oriented himself for the run back to the Mahar encampment.

Using the meandering river that flowed by the compound as his highway would take time, but he didn't want to try running the clapped-out skimmer over the treetops. If one of the fans gave out, they would have an uncomfortable few seconds before thundering in.

"One of you guys keep your head out and watch for anything coming up our ass," he said. "The other two can come in."

"I'll play sentry," Langton immediately replied. "Tiny's done enough for one evening."

Tiktin and Steiger dropped back into the cab, the latter with a sigh of relief.

"That was fun. Whatever are you going to do for an encore?"

"You enjoyed the little volcanic eruption I laid on, did you?" Decker grinned at her over his shoulder. "Howe should be happy Naraka itself disrupted the Qhazd's operation permanently, and left no proof pointing back at Frontier Solutions."

"Other than us stealing this skimmer and its contents. Speaking of which, shall I see what we're hauling?"

"Knock yourself out."

A few minutes later, Steiger climbed back into the cab.

"I think the Arkanna's bosses are going to be seriously pissed, and if they're Shrehari corsairs, that could be painful."

"Why?" Decker asked.

"We're carrying what's probably their entire armory, and it looks to be of Shrehari manufacture."

"Nice. Maybe they'll pay us a bonus." Tiny's face lit up at the thought.

"Sure," Decker said. "A bonus debrief by the boss after a great big 'what were you thinking?' We were supposed to disrupt, not steal."

"So we ditch this thing a few klicks before we reach home base, then walk the rest of the way," Langton said from his perch. "What happens on patrol stays between us."

"Just how are we going to explain returning so fast without a ride?" The Marine shook his head, smiling. "No wonder they made me the team leader."

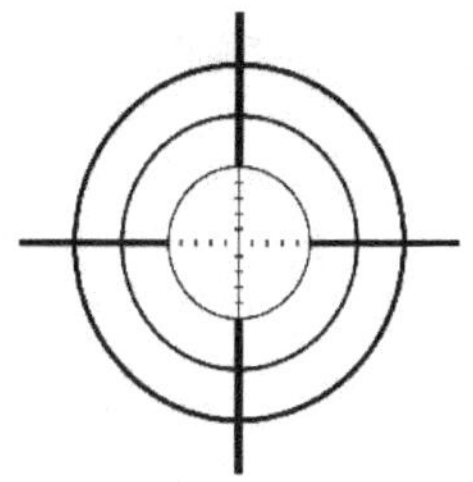

—TWENTY-ONE—

"Don't look now, but Kozlev came back early from her daily fun fest in town," Tarra's wingman said, nudging him in the ribs. "And she's glancing at us."

A noisy crowd of hungry troopers had taken over the chow hall, looking for a hearty breakfast, but they gave the Frontier Solutions' intelligence officer a wide berth, leaving her isolated in a sea of uniforms.

"If Gerin didn't pass my report on to her office, I'm going to reach down his throat with my dagger and recover the shots of whiskey I fed him last night." Tarra's eyes darted to where Kozlev stood, surveying the hall as if undecided on whether to grab some food or speak with the Marine. "I hope her Nibs decides to go suck on a pork sausage instead of bothering us."

"Nope," the wingman replied. "She's coming for your non-vat meat, Hal."

"Please. Not even as a joke. That woman is fucking evil." When he realized what he'd just said, Tarra grimaced. "In more ways than one."

He raised his head just in time to meet Kozlev's basilisk stare.

"I want you in my office at eight, Tarra," she said.

"Didn't Gerin give you my after-action report? I'm officially on day one of my four days off."

"My office at eight," Kozlev repeated. "I need to see you for something other than your AAR."

Without waiting for a further reply, she turned on her heel and joined the food line at the buffet.

"Her Nibs needs you," one of Tarra's teammates chortled, wiggling his eyebrows. "She's still hungry from last night."

"Sure." Tarra nodded agreeably. "Except I'm not her type when it comes to non-military matters."

"Oh? What is her type then?"

"Oversexed, ambitious and powerful. I don't qualify on any of them."

"I can see you not being ambitious. Heck, you're here with us, aren't you? Power, check, you ain't got any of that either, but I've always figured you for an oversexed jarhead."

Tarra mimed a punch at his wingman, who asked, "You going to visit the Queen of Psychos at eight like she said?"

"If that'll keep her off my back for the rest of our stay here, sure."

When Tarra entered the intelligence section's office half an hour later, Kozlev looked up from her screen and directed a chilly smile at the barely concealed spark of insubordination in his eyes. She pointed at a chair in front of her desk.

"Sit."

He complied, asking, "And what can I do for our charming Acorn this morning?"

A satisfied smile twisted his lips when he saw the inevitable flash of irritation cross her narrow face. The Marine Corps used Acorn as the universal call sign for intelligence officers, and for some reason, Kozlev seemed to have an allergy to anything Corps related.

"I've heard it said that in your former outfit, every noncom is only two degrees of separation away from any other noncom, meaning you either know each other, or you know someone who knows someone."

"Not entirely true, but yeah, among the senior noncoms, there's a lot of that," Tarra replied, realizing why she'd called him in. "What of it?"

Those cold eyes searched his as if establishing a baseline before the real questions started. He felt a chill run down his spine.

"Gerin told you we have a new team of operators, didn't he?"

"Sure. They're out playing cowboys and aliens on the Mahar peninsula."

"Did he also tell you a Marine's running that team?"

"He didn't have to. In any unit where there's one Marine and a bunch of lesser military beings, the Marine always ends up in charge." This time, he didn't restrain an urge to smirk. "It's an immutable law of nature."

Kozlev's look of pure disgust only served to widen his smile.

"You know what I mean, Tarra."

"As a matter of fact, I don't. We mere mortals are unable to fathom the mysteries of the Acorn's brain." Or the crazy officer brain for that matter, he thought.

She turned her screen around for him to see.

"Tell me about this one."

"Why? Didn't Gerin give you a peek at his service record?"

"You try my patience, Tarra. Most people seem to realize doing so is a bad idea."

He shrugged with an air of supreme indifference.

"How about you ask your question? While I enjoy the banter, it is eating into my intercourse and intoxication time."

"Who is this guy?" She tapped Decker's image with a manicured fingernail. "I mean who is he really?"

"Jack Lorenzo." Tarra drawled out the name, examining his fingernails with languid gestures of a man bored to tears. "Asshole owes me money, by the way."

"And how did you two meet? Lorenzo's service record doesn't show any assignments with special ops, while yours shows pretty much only time with special ops in the last two decades."

"The Corps does allow Pathfinders and lesser breeds to mingle, you know. Jack's good with things that go kaboom, among others, and we worked together on a few missions. He's a stand-up guy, so we became friends until he borrowed fifty creds from me just before I shipped out.　Next thing I know, he's a civilian and unreachable, and I'm out fifty smackers.　Why the interest?"

He met her icy stare with a noticeable lack of concern.

"Your friend Jack Lorenzo looks very much like a man who crossed my path.　He went by a different name, of course, and didn't quite have the same appearance, but something tells me they're one and the same."

"You make it sound like he ran out on you after a whirlwind romance.　Jack's been known to love 'em and leave 'em."

"Oh, the man in question did run out on me, but not in the way you mean.　I still owe him for that."

Lisk came into the office at that moment with a steaming cup and stopped in his tracks.

"I thought Tarra's report had everything we need," he said.

"Well, well.　If it isn't Acorn Minor." Tarra sketched a salute in Lisk's direction.　"How are they hanging?"

"Same old, same old." The intelligence section's second in command seemed distracted.　"Did you see the report from Howe over in Mahar yet, Rika?"

"No, but coincidentally, I was just having a friendly conversation with Hal concerning the man running the Mahar Special Assignments team, Jack Lorenzo.　Since you've already interrupted us, why don't you tell me what's going on?"

Lisk sat on the corner of his desk and took a sip of coffee, eyes darting from Tarra to Kozlev, trying to figure out the undercurrents he could sense.

"The Qhazd operation on the peninsula is gone, completely and utterly gone, buried under meters of ash. Lorenzo's team had it under observation after booby-trapping one of their skimmers that went out to find a missing patrol which, by the way, Lorenzo and company made vanish.　One of the mountains inland from the mine blew its top and spewed out a pyroclastic flow that took out most of the countryside between the central range and the bay in that area.　Our guys made it out by hijacking one of the Qhazd skimmers evacuating the encampment. Apparently, they managed to fuck up the convoy quite a bit before heading for home with most of the guard detail's armory. Shrehari stuff, not made for export. Lorenzo figures Shrehari corsairs owned that mining operation."

Tarra repressed a smile. That sounded like Zack Decker all over. His old troop leader and best friend still knew how to make an impression.

Kozlev sat back, eyes resting on Decker's image and purred, "Interesting. I think it's time I went up to Mahar and spoke with Lorenzo in person. If the boneheads are involved on Naraka, that could change the balance of power. Ask operations to arrange for a flight within the hour, Raj."

"Can I come?" Tarra asked, feeling a sudden urge to be by Decker's side when Kozlev met with him. Whatever his old friend had done to her, it seemed to have left an indelible mark, and not in a good way.

"Why?"

"He still owes me fifty creds."

"What happened to, as you so crudely put it, intercourse and intoxication?"

Tarra shrugged. "Who says I won't get lucky up at Mahar. Besides, knowing Jack, he'll have the intoxication part sorted out already."

"That's not a bad idea," Lisk interjected. "Hal has plenty of experience fighting Shrehari corsairs when he served in the Corps. Maybe having him check out the stuff Lorenzo captured along with sitting in on the mission debrief will allow us more insight into the Qhazd clan, considering they still have a few other operations running on Naraka."

"Very well," Kozlev replied after a few moments of thought spent staring at Tarra. "Go prepare. We can continue this conversation at another time."

*

Alun Howe, the Mahar garrison commander, poked his head into the Special Assignments team hut, eyes searching for Zack who lay spread eagle on his cot, digesting a heavy breakfast. They had spent the night alternately sleeping and keeping watch from within the skimmer, tucked away in a hollow a few kilometers beyond the Mahar camp perimeter. Decker had decided to wait for daylight before approaching, to avoid any misunderstandings with the guard detail.

"You're going to have company in a few hours, Lorenzo."

Decker raised his head and opened one eye.

"It's good to be wanted. Tell 'em to bring a few steaks and maybe some entertainers."

"I doubt our beloved intelligence officer will find that amusing."

The Marine sat up with a start.

"Come again?"

"Rika Kozlev is on a thopter headed our way. She wants to hear about the Qhazd directly from you, and inspect the Shrehari hardware you brought back."

"Fuck." Decker's curse sounded so heartfelt that Howe at him in surprise. "We need to head back out on patrol before she gets here."

"Sounds like a plan," Steiger said, jumping to her feet. "Where's the next wildcat mining operation that needs our tender loving care?"

"Sorry." Howe shook his head. "No can do without orders from Moria. The Queen of Darkness wants to see your tender pink butts up close, and see them she will."

"Why do you call her that?" Langton asked, also rising to his feet.

"Look into her eyes when you meet her and tell me there's a soul behind them." Howe grimaced. "Plus, there are all those rumors about her proclivities when it comes to interrogating prisoners."

"All of which are true," Steiger said. "Leastwise, they were the last time I saw her, on Garonne. I witnessed Kozlev in action and it completely ruined my appetite for intelligence work."

"What was she doing on Garonne?" Howe asked.

"Kozlev, along with a lot of other officers, served there on loan from Tiny's former employer, to run the Garonne militia and squash the rebels. They lost, the rebels won, and all of those officers were stripped of their commissions after the new government shipped them home."

"Oh."

"So you fought on the rebel side, is that it?" Howe asked.

"Not just fought on the rebel side," Steiger replied. "I infiltrated the militia on the rebels' behalf and ended up in Kozlev's section, which gave me the opportunity to turn an entire district capital over to the insurgents without a fight. She's not the type to forgive and forget on that scale."

"And you?" Howe asked Decker. "On the rebel side as well?"

"So to speak. I found myself on the wrong end of an interrogation after the Militia captured me. I managed escape, but not without stirring up a lot of crap and turning the feared Rika Kozlev into a bit of a joke. Miko saw it go down."

"Stirring up a lot of crap is an understatement," Steiger said. "Causing havoc is a more apt description. That night proved to be the beginning of the end for the Garonne militia."

"She may or may not remember me," Zack continued, "but if she does, things might become a bit tense. After losing Garonne, Kozlev lost her career, so I think she'll be less than thrilled to see us again."

"In the private sector, bygones are bygones, once a contract is over," Howe said. "Even the Queen of Darkness needs to respect that if she wants to keep working for Frontier Solutions."

"The only thing Rika Kozlev respects is Rika Kozlev, and I'm afraid I disrespected her in a very public manner — twice." Decker climbed to his feet. "Psychos like her never forgive and never forget."

"I'll sit in on the debrief," Howe replied, "to help keep things on an even keel. Besides, she's bringing another Special Assignments team leader with her, someone who's fought Shrehari corsairs before. You might know him, Jack. He goes by the name Hal Tarra."

Oh good, Decker thought. It'll be old home week, except Kozlev and Tarra know who I am and what I am. He caught Steiger's eye and saw her fear at what might happen once that thopter landed.

"Okay, Alun," he said, "thanks for the heads up. I'll have a quiet chat with my folks before the royal presence arrives."

"What happens now?" Langton asked once the garrison commander had left them. "As Alun said, bygones are bygones in the mercenary trade. Surely Kozlev wouldn't risk her job by taking revenge on the two of you for what happened in another place and at another time."

There, in that one sentence lay the crux of Zack Decker's problem. If Kozlev outed him as a Fleet agent, his life wouldn't be worth a busted cred chip. And he had only himself, and his big mouth to blame. If he had resisted the temptation to speak with ex-Colonel Harend in the prisoner stockade on the morning after the decapitation attack, things wouldn't be quite as dire.

"In my case," he replied, "I can assure you that she would. Remember what I told you about my counting coup on her. It was not the wisest choice I ever made."

"Indeed." Langton nodded. "Haven't you ever heard of the truism that you should never cause an enemy a small injury? And so, to repeat myself, what happens now?"

"We'll have to play it by ear." He met Steiger's eyes again, and then turned back to Langton. "I hope you and Tiny aren't squeamish."

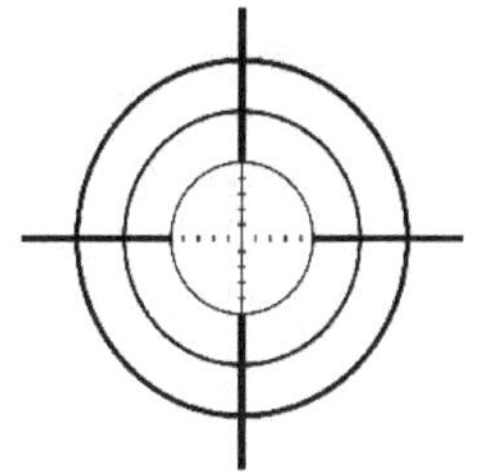

— TWENTY-TWO —

"Tell me more about your buddy Jack," Kozlev demanded once the thopter had lifted off.

"What's to tell?" Tarra shrugged, the motion almost indiscernible beneath his battle armor. "He's a good Marine, a good buddy, and a bad drunk."

"And he owes you money." She glanced out the window at the rapidly receding Moria settlement. "Please. There's more to Lorenzo than meets the eye."

"Sure. And if you're nice to him, he might even show you."

"What if I said Lorenzo is really a serving Marine called Zack Decker?"

"Then I'd say you've been sniffing too much of that shit you feed the prisoners before interrogation." Tarra turned his eyes to the carpet of jungle below their aircraft, wondering what was going on.

"Perhaps your Jack Lorenzo has a double, a twin."

"Or a clone. Welcome to the twenty-sixth century. I still don't understand why you have a fixation on Jack. As Marines go, he's entirely unremarkable, though he does have this thing with the ladies that I'd like to copy."

"I might have seen his thing." This time, she looked up and turned a feral smile on Tarra. "I found it to be utterly unremarkable, but then pretty much everyone's is when they're strapped to the interrogation chair. Perhaps I'll get a look at yours one of these days."

"Dream on, sister."

"So you don't know anyone by the name of Zack Decker?"

"Nope." He shook his head, avoiding her gaze.

"I'm sure you realize that our employers will be chagrined to find Frontier Solutions has been infiltrated by your Marine Corps, right?" When he didn't answer, she continued. "They'll be equally saddened by employees who failed to tell their supervisors about it, though now I'm beginning to wonder why two long-service Marine noncoms ended up here within weeks of each other. Oh — pardon me, I meant one noncom and one chief warrant officer."

"Sorry, I'm still not tracking." Tarra looked up at her with hooded eyes. "The only chief warrant officers I know are administrative or technical types, not operators."

"So you admit that Lorenzo used to be an operator?"

"Sure. He was a heck of an operator in his own way." An ironic smile lit his face up for a few seconds. "You should have seen him on shore leave. He always left a swath of destruction wherever he went."

Tarra indicated the distant volcano, still crowned by its dark plume of ash.

"It seems like he hasn't changed much if that's an example of his more recent work."

"You're a funny man," Kozlev replied. "It's a shame I'm not particularly inclined to appreciate the humor. When we land, and I see Jack Lorenzo face-to-face, I'll know if he's the Fleet agent who fought on the side of the Garonne rebellion against the legitimate government."

"What happens if you have a crazy acorn moment and decide he's the ghost who's been haunting your nightmares?"

This time, Kozlev's face twisted into something so cruel and rapacious that Tarra almost looked away.

"Then I'll pick up where I left off on Garonne."

"Good luck with that," he muttered, turning his attention to the tortured landscape beneath the speeding thopter. *I hope you know what's coming at you, old friend,* he thought, *and have planned accordingly.*

*

Alun Howe volunteered to greet Kozlev on the landing pad by himself, leaving the team to wait in their hut.

They heard the thopter land and Tiny, peering through a window, announced that two people had climbed out, one tall guy wearing armor and one woman in regular clothes.

"Trust Hal to come here ready for a fight," Decker chuckled. "But I'm glad to see dear Rika is still arrogant enough figure her reputation and importance to the organization are all the armor she needs."

"After Garonne and dismissal from the Celeste National Guard, she might be even less mentally balanced than when either of us last saw her," Miko cautioned.

"True." Decker checked that he could draw his dagger from its forearm sheath once again, the fourth time since Howe delivered the news.

Steiger leaned over to whisper in his ear.

"Nervous, lover boy? I can't see Rika Kozlev scaring you. She's just a wee psychopath."

"I'm not worried about her," he replied in the same tone, "but at the repercussions, if things go sideways, as I figure they will the moment she sees my ugly mug."

He leaned against one of the double-decker bunks, arms crossed and waited for the door to open.

When it did, the first thing Zack saw was Hal Tarra's face beneath the open visor, a face he hadn't seen in almost five years. Their eyes met, and he could read a clear warning in them.

Then, Kozlev entered the hut, a smile of anticipation revealing small, white teeth. She seemed older and leaner than when he had last seen her, hungrier even.

"Well, well, well." Her eyes found Miko, and she tilted her head to one side, like a demented bird. "If it isn't my old comrade Staff Sergeant Steiger, who handed Tianjin to the insurgency. I'd have thought you'd still be working for the provisional government, considering how much they owe you."

Her serpent's stare turned to Zack. "And who have we here? Frontier Solutions' records say Jack Lorenzo, but you remind me very much of someone who spent a bit of time in my custody, a man who went by Mark Skeen, or was that William Whate? Or is it really Chief Warrant Officer Zachary Decker, who, from what Colonel Harend told me on our return trip to Celeste, is emphatically not retired from the Marine Corps?"

All present, except Decker and Tarra, tensed at her words. Steiger's eyes went from Kozlev to Zack and then back again, wondering, waiting, while Langton, who still had that infuriating smile plastered on his rat-like features, watched Tarra. Howe seemed puzzled while Tiny appeared to have acquired a sudden headache, based on his pained expression.

"It's Jack Lorenzo." Zack met her cold stare without evasion or hesitation, knowing he wasn't a good enough liar to fool the likes of Kozlev. He had no choice but to brazen it out. "I have no idea who those other jokers are. If you're here to debrief us on the Qhazd mission, we're ready, so let's get going. We all need some sleep. If you're here to accuse me of being someone other than Mama Lorenzo's boy, you might as well climb back into that thopter and fuck off." Decker shrugged. "It makes no difference to me. I gave Alun my report, which he's obviously sent on to Moria, so my job is done for the day."

Then, ignoring Kozlev startled expression, he turned to Hal Tarra and frowned.

"I suppose you're here to collect those fifty creds I owe you?" He pulled Tarra into a bear hug and whispered in his ear. "We have a problem."

"It figures. Kozlev has a hard-on about you. Whatever you've planned, I'll play along."

"Folks," Zack released him and turned to the others, "this here is Hal Tarra, one of my oldest and best friends, even though he's overly fond of his money. We've saved each other's ass more times that I can remember. He's the one Marine who I'll gladly say is a better and meaner fighter than I am. Hal, meet Tiny Tiktin, Alex Langton, and Miko Steiger, a friend of mine from before this contract."

By calling Miko a friend of his, Decker had signaled that she could be trusted but didn't know everything. If he had used the expression 'a friend of ours,' then Hal would have known she was all in with the two Marines.

"It's a pleasure to meet you all." His eyes came to rest on Decker again. "The acorns said you'd come back with a bit of Shrehari hardware. I'd like to give it my master gunner's once-over."

"After the debrief," Kozlev said, visibly angry at having her grand entrance interrupted. "Besides, I'm not done with Lorenzo yet."

"You get the debrief and the hardware exhibition, then you fly back to Moria," Decker replied in a calm tone that nonetheless carried a hard edge Tarra remembered only too well. "Or you get neither and leave now. It's your call, Acorn."

It suddenly dawned on Kozlev that the power she thought she wielded within Frontier Solutions seemed diluted here inside the Special Assignments team hut on the Mahar peninsula.

She had stupidly let herself be surrounded by armed troops whose attitude conveyed little respect and no fear, and for the first time in months, she began to feel like she had made a grave error. Not about Lorenzo's real identity — she remained convinced he was the man who had sliced her throat in the prisoner stockade on Garonne.

No, her mistake was in being too eager. She should have let Lorenzo/Decker return to Moria for rest and relaxation, and taken him on her home turf. Perhaps she still could.

"The debrief, then." She looked around the converted container. "In here?"

Decker gestured at a set of lower bunks.

"In here. Have a seat, and I'll tell you the story of how Jack Lorenzo caused a volcanic eruption to finish off the Qhazd clan's operations in this region."

Kozlev obeyed, but her eyes held the promise that this wasn't over, that she would collect the debt Zack owed for Garonne, at another time and in another place.

Decker nodded once at her, a gesture signifying he understood. He switched on a holographic map projection and launched into his report. For some reason, he felt unexpected amusement at seeing Kozlev sit helplessly among his team, pretending to listen, while her thoughts revolved entirely around him.

At one point Decker winked at her and had to repress a burst of laughter when he saw the intelligence officer's disgusted expression. It almost made up for the treatment he had suffered at her hands. Almost, but not quite.

When he fell silent, Kozlev climbed to her feet without a word of acknowledgment. "The hardware now, I think. Tarra pronounced himself an expert, and I'd like to test that expertise."

"Sure." Decker nodded at Langton. "Take them to the hangar, please. I need to have a brief chat with Alun about administrative crap. Miko, Tiny, why don't you go along as well."

"What's up?" The garrison commander asked once they were alone in the hut.

"Send us back to Moria."

Howe seemed taken aback. "Why?"

"Your Qhazd problem is solved, and you don't want Jack Lorenzo festering here, not with the Queen of Darkness thinking I'm some other guy who might be actively connected to the Commonwealth military."

Decker could see the questions stumbling over each other in Howe's eyes, but to his relief, the man merely nodded.

"I'll give Moria a shout," he said.

"Talk to Jon Gerin. Tell him we could fly back on Kozlev's thopter so he can reassign us to a higher priority without waiting."

"Are you sure about this, Jack?"

"Oh yeah. Me and Kozlev, we're a problem you don't want inside your security perimeter."

"Does that mean you really are a serving Marine officer on a mission?"

Decker snorted. "Right. I'm on a mission. On Naraka, the ass end of the galaxy, where our beloved Commonwealth had no jurisdiction and even less interest. Kozlev hates my guts and wants to get even for a bit of past history that doesn't concern anyone around here. I'd rather she didn't, and for that, it's better that I'm in Moria, where she has to watch her step. Just have HQ order our return on her thopter, and you'll have done both of us a favor."

Howe must have sensed the truth in Decker's words, even though his explanation seemed incomplete.

"Consider it done," he replied after a few moments of reflection.

"Good man. I'll catch up with the royal tour. When you receive HQ's okay, make it look like Gerin's the one who thought of pulling us out of Mahar."

"That's what I intended." Howe gave Decker a tight smile and then sketched a vague salute before trudging off to his command post.

When Zack caught up with the others, Hal Tarra had already opened a crate and hauled out a large, heavy piece of weaponry. He examined it from all angles before pronouncing himself.

"This gun isn't an export model," he said, "and it's new enough to have come directly from the manufacturer, or perhaps via their Deep Space Fleet war stocks, and not from the used armaments trade." Tarra looked up at Decker. "You might be on to something, calling the Qhazd a Shrehari corsair-backed operation. I can't see the boneheads selling stuff meant for the home market to non-Shrehari. For one thing, the penalties are pretty stiff, not like the tap on the wrist our supply people get when they're caught making extra money via the back door."

Brilliant, Decker thought. Current generation ordnance from both the Commonwealth and the Empire is ending up in private hands.

"Let's look at the rest before we jump to conclusions," he said, indicating the other crates.

Fifteen minutes later, they had their answer.

"If we agree that we're likely dealing with Shrehari corsairs, I guess the next question," Decker glanced at Kozlev, "is figuring out whether they have government backing or not. Seeing stuff that shouldn't have left the warehouse in the first place makes me wonder whether the Empire is slowly making a play in the Protectorate. Do you have any comments or opinions on that matter, Rika?"

He smiled at the flash of annoyance in her eyes upon hearing him use her first name. Sometimes, you simply couldn't beat the officer-type arrogance out of a commissioned asshole, even after dismissal with disgrace. Decker wondered what Kozlev would say if she knew he held the rank of major, and not merely that of chief warrant officer, as she suspected.

"This is a new development. I shall have to think about it. Of course," her malicious smile returned, "Frontier Solutions and our employers of the Confederacy don't necessarily hold the same views as the Commonwealth when it comes to imperial shenanigans in this part of the galaxy, wouldn't you agree, Zack — sorry, I mean Jack?"

Decker made a dismissive gesture, retaining his air of utter detachment.

"Perhaps, but I can't see how something that's good for the Empire would bring anything but grief to the Confederacy. If the boneheads start throwing their weight around here in earnest, it'll become unprofitable for humans very quickly. A lot of 'em still haven't forgotten that they technically lost the last war. As species go, Shrehari are pretty good at holding grudges. If Frontier Solutions wants to make use of this stuff, Hal and I can teach the troops. Otherwise, I'd suggest handing the whole kit and caboodle to the Confederacy with the recommendation that they sell it as far away as possible from the Rim so no one can trace it back here. Of course, you could always dump it in the ocean."

"Why?" Kozlev sounded genuinely curious.

"Like I said, the boneheads hold grudges longer than an average human lifespan. Then, there's Fleet intelligence, with its uncanny ability to dig up stuff you thought buried kilometers deep. The one thing neither Frontier Solutions nor the Confederacy want is to get some Navy spooks on their ass."

Although that ship has sailed, he mentally added. Hearing footsteps behind him, he turned around and saw Alun Howe enter the pop-up shelter. He gave Decker a nod.

"Since the Qhazd are toast on the Mahar peninsula," Howe said, joining the group, "and there are no other immediate threats, Jon Gerin is redeploying your team, Jack. You're flying back with our esteem intelligence officer once she's done here."

Kozlev's icy stare alternated between Decker and Howe for a few seconds, suspicion clearly visible on her pinched features.

"Really? That seems rather convenient."

"Of course it's convenient," Zack replied with a grim chuckle. "Transport is already here. It saves Jon the bother of sending another aircraft. Flying time costs money, and this is the private sector, after all."

"Oh, I didn't mean that. I'm merely surprised about your team being redeployed after only a week, and just after I expressed my contention that Jack Lorenzo isn't who he claims to be."

"You should mention that to Jon when we're back in Moria. He'll be thrilled to hear that an acorn figures his command decisions are based on something other than the needs of Frontier Solutions' wider mission on Naraka."

Then, Decker turned to Tarra.

"Hal, why don't you go talk to the pilot? Ask him how much of this Shrehari crap he can haul along with six passengers. I think Alun would be glad to see it vanish.

And tell him I'd like an overflight of where the Qhazd mine used to be, maybe even a quick landing to see if we might have missed something. Since it's on the way, I figure we may just as well. You never know what could have happened since we left the area."

"I'll decide whether or not we should land," Kozlev said with a dangerous edge to her tone. "After all, I'm the senior officer on that flight."

"And the pilot is the boss once we're aboard his craft," Decker replied, smiling. "Off you go, Hal."

He jerked his thumb at the shelter's open door.

"Time to pack, folks. I hear the bar back in Moria calling your names."

"But not yours, Jack?" Steiger asked. "How long are you going to stay on this sobriety kick?"

"As long as I have to."

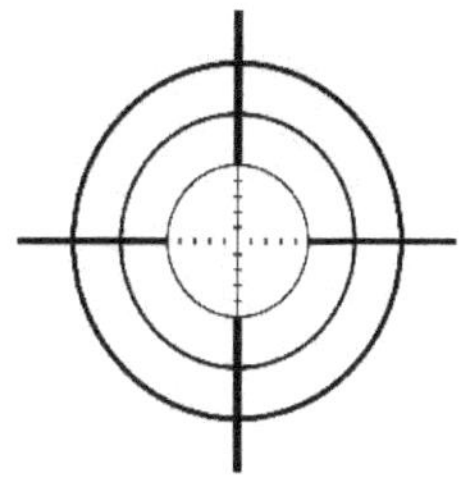

— TWENTY-THREE —

The thopter felt sluggish as it broke free of the landing pad and worked to gain altitude before turning east. A third of the stolen ordnance accompanied them, the most their pilot would allow along with all the additional passengers. Alun Howe would sit on the rest until transport from Moria came up to fetch it.

Kozlev sat on a rear-facing bench, stuck between Tarra and Decker, across from the rest of Zack's team. Tiny seemed increasingly puzzled by the turn of events and Steiger alarmed, but Langton wore the face of a man who thought he had figured things out.

They flew a few meters above the treetops for the better part of an hour in relative silence. Decker would have liked to study Kozlev's eyes, to gauge her comfort at being stuck between two large, armored men, one of whom she had threatened to geld when she had him in her power, but he refrained from turning to glance down at her.

Rika Kozlev was a thoroughly evil woman, a war criminal who deserved a long prison sentence, if not death, for what she did on Garonne, but somehow, she had managed to avoid just retribution. Decker suspected the intelligence officer knew enough about a few sufficiently powerful people within the Celeste National Guard to be allowed self-exile and a new life in the private sector, where she could continue to ply her trade unfettered by government oversight.

He knew she itched at the chance to see him back in her interrogation chair and finish what she'd started back then.   Frontier Solutions wouldn't be happy with the notion that a serving Marine officer had infiltrated their ranks, and here, beyond Commonwealth jurisdiction, they could do whatever they wanted with him. Or, to be precise, whatever Kozlev wanted, which would only end with his death since the conditioning he'd received after joining intelligence effectively made him immune from interrogation. His body would simply shut down if it suffered enough abuse.

The volcano, topped by its ever-present plume of ash, grew rapidly in the distance and the pilot swung his craft further out over the bay as a precaution, giving them a bird's eye view of large aquatic predators lurking in the shallows, just beneath the surface. Soon, the vast swath of destruction wrought by the pyroclastic flow came into view, cooler now, its surface hardened. Decker could see no trace of the mining operation beneath the ejecta.

When the thopter swung into shore, aimed at the edge of the flow, Kozlev looked up at Zack and said, "I see no need to land. It's quite obvious that nothing remains."

"We're landing, Rika." He turned towards the pilot and pointed downward. When the man caught his signal, he nodded and cut the craft's airspeed until it came to a hover over the beach. Then, without so much as a lurch, they touched down.

"I'm going to take Hal and Kozlev on an inspection tour," Decker told his team. "You will remain right here, understood?"

Steiger flashed him a concerned glance, but he ignored her. Tarra jumped out and, without prodding, Kozlev followed. Zack dropped to the ground on their heels.

"Let's go up the outer edge of the flow and see if anything escaped," he said.

When they reached the tree line, Kozlev stopped.

"So this is how you'll do it, Decker?" She asked. "A quick assassination, out of view, with only your old buddy Hal Tarra as a witness? Is he another active service member of the Marine Corps?"

Zack removed his helmet and tucked it under his arm.

"I'm sure you appreciate the concept of irony, Rika. Every intelligence puke I've ever met loves it. One of your breed's major failings, I suppose."

She crossed her arms and cocked an eyebrow at him. Nothing in her stance or expression hinted at fear.

"Do tell."

"Hal and I are just passing through while working on a personal matter. Neither of us gives a shit about what the Confederacy and its hired guns are doing here or anywhere else beyond the Rim. We're certainly not on the Fleet's or anyone else's business. If you had simply let bygones be bygones and ignored me, I would have ignored you. That means we wouldn't be having this conversation right now and you wouldn't be about to make your peace with God, or Satan, or whatever being your kind worships. Ironic, isn't it?"

"My kind?"

"Psychopaths."

"My, my." She smiled. "You're able to diagnose psychiatric conditions as well as fight. Impressive. Tell me, Chief Warrant Officer Decker, how are you going to explain my death?"

Zack shrugged.

"From what I've seen, there aren't too many people who'd give a shit if we returned to Moria without you. This area is full of fun-sized six-legged critters who haven't figured out human flesh isn't good for them. By the time they're done, no one's going to find anything more than bite-sized pieces of you, perhaps half-digested, if not excreted. It's a shame a hexacroc attacked you, but we weren't able to fight it off before it dragged your body away."

"I know for a fact that the Frontier Solutions' CO is going to miss me. And not just her but a lot of the command staff."

"You fucked your way through the entire chain of command?" Decker raised an ironic smile. "Impressive. The private sector seems to have its advantages."

"Is everything related to sex with you, speaking of mental issues? They find my services valuable, for the organization and for the mission. I obtain results, which their former intelligence officer didn't. They won't take the animal attack excuse at face value, I can guarantee that."

"Do they know you're a war criminal?"

"Am I?" Her smile took on a derisive twist. "Legally, I'm a retired Celeste National Guard officer who's never been found guilty of any wrongdoings, and my service record is perfectly clean. Therefore, whatever I may or may not have done while seconded to the Garonne Militia doesn't concern Frontier Solutions."

"I find it hard to believe that your bosses in the Guard would give you a pass after everything that happened. Who did you blackmail to secure an honorable discharge?"

"No one. I just let it be known that certain bits of information would be released in an entirely anonymous fashion if I faced charges or died before obtaining an honorable discharge. It's amazing what one can ferret out in my line of business. Of course, I offered self-exile as a quid pro quo, and a means to stay beyond the reach of those whose indiscretions fed my treasure trove of data. So go ahead, accuse me of whatever you want. It never happened. Garonne was unfortunate, but such is war. No matter what you might claim about me, you'll still find it impossible to explain how three of us went up the beach and only you two returned."

"As I said, Hal and I are just passing through on personal business. We don't plan on sticking around for any lengthy discussions." Hidden from the thopter by Tarra's bulk, Decker drew the blade he had carried on Garonne. "Remember this? It left that nice white line across your throat. I should have killed you then, a mistake I'm about to correct."

Kozlev took a step backward, but Tarra grabbed both her arms from behind, immobilizing her.

"Try not to get any blood on my armor," he said. "I don't feel like taking a dip in the water, not with the critters living there."

Kozlev's confident expression evaporated, yet she didn't struggle.

"Through the ear, then?" Decker asked. "That doesn't produce much blood, though it won't be anywhere near as satisfying."

When he saw fear in her eyes for the first time, a broad smile split his face.

"Beginning to feel a shiver of anxiety, are you? That's pretty much how your victims felt once the militia goons working for you strapped them into the interrogation chair. By the way, what did your body count on Garonne add up to?"

"I didn't bother keeping score."

"You know the exact number, Rika. Murderous lunatics like to keep track of their victims."

"Are your speaking from personal experience?" A bit of her previous confidence returned, along with a small, knowing smile. "I'd be curious to find out about your body count. Marines aren't famous for taking a pledge of non-violence."

Decker glanced up to ensure that Tarra still blocked the view from the thopter, then grabbed Kozlev's hair with his left hand and twisted her head around, to expose an ear to his waiting blade.

"Whatever my total is, I'm about to increase it by one."

"No, wait," she said in an urgent tone. "Maybe we can make a deal."

"I don't deal with war criminals," Decker growled, but he made no further move to carry out the planned execution.

"You're no cold-blooded killer," she replied. "I, of all people, should know. You didn't kill the guards in my interrogation suite back on Garonne when you escaped, and you didn't kill me after the rebellion seized control. Your Marine Corps doesn't promote sociopaths to chief warrant officer."

The near panic in Kozlev's voice would have been amusing, but for the fact that her words rang true. He released her hair and lowered his knife.

"Offer me a deal. If I don't like it, we'll see if the Corps fucked up and promoted a stone cold killer."

"You mentioned a personal quest. Since you signed up with Frontier Solutions and came to Naraka, it means the road to your goal is either through this outfit, the Confederacy of the Howling Stars, or Naraka itself. I'm an intelligence officer and a damned good one. Tell me what you're looking for because I can probably help you. And once I do, you'll have leverage on me to ensure I won't try to rat you out. Does that sound like a deal?"

Decker looked up at Tarra and cocked his head to one side in question.

"It's your call," he replied. "Kozlev has nothing on me. I wasn't on Garonne, and I'm out of the Corps for good. But if she can help us, then letting her live will have been worthwhile."

Zack locked eyes with Kozlev again to impress upon her that she would die at the first attempt to resist.

"I might not be cold-blooded enough to shove my blade into your brain here and now," he finally said, "but the slightest hint of betrayal on your part will count as being in the heat of action. If you need a visual of what that would look like, remember the night of my escape and the havoc I caused. Do we understand each other?"

"We do."

Decker raised his blade again, making Kozlev flinch. Then, he lovingly drew the tip over the white scar at the base of her throat, pressing just hard enough to make her feel it, but not hard enough to draw blood.

"You can let Rika go, Hal," he said stepping back to sheath his dagger.

"Are you sure you can trust her?" Tarra asked, still holding Kozlev.

"Not in a million years, but she has a highly developed survival instinct, and I can trust that. She knows I won't have any scruples about killing her to ensure my own survival." Decker's face twisted into an unpleasant smile.

"Besides, I've let darling Rika live twice now. She knows there won't be a third time."

Tarra released Kozlev, and she immediately began to rub her arms where his gloved hands had squeezed her flesh hard enough to bruise.

"So what's this personal mission?" She asked. "I'd like to get on it the moment we're back in Moria. The sooner you're gone, the happier I'll be."

Zack looked at Tarra with a cocked eyebrow.

"Over to you, buddy. I'm here because of your message that said she's alive. Please tell me she is Elyce Sakal. Otherwise, I'm going to knock you into the next century. Do you have any idea of the kind of shit I had to go through just to make it here?"

Tarra snorted. "You think it's been fun marking time and enjoying corporate warfare while I waited?"

"Gentlemen," Kozlev raised a hand. "At some point, we must return to the thopter. I don't think you want the others to overhear your story, so please, let's discuss the issue at hand."

"About six months ago," Tarra began, "my squadron was ordered to raid a suspected reiver base a few light years outside the Commonwealth sphere, in the Protectorate badlands. We were looking for the crew of a ship that had been found abandoned after it sent out a distress signal. Unfortunately, our intel had a few major holes in it. What we struck instead turned out to be an unregistered colony, not much different from Moria, meaning one of those resource exploitation deals living on the edge. Since it lay beyond the Rim, Commonwealth law didn't come into play, and all we could do was excuse ourselves, give them a few supplies to make up for any damage and bugger off. Except we found a Confederacy ship on the ground when we hit the place, so the boss had to do a bit of negotiation to keep everyone calm while we extracted our sorry asses from the place. Part of the deal included letting the Jackals fly out, unharmed and I watched them load up merchandise and people. That's when I spotted her, clear as day, climbing aboard with a bunch of the tattooed freaks. She looked exactly like she did when we watched her being kidnapped six years ago.”

“And you’re convinced of that?”

“Buddy, I stood no more than thirty meters away, at the edge of the landing strip. I saw Elyce Sakal. Heck, I took images of her and showed some of the guys in my troop who’d been with us when it happened, and they agreed.”

“And what happened then?”

“What do you think? I told the old man. He, in turn, sent it up the line while we tracked the Jackal ship until it went FTL, headed deeper into the Protectorate Zone where we couldn’t follow. What came back from HQ was a great big yawn. No one seemed to care.” A disgusted expression transformed Tarra’s face. “When they rotated us home for our turn at rest and reconstitution, I had a very nice chat with the regimental sergeant-major. Apparently, some folks higher in the food chain than the CO weren’t happy that I dredged up ancient history and wondered if I had considered that with no further promotion opportunities in sight, a twenty-five-year pension might be a good option.”

“The RSM said that?” Decker sounded incredulous.

“He was just passing on a message as ordered. In his considered opinion, as the top kick of the 9th Marine Regiment, I should tell them where to shove the pension and stick around until I had my thirty-five years in.”

“So you decided to retire anyway and chase Doctor Sakal.”

“That’s pretty much it.” Tarra shrugged.

“And what makes you think this Elyce Sakal might be on Naraka?” Kozlev asked. “I haven’t come across the name, and I do check everyone related to Frontier Solutions or the Confederacy who passes through. Unless they have her in the records under another name, I doubt we’ll find her here.”

“I don’t really have anything concrete other than her being in Jackal hands, so I decided to follow the Howling Stars angle and made my way to Kilia Station. Once there, I spent a couple of days blowing through my pension and listening. Then the damn ship I saw Doctor

Sakal board docked at Kilia. So I asked around some more and found that it had come in from the Protectorate after shipping out some fresh recruits for a mercenary operation controlled by the Confederacy. I signed up, and a few weeks later, I found myself running a Special Assignments team on Naraka without seeing a hint of the good doctor."

"For fuck's sake, Hal," Decker snarled. "You dragged me into the galaxy's armpit on evidence that thin? No wonder the Corps told you that further promotion was out of the question. Of all the idiotic stunts." Decker turned around to stare at the hardened lava flow, barely visible through the curtain of trees. "She could be on Asgard or on any of three dozen worlds for all we know."

"I assume that you still remember the ship in question," Kozlev said. "When we're back in Moria, give me all of the details, and I'll see about tracking its movements over the last six months. I'll need Doctor Sakal's physical description as well so I can check if she's on Naraka under another name."

"What if that doesn't produce any results?" Decker asked, turning back to face Tarra. "We signed up for an initial six months contract. I doubt they'll allow us to board the next ship when we say, sorry chaps, wrong planet, but no hard feelings."

"One thing at a time, gentlemen. I'll do my magic, and then we'll regroup to figure out the next steps. If we're done here, let's return to the thopter. We still have a four-hour flight ahead of us and daylight's wasting."

Without waiting for an answer, she headed back down the beach, confident that she wouldn't feel Decker's blade slice through her spine. The two Marines wordlessly followed her.

When they climbed back aboard the thopter, Steiger gave Zack a look that combined relief and incredulity at seeing Kozlev unharmed and visibly relaxed. He replied with a barely perceptible scowl before taking his seat, knowing she would want a full accounting the moment they had a bit of privacy.

Langton, on the other hand, wore his usual sly smile, as if the Marine had continued to prove him right. Tiny hadn't noticed anything amiss and just kept on staring out a window at the flying critters surrounding a dead hexacroc two hundred meters away.

No one spoke for the remainder of the trip.

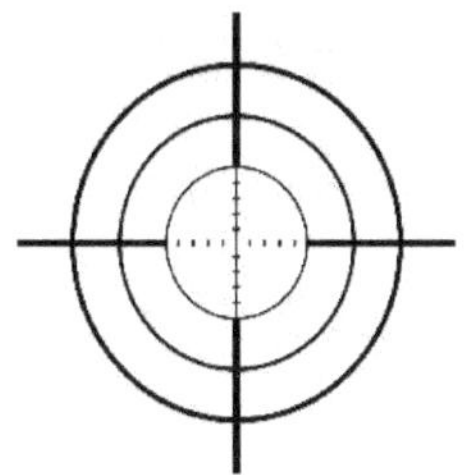

— TWENTY-FOUR —

Naraka's sun, turned blood red by volcanic ash, hung low on the horizon by the time they landed in Moria and stepped out into the suffocating mugginess of a late afternoon.

"Meet me in my office when you've dropped off your gear," Kozlev said. "We might as well start before the evening meal."

She wiggled her fingers by way of a wave and left them standing on the tarmac.

"Get started?" Steiger hissed in Decker's ear. "I thought you and your buddy were going to take care of Kozlev. What the hell is going on?"

"We made a deal," he replied. "She helps us with our quest and gets to live."

"What? Wait a minute." She grabbed Zack by the arm. "Let me get this straight. Kozlev will help you track down the doctor you're chasing. How does that work in your upside down universe?"

"Hal doesn't have a clue beyond the fact that Sakal is in Howler hands, but Kozlev has access to information we can't obtain on our own."

"I see. You know she'll eventually betray you, right?"

Decker nodded. "Yeah, but in the meantime, I'll use her. Hal doesn't exactly have a firm idea of where to find Doctor Sakal, and by that, I mean in which part of the galaxy." He gave his friend a dirty look. Then, in a voice loud enough for the others to hear, he said, "Off to the barracks, guys. Hal and I have business with intelligence, but you're free to relax for the rest of the day."

"Business?" Langton cocked his head at Decker as they walked towards the company lines. "I thought Kozlev represented a clear and present danger to Miko and you. Is there anything you'd like to share with us?"

"Not particularly. This has nothing to do with the team or our job for Frontier Solutions. It's personal."

"And yet, whatever you and your buddy Hal are up to will affect the team. After Kozlev's performance back in Mahar, I can't believe that you've suddenly become best friends. Staring into her eyes gave me the willies, and I've seen some of the worst criminals the Army can produce."

"You're not going to leave this alone, are you?" Decker growled.

"No."

They entered the Special Assignments Company hut and trudged through the office to the team room set aside for them.

"I'm going to say hi to my guys," Tarra said, peeling off towards the rear of the building.

"Alex has a point," Steiger said once the four of them were alone. "I don't think telling him and Tiny is going to hurt matters, and since we're supposed to be a team, they deserve to know at least as much as I do."

Decker didn't answer while he took off his armor, piece by piece. Once down to his battledress uniform, he turned around to face them.

"Hal and I are looking for a woman taken by reivers six years ago, while we watched, unable to prevent the abduction. On his last mission, before he retired from the Corps, Hal saw her climb aboard a Confederacy of the Howling Stars sloop which headed deep into the Protectorate. No one in the Fleet wants to do anything about it, so we're going to find her."

"Why?" Langton asked.

"Because neither Hal nor I have been able to forget the sight of her being hauled off, screaming, by a bunch of ugly critters. The only way we stop the nightmares is to go for a do-over, especially now that we know she's still alive. Or at least we know she was alive six months ago. Besides, neither of us have anything better to do, now that we're retired from the Corps."

"So you enlisted with Frontier Solutions on the premise that it might get you closer to finding this person since the Confederacy is our employer's majority owner." Langton's tone made it a statement rather than a question. "It makes sense in a crazy way, but I don't see how you intended to go about narrowing down the possibilities. There are many habitable worlds in this sector, likely many habitats tucked away on airless moons or asteroids, and the Confederacy probably has people on most of them. Is that why you spared Kozlev's life, so she could use her special connections to narrow it down?"

"Not exactly. I had my knife at her throat when she figured out Hal and I were after something totally unrelated to the commerce war on Naraka. She offered us a deal — her life for her help and a truce between us."

"A deal you apparently took." Langton paused, eying Decker. "Tell me something, Jack. If the Fleet isn't interested, but you're here, does that mean Kozlev's wrong about you, or have you gone rogue?"

"Does it matter?"

Langton stared at Zack for a few more seconds before shaking his head.

"Probably not. I have pretty good bullshit detectors when it comes to people. You have to, in my former branch, and those detectors are telling me that you're not the kind to screw the rest of us over if it suits your purpose. Besides, I could see that you intended to leave Kozlev's corpse in the jungle, for a hexadragon to snack on, but I didn't think you'd actually do it. You don't strike me as the cold-blooded type."

"You sound just like a lady I hang out with from time to time," Zack grumbled, eliciting a laugh from Steiger.

"Ah yes, the redoubtable Pru Pasek, who also goes by the *nom de guerre* Hera," she said. "Her little starship would be pretty useful right now, and she's also the only person I've met who's potentially more dangerous than Kozlev."

The former MP gave her a quizzical look.

"It's another Garonne war story, Alex. Jack likes to surround himself with dangerous ladies."

"Present company included?" Langton asked.

"Of course."

Tarra poked his head into the room.

"Let's go see if the Queen of Darkness intends to hold up her side of the deal." He patted his holstered blaster. "Or whether we're about to go down in a blaze of glory."

"Want us to loiter around the HQ building?" Langton asked. "Just in case."

Decker gave him a skeptical glance. "Why would you want to make this your business?"

"Maybe I've decided this mercenary gig isn't as fun as seeing where you're going."

"Hah." The Marine's laughter sounded like a bark. "My natural leadership in action again."

"Yep." Tarra grinned at him. "You have a knack for attracting folks who want to follow you out of sheer curiosity, just to see what happens next. Some things never change. C'mon, buddy."

As he walked out, Decker said, over his shoulder, "Take it easy. We'll be fine."

"I hope it occurred to you," Tarra said, once they were outside, "that Kozlev is playing her own game, trying to figure out who Doctor Sakal is, why we're after her and what she might have been doing when the reivers kidnapped her."

"Please. You obviously know who I work for these days. Otherwise your message wouldn't have reached me. I'm no longer a dumb, happy Pathfinder. Having my ass kicked halfway across the Orion Arm and through the Coalsack has taught me to never, ever trust the likes of her."

The other Marine agreed wordlessly, and Decker continued.

"It's a given she'll want to see if she can play this thing to her advantage. She has no intention of rotting on Naraka, but wouldn't mind if our dead bodies did. What Dear Rika doesn't know is that neither of us has any idea what Sakal and company were doing in the 31 Aquilae system. When I tried to raise the matter with my chain of command after seeing your message, they shut me down quicker than you can say taboo. I was told that the whole business had vanished down the memory hole and would never see the light of day again." He shook his head. "I have no illusions about Kozlev. She's already playing her own game. The trick will be to extract what we can before she decides we've outlived our usefulness."

"The real trick will be to realize when that happens," Tarra replied. "I'd suggest you try the old Decker charm on her, but I'm afraid you might not survive a single night in her bed."

"She's not my type anyway."

Tarra snorted in disbelief. "Female isn't a type anymore? You *have* changed. I remember a time when you'd have considered dangerous and crazy as a challenge."

"In my new line of business, you choose your challenges carefully. Dying isn't always the worst part of a fuck up."

Tarra glanced at Zack and frowned, surprised by his dry, humorless tone.

"What?" Decker asked.

"Who are you and where is the guy with temper problems and an outsized zest for life I used to know?

"He grew up, Hal. The Corps expects its majors to behave as adults."

A loud guffaw escaped Tarra's throat, and he stopped in his tracks.

"Oh shit. Now I really know the universe is off kilter. Major Zack Decker. What happened? Did the Commandant have a momentary lapse of reason?"

"He had a surge of sanity, asshole." Decker punched his friend on the arm. "And no, I haven't run across Sarratt yet. I don't even know where the careerist prick works nowadays, but the day I do, I'm going to enjoy every moment of him calling me sir."

"I'll bet." Tarra's amusement vanished just as quickly as it had appeared. "Is coming out to help me going to cost you? If they shut you down after mentioning 31 Aquilae, I can only assume you're not on a sanctioned mission, and I seem to recall that the Corps tends to punish its senior officers a lot more than noncoms for going rogue."

"I took an extended furlough, Hal. This is on my own time and my own resources. But I'm picking up useful intelligence that'll keep my bosses happy when I return home. Just finding out that a Chisger Mining subsidiary is operating here will be worth its weight in platinum."

"Why?"

"Chisger is a conduit to finance some nasty guys. Since we — and by that I mean my partner and me — shut down all of their operations in the Alpha Cephei system, Naraka is going to become one of their primary sources of funds. Call the information my peace offering if I don't report for duty the day after my furlough expires."

"It sounds like you live in a strange new world these days."

Decker clapped him on the shoulder.

"You have no idea. It's enough to make a good Marine weep."

*

Kozlev was alone in the intelligence section's office, frowning at her computer screen when they walked in. She glanced up at them, gesturing towards the chairs in front of her desk.

"I've run the name Elyce Sakal through the database, with no results," she said, "which means Sakal either never set foot on Naraka or came here under another name. My access to other Frontier Solutions databases via subspace link is pretty limited, and if I send a query to a place like Asgard, it might raise questions we don't want, and it would take a few days anyhow. Which one of you wants to give me a physical description and tell me where someone last saw her?"

"I guess that would be me," Tarra said, "seeing as how I've had the most recent sighting."

He spent the next five minutes describing her in excruciating detail, to the point of earning Kozlev's grudging approval. When he gave her the location where he'd witnessed Sakal climbing aboard a Confederacy ship, the intelligence officer nodded.

"Krommor, an unregistered colony, but allied with the Star Wolves, or Jackals as you like to call them. It's in my database. The Confederacy is their primary shipping agent. I can't see what they produce that might be of interest, but it'll probably be both highly valuable and highly portable, but not necessarily illegal in the Commonwealth."

"We didn't stick around long enough to find out."

"Tell me about the starship."

"It was a Jackal sloop, with the usual howling wolf insignia on its nacelles. It had a Commonwealth registration number, MVF921670 and went by the name of *Lupus Arctos*."

"Arctic Wolf," Decker said, "cute. Their newer ships are all *Lupus* something or other along this part of the Rim nowadays."

Kozlev gave him an amused smile. "You're very knowledgeable for an ordinary grunt."

The Marine shrugged, and then tapped his forehead with his index finger. "There's an incredible fund of useless trivia in my skull. It's a guy thing."

"Of course." She turned back to her screen and entered the information. "You're in luck. We have extensive records of *Lupus Arctos* in the system. She regularly touches down on Naraka and gives me a data dump, just like every other Confederacy ship."

"Convenient," Decker said, not bothering to hide his skepticism.

"Indeed, but it is company policy. Intelligence can't function properly if it doesn't have a steady stream of information about this sector so we can analyze potential threats to Naraka. But before you become overly excited, they scrub the dump according to some internal Confederacy rules they haven't shared with Frontier Solutions. There's such a thing as too much information in the private sector, apparently."

"Ain't commercial warfare fun. Does your data dump include crew and passenger lists?"

"Of course not." Kozlev shook her head, chuckling. "That would have been too easy. Six months ago, you said."

"Give or take a few weeks. Mostly give."

"Okay, I have *Arctos* at Krommor, the unregistered colony, thirty weeks ago. No report of a raid during her layover, though. Nothing on cargo or passengers either. It might well have been scrubbed out, but let's pick up the thread and run with it for now." She nibbled on her lower lip while reading the data on her screen. "Asgard. No specific mention of cargo or passengers, but she picked up a draft of recruits for Naraka, the next stop. This time, we know she took refined product from Moria. After that, Rakka, before heading back to the Rim and Kilia Station. From Kilia to Marengo, Valeux station to be precise, and then back to Krommor two months ago and here last month when I received this data dump."

"So Sakal could be anywhere by now." Decker scowled.

"She's still in Jackal hands," Tarra replied. "The way they hustled her aboard *Arctos* seemed pretty damn possessive as if they owned her ass."

"Or they could have sold her somewhere along the way."

"Doubtful." Kozlev shook her head. "The Confederacy tries to stay reasonably clean when it comes to capital offenses under Commonwealth law, and slavery is the one sin that will see them hang the moment the Navy finds out, even if it happens beyond the Rim."

"Doubtful but not impossible," Decker said. "You can coerce someone to selling their services and not make the act meet all of the requirements for an accusation of slavery."

"Perhaps. What was Doctor Sakal doing before her abduction?" Kozlev asked.

And here we go, Decker thought.

"We have no idea."

"Really?" Kozlev's right eyebrow shot up. "That's not terribly helpful, is it?"

"I'm serious, Rika. We never found out what she and her colleagues were doing when reivers struck the outpost. By the time we landed, she and possibly two others had been kidnapped, the rest killed and the place wrecked beyond recovery."

"So they took more than one prisoner."

"That's what it looked like. We only spoke with Elyce Sakal during our final approach, after we received the distress call. Plus, she's the only one we saw physically hauled away by reivers, but when we did a head count of the bodies, two more appeared to be missing, based on the nominal roll Sakal transmitted, a Sister Anca and a Doctor Antoine Mazkow."

Kozlev's head whipped up, and she blinked at Decker. "Run that last name by me again."

"Antoine Mazkow."

"Chisger Mining has a Doctor Anton Maslow on staff in the Moria medical facility." She turned back to her screen. "The personnel records show that he's been here since they opened the mine last year, but not what he was doing before then. Both your guy and this one have unusual names that sound very similar. When he's in his cups, he'll tell you the Star Wolves own his ass now and forever. And he's often in his cups. Make of that what you will. You don't have anything more than the name, per chance?"

"No. We don't have a clue as to who he was, what he looked like, nothing," Tarra said. "Why don't we go collar this Maslow guy and shake a few answers out of him?"

Kozlev glanced at the time.

"Not today. He's already started happy hour and then, it's an even toss whether he'll tell you to fuck off or offer to do a rectal exam with a laser drill."

"He sounds like a nasty drunk."

"I'd say he's more of an unhappy drunk, the kind of guy who goes through life pissed that he doesn't have the guts to off himself. We'll go visit the infirmary mid-morning tomorrow, once he's recovered from his daily ingestion of a hangover pill."

"This Maslow sounds like he's more of a danger to his patients than a healer."

"When Maslow's sober, he's brilliant. When he climbs into a bottle, he's smart enough to stop practicing medicine. Screw up with one of the miners on the examination table, and you end up doing a whole lot of self-diagnosis."

"I guess that means we go sample the bar's inventory before hitting the chow line." Tarra stood though his eyes stayed on Kozlev. "Unless you have any other ideas to explore."

"No." She switched off her computer. "We'll talk again tomorrow and see if we can't tease out some additional information still hiding in your subconscious."

"As long as it doesn't involve sitting naked in an interrogation chair," Decker replied, deadpan, glaring down at her.

He could have sworn Kozlev's laugh betrayed more than just a hint of nerves and had to repress a smile when he saw her hand touch the pale white line at the base of her throat in a gesture that had to be involuntary.

At that moment, Raj Lisk entered the intelligence section's office. He came to a sudden stop when he saw Decker and Tarra standing in front of Kozlev's desk.

"I see that you're back safe and sound from Mahar." Lisk raised his coffee mug in salute. "A nice bit of success for your first outing, Jack, even if a volcano did the heavy work. From what radio transmissions we've been able to intercept and decrypt, there's some serious butt hurt in the Qhazd camp and they don't know who screwed them over — other than Naraka itself. Well done."

"Thanks, Raj. I need a cup of coffee, so bye Raj," Decker replied, sketching a vague salute. Then, he and Hal made their exit.

When they had gone, Lisk sat down on a corner of Kozlev's desk.

"And? Is Jack Lorenzo a ghost from your past, the dangerous pro you mentioned, or is he just someone who looks like an old acquaintance?"

"Lorenzo is dangerous, no doubt about it," she said, staring at the door. "Very dangerous in fact, as the Qhazd learned. As to being a ghost from my past? No. Lorenzo is real, but he's only a threat to the opposition. That being said, I'll still keep my eye on him because he may turn out to be very useful indeed."

She could see a glimmer of skepticism in her deputy's eyes. Lisk was no one's fool, least of all Kozlev's, and in due course, he would start digging. Hopefully, that wouldn't happen until she'd extracted enough from Decker and Tarra to serve them up as Fleet spies.

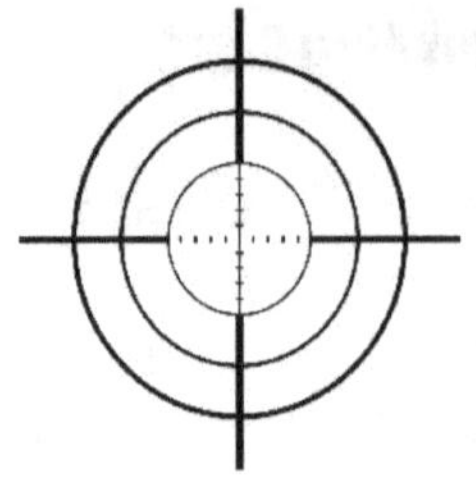

— TWENTY-FIVE —

"You're alive and well, I see," Steiger said when they emerged from the headquarters building. Langton and Tiktin sat on a nearby bench, the former snoozing, and the latter playing with his knife. When he saw Zack, the Celestan nudged Langton, and both rose to join the others. "Any claw or bite marks that might become infected?"

Decker shook his head. "No. So far, she's playing the game."

"You do realize that…"

He held up his hand.

"Hal and I have already had this discussion. You of all people should know how suspicious and distrusting I can be. The moment Kozlev reneges on her side of the deal, she dies. It's as simple as that."

"Good. Part of me hopes she does so. The bitch needs to pay for Garonne, but that would mean you and Hal will land in a pile of shit deep enough you'll need wings to get out."

"One thing at a time." They headed across the open ground towards the chow hall. "She did find us a possible source, someone who might have been with Sakal at the time of the abduction. We'll go see him tomorrow after his daily hangover's gone. Apparently, our man is the epitome of the alcoholic frontier doctor, a true to life, walking stereotype. He works over at the mining operation's medical clinic."

"And this is not a ploy by Kozlev?"

"No. My money's on Rika being intrigued enough to let us track Sakal down as best we can, in case there's some advantage in it for her. Then, she'll stick the knife in. I'm not convinced she's all that enchanted with her new lifestyle."

"Torturing — pardon me, interrogating non-humans doesn't appeal to her? I'm surprised our Rika isn't a big fan of diversity."

"My money's on her wanting to climb up the greasy pole and become a somebody at Frontier Solutions' head office, or even find a spot within the Confederacy, but there's not much on Naraka to help further her ambitions."

"Enter Zack Decker," Miko murmured, "with his charisma, charm, and secret identity. Not to mention his quest for the mysterious and ravishing Elyce Sakal."

"Laugh all you want," he growled. "If I get what I need from her, then I'm fine compromising my values just this once."

"You really have it bad, finding this woman, don't you?" She nudged him with her elbow. "I'd love to inspire that kind of devotion."

"Get kidnapped by reivers, and we'll talk." Decker pulled the door to the bar aside and ushered his team in, followed by Hal Tarra. "It's an unforgettable experience you'll not wish on your worst enemy."

"Why would you want to see the delightful Miko taken by scum?" The latter asked. "After you've already exercised your Decker charm on her, that is."

"And how would you know?"

"She has that look in her eye." Tarra laughed. "Now haul your ass to the bar and buy us something. As I recall, you still owe me fifty creds."

"Cheap bastard."

"Hey, my parents were married."

"But not to each other." Decker punched his friend on the arm. "That joke never gets old."

"Actually," Steiger said, face wrinkled as if she'd just inhaled a whiff of sewage, "it's become terribly ancient.

And it not only died but also rotted. I can smell its corpse from a parsec away. And yes he's tried his charm and yes, it's overrated."

"Everyone's a critic," Decker grumbled. "Just for that, you can buy the first round."

"I don't recall owing you any money."

He snorted. "You still haven't paid for the starship ride from Rakka to Garonne, sweetheart."

"Only because you shanghaied me." She leaned on the bar and examined the dispenser menu. "Still no Shrehari ale, but you gave up booze, so you don't care. Okay, people, it's swill for everyone except Jack, who gets the kiddy pop of his choice. Just remember that I paid the first round."

While Steiger drew five bulbs, Decker glanced around the mostly empty room. "You team's not here?" He asked Tarra.

"They're looking for shits and giggles in the settlement. Hanging out with rock moles isn't my style."

"No." Decker accepted a pink juice. "Your style is looking for a fight. But you're smart enough to know that a room full of miners is a losing proposition you'll only consider if you're really drunk. And I'm too old for that kind of shit, so you'd be on your own. Skoal."

"Skoal." Tarra raised his bulb. "And thanks, Steiger. You're a real lady. Too bad you're hanging around with this character." He nudged Decker with his elbow.

"I'm no lady, honey," she replied, smiling. "Besides Jack's kind of cute in his own way."

"Ugh." Tarra made a disgusted face, drawing amused chuckles from the others. Then, he looked around the room again. "I'm surprised Jon Gerin isn't here, what with your team's return from the wilds of Mahar."

"Maybe he's having a chat with Rika." Decker shrugged. "I have no burning desire to speak with him tonight anyway, just in case he comes up with something for us to do tomorrow morning. We have an appointment with Doctor Anton Maslow, remember?"

"And if he turns out not to be Antoine Mazkow?" Tarra asked.

"Then we're no further ahead." Decker took a swig of his alcohol-free cocktail and grimaced. "But also no further behind either. Kozlev smells an opportunity, and she'll use everything she can think of to help us. Until we're no longer useful, that is," he added before either of his companions could. "If she's no help, then we'll have to make our way back to the Rim and either give up or sniff out another trail."

"I'm not giving up," Tarra replied with a somber expression. "You have no idea what seeing Doctor Sakal at Krommor did to me."

"Actually, I do. But I've also learned that sometimes, you need to step back and re-evaluate your decisions in light of the universe not giving a flying fuck about what you want."

"I think I liked the old you better. Maybe turning teetotaler wasn't such a splendid idea."

Decker snorted. "You do remember what being the old me ended up costing, right?"

"Sure, but you came back stronger than ever, in a really major way." Tarra's eyes danced with mischief. "Except for this strange booze-free lifestyle you've adopted, not that it'll excuse you out of buying the next round."

*

The following morning, Kozlev intercepted Decker at breakfast, just as he was about to discard his empty tray.

"My office, one hour. You and Tarra only. Tell Steiger and the others to steer clear. Spooking Maslow won't get us anywhere."

Decker smiled at her use of the word 'us.' She had already taken a proprietary interest in finding Sakal. Her life as an intelligence officer for Frontier Solutions on Naraka must really be tedious compared to the excitement on Garonne.

"Understood."

He walked back to where his team and Tarra's milled about and caught the latter's eye.

"One hour in the Queen's antechamber, just you and me."

"What if we want to go into town?" Steiger asked.

"Steer clear of the medical center." He stared at her with hard eyes until she nodded.

An hour later, Kozlev intercepted them at the HQ building entrance and waved towards the main gate.

"Shall we?"

The Moria settlement turned out to be everything Decker had expected: primitive rammed earth roads, bordered by many battered, blackened containers transformed into offices, commissary stores, hydroponic greenhouses, and lodgings for the miners and support staff, all dominated by the large metallic excrescence of the mine itself stuck to the cliff side.

A deep rumble seemed to permeate everything as they neared the medical center, evidence of machinery digging through hard rock beneath the surface. Though the ore refining plant, sitting next to the mine head, was fully enclosed, dust lay everywhere, stirred up here and there by an anemic breeze, giving the air a flinty tang. Few humans walked the streets, though a fair number of skimmers passed them, shifting unmarked crates to the landing strip, and coming back empty.

"I gather there's a ship inbound?" Decker asked, eying the flatbed vehicles.

"Yes, later today," Kozlev replied. "It dropped out of FTL thirty-six hours ago."

Tarra and Decker exchanged glances. If Anton Maslow was Antoine Mazkow and gave them a lead on Sakal, and she wasn't on Naraka, that ship might be their earliest chance to escape. A lot of 'ifs,' but both ex-Pathfinders had a gut feeling that things were about to move very quickly, as they always did at a certain juncture.

The medical center turned out to be an array of large metal boxes forming a rough cross, with perpendicular units at the end of each arm. Decker stopped them short of the entrance, where the four arms met.

"I'm assuming Doctor Maslow knows who you are?" He asked Kozlev. "And what you are?"

"Of course." Her smile made the ambient temperature drop by a few degrees.

"That's what I fear. Hal and I are going to speak with the good doctor alone, at least until we know whether or not he can help us. Having you along is bound to unnerve him, especially if Maslow isn't his real name."

"You'd deprive yourself of a skilled interrogator?" She tilted her head to one side like a curious bird. "Don't forget that I can make even the most recalcitrant customers talk."

"Present company excepted," Decker growled.

Kozlev's direct gaze didn't waver. "Present company excepted. I assume your friend Tarra has also received conditioning."

He hadn't. That treatment was reserved for intelligence operatives, but the lie came easily to Zack, and so he went with it. "Of course. Now back to Maslow. You'll stay in the corridor, Rika. Listen from a distance if you want, but don't join us or otherwise interfere unless and until I say so."

"Actually, buddy," Tarra said, "maybe you should go in alone. Even the two of us might be overwhelming if the guy is hiding away from what happened six years ago."

Decker heard the implicit suggestion that his friend could then also keep an eye on Kozlev.

"Good point. We'll play it that way." He jerked his head towards the door. "Where to?"

"The outpatient section. I'll be to the right when we walk in. His office is at the far end of the arm." Kozlev pulled the door open and waved them through.

An eerie silence greeted them, along with the strong smell of antiseptic. A bored technician, sitting at a console by the entrance, glanced up.

"Can I help you?" He asked in the tone of a man who wanted to be anywhere but here.

"Visitors for Doctor Maslow," Kozlev said, pointing at the outpatient corridor with her chin. "I assume he's in by now?"

"Yep. And reasonably awake too. Office twenty-three."

Without a further word, Decker headed in the indicated direction, the others following at a more leisurely pace. The medical center carried a distinct frontier vibe, its origin as an assemblage of containers dropped from orbit still visible in the decor, where bare metal warred with scarred beige plastic, and where gray-sheathed conduits ran along the ceiling.

Doors pierced both sides of the corridor at regular intervals, each with a large rectangular label that identified its function. He stopped at the door with a sign that read Doctor Anton Maslow and knocked.

A muffled voice called out, "Come."

The door slid aside at Decker's touch, and he stepped into a sparsely furnished office, dominated by an examination table. A wizened human male sat behind a cluttered desk, clutching a steaming mug.

He could have been any age between sixty and a hundred and ten, with thin white hair, eyes the color of a washed out sky and the posture of someone who has been carrying the weight of several lifetimes on his frail shoulders. The network of broken veins crisscrossing his cheeks and nose spoke of a hard-core toper while his expression was that of a man who stopped caring long ago.

"I don't believe we've met," he said, carefully putting the cup down. His voice sounded remarkably healthy for a man who looked like he had one foot in the grave and the other stuck in a bottle of ethanol. "I'm Anton Maslow. You are?"

"Jack Lorenzo, doctor." Decker pulled up a spare chair and sat down facing Maslow. "We might not have met, but we may have acquaintances in common."

"Oh?" Maslow sat back, a skeptical eyebrow cocked at the Marine. "And what common acquaintances might I share with a freelance soldier?"

"Doctor Elyce Sakal." Though Maslow showed no outward reaction, Decker could swear that he saw a brief flicker of alarm in his eyes. "I believe you used to work with her six years ago."

Another flicker of alarm, this one stronger than the first.

Maslow shook his head. "Sorry. I have no idea who this Doctor Sakal is. You're quite mistaken, Mister Lorenzo."

"May I tell you a story?" Decker asked in a gentle tone. "To demonstrate that I'm not mistaken?"

The doctor shrugged with the weariness of a man who had heard every tale ever told. "I have no patients lined up this morning."

"About six years ago," Decker began, "while I was serving in the Commonwealth Marine Corps aboard a patrol vessel, we received a distress call from an outpost in the 31 Aquilae system. It was under attack by reivers. We tried to get there at best speed, but the laws of physics are what they are, and so having established contact with outpost, we couldn't do much more than offer advice and reassurances. Doctor Elyce Sakal was manning the communications station, and we spoke with her for hours on end until the attackers managed to break in. By the time we entered orbit, they had gone, leaving behind a pile of bodies and a trail of destruction. Except we weren't able to account for three people based on the personnel list Doctor Sakal provided. Besides Sakal herself, we found no trace of a Sister Anca, and another doctor, Antoine Mazkow. The government wrote the outpost off and declined to pursue the abductors, effectively writing off three lives as well."

While he spoke, Decker held Maslow's eyes and could see the effect of his words behind the stoic facade. Pain, fear, and regret, they all chased each other.

"Then, about seven months ago," he continued, "someone who was at 31 Aquilae with me saw Doctor Sakal in the company or more likely in the custody of the Confederacy of the Howling Stars on an unregistered colony called Krommor. That was the first sighting since her kidnapping, the first confirmation that she was still alive. Unfortunately, the Howlers lifted off in their starship before he could follow up. And now, here in Moria, a mining settlement owned by the Howlers, I find

Antoine Mazkow going by the not very original alias of Anton Maslow."

"A very amusing story." For the first time, he heard a sharp edge of emotion in the doctor's voice. "But it's none of my concern. If that was everything, then I'll wish you a good day, Mister Lorenzo, or whatever your name is."

"Three people were abducted before our eyes, Doctor. We Marines have a habit of remembering things like that and jump at the chance for a do-over, in this case bringing three Commonwealth citizens back to their families and friends."

"That all sounds very noble, I'm sure." Maslow shrugged again, with the same air of defeat. "But it still doesn't concern me. I'm a contract employee of Chisger Mining, here to provide medical care to its employees and to those of its partner operations, the Confederacy among them."

"And yet I hear you like to claim the Star Wolves own your ass, which is a weird thing to say, considering they steer clear of anything that might be seen as involuntary servitude."

Maslow made a dismissive gesture with his right hand. "We all say strange things after a bit too much ethanol."

"Except in your case, I'm told that we're talking about enough for an early funeral. You say you're merely a contract employee for a mining company, but I see a man killing himself because he can't kill his demons, and I wonder what those demons might be. Naraka is the back of beyond, a perfect place to hide from the past and pickle yourself. I understand. Sometimes, being kidnapped by scum will make a man snap, but slow suicide isn't the answer."

Maslow's face suddenly blazed with anger. A reaction at last.

"You have no idea what I've lived through," he said between clenched teeth.

"Try me. I served as the first mate on a starship that was taken by pirates and saw my partner die. I spent quality time as a prisoner of those pirates and then as a slave on an alien world before fighting my way home. After I returned, I found the assholes who did it and killed them." He held out his hands, palms upward. "No more demons riding me, no more daily bottle to drown out the pain."

"Bullshit."

"Look me in the eyes, Doctor Mazkow. You know I'm telling the truth. You've known all along. Now help yourself by helping me."

"I told you, it's Maslow."

He abruptly stood and turned to look out the window, his expression hidden from Zack, though by the set of his shoulders, he knew the man was fighting an internal battle. Brief headshakes bore witness to the intensity of the silent debate.

Several minutes passed, but the Marine knew he had set the hook deep enough to reel in his catch. All he had to do was wait. Finally, Maslow spoke, eyes still on the medical center's forecourt. He said one word.

"Asgard."

"Thank you, doctor." Decker stood, knowing he wouldn't get anything more. "Did you wish me to arrange for your repatriation? Antoine Mazkow might be officially listed as deceased, but that's a mere formality. I could arrange for your resurrection."

Maslow shook his head. "I can't leave Naraka."

"So the Jackals do own you."

"For reasons you'll never be able to understand, I owe them my life. What little is left of it." He shrugged, still facing the window. "This time next year, I'll be dead, and it won't be from alcohol, Mister Lorenzo. You see, I acquired a permanent reminder of the time we spent as prisoners of the reivers, an incurable disease no one back in the Commonwealth has ever heard of, the result of some rather undignified treatment on their part. Alcohol is one of the few ways I can keep the worst of the physical and psychological symptoms at bay. Ironically, I was a teetotaler before we were taken."

"I'm sorry to hear that. Is there anyone back home you'd like me to contact?"

"They think I'm dead. Let's leave it that way." Maslow paused. Then, surprising Zack, he turned around and faced him. "If you find Elyce, take care that you choose wisely when it comes to matters of trust. Now please leave me."

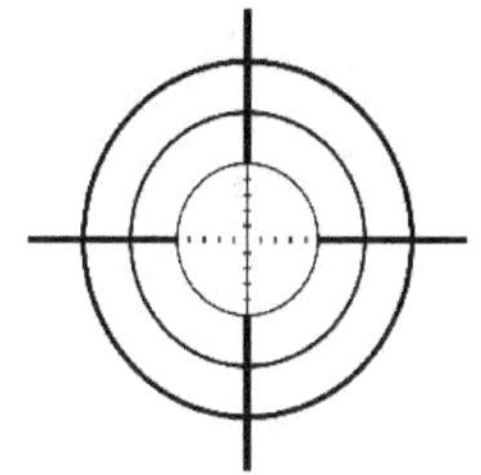

— TWENTY-SIX —

When Decker emerged from Maslow/Mazkow's office, leaving the doctor to contemplate his imminent demise, he almost ran into Tarra.

"Asgard, eh?" He said. "When I went through there, I didn't see anything that might point at Elyce Sakal. Shit. If we'd known, we might not have had to make the long trip to Naraka, never mind spending so much quality time in the Protectorate's ass crack fighting off oversized lizards."

"He could be pointing at Asgard to get you off his back," Kozlev noted. "It's a common tactic."

"True, but my bullshit detectors tell me he wasn't lying. Maslow believes Sakal is on Asgard." He led the way back to the reception area.

"So you're a trained interrogator as well?" Disdain colored her tone.

"You'd be surprised at what I am, Rika."

"I can guess." She gave him a nasty sneer. "It's a shame you're conditioned against interrogation, but back to our primary objective. What do you intend to do with this information?"

"Hitch a ride to Asgard and continue the search there," he replied, his tone making it clear the answer was so obvious it didn't need spelling out.

Once they had left the medical center, she said, "That will more complicated than you might think."

"Do tell."

"Obtaining permission to board a ship bound for Asgard, outside of a duly authorized personnel transfer, is going to be tough. Doing your own snooping once there will be next to impossible. The Confederacy owns the place, so if Doctor Sakal is indeed on Asgard, she'll be held somewhere mercenaries aren't welcome except by invitation."

Decker chuckled. "Hal and I spent most of our adult lives going where we weren't wanted and fucking up the guys who didn't want us."

"Have you considered how the Confederacy will react once someone finds out about your interest in a person they're holding for reasons we cannot even guess at?"

"They'll be howling mad?" Tarra asked, with an innocent look on his face.

"Very amusing," she said, ignoring Zack's hearty laughter. "Let me mull this over for a while and do some digging. I still think there's a good possibility he lied to you."

"It's a lead," Decker replied. "The only one we have, short of putting Maslow in your chair, which is not going to happen. And I'm not just saying that to shield him. I very much doubt our ultimate employers, the Jackals, will let that kind of unauthorized mistreatment go unpunished. Not that I care about your hide, Rika, but I care about my own, and we've been seen visiting Maslow together."

They spent the rest of the walk back in silence. Once through the main gate, Kozlev peeled off towards the headquarters building while Decker and Tarra took a stroll around the perimeter, far from prying ears.

"Why do I have the feeling you're about to tell me that we're taking an unauthorized ride on that inbound ship?" Tarra asked.

"Because you're a psychic. Besides, neither of us has a reason to complete the initial six months in our contracts. I certainly don't, seeing as how I'd rather get back home before my furlough runs end, and after speaking with Maslow, I'm really curious to find out more about Asgard. You know, stuff my bosses might find interesting, such as what kind of operation the Jackals are building for themselves beyond the Rim, and how that helps the Coalition cretins."

"Who now?"

Decker sighed. "Okay. What I'm about to tell you stays between your ears. There's a bunch of high-powered people on Earth and the Home Worlds who'd like to undo the changes of the Second Migration War and re-establish control over the Out Worlds. They plan to do this by eroding what still passes for democracy in the Commonwealth, one piece at a time, so that the ordinary folks don't notice. I don't exactly know what they want as the end result, but I bet it'll look a lot like an empire. We're talking senators, planetary politicians, business people, even some within the Fleet and the Constabulary. They convinced the SecGen to establish a new version of the old Special Security Bureau that Admiral Kowalski wiped out at the turn of the century. They call it the *Sécurité Spéciale* now. Don't ask me why they decided to use the French spelling, but I've butted heads with them, and they are a revolting bunch. I've been spending most of my time since I returned from the Coalsack in the guts of a nasty undercover struggle to block the Coalition's schemes. Our Confederacy friends often do the *Sécurité Spéciale*'s wet work, and I figure they contribute to the Coalition's fundraising as well if I'm right about the reason why they've entered into the mining business. And that means right now, I'm in the middle of enemy territory."

Tarra let out a long whistle. "You really do live in a different world, old buddy. I'm surprised you gave up drinking. Let me guess, you're worried that Sakal might be involved in something cooked up by this Coalition, via their Howler operatives."

"Got it one. And if Kozlev finally puts all of the pieces together, I'm screwed, and so are you. Her analysis will inevitably point to only one possible option that lets her survive and keep a place within Frontier Solutions. She needs to shop us to her bosses and through them, to the

Jackals. That's why we're leaving when that ship lifts off again."

"It means she needs killing before we skedaddle, you realize that, right?"

"She needs killing before she has a chance to come to that conclusion, and she's smart enough to already be weighing her options, now that Maslow has steered us towards Asgard. Fuck." He shook his head. "I should have taken her in the jungle when I had the chance."

"You would have missed the drunk at the hospital," Tarra said. "Kozlev earned that extra day of life for finding Mazkow."

"What do we do with our teams?" Decker thought mainly of Steiger, who knew his real name since their time together aboard *Phoenix* running guns for the Garonne rebellion, but not his identity as a Fleet operative.

"It's not their game, Zack. We haul ass and leave 'em wondering like the rest. Of course," he rubbed his chin, grimacing, "how we haul ass is another question altogether."

"I have an idea or two, but we'll need to move quickly. They're not going to have a sloop sitting on the ground any longer than it has to, not with competing operations that might just decide to sacrifice an unmanned shuttle to score a major hit."

Tarra snorted, pointing at the broad, flat dome in the center of the camp. "Good luck with that. The aerospace defense array can shred anything larger than a gnat."

An evil leer spread across Decker's face. "Yep, that it can."

Zack's exaggerated grin seemed all too familiar, and Tarra contemplated him for a few moments, frowning, then he shook his head. "I do believe I won't like what you're plotting."

"Think of this as war, buddy." Decker slapped Tarra on the shoulder. "Confusion to the enemy has always been my favorite toast, and I've become pretty good at causing chaos to cover my escape."

"And how many bodies will you leave behind?"

"Are you turning soft in your old age? I just told you we're standing in enemy territory, that the Jackals work with traitors and that Moria funds treasonous activities. As a serving officer in our beloved Marine Corps, I have an obligation. Besides, as someone once said, never cause an enemy a small injury."

"All fine and dandy for you," Tarra replied, unconvinced. "But I'm retired and would rather avoid becoming a hunted man for the rest of my life. The Howlers won't forgive what you have in mind."

"Did you transfer to the inactive reserve, like a good boy, when you took off the fancy suit?"

"Sure. A twenty-five-year man owes the Corps a few more years on stand-by."

"Then as the senior Marine Corps officer on Naraka, heck make that the senior officer in the Protectorate, I'm calling you back to active duty for the duration of this mission, plus a month, with an assignment to Naval Intelligence. There. Done. We'll handle the administrivia once we're home."

"I don't think you can do that, Zack."

"Think what you want, but I just did it, Command Sergeant Tarra. Welcome back."

"Asshole."

"That's Major Asshole, sir, to you, Sergeant."

"Shit." He shook his head, but then gave Decker a thump on the arm. "They might have commissioned you, but it suddenly feels like old times again."

*

"So?" Steiger glanced up at Decker when he entered the team's quarters.

"Nothing doing. Maslow's not our man, so we're no further ahead. Actually, at this rate, we may never catch up with Doctor Sakal." He sat on the edge of his bunk and kicked off his boots before stretching out on the hard mattress. When Steiger failed to reply, he turned his head to glance at her, only to be met with a skeptical stare.

"Really?" She drawled. "You spent an awfully long time speaking with your friend Hal after Kozlev buggered off. And yes, I watched you guys through the window."

"Where are Tiny and Alex?" He asked, in an attempt to change the subject.

"They're sampling the joys of the recreational facility, seeing as how we'll have no new orders until Gerin returns from his liaison visit." She stood and walked over to his bed, and then, without warning, climbed over Decker until she straddled him. Her rough hands took hold of his shoulders, and they locked eyes. "You're so full of shit, Zack Decker, that if they kicked you out of a shuttle at thirty thousand meters, you'd thunder in like a fucking asteroid."

"If you want to have sex, you might consider removing your clothes," Zack replied. "Although the risk of someone walking in and getting an eyeful is pretty high, and I don't like providing entertainment for the deprived masses."

"You and Tarra are cooking up something. I can feel it. Does it have to do with finally giving Kozlev what she deserves?" When he didn't reply, she reached behind her with one hand and squeezed him. "Hey, lover boy, it's me, the woman who's watched your back since we left Kilia, the one you joined in fighting the good fight for Garonne independence. If you're about to pull a nasty, I deserve to know, if only so I can protect my own ass. You owe me at least that."

Decker grabbed Steiger's upper arms and yanked her down so that his lips touched her ear.

"Hal and I are leaving Naraka tonight. There's a ship coming in, and we aim to be on it when it lifts again."

"Deserting and then stowing away? Are you forgetting that the Star Wolves aren't fools?"

"You of all people should remember what I'm capable of pulling off."

"That sounds ominous, considering what you did to the Garonne militia."

"It's threatening only to the Jackals." A soft, almost inaudible chuckle escaped his lips. "By the time they figure out what's going on, we'll be headed for the hyperlimit if we're not already FTL."

"And you'll have walked out on me again." She nipped his earlobe. "Bastard."

"My parents..."

"Yeah, yeah," she interrupted. "You've said so more often that anyone can stand. Still, I'm beginning to wonder what I'm doing wrong if I can't keep you around."

"I'm a wanderer, honey. You can't hold me down."

"How about I come with you this time?" She asked.

"This is a personal matter for Hal and me," he replied. "We don't actually care if we step on any toes or blow up stuff that belongs to friendly folk like the Jackals. You come with us, and you'll never work as a freelancer again, at least not without looking over your shoulder all the time. That's if you survive the experience."

"Maybe I'll reinvent myself. It seems to work for you."

Decker grunted. "Yeah, that's me. The man of a thousand faces, none of them mine. It's not a life for you." He pushed her up, and then with a twist of the hips, dumped her on the bunk beside him. "If you want to help, keep Tiny and Alex busy until we're gone."

"You don't actually think Frontier Solutions is going to give the rest of us, and I include Tarra's team in that, a free pass after the two of you bust out? We'd be tainted by association and suffer the consequences."

"I doubt you'll have anything to fear." He turned his head to look at her. "Just keep your heads down once we vanish. Stay in this hut and ignore everything that might happen outside."

"May I assume that you're planning a major production?"

"Let's just say that we intend to leave in style." Decker winked at her. "Now, unless you have impure intentions, how about you give me some space?"

"Oh, I have wicked plans alright, but I have the feeling this isn't the right place for them, nor the right time."

She climbed to her feet. "I think I'll join the others and see if there's more fun to be had elsewhere, and perhaps try to get a party going until things quiet down. Promise me you won't do anything stupid, Zack."

"I never do anything stupid, even though it might seem so at first." Decker turned on his side and, like every infantryman throughout the ages, when faced with some down time, he promptly fell asleep.

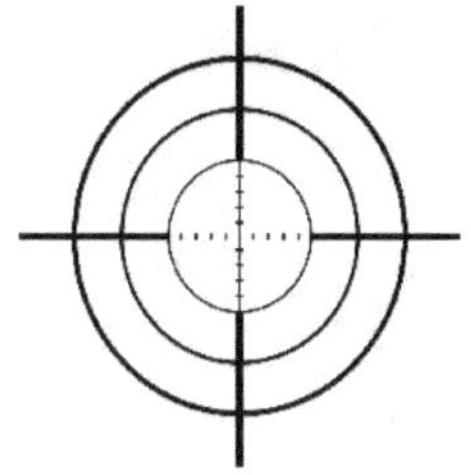

— TWENTY-SEVEN —

Sometime later that afternoon, a rolling thunder in the distance disturbed Moria's dusty frontier town stillness. The sound increased at an alarming rate until it drowned out everything else, including the gentle thump of Decker's own heartbeat.

The barracks began to vibrate in sympathy with an atmosphere torn asunder by the mighty pressure of an FTL-capable starship slicing through the clouds, riding on its braking thrusters.

Decker had taken lunch with Hal, two solitary figures wolfing down food without tasting it, sitting apart from the rest of the mercenary garrison. Neither of their teams so much as looked in, confirming Zack's suspicion that they had decided to spend the day anywhere but within the mercenary base.

Now, five hours later, just as the last rays of Naraka's sun tried to break through a horizon turned murky with dark rain clouds, the two Marines stirred as if by mutual agreement. Tarra joined his friend in the latter's team room shortly after the noise faded away.

"Are you convinced you still want to do this?" He asked. "We'll have one chance, and if it goes sideways, we're fucked beyond all recovery."

Decker sat up, grinning. "Two Master Gunner qualified Pathfinders flubbing a straightforward operation? I'd probably slit my own throat in shame."

"You're paid to take that kind of risk. I'm not anymore."

"Didn't I recall you to active duty a few hours ago? You are paid for it again, including my kind of danger pay, seeing as how I've attached you to my command."

"And I still don't think you have the authority to do that."

"How about we pretend I do for now." He climbed to his feet. "Not that I heard any better ideas from you or any ideas at all for that matter."

Tarra rolled his eyes upward. "I'm not the guy who turned skullduggery into his number one professional accomplishment. To think you used to be an honest Marine once upon a time. You want ideas? How about we go mosey on over to the landing field and scope out our ride, maybe find someone who can tell us when she's due to lift again, so we can time your super-duper spy plan correctly."

Decker clapped his friend on the shoulder. "That's my boy."

They found Raj Lisk standing at the edge of the spaceport tarmac, hands joined in the small of his back, waiting for something or someone. Decker and Tarra stopped on either side of him, adopting his posture.

"Got some good hooch coming off her?" Decker asked, squinting at a ship's name half covered by black streaks from repeated passage through the atmosphere. "*Lupus Arctos*. Seems familiar."

"No hooch," Lisk replied, "and *Arctos* is one of the regulars on the Kilia-Asgard-Naraka route so you might have seen her during your voyage here."

A caterpillar-like string of flatbed skimmers headed for the belly ramp as soon as it touched the steaming ground, ready to take off the inbound cargo. Some of the outbound crates already sat in a neat pile nearby, waiting to be loaded.

"Efficient," Tarra commented, watching the well-choreographed movements.

"It has to be. We can't afford to have her spend the night on the ground. One of our competitors might get it into their heads to send a raiding force just so they can fuck up one of our employer's ships. It would be worth the causalities for some of them."

"How long before she lifts again?" Decker asked.

"Four hours, give or take. That's the usual turnaround time. The crew doesn't step ashore other than on business. No liberty here."

A man stepped down the ramp and headed for them, carrying a case under his arm.

"I guess that's for you." Zack tilted his head towards the main road. "It's time to hit the chow line, Hal."

"Yep."

Once out of Lisk's earshot, Decker said, "We take the AD dome at nine; give ourselves a forty-five-minute delay and then show up just before ten."

Tarra grimaced. "Tight. Very tight. They might have buttoned her up by then. We need to board with the last load."

"Which will probably be thundering past the gate at around quarter to ten. They'll try to squeeze every last bit aboard, including stuff that's still going through the refining mill right now. There will be a last minute truck, trust me. I've run one-half of a freight hauling operation, so I know how they think. It's cheaper to lift off as loaded as the thrusters can handle than to tack on an extra twenty light year run every six months."

Jon Gerin intercepted them in the mess hall.

"Gentlemen, just the two I wanted to see. We need to discuss your next deployment. I visited the Barayan Lake operation today, and the local garrison CO could use a few extra teams. Since both of yours are available or will be once you've had your rest and recuperation, I thought of sending you there at the end of the week."

"Can we talk about it tomorrow morning, first thing?" Decker asked. "Tonight, Hal, and I are planning to get thoroughly soused in memory of the good old days."

"Sure, tomorrow works." Gerin smiled. "Try not to destroy the bar."

"No fears, boss. The bar is the one thing we take care to never damage." Decker gave Tarra a quick wink.

"Until tomorrow, then." Gerin dropped his tray in the return slot and left the building.

Once they had collected their food and taken a table, Tarra glanced around. "What happened to the rest of our folks, I wonder. They've been out in town for a long time."

"Miko sort of hinted that she might keep them busy and away from here for the balance of the day."

"You told her?" Tarra's words came out as a low growl.

"She had me pinned down, literally, as a matter of fact. Don't worry, all she knows is that we intend to leave aboard *Arctos*, effectively deserting Frontier Solutions. She wanted to come along, but I convinced her that it wouldn't be a good idea to make the Jackals mad when you're a real freelancer."

"Tell me again how you convinced her to jump in the sack with you, both literally and figuratively."

"Which time would you like to hear about?"

"Never mind."

They finished eating in silence before returning to the barracks to prepare. There would be no alcohol for Tarra tonight, not until they had successfully stowed away, though Decker had been sincere when he told Gerin that he would spare the bar. He held no beef with Frontier Solutions. Chisger Mining and the Confederacy, on the other hand...

By nine, full darkness had fallen, broken only by a faint volcanic glow to the west. Moria, both the town and the base, had minimum illumination. Most of the artificial light sources were turned outward, to prevent anyone from approaching the perimeter unseen by the naked eye because sensors could fail, and often did, with a bit of encouragement from the enemy.

Working in silence, they donned battle armor, strapped on their weapons and slipped packs containing all of their possessions — at least those they were not leaving behind — over their shoulders before checking each other. Then Tarra slapped an armored hand on his friend's helmet.

"You're good to go, jumper. Just like old times."

"Remember," Decker said, leading the way to the door. "We don't fuck up the guys in the dome."

"Unless they try to do us first." Tarra nodded. "Gotcha."

They walked across the compound as if on a regular guard patrol, hoping no one would think it odd that the evening sentries carried backpacks. Once at the aerospace defense dome, Decker rapped on the recessed door and waited, knowing one of the two men inside would scrutinize them via an external sensor.

"What do you want?" A disembodied male voice asked.

"Jack Lorenzo and Hal Tarra from Special Assignments. Intelligence has a hair up its ass about some idiot trying us on while *Arctos* is on the ground, so we've been sent to back you guys up."

The man sighed. "It's always the same paranoia when a ship is sitting on the tarmac, but whatever. Ours is not to reason why ours is just to break out a deck of cards and fleece each other. By the way, Hal, you still owe me for that bet you lost the other day."

"I certainly do not, Jensen." He replied. "You're just trying to mooch again, as always."

Jensen laughed. "I am not, you cheap liar. However, if you're carrying a flask, all is forgiven."

The door slid open, admitting them into a tight airlock. Once both Marines had stepped inside, it closed again. Then, the inner door vanished into the wall, revealing a control room that wouldn't have been out of place on a starship.

Screens covered the walls, giving the two men inside a three hundred and sixty-degree view of the entire Moria area. They called it a dome for a reason. To one side, a round hatch marked the ammunition bunker's entrance, while another on the opposite side led to the missile launchers. Self-contained, armored, and lethal, it would be perfect for what Decker had in mind.

One of the men, Jensen, climbed to his feet and smiled at the newcomers. "Welcome to our house of horrors."

He nodded towards his partner. "You know Yee, don't you, Tarra?"

"Yep. This here's Jack, my old buddy from the Corps." Tarra jerked at thumb at Decker. "Mean fucker, especially with a few in him."

As they spoke, Tarra walked up to stand behind Yee, still sitting at his console, while Decker stepped within striking distance of Jensen.

"Pleasure," he said, grasping the other man's arm and pulling him off balance. A strike with the side of his hand on the back of Jensen's skull sent him sprawling on the metal floor, out cold.

Tarra gave Yee a similar treatment, then hauled him out of his chair and dumped him beside Jensen. Decker pulled out thin plastic restraint strips and bent over to tie their hands and feet.

"That was almost too easy," he said straightening up.

"Private sector pukes," Tarra said with disgust. "I don't think we'd ever catch Marine artillery guys that easily."

"We would if they thought one of us was an on-and-off drinking buddy instead of a treasonous sonofabitch." Decker indicated Yee's chair. "Let's see if you remember how to break through the safety protocols that keep these guns from depressing down low enough to shoot up the joint."

Tarra laced his fingers and made as if he was cracking his knuckles, then rubbed his hands together while he sat down. "Child's play. This is a Sachsenwerk MANTIS Mark Six self-contained aerospace defense array. Twenty-five-millimeter eight-barrel calliope married to a four-tube auto loading missile launcher. The Corps used them until about ten years ago when they ended up on the surplus market. It's an excellent system, pretty much soldier-proof."

"Thanks for that dissertation, Command Sergeant. I didn't need an abbreviated sales pitch seeing as how I'm quite familiar with this pod. How the hell do you think I came up with our plan?"

Tarra gave Decker the rigid digit salute, which the latter had expected.

"I'll chalk that piece of insubordination up to combat stress," he said, chuckling. "Otherwise, I'd have to charge you under half a dozen articles of the code of discipline. I am, however, disappointed that you didn't find anything more inventive than giving me the finger."

"You want to do it yourself, be my guest." Tarra snarled, eyes on the control screen. "This was your idea, and you *are* two years ahead of me on the Master Gunner honor roll."

"Sure, but I've discovered I'm better at fucking with people than with machinery. Besides, you're more recent than I am."

"And better looking, which isn't hard to do." Tarra pushed his chair back and smiled. "I'm in. God bless the pointy heads who left one or two active back door codes after they scrubbed this thing's AI for surplus sales."

"The real question is can you sweet-talk the AI into blowing away its master's creations?"

"Yup. I can even program the thing so it doesn't hit the mess hall or the bar."

"You're a prince among men." Movement on one of the screens caught Decker's eye. "Another string of trucks is leaving the enrichment facility."

He stared at the flatbeds for a few moments, trying to calculate how much time they had left before the last one swung by the gate, and missed the shadowy figures approaching the dome. Tarra, busy teaching the fire control system new tricks, saw nothing at all.

Decker whirled around at the sound of both airlock doors opening at once and pulled up his carbine in a smooth movement, only to face an equally well-armed Rika Kozlev. Two armored men who, judging by what he saw through the open visors, looked like the kind of goons she had preferred for her dirty work on Garonne, backed her. The outer door slammed shut again.

"Put that gun away, Jack. Or rather, Zack," she said. "You and Tarra aren't going to fight your way out of Moria, and even if you manage to do so, you'd have no place to go. It's hostile jungle for hundreds of kilometers on all sides."

With three large bore plasma guns aimed at his chest, he obeyed. At this range, they could cause some serious harm, even punch through his armor, but he worried more about damage to the controls that might prevent them from carrying out the plan. He heard Tarra, behind him, swivel his chair.

"I figured you two would try something," she continued. "I've had you watched since we returned from visiting Doctor Maslow this morning. Imagine my surprise when the security cameras showed you entering the air defense dome. So I asked myself why, and the answer came to me almost immediately. Two Marines, highly skilled with weapons can use this beautiful defensive ordnance for some very nefarious purposes. The one that struck me as most likely revolved around the creation of a massively destructive diversion while they stow away on the *Arctos*. It's due to lift soon, and possibly, thanks to the distraction, will do so in enough of a panic to ensure you pass unnoticed until it's in hyperspace. How am I doing so far?"

Her indolent, feral smile made Decker think of a predator who knows she's cornered her prey and was already choosing which part to devour first. She pointed at the bound and gagged artillerymen with her gun. "If you had legitimate business here, you wouldn't have knocked out the crew."

"Interesting theory," he replied. "But then, people with twisted minds like yours are naturals when it comes to spinning wild tales. What do you intend to do now? The way I see it, we're in a standoff. Blasters start pumping out plasma, and there's going to be a lot of damage that your bosses won't like, starting with this control room and ending with a lot of Frontier Solutions troopers dead, you included. Besides, I think you're still working on some plan of your own. Otherwise, you'd have the better part of the Moria battalion surrounding us, not a handful of dungeon goons."

While he spoke, he shuffled to one side, out of Tarra's line of fire, while his right hand hovered near his dagger's hilt. "So what is it? You get a crack at interrogating us, and then present the whole Elyce Sakal story to the CO, along with a pair of Marine Corps infiltrators? Perhaps you figure it'll be the first step to a better position in the corporation. What I don't understand is why you'd think we would cooperate in our own demise. After what I did to your operation on Garonne, I would have thought you'd be more careful."

The feral smile broadened, revealing her teeth.

"I have your friends in custody. If you don't cooperate, Steiger, Langton, and that oaf Tiktin will have a series of unfortunate accidents."

"Bullshit. They're in town."

"Not anymore. They're in my cells." Kozlev pulled a tablet from her pocket and held it up so Decker could see his three teammates staring back with palpable hate from inside cells. She jerked her head towards the door. "Shall we?"

Tarra coughed as if clearing his throat, giving Zack a signal that went back to a time when bar brawls provided them with much of their entertainment, before they became respectable senior noncoms.

In a movement almost too fast for the eye, Decker drew his dagger and threw it at Kozlev, the blade piercing her throat millimeters from the scar he'd given her in the stockade. One of the two goons behind her suddenly sprouted a hilt from his left eye and crumpled to the floor almost at the same time as his CO. The third, too stunned by the rapid turn of events, took a plasma round in the face and died instantly.

Decker leaped towards the airlock, to drag the bodies inside in case any of Kozlev's troops still outside decided to enter uninvited. Kozlev, her windpipe severed, stared up at him with astonishment as her life rapidly bled out.

"I should have done that back on Garonne and saved us a world of grief," he said, watching the light fade from her eyes. "Good riddance to bad garbage."

He pulled his dagger from Kozlev's throat and carefully wiped its blade on her tunic before returning the weapon to its sheath.

"What about your team?" Tarra asked, imitating his friend. "Are you going to leave them in Kozlev's cells for Lisk to find tomorrow, after we've buggered off in the most spectacular way possible? That's not the Zack Decker I know."

Zack sighed. "Of course not, you dumbass. I'm going to leave you here to finish the job while I break them out."

He shut his visor, stepped around the pools of blood, and slipped out the door. Two armored troopers stood on the opposite side of the road skirting the dome but didn't make a move to intercept him. A single man exiting probably failed to meet whatever mission parameters Kozlev had given them, and knowing her, he wasn't surprised that they would take pains to obey orders to the letter.

He entered the darkened HQ complex and gave the folks on night duty a friendly wave as he walked by on his way to the intelligence section's empty office suite. Once there, he searched for the interrogation cells, finding them in a container array attached to the rear of the building. A quick shot with his blaster took care of the lock, and he stepped in, raising his visor so the others could identify him.

"What the hell is going on?" Steiger asked the moment she recognized the big man inside the battle suit. "We were minding our own business when Kozlev and some goons arrested us."

"She decided the game was up. Bad decision, as it turned out. Unfortunately, that means you three will have to come with Hal and me. Once they find her body and those of her men and figure out we did it, your time in Frontier Solutions will run out, permanently."

"So you finally killed her." Langton winced. "I knew it would happen sooner rather than later. And now what? We run for the hills and offer our services to the nearest reiver clan?"

"No." Decker found the controls to the cells, and three doors slammed open in unison. "We're booked on the *Lupus Arctos*, departing within the hour. You're welcome to join us unless you'd rather take your chances with Kozlev's deputy."

"I'm with you," Steiger said. "And if you'd let me join your conspiracy earlier, we might have avoided this jailbreak."

"Me as well," Langton added. "I'm tremendously curious to see the end of this quest you've undertaken. Raj Lisk strikes me as a saner version of Kozlev, and I'd rather not take the risk of having a conversation with him while sitting in one of those interrogation chairs."

"Tiny?" Decker looked at the Celestan.

Tiktin shrugged. "I guess I don't have much of a choice."

"In that case, haul your asses to the barracks at the double, put on your armor, pack your crap, and meet us at the gate. We're going to jump on one of the last trucks and ride it aboard while my buddy Hal triggers a wee diversion."

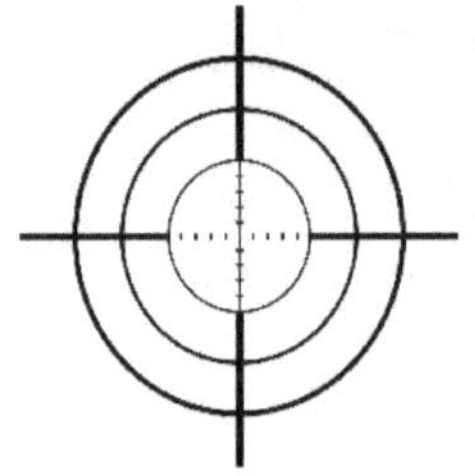

— TWENTY-EIGHT —

Tarra still sat in the control chair, surrounded by bodies, both living and dead when Decker re-entered the dome. The odor of spilled blood and voided bowels seemed almost overwhelming in the confined space.

"All good?" He asked Zack over his shoulder.

"They're suiting up and packing as we speak. We'll regroup at the gate. How are your tricks coming?"

"I'm just about done." He held up a small, boxy instrument. "I've linked my sensor to the controls. One command and the program kicks in. That means we can trigger it whenever we want. Or not trigger it at all if we can board without a diversion."

"All five of us? Not a chance. We'll use it."

"It's a damn shame." Tarra climbed to his feet.

"For the last time, Command Sergeant, this is war, be it ever so undercover, and Moria is a legitimate target."

"Yeah, yeah, so you keep saying. But there are good people here no matter what your beef with the Confederacy and this Coalition of yours might be, and mining on a planet at the ass-end of the galaxy isn't criminal."

"But the proceeds will be used for criminal ends." Decker slapped Tarra on the shoulder. "Cheer up and consider this — you lost the right to object the moment you called me into this mess."

"Yep. I should have known you'd take over. You always had a bossy streak, Major, sir. What about the guys Kozlev left out there?"

"They're still fat, dumb, and happy, waiting for new orders that'll never come. Kozlev has them properly whipped." He glanced down at her body, pale in death, lying in a pool of rapidly congealing blood. She seemed much smaller now, almost deflated, and utterly harmless. "Dumb fuck should have left well enough alone instead of renewing her acquaintance with Uncle Zack. She'd still be alive, happily screwing and torturing her way up the chain of command. Are we ready to go?"

"We are. I've set it up so that once we leave, the doors won't open to anything short of cutting through the locks, and they're armored."

"You're always thinking of the important details. Good stuff. Now try to look casual, as if dear dead Rika gave us a kiss and a pat on the ass. I'd rather not make the body trail any longer. At least not right now."

They emerged from the airlock into the humid Naraka night. Over to their left, the landing strip lights still burned brightly, outlining the shape of the Star Wolf sloop, proof loading hadn't quite ended, though Decker's trained ears could hear the thrusters spooling slowly, warming up.

He waved at Kozlev's men and then, carbines slung, the Marines headed for the gate. Two pairs of curious eyes followed them, their owners torn between obeying orders and an urge to intercept the armored troopers wandering off into the darkness as if they had no care in the world.

When they reached the road running between the ore refining complex and the improvised spaceport, the others hadn't yet appeared. Decker glanced back at the barracks with a measure of impatience, knowing that the next hauler to pass by could be the last.

Finally, just as he turned to head back into the compound and look for them, three shapes in battlesuits, carrying weapons and packs, emerged from the shadows at a running pace. They slipped through the gate and skidded to a halt in front of them. Steiger opened her helmet visor.

"Something's stirring around HQ, guys. We saw Raj Lisk walk into the building like a man on a mission."

"Shit. Did anyone see you slip away from company lines?"

"Nope." She shook her head. "At least I don't think so."

"Okay." Decker looked up the road at the mining complex, trying to gauge when the next and hopefully last truck would show up. If it wasn't the last one, *Lupus Arctos* would lift with a smaller cargo than planned. Once Tarra's diversion kicked in, the ship's captain would order an emergency liftoff. "Next hauler that goes by, we hitch a ride."

*

"Damn Rika and her bloody schemes." Raj Lisk muttered, barely acknowledging the duty officer's wave as he entered the headquarters complex.

One of his friends had tipped him off about Kozlev taking three Special Assignments operators into custody without much ado, and he had cut short his foray into the mining settlement.

He felt sure that the former Celeste National Guard officer was playing some game involving the folks she remembered from Garonne, a game she had declined to share with her deputy. Arresting most of Jack Lorenzo's team without obtaining approval from the boss, as per standing orders, took it up another notch.

Jon Gerin would be beside himself the moment he found out, and Lisk knew he had to fix this before morning. His own neck wouldn't be safe from the grasping hands of irate commanding officers.

The intelligence section's offices were empty, computer screens dark and he headed for the custody pod, wondering what he would find. It had better not be one of the operators strapped to an interrogation chair.

He stopped short of the door the moment he saw blast marks on the now destroyed lock. Perhaps Lorenzo had come to break his people out. Perhaps he would find Kozlev strapped to a chair, alive or maybe even dead.

The former Marine had struck him as a man who wouldn't hesitate to kill when necessary.

But the space was empty, clean and the systems shut down. If not for the damaged lock, he might have believed someone had pulled a prank. He chewed his lower lip for a few moments, trying to decide on his next steps. Find Kozlev, or find Lorenzo?

His long stride took him through the corridor warren and back outside. He crossed the quadrangle, headed for the Special Assignments Company barracks, eyes scanning the darkened base for any sign of life. Only the noise of mine haulers trundling by the gate and the lights adjoining the landing strip kept his immediate surroundings from appearing lifeless.

The barracks turned out to be as empty as the cells, all the resident operators either in town or in the mess hall. So much for finding Lorenzo and his team.

He entered the bar and searched for a face that might provide him with badly needed intelligence. One of the men at a corner table raised his hand and waved him over.

"Are you looking for someone, Raj?" He asked once Lisk came within earshot.

"Yeah, my boss and a special operator by the name of Lorenzo."

"The Queen of Darkness is apparently doing something in the vicinity of the air defense dome. Charlie saw her and a few of her henchmen loitering around there less than half an hour ago."

"Thanks, Vern. I appreciate that."

"What can I say?" The man shrugged. "It doesn't hurt to keep tabs on her."

"That's what I'm trying to do." He tossed off a mock salute. "See you later."

As soon as he came within sight of the dome, he noticed two of Kozlev's men standing in the shadows, but no sign of her, which meant she had to be inside. Lisk walked up to the troopers, eyes darting from one to the other.

"What's going on here?" He asked.

One of the henchmen shrugged. "No idea, sir. Kozlev told us to wait here for orders before she went inside with Karl and Yann. They haven't come out yet."

"Did anyone else come out since she went in?"

"Yeah. One guy left on his own then came back ten minutes later, then ten minutes after that, two guys came out."

"Who were the guys?" Lisk's voice took on a dangerous edge.

"I think they were Special Assignments."

"It didn't occur to you to stop them and find out?"

"Kozlev gave orders to wait here, and you know what she's like when you don't obey her to the letter."

Lisk swallowed a sigh. Rika liked her goons big, strong, and stupid. Smart ones would question her methods, if not her orders.

"Where did the two operators go?"

The man waved in the general direction of the road to the landing strip. "Somewhere over there. I stopped looking once they turned the corner."

Indecision struck Lisk once again. Figure out why Kozlev had entered the dome? Or follow the operators, one of whom he assumed to be Lorenzo and the other, Tarra?

He crossed the street and touched the pad by the dome's door. It didn't budge. He entered his override code, which allowed him and a few select HQ staff officers access to any Frontier Solutions facility on Naraka, but without luck. After a minute or so of fruitless effort trying to communicate with anyone inside, he stepped back and chewed on his lip again.

Something felt wrong about the situation. Kozlev's secretiveness wasn't new, but her unexpected involvement with the two former Marines after the trip to Mahar seemed uncharacteristic, as did her activities tonight when she would normally be in town performing her half of the beast with two backs.

He glanced towards the landing strip lights again, suddenly seized by a nagging worry that didn't, as yet, dare speak its name. Conscious of his unarmored state and the fact that his entire firepower hung in a holster at his hip, he stepped out of the dome's shadow and headed for the gate.

*

"This is the one," Decker said, waving towards the oncoming flatbed truck. "Get ready."

Automated, like the rest of the hauler fleet, it didn't need lights to navigate down the darkened road, nor did it have a driver who might become curious at a handful of mercenary soldiers hitching a ride.

It moved at little more than a walking pace, and they hopped onto the open platform with ease, trying to look like an escort for some high-value cargo. After a short ride, they emerged from the darkness and turned onto the brightly lit strip with the grounded sloop at its center.

A small, sleek starship, ideal for commerce and raiding in the wild frontier beyond the Rim, it sat on stubby legs, its belly ramp still touching the ground, though Decker could sense its drives gathering more and more power.

Their truck shot up the ramp, under the eyes of two astonished spacers and came to a halt at the threshold of the cargo bay, where a gantry waited to transfer the last few containers to their allotted slots in the packed hold.

"What the fuck are you guys doing here?" A Star Wolf wearing faded coveralls shouted from the controls. "I didn't hear anything about passengers."

"Transfer to Asgard," Decker yelled back. "We had five minutes to pack our gear and show up. Don't know why, but that's our orders."

"Captain's gonna have words to say about that." The man finished shifting the crates, releasing the flatbed which promptly trundled out of the hold and down onto the tarmac. "You guys just wait right here."

He waved at the two crewmen walking up the ramp. "Watch these jokers. Last minute passengers, eh?" Then he vanished into the bowels of the ship.

Decker nudged Tarra and murmured, "Now would be a good time."

"I'd rather wait to see what his captain will say," the other Marine whispered back.

"He'll say to check with the Frontier Solutions duty officer to confirm the last minute personnel transfer. Do it."

Reluctantly, Tarra took out his sensor, using his body to shield it from the crewmen's eyes, and entered a sequence of commands. "There."

A few seconds passed while the Star Wolves and mercenaries eyed each other with the boredom of folks used to administrative screw-ups, then, unseen by anyone but Kozlev's two troopers, the air defense dome split open and turned Moria into an antechamber of hell.

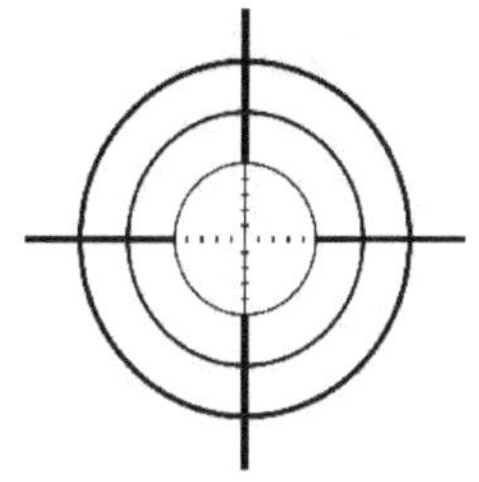

— TWENTY-NINE —

Raj Lisk made it almost halfway to the landing strip when he heard the rapid fire of air defense guns behind him. He froze for a few heartbeats, feeling a surge of adrenaline shoot through his veins, then he turned back to see the calliope spit plasma, but not at any aerial target.

Out of instinct more than rational thought, he ran back towards the dome, fearful that they might all be doomed unless someone managed to shut the gun down before it slewed around and took out the grounded sloop. Whatever Kozlev might have been up to, he couldn't believe this was her doing.

Torn apart by a torrent of sustained fire, the ore refining plant collapsed before his eyes into a glowing mass of superheated metal. Shifting its fire, the calliope ripped through the mine head and ate into the rock behind it, sending fist-sized stones flying through the air like so much solid rain.

Aboard *Lupus Arctos*, a klaxon, very much like that of a warship's battle stations siren, blared and the ramp rose with no regard for any remaining cargo or personnel.

A voice sounded through loudspeakers, alerting the crew to prepare for an emergency take-off. Seconds later, the deck beneath Decker's feet began to vibrate, and one of the two crewmen told them to lie down on their backs and grab the nearest stanchion before both ran off to their duty stations.

"What have you done?" Steiger asked once the Wolves had gone.

"We created a diversion that's going to put the Moria operation out of commission until they can ship in an entirely new mine head and refining plant. I figured that if we stampede the captain of this fine ship into an emergency lift, he won't be so keen to check our transfer orders." He winked at her. "And we do the Commonwealth a solid by cutting off some of the bad guys' cash flow."

"You're a fucking maniac, Decker," she growled over the rumble of the thrusters.

"That's what I keep telling him," Tarra shouted, "but he likes to blow up stuff."

The noise in the hold rose to a level that prevented any further conversation. Then, they felt the pressure on their bodies increase while the deck beneath them swayed when *Arctos* broke free of the surface. A pleased smile spread across Decker's face while he contemplated the vibrating deckhead above.

*

Lisk heard the sloop lift with a roar that drowned out the ripping sound of the calliope's eight continuous plasma streams. Hopefully, *Arctos* would escape before the guns turned on her.

Then, a missile erupted from its launcher, followed by another and another until a full brace streamed up into the sky. He turned to watch the rapidly receding shape of the sloop, riding up into the low clouds on pillars of brilliant light and felt sick to his stomach

But within a few seconds, he realized that none of the missiles was chasing it. Instead, each flew off in a different direction, and it didn't take the intelligence officer long to understand that they had been aimed at the remaining Confederacy mines scattered over this continent.

The gun fell silent, and time seemed to stop for a few moments, while all over the base, troops froze in place, wondering what would happen next. Then, a streak of flame erupted from the open dome. He moved away on the run, to escape the sudden onslaught of heat until he could turn back to watch the sophisticated, expensive air defense array crumple into wreckage around the control pod.

Lisk didn't see Wolski, the Frontier Solutions commanding officer, until she stood beside him, gaping at the sight with a look of disbelief on her face.

"What in all that's holy is going on here?" She asked in a raspy voice.

"I have no idea, except that according to those two clowns with the stupid faces over there, Kozlev and a pair of troopers went inside and never came out. I tried to go in before the thing went haywire, but someone's locked out all of the command codes."

"I can't believe Kozlev would be dumb enough to destroy Moria."

"We'll find out when we break through the airlock," Lisk replied. "The control room is an armored pod built to withstand a direct hit. It should survive more or less intact."

"You realize what's going to happen to Frontier Solutions if the Confederacy decides we're guilty of letting one of our own ruin their operations, right?" Wolski asked.

"We're going to wish we joined Avalon instead, happy for the crappy pay, or had gone into a different line of business altogether."

"At least *Arctos* didn't get hit."

The flames suddenly vanished under the smothering of a much-delayed firefighting system, belatedly coming online courtesy of Hal Tarra's sabotage, now that the weaponry had been damaged beyond repair.

Then, with loud clicks the locks released first the outer door and then the inner one. Wolski and Lisk cautiously approached the dome, their need to know winning out over the heat radiating from tortured metal.

Lisk took the first tentative steps towards the control room, stopping in the airlock when he saw five bodies littering the floor. It took him a few seconds to realize the two who had been tied up were still breathing.

However, there was no doubt Rika Kozlev and her henchmen had died in a most bloody fashion. Lisk thought he knew who might have done it, but held his tongue. This mess belonged Wolski. Frontier Solutions paid her enough for it.

When she peered over his shoulder, Wolski grunted. "Lovely. Part of me doesn't actually want to know what happened. Have the gun crew interned and speak with them yourself. Ensure that no one else hears what they have to say. I think the way we'll play this is by reporting that Kozlev turned out to be an operative for one of the competing syndicates who want to eject the Confederacy from Naraka — you figure out which one is the most plausible. She's responsible for this mess."

Wolski pulled out her blaster and nudged Lisk to imitate her.

"Aim for the wounds. We'll say we killed them. Then have the gun crew back up our story. Maybe, just maybe, the Wolves will stop short of having us shot."

"And what about the real culprits?" He asked. "I have the feeling they might have stowed away aboard *Arctos*."

"Who?" She gave him a hard stare. "This is Kozlev's doing, you read me Mister Lisk?"

"I read you." Then, as if to underscore his agreement, he aimed at the gaping wound giving Kozlev a second smile at the base of the throat and fired. "There. I've dealt with the real culprit. The report will be on your desk before morning."

"I know it'll be complete, precise, and utterly unimpeachable." Wolski shot each of the dead troopers once, obliterating the wounds that had killed them and then holstered her gun. "Get someone to remove the bodies. I don't think this dome is recoverable, but maybe the control room is."

*

"I probably shouldn't be surprised at this last minute personnel transfer," *Arctos'* first mate said, examining the five mercenary troopers standing in a single row by the stacked containers. The sloop had broken orbit a short time earlier and was accelerating towards the hyperlimit, its crew now at cruising stations. "But I find it annoying nonetheless. We like to run an efficient operation and adding five bodies, even if it's just for the run to Asgard, is messy. I don't suppose you're actually carrying transfer orders."

"No. All we have is a verbal from the commanding officer to report to Flora Barzee when we show up at Midgard base," Decker replied. "We're as surprised as you are, sir, but this kind of shit isn't exactly unusual."

The first mate snorted. "Ain't that the truth? Okay. You get the spare cabin. Six bunks, so you can use one of them to stow your gear. Do I need to inspect your weapons and check that they're not loaded?"

"We're clear, sir," Decker replied. "But if you want us to put 'em in your weapons locker, that's fine."

"Why don't we do that?" The Star Wolf said. "I'll have the bosun come around to collect them and sort out your rations and quarters. Until she shows up, you stay here."

"Whatever you say, sir." He paused for a fraction of a second. "May I ask why we did an emergency lift-off?"

"Moria came under attack. Last we heard, the mine and refinery are gone, as is the air defense dome. From the way it went down, it looks like it might have been an inside job from the competition. Or at least that's what the last transmission from Moria said. I guess we were lucky to escape away unscathed. It looks like you folks missed a heck of a show."

Then, he turned on his heel and left.

Steiger nudged Zack. "You don't mess around, do you, big boy? I can't wait to hear that story."

"When we're in a place where the bulkheads don't have ears. Besides, in the Decker-Tarra team, I'm the ideas guy. Hal's the one who made my beautiful plan work."

"Sure, blame me," Tarra grumbled. "I tried to talk him out of it, but no, Mister Wonderful wants his fireworks display."

"You should have seen him on Garonne," Steiger replied, chuckling. "Speaking of which, what about Kozlev?"

"I finally got around to doing the job I should have finished back then."

"Good!" She patted him on the shoulder. "That bitch needed killing since the day she drew her first breath."

A barrel-shaped woman with a mean, seamed face beneath a hairstyle that reminded Decker of a Shrehari's crest, stalked into the hold a few minutes later. She sized up the five mercenaries and grunted.

"Any of you gonna be trouble?" She asked.

Decker, who had decided this one would likely be a dangerous adversary in a hand-to-hand fight, shook his head. "No. We'll be as quiet as mice. Point us to our bunks, tell us when and where we eat and you won't hear a peep. By the way, the name's Lorenzo. Jack Lorenzo."

She locked eyes with him for a few seconds. "You keep it that way, and we'll have not problems with one another, Jack Lorenzo."

Then, she turned towards the exit and waved at them to follow her. They went up a short spiral staircase and down a narrow passageway before stopping at the door marked armory, which opened at her touch. She indicated a row of rectangular boxes affixed to the bulkhead.

"Take whichever empty one you want, remove the magazines and power packs, then stow everything. Don't worry, won't nobody mess with your stuff while we're in space. I'll bring you back here just before we land on Asgard."

Once they had complied, she led them aft to the cabins, waving them into one with six bunks, stacked in two sets of three on either side of the door.

"Make yourselves comfortable. I'm gonna lock you in until we're FTL, then someone will show you to the saloon."

When the door closed, shutting them off from the rest of the ship, Steiger smirked at Zack. "Your turn to be confined to quarters, eh? How does it feel, big boy?"

He shrugged, refusing to rise to the bait. "Like the bosun knows her business. How about we climb out of our tin suits and settle in? We might as well make ourselves comfortable, seeing as how we won't have much entertainment for a while."

Decker caught Tarra's eye and glanced at the deckhead. Tarra nodded and pulled out his sensor while the remainder tried to strip off their armor without knocking each other out. After almost two minutes, Tarra gave Decker thumbs up. "It seems clean, which doesn't mean that there's nothing, it just means that there's nothing active."

"Thanks." Decker shoved his gear into one of the lockers set against the far bulkhead. "Folks, I'm sorry that we dragged you into this, but after Kozlev had decided to use you to blackmail me into cooperating, we didn't have too many options. How did that happen anyway?"

"We were minding our own business in one of the miner dives just outside the main gate," Langton began, "when a guy came in and said you wanted to see us in the HQ building. Something had come up that the guy couldn't discuss out in the open. It sounded genuine, what with your quest and working with Kozlev, so we followed. Next thing we know, walking into the intelligence section's office, we found ourselves facing four gun barrels. From there, they took us to the cells and Kozlev took our picture for posterity. Then you showed up. The end. Let me ask you a question, though. Will the powers that be on Naraka track the trail of destruction back to you?"

Decker shrugged. "A smart guy like Lisk probably has us pegged for it right now. Hal set the air defense dome to open after the guns and launchers self-destructed, so they could extract the gun crew. Unfortunately, they'll find Kozlev's body with her throat cut, lying in a pool of blood, alongside two of her goons, also dead."

"Then why did the first mate say that Moria called it an inside job from the competition?" Tiny asked, his broad face twisted into a question period.

A sly smile tugged at Langton's thin lips. "I may have a theory or two on that. Who do you think the Confederacy will blame for the destruction of the Moria mine head and refinery?"

"And all of the outlying operations," Tarra added. "Or at least I hope we damaged them. Those air defense missiles might make decent kinetic strikes, but they don't have much by way of explosives."

"What?" Langton started to laugh. "You mean you launched at Mahar and the other places? Oh man, the Confederacy is going to be livid. Frontier Solutions might not survive. But what I wanted about to say is this, if our employers can blame a competing clan, rather than admitting they hired a pair of former active duty Marines who turned out to be the kings of chaos, they might save their necks."

"Yeah, but the gun crew knows we knocked 'em out," Tarra said, "and there are the three bodies."

"So they blame Kozlev," Langton replied. "She already has a reputation for being horrid, she hasn't been with Frontier Solutions for very long, and she's the one who's been talking to captured reivers the most. Raj Lisk strikes me as smart enough to spin a story that'll hold up, and I'm convinced that the Frontier Solutions CO will be looking for a way to shift the blame off her shoulders."

"It fits." Decker smiled with grim satisfaction. "And once they head down that path, we're home free because they can't suddenly turn around and blame us, which means that if Asgard sends a message to Naraka concerning our orders, they'll be told everything's copacetic."

"Even dead, Kozlev's done you a favor." Langton's sly smile returned, and Decker found himself wondering about the man's motivations once again. Langton seemed too smart for the average army cop, and smart guys didn't join mercenary units operating beyond the Rim. They found cushy jobs doing corporate security after retiring from the Service.

"Three cheers for Rika Kozlev," Tarra said with a mocking leer. "Wasting her wasn't a wasted effort."

"The real question is what next?" Langton said, climbing into one of the upper bunks. "I hope you two have a plan. Asgard's a big place — heck, it's a whole planet — and we've only seen Midgard base. If your Elyce Sakal isn't holding surgery hours there, we're rather screwed. Besides, what will we tell Flora Barzee when she asks why they shipped us back?"

Decker made a dismissive gesture with his hand. "We have time to figure it out. Right now, my internal clock says it's time to sleep, and since I doubt they'll let us out for a few hours yet, I suggest we catch up on our rest. It's been a fun day."

"A shot of something would be nice, though," Tiny said.

Tarra dug into his bag and pulled out a bottle containing amber liquid. He raised it high in a triumphant gesture.

"I figured someone who's not on the wagon might ask. This comes from Jon Gerin's private stash. He needs to find a better hiding spot and booby trap it or something. I suspect it's some sort of rotgut made with alien crap, but from the whiff I got, it might taste just a bit like whiskey."

He took a sip and grimaced. "Take it easy on this stuff, folks." He offered the bottle to Steiger. "Ladies first."

"She's no lady," Decker protested.

"But she is better looking than you are, by a dozen parsecs." Tarra sketched a small bow towards her, winking.

"From the aroma I'm getting, we'll all be better looking after a few slugs," Zack growled.

"And our predicament will seem a lot less dire," Langton added. "Though I must confess that I'm intensely curious about what happens next, so I'm not exactly devastated at being in this situation."

"That's my buddy alright." Tarra recovered the bottle from Steiger and offered it to Tiny. "I may have mentioned this before, but he exercises the most natural form of leadership ever devised — people follow him out of sheer curiosity."

Steiger groaned theatrically. "What is it with you Marines always repeating the same tired old jokes? Do the universe a favor and expand your repertoire."

"Why?" Decker winked at her. "The classics always leave 'em laughing."

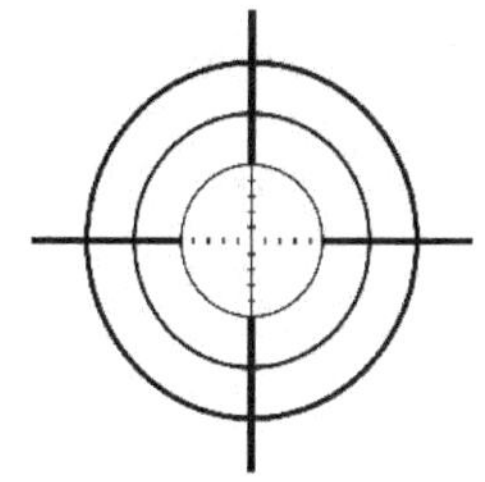

— THIRTY —

"It doesn't look or smell any better than last time," Decker remarked, striding down *Arctos'* belly ramp and into the miasma that passed for Asgard's atmosphere.

"Nope." Tiny shook his head. "But I'm glad to be here anyway. What a painful trip, stuck in a tiny cabin with no chance to exercise or even get a good drunk going."

"Cheer up." Decker thumped him on the shoulder. "You didn't have to pay for your passage and the food was edible."

He glanced around, trying to find evidence of a reception committee, like last time, but all he saw were crates waiting to be loaded aboard *Arctos*. Spotting the trail that led to Midgard, he slung his carbine and led the team through the violently green strip of jungle that separated the tarmac from the base.

Puzzled sentries let them through the main gate after checking that they knew where to report in.

The clerk manning the orderly room didn't quite know what to make of them and, with Flora Barzee away at another location, he assigned them barracks after taking down a summary of what Decker claimed as the verbal orders given to them before leaving Naraka.

Thankfully, he didn't seem overly surprised at last minute troop movements done without the benefit of written orders, thereby mirroring the reaction of *Arctos'* first mate.

"So where's this other location, good old Flora has gone to?" Decker asked in a conversational tone.

The clerk waved towards one of the windows overlooking the bay. "She's at the Confederacy stronghold on the other side. It's out of bounds to our kind, except by invitation."

"Have you ever been there?"

"Me? Never. But she's been frequently going these days. I guess the Confederacy have themselves some sort of human resources problem." The clerk cackled. "Not that Flora can help 'em, but it gets her out of my hair."

"Why can't she help them?" Langton asked.

"Because she knows dick-all about it." The clerk looked up at them in surprise. "I guess you didn't know she had another job as the Star Wolves representative within Frontier Solutions, did you?"

"No." Decker shook his head. "But it doesn't surprise me. She didn't look like she had a single day of useful military service on her record."

"It makes working around here so special." The clerk's voice dripped with sarcasm. "She'll want to see you when she gets back, but that likely won't be today. You might as well settle in and report to the battalion adjutant after breakfast tomorrow. Since he isn't expecting you, there's no point in hurrying, right?"

"Right."

They were assigned a twelve-bunk squad room to themselves, away from the current draft of recruits undergoing training, and after Tarra's sweep for listening devices, they took the clerk's advice and settled in.

"So," Langton asked, after stretching out on his bunk, "now that we're here, are you going to share your plan for the next step?"

"You want to hear my plan, eh. Well, it's pretty simple. Foolproof, really. We need an invitation to visit the Jackals. If Sakal is on Asgard, it's the best place to start."

"That's your plan?" The former military policeman sounded incredulous.

"It's better than what I had fifteen minutes ago, which approximated the square root of sweet fuck-all."

Steiger snorted. "Hey Hal, has he always been like this or are we getting special treatment because we didn't serve in the Corps?"

"Believe it or not," Tarra replied, "Zack's the king of improvisation. It used to drive the CO nuts."

"You've all heard that no plan survives contact with the enemy, right?" Decker beamed at his comrades as if bestowing a special blessing on them. "And when a plan goes sideways, the one who improvises best usually wins. It's simple logic. And it's the height of tactical flexibility."

"Sure. Keep telling yourself that." Tarra slammed his locker shut and turned to face Zack, hands on his hips. "The sun's almost kissing the horizon, which means it's time to go kiss a cold bottle."

"Sounds like a plan and as far as I remember, no booze has ever survived contact with you."

*

Tarra had just put down a tray with the second round when a gray-haired man in the ubiquitous Frontier Solutions uniform approached their table.

"Are you guys the Lorenzo team?" He asked.

"We are." Decker sat back in his chair and looked up at him. "I'm Jack Lorenzo. What can I do for you?"

"A lot, actually. Mind if I sit?"

Decker kicked out a chair. "Go ahead."

"My name's Doug Marson, and I'm the training battalion's adjutant," he said, taking the seat. "Tomas told me you're a Special Assignments group freshly back from Naraka."

"Tomas?"

"The orderly room clerk."

"I see." Decker gestured at Marson to continue.

"He said you were being reassigned to my outfit so we can train more and better operators for Naraka."

"That would be the case, yes. Naraka's a crappy place. A team's gotta be on its toes to survive in the wilds."

"And survive the opposition," Marson replied. "We heard rumors from *Arctos* that Moria was shot to hell by infiltrators."

"Sounds like it." Decker shrugged. "We were already aboard when it happened, so we know barely as much as the crew does, if that."

"Jon Gerin won't be happy, but I don't have anyone good enough for Special Assignments in the training pipeline right now, though I suppose the entire Naraka garrison has other problems on its hands these days than going out to harass the competition."

"Really?" Decker cocked an eyebrow. "Tell you what, we can evaluate the folks you do have and see if any of them might make useful operators with some of our gentle training methods."

"You could, but I have instructors capable of doing those evaluations, and they've already come up blank. However, you could help me out of a pickle."

"Oh?" Decker reached for a fresh mineral water bulb and took a gulp. "What would that pickle be?"

"You know Flora Barzee, I presume?"

"Sadly, yes. I seem to recall her telling me to zip my lips. The lady doesn't like to be interrupted."

"She's a pain in the neck, but since she's the Confederacy's eyes and ears around here, we just smile and agree with her." Marson suddenly had the look of a man with a deep thirst.

Decker caught Tarra's eye, then looked down at the tray. "Slide one of those to our new friend here."

Marson's look of relief when he took the first sip seemed almost comical, but he raised his bulb in thanks. "You're a true gentleman, Jack Lorenzo."

"Not really," Steiger quipped, "but he's known to show compassion once in a while."

"Then I appeal to your compassion and ask that you listen to my proposal," Marson said.

"I'm all ears. You mentioned everyone's favorite HR officer."

"It's not actually her, but her Confederacy bosses."

"We heard she's been spending a lot of time wherever their stronghold is."

"That's at the heart of my problem. You see, Frontier Solutions also provides security to Confederacy operations here on Asgard, among others, and we're just not capable of producing enough troops with the right qualifications, or at least the kind of skills our employers are looking for in some particular jobs. It's a case of expanding too much, too fast. Heck, we didn't exist eighteen months ago."

"And suddenly you have five high speed, low drag operators dumped in your lap by gods of war, and you don't have any high-speed work for them right now."

"Exactly." Marson took another sip of his beer. "What I'd like to do is offer your team to our employers and see if you fit the bill for some of their particular jobs. If they're happy, you go and work one of those assignments, then tell us what exact qualifications and experience they want so we can tailor one of the training pipelines to feed them. Rotate through all of their particular jobs and we don't have to suffer through Flora Barzee trying to tell us our work, and by the time we can deliver fresh meat to replace you, we might have operator training work. How does that sound? It beats wasting your time running regular grunts through the workup program."

Decker glanced around the table at the others. Tarra and Langton seemed in agreement, Steiger skeptical and Tiktin uncomprehending. Sometimes the universe throws an opportunity your way, he figured. They wouldn't have a better chance of searching through the Jackals' Asgard operations for Elyce Sakal than this.

"Sure. Why not," he said, smiling at Marson. "But you'll owe us one."

"I'll owe you several." The adjutant drained his bulb and stood. "Thanks for the drink and for taking me up on my proposal. I'll sort out the details with Flora when she gets back and let you know what's what. In the meantime, you're off duty, so feel free to tie one on and sleep in tomorrow."

When he was out of earshot, Steiger leaned over the table and whispered, "We've only been on the ground for a couple of hours and a way to implement Zack's one line plan shows up, just like that. A bit of a coincidence, no?"

Decker gave a half shrug. "Maybe it is, maybe it isn't. The Mendicant Priests of the Void say that a coincidence is God's way of opening a path towards salvation."

"I'd have never figured you for the religious type," Langton said.

The Marine smiled. "I'm not, but some things just cry out for a bit of faith, don't you think? Like the fact that I followed Hal here on faith that he had a good lead, and guess what? He did, even if it wasn't immediately apparent. It may not have been the greatest lead, but we did get somewhere. And along the way, I managed to correct a mistake from my recent past."

"I seem to recall your faith being weak until Doctor Mazkow popped up on our sensor screens," Tarra remarked.

"We all struggle from time to time. It's what makes us stronger." Decker conferred a paternal smile on his team. "Now, whose turn is it for the next round?"

"That would be yours, O Great Leader," Steiger intoned, "but make mine a whiskey. I need to wash the taste of this horse piss out of my mouth, and there's not enough privacy around here to do it in the biblical fashion."

"Then you shall have it, with my benediction."

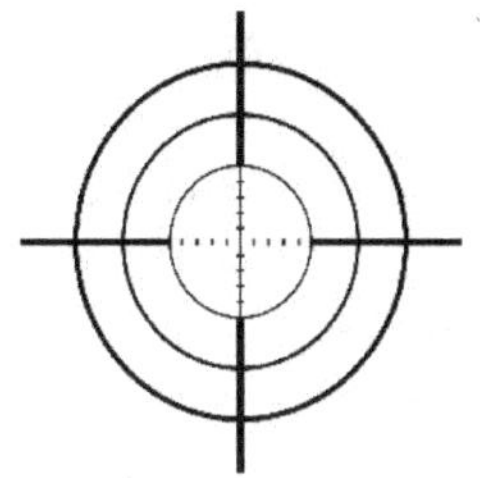

— THIRTY-ONE —

The next morning, Flora Barzee emerged from her office to find Decker and his team waiting patiently in the pale light of Asgard's sun.

"Well, well, well," she said, "Jack Lorenzo. I remember you. The man who couldn't keep his mouth shut. Did the CO on Naraka find you too much? Is that why you're back?"

"Actually," Zack grinned, "he's not happy with the product coming out of the selection process you're running and sent us back to sort things out."

Steiger almost choked trying to repress a burst of laughter. Tiny couldn't hide his smile, but at least he remained silent.

"Cute." Barzee seemed wholly unfazed by the Marine's flippant attitude. "We'll see how good your performance is when I send you out to work directly for the Confederacy of the Howling Stars. They don't have my forbearance and won't tolerate your sort of attitude."

"Then we should get along just fine. I don't tolerate people with my attitude either." His smile widened. "What's the mission and when do we go?"

"Why so impatient?"

"Doug Marson mentioned our employers were showing impatience at the delay in obtaining soldiers that can cater to their needs. Hence you not being here to welcome us yesterday. Of course, I'm assuming the needs in question are legal. Otherwise, we'll have a problem."

"This is the Protectorate, Mister Lorenzo. There's no Commonwealth Fleet to enforce Commonwealth law. We make and enforce our own." Barzee sniffed. "Legality is entirely what our employers say it is."

"Then I'm assuming their needs are morally acceptable. Morality is pretty much universal among us human beings, or at least it should be."

"Tell me, Mister Lorenzo, are you trying to be a barracks lawyer or are you a philosopher? Because I can't stand the former and have no use for the latter."

"I'm merely setting out the ground rules. The Confederacy likes to skate close to the edge of what'll earn them a shipload of Marines dumped on their heads, and coming from the Corps myself, I don't want to be on the receiving end if my former buddies come for a visit."

"No one wants the Fleet to intervene," she replied, sounding as if she was speaking to a rather stupid child, "but as I said, this is the Protectorate and your precious Fleet isn't allowed to operate beyond the Rim, thanks to the treaty that ended the last Shrehari War."

Hal Tarra grunted. "You'd be surprised at what can happen if the stakes are high enough, whether or not the powers that be back on Earth approve."

Barzee stared down her nose at Tarra for a few seconds before dismissing his words with a shake of the head.

"You'll be taken to Valhalla, the Confederacy stronghold across the bay, where your assignment will be explained."

Decker guffawed. "Valhalla? On a planet called Asgard, near a base called Midgard? You guys are really laying it on thick. Is the Confederacy boss called Odin, by any chance?"

"Don't knock it," Tarra said, nudging his friend, "any place called Valhalla has to have a bunch of Valkyries on staff and that means party time."

"Mister Lorenzo, Mister Tarra, please shut up while I'm speaking." Her nostrils flared for a brief moment. "As I was about to say, you'll be taken across the bay after the midday meal, so report back here as soon as you've eaten, with all of your gear and a basic load of ammunition.

Once in Valhalla..." Decker hiccupped, earning himself a hard stare, "...you'll report to Lars Harad, the man running operations. He'll be your CO for the duration of your detachment from this command. Rations and quarters will be provided, and in case you're required to expend ammunition or obtain replacement parts, he will make the arrangements."

"Are any other Frontier Solutions troops in Valhalla right now?" He asked. This time, Tarra hiccupped.

"Yes, but they're none of your concern," she replied, stabbing Hal with furious eyes. "If there are no further questions, you're dismissed."

*

The troop skimmer that took them across the calm waters that afternoon was one more piece of Commonwealth military gear that came straight from Army war stocks. Decker nudged Langton, drawing his attention to a data plate by the door.

"Does that look familiar to you, Alex?"

"I sure does. This thing must have fallen out the hatch of a quartermaster transport pod."

"Big as it is, that means some corrupt logistics puke pushed hard."

"We've been fighting this kind of crap for years," Langton replied in a resigned tone.

"We?"

"Figure of speech. The uniform might come off, but the thought patterns remain."

"Gotcha."

Soon, they approached a narrow strip of land separating the bay from the open ocean. What had seemed like a dark lump of stone at its tip from afar turned out to be a massive, brooding fortress.

"Nice," Steiger said, indicating granite ramparts smooth enough to reflect the drab light of a cloudy day. "A bit overdone, but a girl's got to love a castle on a savage alien planet."

"If you like that kind of thing, I suppose," Decker replied. "It's probably a L'Taung era outpost, which makes it about a hundred thousand years old."

"A what era outpost?" Tarra asked.

"The L'Taung were a proto-Shrehari civilization that vanished while our ancestors still roamed the African savanna back on Earth. They had colonies all over this part of the galaxy, but their empire collapsed for unknown reasons. A lot of the present-day Shrehari consider them a myth."

Tarra grunted. "Huh. Can't say I've ever heard of them. The architecture's impressive but a couple of kinetic strikes from orbit and you'll be polishing rubble."

"When the gods handed out a sense of awe at the universe, you slipped away to the latrine, didn't you?" Steiger made a face at Hal.

"When a man's gotta go, he's gotta go. Though I suppose the Jackals setting up shop here and calling it Valhalla makes a weird kind of sense."

"Maybe to you. I still think they're too cute by half with their naming conventions, if not showing an outright streak of megalomania," Decker said.

The skimmer pulled up and away from the water, cresting the stone rampart before settling down on a brilliantly marked landing spot in the center of what might have been a parade ground all those millennia ago.

Within the walls, blocky towers built with reddish stone occupied four of the hexagonal structure's six corners, their gaping windows, and doors filled with translucent plastic sheets while a smattering of Frontier Solutions troops wearing battle armor and carrying slung carbines patrolled the walls in pairs.

Before they could climb out of the troop carrier, a Confederacy member emerged from one of the buildings and headed towards them. He had a face seamed by a lifetime spent aboard ships with poor shielding beneath a bald pate and looked twice Zack's age and half his size. The mercenaries dismounted and lined up, if not quite at attention then with a certain amount of pride.

The Star Wolf stopped a pace in front of Zack and examined him with deeply sunken dark eyes, then subjected the others to the same scrutiny. Finally, he spoke, his voice a deep rasp.

"The name's Lars Harad. I'm the operations boss around here. You must be Jack Lorenzo and team. Flora Barzee holds you out to be serviceable Special Assignments operators, veterans of the regular Commonwealth services. We'll see."

Decker snorted. "I'm surprised that Barzee has such a high opinion of us."

Harad considered him for a few heartbeats, his jaw muscles working. Then, he said, "Flora's a pain in the reactor core, but she knows her business. I hope she's right because I'm tired of Frontier Solutions sending us nothing better than garrison troops."

"Naraka's sucking up the cream, is it?"

A harsh laugh escaped Harad's throat. "Hasn't done us much good, from what I've heard. You were there when it happened, weren't you?"

"We were." The Marine nodded. "But we were already aboard *Arctos* when it went down, so I don't know much."

"That's what *Arctos*' captain said." Harad locked eyes with Decker. "Lucky for you."

"Why so?"

"Gonna be a wholesale purge of the Naraka Battalion if it was infiltrated by the competition."

Decker shrugged. "Some parts of the operation were lax. Some house-cleaning won't hurt."

"You figure, eh?" Harad cocked a skeptical eyebrow at Zack. "On the other hand, I think you escaping as it went down was convenient."

"No arguments here." Zack smiled. "It got us out of the line of fire, the real one, and the one from the house-cleaning."

"Flora did mention you were a smart ass. I hope your mouth doesn't promise stuff your team can't deliver."

"Try us. Now, do we keep shooting the shit out here like a bunch of useless twits, or is there a place we can dump our gear before we get our bearings?"

Harad barked a laugh. "Funny guy aren't you? Come on then, Jack Lorenzo."

He turned towards one of the squat structures and motioned with his hand. "Follow me."

Decker fell into step beside him. "What's the job?"

"Close protection."

"Really?" The Marine laughed. "You're going to use a rare Special Assignments team as plasma catchers?"

"This *is* a special assignment."

"Touché. Besides, it doesn't look like the training battalion will need us for a while. Who are we protecting?"

"I'll let you know once I've had a chance to see you in action, and if the people you'd be protecting accept your team. Mind you, it might help that one of your troopers is a woman."

"I'm guessing that if I ask why it might help," Decker said, "you're going to tell me it's none of my business."

"Smart guy." Harad glanced up at him, dark eyes shiny in his wizened face. "You're already a lot better than the previous candidates Flora's tried out."

Close in, the stone building appeared even more oppressive. Harad snorted when he noticed Decker's critical examination of the polished stone.

"If you're worried that it'll come down on your head, don't. This place has been here since before our species built its first lean-to. I reckon it'll be here long after humanity goes down into its version of the long night of barbarism, which is what happened to the original owners."

"And their descendants came back as the Shrehari. I hope our species doesn't become as ugly and ornery as the boneheads while they're trying to figure out the basics of technology all over again," Zack made a face. "It just seems better preserved than the other L'Taung sites I've seen."

"We found it this way. Mind you, we found nothing but stone. If they left anything else behind when they vanished, it didn't survive. But don't worry. We have the place wired, windowed and about as comfortable as you can get on Asgard."

He pushed the plastic door aside and led them into a brightly lit corridor where sheathed conduits ran along the ceiling, and glow globes hung at regular intervals.

"Barracks for the security detail. You'll have your own room, but eat, drink and relax with the rest of the troops. The other buildings are out of bounds for now, but feel free to wander around the remainder of the place. Flora did tell you that I'm your CO, right?"

"Sure and she said the rest of the Frontier Solutions troops aren't in my chain of command."

"Exactly. If the company commander wants to order you around, tell him I own your ass directly." Harad led them up a broad, winding stone staircase. "If I keep you for the close protection job, you'll probably move out of here, so don't get too comfortable."

They emerged on a second-floor landing and entered a corridor identical to the one below. The Star Wolf stopped at a door near the stairs and gestured towards it.

"Your team bay. Unlike a lot of places on Asgard, this one doesn't come with hot and cold running critters." He then pointed towards the end of the corridor. "Facilities are down there. Door's marked. Mess, bar and rec room are on the ground floor to the left of the stairs. We'll start you off tomorrow."

Then, without so much as a goodbye, he trudged down the stairs and vanished.

*

"Close protection, eh?" Tarra glanced around the room with a disgusted look on his face. The furnishings were basic: bunks, lockers, a table, and some chairs. A single broad window allowed natural daylight to brighten the otherwise dull space. At least they had a beautiful ocean view. "That's more of a job for Alex's mob, not finely honed Marines."

"Don't knock it, Hal." Decker selected one of the beds and dumped his pack on the floor before stripping off his armor. "At least until we know whose ass we're supposed to keep safe from stray plasma rounds. We might find the assignment suits our purposes."

Tarra turned back to look at his friend. "Point taken." He looked up at the ceiling. "Do you want me to...?"

"Sure. Go ahead, though I figure we can take advantage of the ocean air when we feel like shooting the breeze." Decker gave the others a significant look until they signaled their understanding. "For now, I'd suggest a stroll around the castle to get our bearings."

"And slake our thirst." Tiny rubbed his hands together. "A Confederacy hang-out must have better booze than Midgard base."

"If they're sticking to the theme, you might be disappointed," Langton said. "In the Valhalla of myth, they drank mead and nothing else."

"What the hell is mead?"

"Fermented honey."

Tiktin grimaced. "You mean from bees?"

"Yep."

Decker clapped the Celestan on the shoulder. "There's nothing like booze fermented from insect puke to make you appreciate the finer things in life."

On their way out, Decker poked his head into the rec room. He snorted when he saw the men relaxing by one of the windows.

"I can understand why our new best friend Lars isn't happy with what he's been sent before we showed up. Our two favorite embarrassments to the Commonwealth Marine Corps are here. I'll bet Flora saw their service record and figured they might make good plasma catchers."

"Parker and Barrow?" Steiger asked. She squeezed by Zack and took a look. "Yep. In the flesh and no better looking."

Tarra gave Zack a quizzical look. "Who are they?"

"Guys on our draft of recruits," Langton said. "They didn't meet Jack's standards. Didn't meet mine either, and as you jarheads are fond of saying, the Army's standards are lower than a snake's belly in a pothole."

"That bad, eh? The buggers probably ended up in the private sector because the Corps didn't renew their enlistment contract."

They stepped out of the barracks and into the damp sea air. Decker took a deep breath and looked around.

"Impressive. I'm not convinced it would last forever under the pounding of some Fleet artillery, but if it's lasted a hundred thousand years by the seaside, it can probably take a lot of damage before showing cracks."

"A five-megaton warhead launched from orbit would do the job," Tarra replied. "And vaporize the peninsula we're standing on at the same time. I wonder why they built this place here. There's nothing but jungle between it and the mainland."

Decker shrugged. "The area probably looked a lot different back then. The seaside might have been kilometers away and the bay a nice lake beside which any bonehead would want to build a little cottage."

He started walking towards a staircase leading to the top of the towering ramparts. Here and there, the silhouettes of sentries cut dark shapes against the pearly gray sky.

"I wonder what they're afraid of that a decent sensor net can't handle," Langton remarked.

"Sentry duty keeps the troops busy, I suppose," Decker replied. "Besides, a sensor net can be spoofed. A set of eyes connected to a sharp brain generally can't. I snuck into many places that wanted to keep me out by turning their electronics into broken toys."

"It still doesn't tell me what they're afraid of."

"Until we know more, I'd suggest we go with the assumption that the Jackals have some good reasons," Tarra said. "Considering they're mostly business people, wasting money isn't one of their failings."

Decker snorted. "Business people. I guess that's one way to see a gang used to skirting the edge of the law and climbing into bed with unsavory folks."

"You also climb in bed with unsavory people," Tarra pointed out.

"Hey!" Steiger punched his arm. "I'm very savory."

"Especially after three days without a shower."

The top of the rampart was broad enough for a combat skimmer and for the first time, they noticed the walls had a distinct slope. Waves crashed against the base on the outer side, sending up clouds of spume that almost reached them.

"I can't believe that anything would last that long against the action of the water," Langton commented. "Your notion that the ocean must have advanced in more recent times seems apt."

They walked along the edge, headed towards the next corner, also occupied by a squat tower. Like the rest, its openings had been filled with clear panes, polarized to allow those inside to see out while preventing those outside from seeing in.

Langton was the first to point out that each of the rectangular keeps had a dome on its roof, similar to the one Decker and Tarra had destroyed in Moria.

"It seems well protected for a gangster hideout," he said.

Tarra stopped and examined the domes, looking from rooftop to rooftop. "I make out two air defense modules. The other two are probably communications arrays. One could be a subspace transmitter, although, without a relay in orbit, it wouldn't do much good."

"Without a full-scale amplifier near the outer edge of this star system, it wouldn't do much good," Langton added. "And those are usually beyond private means."

"Why do I have the feeling that this place might be the Confederacy's actual headquarters," Decker asked, "and not an outpost? Considering the investment they've made here and on Naraka, and considering that they've set up their own private army under the guise of a mercenary corporation, it's almost as if they're trying to establish the foundations of a sovereign state."

"The Shrehari would yell bloody murder if they found out humans planned to take over a system or two in the Protectorate. It would start a race that could lead to all-out war," Tarra said. "I doubt the Jackals are naive enough to believe they could keep their activities hidden for long."

"Perhaps," Decker shrugged, "though it's not really our business. We're here for a job, and once we're done, I plan on kissing Asgard goodbye."

The Marine sounded unconcerned, but he felt far from sanguine at the evidence piling up. What if, he wondered, the Coalition planned to use the Howlers to create an interstellar crisis? He felt a pang of longing for Hera, who would be in her element picking doom and gloom scenarios apart.

"Are you okay?" Steiger asked him. "You had that thousand parsec stare for a moment."

"Yeah, I'm all right." He gave her a quick smile. "I'm just wondering what the Jackals are up to. I reckon it's time to see if they actually have something good in the cooler or if you borderline alcoholics are stuck with mead until the mission's over."

Then, he felt something touch his mind, something soft, almost imperceptible, like the brush of a butterfly's wing, and it took all of his willpower to keep from reacting. He turned away from the nearby tower and headed back towards the stairs. The touch didn't return, but he knew what it meant. Somewhere within this fort, a Sister of the Void had her eyes on him.

The nominal roll Elyce Sakal had transmitted before her kidnapping didn't specify whether Sister Anca belonged to the Order of the Void. Yet he was willing to bet she not only did but also stood behind one of the polarized windows at his back, curious about the newcomers.

None of his companions seemed the slightest bit distressed, but that didn't mean he was the only recipient of the Sister's attention. After all, he was one of the few males who could actually sense them probing, and as he had discovered on Garonne, he could not only make them see images in his mind but also block them out entirely, something that had terrified the Sister who first triggered the ability in him.

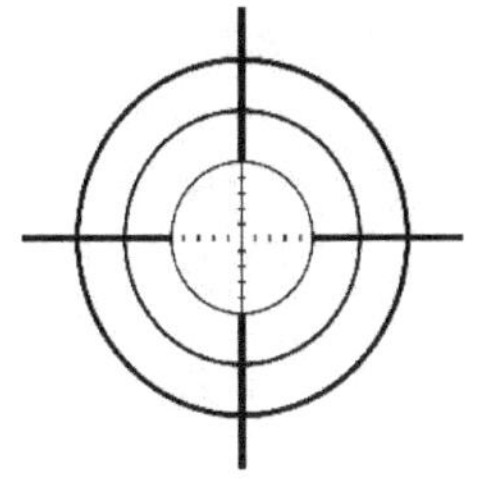

— THIRTY-TWO —

"Are those the next iteration of this close protection team you wish to foist on us, Lars?" The lean-faced woman wearing black robes asked, gesturing towards the window.

"Flora Barzee tells me these are the best that have come through so far," the Star Wolf replied. "Four of the five are veterans of the Commonwealth Fleet, one of them a woman, which should please you."

"A woman of war? Why should that please me?" Her tone held a hint of mockery. "I am devoted to peace, as you well know. The Void prides itself on eschewing violence."

"Perhaps you can convert her to your mysticism and develop a more useful creature — a mind warrior that can also defend herself and not need close protection."

"Take care." The Sister lifted an eyebrow. "You're coming dangerously close to heresy."

"Pardon me if I don't believe in your mumbo-jumbo, Sister." The Star Wolf's expression seemed anything but contrite. "I'm just a simple man, tasked to ensure Valhalla and by extension Asgard, function as desired by my superiors. Part of that is providing for your security since they believe you and Doctor Sakal can contribute something of great value to the Confederacy's future."

"We most assuredly will." She bestowed a chilly smile on him. "I can sense your skepticism fight with fear that I might actually be able to touch your innermost being."

Harad snorted. "Sure."

"And now you're actually wondering."

He shook his head. "Enough, Sister. I wanted to tell you about the new team, and I have done so. Tomorrow, I will test their abilities. If they pass, you'll have your chance to exercise whatever witchcraft you like on them."

"I already have. They're violent creatures, the woman as much as the men." She tapped her chin with an extended index finger. "Although one of them felt more complicated. I shall look forward to coming in closer contact."

"After I evaluate them. If they stink as much as the last lot, they're going straight back to Midgard."

"Fair enough. If there's nothing else, you may leave."

Harad inclined his head in an abbreviated bow. "Enjoy the rest of your day, Sister."

*

Hal Tarra studied Zack through half-closed eyes while taking an occasional sip. The others were chatting quietly at a nearby table, sensing that the two Marines needed to be alone for a while.

Parker and Barrow had left the rec room the moment Decker appeared as if afraid he would take them to task for one reason or another. None of the remaining off-duty mercenaries had paid them any attention after an initial once over.

"Spit it out, Zack," Tarra finally said in a voice pitched low enough so only Decker could hear. "Something spooked you when we were outside. Neither your girlfriend nor Langton noticed, but I've known you for too long. You were in a heck of a hurry to get away from that tower."

"You're forgetting Tiny," Decker growled back, eyes focused on his coffee. "And Miko's not my girlfriend. My girlfriend, if you can call her that, is a lot of parsecs away, no doubt kicking ass and taking names, which is what we need to be doing here."

"Avoiding the question won't get you off the hook." Tarra took another sip.

Decker grunted but raised his eyes to meet Tarra's. "You know how I've always hated the Sisters of the Void?"

"Sure. You can't stand being near them. I remember that time on..."

"Never mind the trip down memory lane. You know those stories about the Sisters being able to touch minds, not actually read them, but feel them enough to sense emotions?"

"Sure. Mystical hogwash." Tarra shrugged. "They're just another bunch of religious nuts pretending to have some sort of superpower from God."

"No hogwash. I can feel them do it to me. Apparently, it's a very rare talent among males of our species. On Garonne, I had to deal with the Sisters and one of them pissed me off enough that it triggered something. Whatever it was, it suddenly made me able to project images at them and even block them from touching me. It's real, Hal. Take my word for it."

"So what does this have to do with whatever's eating you? Garonne is dozens of parsecs away." Tarra might still have sounded skeptical, but his eyes shone with curiosity.

"There's one of them here. When we were out on the rampart, I felt her touch my mind, very fleetingly to be sure and very delicately, almost as if it didn't happen. Thankfully, I didn't shut her out, because that would have been dangerous for us, but it means the rest of you have been touched as well. She must have been in the tower in front of us. From what I know, and it isn't much, their talent requires a direct line of sight with the victim, and it loses clarity over distance, which is why it felt so faint."

"Okay, let's assume this is for real, what's our angle? I mean other than an empath finding out that we don't hold a lot of love for our employers, and don't intend to stick around for long?"

"Are you being dense on purpose, Hal? Sister Anca. The Troy Station nominal roll didn't specify what order she belonged to, but it could just as well have been the Sisters of the Void. And if she's here, I figure there's a good chance Sakal is as well."

"Excellent. We bust into the place, find them, hijack a skimmer, and make tracks for Midgard, where we do another stowaway operation, fighting off the better part of a battalion as well as a bunch of Jackals." Tarra smirked at his friend. "Extra points if we can sabotage all three air defense domes — the two here and the one in Midgard."

"Now you're just acting like an asshole." Decker drained his cup and used it to point at the dispenser. "It's your round. While you fetch it, try to think, Command Sergeant."

"Yes, sir, Major, sir." Tarra stood and tossed off a mock salute.

When he returned with the drinks, his grim expression had morphed into a thoughtful one.

"What happens if this Sister, whether it's Anca or not, finds out you're immune to their mind meddling?"

"I don't know." Decker wrapped a hand around the coffee mug. "I really don't know, but the idea that a Sister with empathic abilities is working with or for the Jackals won't do much to help me sleep better."

"Maybe you're getting ahead of yourself. Could be she's a prisoner, like Doctor Sakal."

"You'd think that after six years, she would have managed to manipulate them into letting her go if she was being held against her will."

Tarra made a dismissive gesture. "We don't know anything about what happened after the scum buggered off with their captives, and all you have here is the notion that an empath shoved her ghostly fingers into your thick skull. What we need to figure out are the next steps in the real world, not Void mumbo-jumbo. Like how we'll impress Harad tomorrow with our finely honed soldier skills so we can become insiders via the plasma catcher detail."

"That won't be a problem. You and I have loads of experience doing close-in jobs, Langton's ex-military police, which means he probably benefited from formal training and I know Miko can handle herself. She's been around the block a few times. Tiny's the fifth wheel, but he'll do what I tell him and if that means standing still to block enemy fire, so be it." He lowered his eyes to stare into the black liquid. "You know, we never did find out why the Fleet set up a research station in a dead system, one they disavowed pretty quickly, a research station that might have had a Sister of the Void on staff. Considering that we don't have a clue about Sakal's specialty..."

"So? I seem to remember a troop leader who once told me that you need to take some things a day at a time. This is one of them. Don't let your brain twist itself into knots, not tonight."

"And tomorrow? What if this Sister 'sees' what we're up to?"

"If it's Anca, she helps us break her and Sakal out. It'll be as easy as slitting a pirate's throat."

"What if the pirate, in this instance the Jackals, slit our throats?"

Tarra stared at him, nonplussed. "That mind touching incident really spooked you, didn't it? Where's the Zack Decker who'll gleefully fight his way through an entire pirate ship armed only with a blaster and his dagger?"

"He's become a thoroughly paranoid spook. My new line of work will do that to an honest Marine. There's too much strange stuff going on with the Confederacy, Hal. This is no longer just organized crime getting better organized. Besides, having someone touch your mind, feeling their fingertips caress your feelings is about as screwy as it gets. Consider yourself lucky you don't have my talent."

*

Lars Harad switched off the simulator and waited for Decker to wind things up with yet another team recap. This had been the sixth scenario since early that morning, and while none of them had ended in a happily ever after for everyone concerned, they had managed to protect their simulated VIP in all cases except one.

Decker slung his carbine and pulled off his helmet. "Nice try, Lars," he said. "After that no-win you threw at us earlier, I have your measure. We aced this one. The SecGen's guards couldn't have done better."

Harad inclined his head, a grudging smile further creasing his already seamed face. "Not bad. The last bunch we tried got their underwear in a twist when I threw a nasty one at them and never recovered. They just became worse with each scenario. Your lot improved every time. I'm not impressed often, but you came the closest to doing so. I know that Langton's ex-police, but I didn't know the Corps gave that kind of training."

"The Corps does a lot of things they don't publicize." Decker glanced over his shoulder and saw his team had fallen in line, helmets tucked under their left arms. The late afternoon sun bathed the fortress' vast inner courtyard with an orange glow that sparkled on the smooth stone. He fought the temptation to look up at the tower where he thought a Sister of the Void lurked, happy that he hadn't felt another mental intrusion. "What's next?"

"A shower, a meal and a glass, and not necessarily in that order," Harad replied. "The fun and games are over. I'm satisfied. Tomorrow you meet the folks you'll be guarding. They have the final say on whether or not you'll get the assignment."

"What if they don't like us?"

"Then it's back to Midgard, no hard feelings. You'd be wasted as garrison troopers here." He scratched the side of his face, squinting at the nearest building. "But I think you'll be acceptable. We're running out of time, and there's no guarantee another group with the right skill set is going to come through."

"Running out of time? May I ask for what?"

"No." Harad shook his head. "Not yet. You'll be told what you need to know when you need to know it."

"That sounds ominous." Decker cocked a quizzical eyebrow at the Star Wolf.

"It'll be all in a day's work for a bunch of warriors like you, have no fear. If you weren't looking for action, you wouldn't have signed up with us, right?"

"Right."

"You're dismissed. I'll find you after breakfast tomorrow." Harad spun around without waiting for a reply and trudged off.

Decker watched the Star Wolf until the gaping maw of a darkened doorway swallowed him. His eyes quickly scanned the polarized upper windows before he turned to face his team. "Well done, folks. Now we wait to see what happens next."

And who we're going to face, he thought.

Just then, he felt a ghostly touch brush his mind again, a contact with no substance but still filled with a galaxy's worth of menace and he barely repressed a shiver.

Something must have shown on Decker's face because Tarra's eyes held a wealth of questions, if not obvious concern.

*

"She did it again," Decker whispered to his friend while they stripped down. "The same as before, a very subtle touch, much more subtle than any other I've felt."

"Is there a problem?" Langton asked from across the room.

The two Marines glanced at each other, then Tarra shook his head. "No problem. The nasty bugger was just razzing me on my performance."

"Why?" Tiny, busy taking off his leggings, looked up. "I thought you kicked ass."

"Because he's a prick and can't stand anyone showing him up."

"Alright, children." Zack held up his hand. "Let's not become too rambunctious. Food and libations are waiting downstairs — after everyone takes a nice, hot shower. I don't hang out with unhygienic pigs."

"Want to play hide the soap?" Steiger gave him her best leer.

"And scandalize the entire contingent? Sure, why not." He grinned at his teammates, giving Tiny, whose eyes had lit up at the idea, a conspiratorial wink.

"You're a bad example for the lad," Tarra said. "Try to behave like a proper team leader." He dropped the last of his clothes to the floor, then, with a towel over his shoulder, he padded off towards the showers. "And by all that's holy, don't do it in front of me."

Steiger and Decker looked at each and shrugged.

"There's no appreciation for live acts anymore," he said. "That's what android porn gets you."

Later, down in the mess hall, where they had commandeered a table well away from anyone else, Decker motioned his team to lean in and told them what he had told Tarra the day before, concerning the Sisters of the Void and their ability to touch minds.

"Whoever the Sister is, she reached out right after Harad walked away, which means she was watching us at play. You might not have felt it, but I did, and if she entered my thoughts, she'll have done the same to all of you."

"I don't know what to make of this," Langton said, sounding doubtful. "Like every religious group, the Sisters of the Void have some beliefs that seem outlandish to ordinary humans, but empaths verging on telepaths? It's a bit hard to swallow. Why share this with us now?"

Why indeed, Decker thought. But he had followed his instinct so far, and might as well continue.

"Because I think there's a chance it might be Sister Anca, who vanished along with Doctors Sakal and Mazkow. We've already found Mazkow and Hal's seen Sakal, both under Confederacy control. It makes sense Anca would be as well. I haven't heard of any contemplative order spreading beyond the Rim, let alone associating voluntarily with semi-criminal organizations.”

“Their male counterparts, the Mendicant Priests of the Void, have no problems moving about the Protectorate and ministering to the wretched refuse of the galaxy,” Langton said.

“Sure, but they’re not a contemplative order. They’re missionaries. All the two share is a common belief in serving the Reformed Church of the Everlasting Universe.”

“Praise to the Void,” Steiger said in a dry tone.

“You’re not a religious type, are you?” Langton glanced at her with amusement dancing in his eyes.

“I’ve seen enough crap to make me believe life is random and not under the influence of a higher power. Considering the billions that died during both Migration Wars, there certainly isn’t a deity watching over humans.”

“Can we return to the subject at hand?” Decker asked.

“I didn’t know that we’d left it. We were discussing mystics and mysticism,” Langton replied.

“And I’d like to discuss practicalities.” When the former military policeman yielded with a nod, he continued. “I wouldn’t be surprised if the Sister’s interest in us is related to the job we’re expected to take on.”

Steiger snorted. “Close protection for a mystic? Sounds crazy.”

“What if the Jackals intend to use her for reasons of their own? Think about the ways an empath could help the Confederacy in their dealings. Wouldn’t protecting such an asset warrant some serious muscle?”

“I suppose.”

“And now we come to the reason why I’m discussing the matter.” He looked at each of them in turn. “You may or may not believe in the Sisters’ abilities, but they’re real. If you trusted me enough to follow me here, then trust me on this. The thing is, we’re going to spend time near an empath, and she’s going to get some seriously precise readings of your emotions. It's not telepathy. She can't read your thoughts, but she'll be able to figure out the general gist of what you're thinking. Remember why we're here. It's not to serve the Confederacy. If that's indeed Anca, one of the three kidnapped under Hal and my eyes six years ago, *she* might be serving the Confederacy, like Mazkow and won't be our friend. You get my meaning?"

"We'll have to be in control of our emotions and our thoughts whenever she can see us," Tiny replied. "Got it."

"What if your Doctor Sakal is here as well and working for the Confederacy?" Langton asked. "Have you considered the possibility that this will turn out to be a fool's errand? After all, Mazkow didn't want you to take him home."

"Then we find out what the Jackals are doing in the Protectorate and vanish at the next opportunity. Some people will pay good money for that kind of intelligence. Or at least Hal and I will disappear. We're not mercs at heart. If you want to continue with Frontier Solutions, we'll try to arrange matters so that our defection doesn't create too much of a problem."

Steiger grimaced. "At this point, I figure I'm better off sticking with you, even if the thought of facing a mind-meddling nun gives me the willies."

"Ditto," Langton said. "And I second Miko's sentiment."

Tiny's head bobbed up and down. "I guess that means me too."

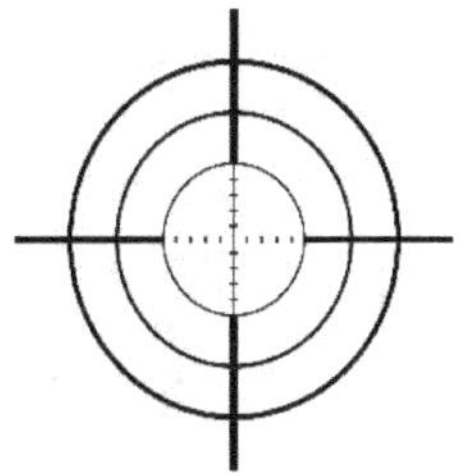

— THIRTY-THREE —

The team was enjoying a quiet breakfast the next morning when Lars Harad came into the chow hall and made a beeline for Zack.

"I see you're not scowling," the latter said after swallowing one last bite of bread. "May I infer that we've been accepted by the folks requiring close protection?"

Harad pulled out a chair and sat. "Not quite yet. Though I've reported that your team passes muster in all respects, they'd like to meet you first."

"They?" Decker cocked a questioning eyebrow. "How many people are we talking about?"

"Two." Harad held up his index and middle finger.

A sudden surge of hope drove away Zack's lingering fears. Sakal and Anca? Would fate really be that generous?

"Men or women?" He asked.

"Two women. They're very valuable to the Confederacy and its allies."

"I had assumed that our charges would be valuable," Decker replied, smiling, "after the scenarios you put us through yesterday. When are we meeting them?"

"In thirty minutes, so you have time to finish your meal. You'll wear undress uniform with side arms." He jerked his chin at Decker's waist. "And you can carry your pig sticker if you want. Any questions?"

"No. We'll be on our best behavior."

"Good." Harad climbed to his feet. "I'll be waiting for you across the courtyard."

Twenty-five minutes later, Decker marched his team over to the tower from where he believed a Sister had been watching them. Their dark uniforms seemed unusually crisp for mercenaries, but the blasters riding in open hip holsters wore the patina of long use. Both Marines sported a long dagger in a black sheath to one side, its hilt stamped with the representation of pathfinder wings.

Zack spotted Harad in the shadows of a doorway cut for a taller species than humanity and called them to a halt a few meters short. After taking the time to make their tunics and trousers look like those of professional troops rather than mercenaries on a rat hole planet, he might as well go through the full soldierly routine.

He barked out, "Jack Lorenzo and four Special Assignments operators reporting as ordered."

Something like a wry smile flashed across the Star Wolf's face. "Nice. You make it look like you actually want the job."

"We have nothing better on offer right now, and I like to give a good show for prospective employers. You obtain more work and better pay that way. Yesterday, we satisfied you on technique, today we'll impress the ladies who are going to be seeing us day in, day out for however long this job lasts."

"Works for me." Harad motioned towards the door. "Come on. Let's do this."

They stepped into a corridor that looked like a mirror image of the one in their barracks and climbed up an identical stone staircase. The lack of decoration appeared to be a common theme and not just an oversight in the tower set aside for the security detail.

On the second level, Harad led them to a doorway marked 'private quarters.' He knocked and a muffled voice told them to enter. The Star Wolf pushed the panel aside to reveal a tastefully appointed chamber that made the utilitarian team room look positively drab.

Two women rose from form-fitting chairs and turned to face them. One, with hard, dark eyes and short gray hair above the narrow face of an ascetic, wore unrelieved black while the other, equally slender and of indeterminate age sported more colorful, yet still somewhat severe business clothing.

Both examined them with emotionless expressions. It took all of Zack's self-control to maintain an impassive facade at the sight of the woman they couldn't save all those years ago, and he hoped Hal would be able to keep his own reactions in check.

Harad bowed his head in a polite greeting and said, "Doctor Sakal, Sister Anca, this is Jack Lorenzo and his team. I'm convinced you'll find them entirely satisfactory. They're the only ones who've been able to meet the highest standards. I daresay they'll be able to protect you with the kind of skill and zeal we all wish to see."

Soft fingers caressed his mind and his eyes involuntarily turned to Anca for a fraction of a second. The fingers vanished, and a look of curiosity softened the Sister's penetrating gaze. The caress returned, but this time, Decker kept his attention on Sakal.

She seemed to have aged more than the half dozen years that had passed since her abduction. Time had etched deep lines into her face and sprinkled her long dark hair liberally with silver strands.

Sakal showed no recognition at the sight of the two Marines, though Decker's disguise could easily throw someone who had last seen him over a communications link for a few hours a long time ago. Hal still looked like Hal, but Decker and the captain of *Ruddigore,* his ship at the time, had done most of the talking.

Sakal inclined her head. "Mister Lorenzo. Welcome. Might I inquire as to the names of your people?"

Zack snapped to attention. "Of course." He introduced each turn and saw a brief flicker of recognition when he named Hal Tarra. She might not remember when or where yet, but he seemed familiar.

Her eyes rested on Hal for a long time before she asked, "Have we met before, Mister Tarra?"

Remembering Zack's last minute warning to hold back until they knew the lay of the land, he replied, "Not that I'm aware of, ma'am."

"And yet there's something familiar about you."

Anca cackled, a derisive sound that raised the hairs on Decker's nape.

"You're familiar to him, Elyce," she said.

Sakal gave the Sister a dirty look. "We've discussed this. Please don't."

"I'm merely observing his body language and facial expression, my dear. Have no fear." Anca's eyes rested briefly on each of the others, and she cackled again. "The remainder has never seen you before, but Mister Lorenzo — he's almost impossible to read. Interesting."

Mental fingers crept back into Zack's consciousness, and he understood that Anca was violating some kind of agreement with Sakal when it came to invading the privacy of others. Without quite thinking it through, he formed the image of himself and Anca engaged in intense sexual congress, substituting his memory of Hera Talyn's naked body for the Sister's clothed one.

Anca eyes widened for a fleeting moment, and she abruptly broke contact. He could tell she wanted to speak, but doing so would expose her disobedience to Sakal's strictures. Decker immediately cursed himself for giving her a hint that he might be one of the few able to sense a Sister's touch.

Then he noticed Sakal examining him, a slight frown creasing her high forehead. "You vaguely remind me of someone, Mister Lorenzo."

"I have that effect on many people," he replied with a self-deprecating grin. "It's probably because of my ugly mug that looks like a lot of other ugly mugs."

"Perhaps." She tilted her head to one side, eyes going from Decker to Tarra and back again. "You and your team seem very confident."

"That's because we're better than most."

Sakal glanced sideways at Anca. "Any comments, Sister?"

"I have plenty, but none that should be uttered at this time or in this place. I see no falsehood in these five. Oh, they're all hiding something, like every human being since the first moment of creation, save for innocents and those without enough wit to dissemble. All except the youngster, the one called Tiktin. Whether that stems from innocence or witlessness, I cannot tell, nor do I care. But if you're asking whether we should accept Lars Harad's offer of this team for our personal protection, then with some reservations, I will say yes but provisionally, to be sure."

"What reservations?"

Anca turned a cold smile on Decker. "The ones I have about Mister Lorenzo himself. Not because I see evil, but because he strikes me as having depths that might contain motivations at odds with our enterprise." That unnerving laugh sounded again. "Curious about what I mean by enterprise, Mister Lorenzo? Your self-control is admirable, but you still give off unconscious signals."

Sakal shook her head with an air of resignation.

"If you accept the task," she said addressing the team, "you'll have to put up with Sister Anca's idiosyncrasies, though once she's discovered all she needs to know about you, things will quiet down."

"Since we have nothing better on offer, we accept," Decker said with a half shrug. "I imagine you're safe enough in Valhalla, meaning you need us because you'll be leaving this place. How soon will that occur?"

"At the appointed time," Harad said. "I will let you know in due course. Meanwhile, you're to fetch the remainder of your gear. As of now, your quarters will be next door to your charges, and you will begin your duties, even if Valhalla is the safest spot on Asgard." He pulled a tablet from his pocket and handed it to Zack. "Here are your standing orders."

"If these orders don't give me — us — the leeway to adapt according to circumstances, I'll retract my agreement."

"You'll have all the freedom you need to do the job. Don't mistake me for a martinet." Harad turned to Sakal. "If you've no other questions for your protection team, Doctor, may I suggest you dismiss them to their duties?"

"By all means." She inclined her head, but her eyes rested on Zack for a moment, then on Hal and an almost imperceptible frown marred the smoothness of her forehead again. "If you'll stay a moment, Mister Harad, we need to discuss some administrative matters."

"Of course."

*

Once back in their soon to be former barracks, Langton said to Decker, "Why do I have the feeling that you and Hal are like the dog who's been chasing a skimmer and finally caught it? Neither of you seems to know what to do next."

"Because you're a suspicious-minded meathead," Tarra replied.

"We don't know what the circumstances are yet," Decker interjected, to stop any argument before it started. "It's still likely that Doctor Sakal and Sister Anca are captives of the Confederacy, or at least forced to collaborate with them. And whatever that collaboration might be, we need to find out. Anca's good at the mind-meddling stuff, better than others I've had the misfortune of meeting, and she neither speaks, acts nor dresses like a proper member of the Sisterhood. There's more going on here than we might think."

"I'm not so sure," Steiger said. "While you were busy having a staring contest with Anca, I watched our pal, Lars. He's clearly deferential to the Doctor — not something one might expect from a jailer. And he's not overly fond of Anca. Wary would be a better word. Again, not a typical reaction for a jailer."

"Perhaps it's a gilded cage," Decker shrugged. "They have something of value to the Jackals and Harad has standing orders to treat them like royalty, even if they're prisoners."

"You seem bound and determined to see Doctor Sakal as a victim, but whatever." She tossed the last piece of armor into her duffel bag and closed it. "Take care you don't place too much trust in her."

"Woman's intuition?"

She scoffed. "Finely tuned bullshit detectors, my ass. Seeing Sakal up close, healthy, and not suffering from ill treatment is blinding you. It's something you didn't anticipate. You figured to find her in chains, locked in a cell, and mistreated, waiting for her savior to appear." When he started to protest, Steiger held up her hand. "You're the last of the romantics, even if you won't admit it to yourself."

Decker made a face at her and grunted, but then he relented. "On second thought, you may have a point. My idea of what we'd find didn't include this scenario. On the other hand, I suspect that we'll be leaving Asgard soon, and that may actually give us better opportunities than if we'd had to bust her out of a dungeon."

"Do you intend to remind her of our last encounter at some point?" Tarra asked. "And if so, did you consider that she might not want to go home, that she's quite happy doing whatever she's doing?"

"I don't know." Zack shook his head. "I truly don't know. The only certainty I have is that I need to tell some folks about what the Confederacy is doing in these parts. There's a bigger picture giving me sleepless nights, and that's even more important than bringing Doctor Sakal home."

"One might almost think you're still working for the Fleet," Langton remarked.

"I could say the same about you," Decker replied without missing a beat.

"Point taken. Some habits remain ingrained despite having hung up the uniform."

*

"Would you care to discuss it with me?" Anca asked once the Star Wolf had left them. "You've apparently seen Tarra and Lorenzo before or men who resemble them. Although, judging by Tarra's reactions, he and you aren't exactly total strangers."

Sakal, facing away from the Sister as she prepared a cup of tea, shook her head. "I don't care to discuss anything right now."

"Why?"

"Because our new protection team or at least the two leading members seem to have triggered some memories I'd rather not resurrect."

"Troy Station," The Sister smiled knowingly, "that fateful day when our lives changed forever. And why would Tarra and Lorenzo have evoked them, I wonder?"

"Because," Sakal said, glancing over her shoulder at Anca, "they remind me of the men I spoke with over the communications link while our attackers were trying to break in, the ones aboard *Ruddigore*."

"Ah, yes, the knights in shining armor with a lousy sense of timing. A few hours later and no one would have known of the events on Troy. What were the names?"

"Decker. Command Sergeant Zack Decker. I remember a Lieutenant Commander Griego as well, the captain of that ship. And a Sergeant Tarra."

"The same Tarra we just had standing in our quarters." Anca's intonation made it a statement, not a question.

"I think so."

"Strange that he'd turn up here after so long, isn't it? Coincidence? Act of God?" Anca walked over to a window and watched the protection team emerge from their former barracks, carrying bulging packs. "Pity I can't push myself to that next level and sift through his memories. I wonder what I might find. The reasons for his almost miraculous reappearance, perhaps?"

Sakal mentally shuddered at the thought of Anca achieving full telepathic powers.

"Pity indeed," she murmured, staring at Anca's back through narrowed eyes.

The Sister turned back to her companion. "Did you know that Lorenzo had a vivid sexual thought about me?"

"What? How?"

"I touched his mind — yes I know, breaking my promise to stay away from the hired help again. At one point, I felt an intense physical desire directed at me, almost as if he sensed my presence and wanted me to leave. It worked, whether the projection was intentional or not. I shall be more careful with Mister Lorenzo from now on."

"Please try to do so. We might rely on him and his team to save our lives in the not too distant future. It wouldn't help matters if you annoyed them."

"Have no fear, my dear. None of the others showed as much as a flicker of awareness."

"Still, I have the impression that Lorenzo isn't the kind of man one trifles with, and he is clearly their leader."

Anca put on a mocking pout. "And where will I find my entertainment?"

"You'll get it soon enough if Harad is right about our impending departure."

"A pity we've not been able to foster more of my kind so far, but it seems that you've been right all along. The talent is innate, which means I'm the Confederacy's only mind spy right now unless they've managed to convince a few more Sisters into freelancing for them. Maybe one day, your detection methods might actually work on those who have the talent but aren't self-aware. It's a pity that we don't have much of a population to screen, but hopefully, that will change soon."

"Perhaps I should try it on the female in Lorenzo's team."

Anca laughed. "A wasted effort. That one is as dull as the males and not much prettier."

"I thought your talent worked only on men."

"Indeed," a sly smile came and went so quickly that Sakal barely noticed. "That hasn't changed, no matter how hard I've tried to overcome the barrier, with your help of course. But Steiger isn't hard to read for someone who's made a proper study of the human psyche. Keep in mind that we Sisters of the Void don't just train our empathic abilities — we also explore other ways of interpreting a person's thoughts and emotions."

"And how to manipulate them."

"The talent wouldn't be of much use otherwise, now would it, Elyce?"

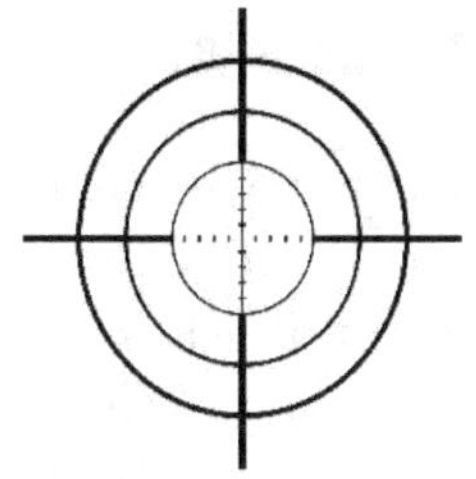

— THIRTY-FOUR —

Two nights later, Zack stood alone on the ramparts, just outside the tower they now called home, staring out at a sea dappled with the reflection of stars. The fresh, salty air felt cleansing after settling into a routine that allowed them to do their jobs while staying out of Sakal's and Anca's way. Preferably out of Anca's sight.

The apostate sister, as he now thought of her because she had become an empathic talent no longer constrained by the strictures of monastic life, hadn't tried to touch his mind again.

He wasn't so sanguine about his companions' mental privacy, however. The routine of patrolling their surroundings, standing guard outside the apartments and monitoring the surveillance devices the Confederacy had put at their disposal, had left him with plenty of time to think about his predicament, but no chance to discuss it with anyone.

Though Tarra had scanned their new quarters for listening devices, he didn't want to risk letting even a single compromising word slip where someone could overhear it. Having a Sister of the Void within arm's reach was bad enough.

He sensed someone coming up the steps behind him and turned in a controlled, fluid movement.

"Good evening, Mister Lorenzo." Elyce Sakal offered Zack a quick smile. It seemed restrained but felt genuine.

"Doctor." He inclined his head instead of a formal salute.

"I always enjoy coming up here for a while before bed. There's something about standing on stones laid long ago by an alien species and staring out at an ocean speckled with the reflection of unknown constellations."

"Agreed. It does have something almost awe-inspiring. Heck, it almost gives you hope that humanity will survive for ages, notwithstanding the civilization-ending stupidities we're prone to commit. If the Shrehari can rebuild their Empire tens of thousands of years after it fell into the long night of barbarism, we'll be able to do so as well. And though I hope it won't happen for a long time yet, some days I think the people who want to run the Commonwealth will do whatever they think is needed, even if it hastens our own downfall, so long as they enjoy a generation or two of absolute power."

"A philosopher-soldier. I'm impressed." Her soft, gentle laugh sounded delightful to his ears. "And a very cynical one as well. Life must not have been easy for you to develop such a jaundiced view of our species."

"I've met some of the worst that humanity can produce." They began walking towards the next corner. "I would have to be a saint to remain cheerful about our future."

"And you don't strike me as the saintly type." That soft laugh sounded again. "Sister Anca thinks you're quite the rogue."

"A rogue sister shouldn't throw stones while sitting in a glass house."

"What gives you the idea that Anca is a rogue sister?" She stopped and looked up into his face. "Some orders aren't monastic and allow their brethren to perform missionary service."

"The Sisterhood of the Void is monastic. They don't let any of theirs roam where ordinary people live unless it's under Chapter rule, something you already know."

"A philosopher-soldier *and* a student of religion. My, my." A mocking note had crept into her voice, in an attempt to drown out what sounded to Decker like worry. "Anca thinks you're a complex man."

"But one without complexes."

"We all need our illusions." She resumed their slow stroll along the top of the ramparts.

"And what are yours?" Zack asked.

"Why would I have illusions? I may not have lived a warrior's life, but I've seen things that'll quash any idealistic notions of peace and harmony among the various strains of humanity."

"Nice deflection, Doctor, but I believe we were talking about an apostate Sister of the Void, one who's abandoned the monastic life. That's not a common occurrence. The Mother Superiors don't like the idea of mind-meddlers stalking normals once they've been fully trained."

After a strained pause, she asked, "And once again, what makes you think Sister Anca belongs to the Void?"

"Your inability to lie convincingly, Doctor."

She stopped again.

"I have the feeling that you're after something, Mister Lorenzo. You certainly don't speak or act like any other mercenary the Confederacy has seen fit to place before me." Then his words registered. "What did you just mean by mind meddlers?"

"Please. It's a well-known fact in some circles that the Sisters of the Void are an order of empaths, a talent that doesn't officially exist. In fact, it's been rumored that the Sisterhood's sole purpose is in removing these empaths from the mainstream of humanity to avoid the chaos they might cause among normals."

He had the pleasure of seeing Sakal blanch.

"How?" She stuttered.

"I'm one of the few males sensitive enough to be aware of a Sister's touch, Doctor. I sensed Anca's fingers trying to sift through my emotions. She didn't much like the primitive sexuality I let her feel." Yet even as he spoke, Decker wondered whether he was making a mistake, lulled by the false intimacy of their private conversation.

"Ah." Sakal looked down at her feet for a few seconds, gathering her thoughts. "This explains a few things. I think I won't mention your particular sensitivity to her just yet.   She would get it in her mind to conduct experimentation that I might find distasteful.”

“And for that, you have my thanks, Doctor. A game of wills between Anca and me won’t necessarily end well — at least not for her.”

“You seem very self-confident, Mister Lorenzo.”

“A lot of people have tried to kill me, yet I’m still here, and they’re not. You do the math.”

They reached the next corner and, as if by mutual agreement, turned back.

She stopped again and put her hand on his arm. “Do I know you? Please be honest. Your friend Hal Tarra’s name echoes something from my past, as does your — not your appearance maybe, but your mannerisms, your way of speaking.”

“Would acknowledging past history be fatal?”

“If it’s shared, I don’t see how.”

“Who do you think I might be?” Decker looked down at her with expressionless eyes.

“You evoke memories of a man who did his best to reassure me while the station I was on came under attack and his ship couldn’t make in time to save us. We never met in person, of course, but spending hours talking over a communications link, while the station’s defenses fell one by one, left a mark.”

Decker had an urge to hold her in his arms, to tell her he had finally come back to finish the rescue he had failed to carry out six years earlier, but something held him back. He knew why seconds later when a silhouette in a Frontier Solutions uniform with a blaster at the hip materialized from the darkness.

“Good evening.” Langton sketched a quick salute. “I’m just doing my round of the perimeter.” Seeing the expression on Sakal’s face, he frowned for a moment. “Is everything alright?”

“The Doctor and I were merely having an idle chat, Alex,” the Marine replied. “Comparing notes about people we might have known in past lives.”

“I think I should go back in now.” Sakal pulled up her shawl as if the night air had developed a sudden chill.

"We should continue this conversation at another time, Mister Lorenzo."

Decker inclined his head. "As you wish. Have a good night."

"You as well." Then she vanished down the steps.

"Has she figured you and Tarra out yet?" Langton asked once they were alone.

"Hal, I'd say yes. Me, almost — not quite, but almost. Perhaps, like her former colleague Doctor Mazkow, or Maslow as he now prefers, she's unwilling to resurrect something she'd rather forget." The Marine shrugged. "It happens more often than you'd think."

"Speaking from personal experience?"

"We all have those experiences. You, me, the doctor, Miko. Well, perhaps not everyone. Tiny doesn't seem to have lived through any regrets, save a few hangovers and they don't count. The joys of being a simple soul, I suppose."

Both men now stood side by side, eyes on the black horizon where an alien ocean met the dark heavens.

"You're quite the philosopher, Jack. And since you're a man of many identities, I can believe that you might have a past that's better left forgotten."

"I could say the same about you."

"How's that?"

"You're not really a retired Army cop, are you? Or rather, you're an Army cop who's not actually retired." When Langton failed to answer, Decker glanced at him. "The usual reaction to a question like that is asking why a mere mercenary would ever think of something so preposterous."

Langton shrugged. "I was wondering how long it would take you to bring the matter up for discussion, one undercover guy to another."

Zack chuckled. "So you figure you have me pegged, eh? What if I told you I'm not on a mission for anyone?"

"And yet, you've openly declared that you had to report the Confederacy's doings to the Fleet. I can only assume it's to whoever you work for in the Corps."

"This is the truth, Alex, or whatever your real name is. Hal and I came out here to find Doctor Sakal. We're not on assignment for anyone but ourselves. Our self-imposed mission is to correct something we were unable to prevent six years ago."

"Active duty Marines have been known to go rogue on personal missions when their superiors refused to act. Some even ended up with a chest full of medals for having been right all along. You believe I'm active duty Army and I believe you're active duty Marines. Do we have a standoff or do we show a little bit of trust? If we're both active duty, then we're working for the same ultimate boss, the Commander in Chief of the Commonwealth Armed Services. Our respective branches have been known to collaborate on occasion."

"Then tell me why you've infiltrated the Confederacy. You already know why Hal and I have. Finding out the Jackals are building an empire beyond the Navy's reach is actually a bonus."

Langton took a deep breath and exhaled. "You may have noticed, from time to time, that the Confederacy seems to be sourcing its military materiel from the Fleet's war stocks, rather than buying used off the surplus market. I work for the Fleet's Criminal Investigation Branch. My job is to collect evidence and trace the pipeline through which our equipment ends up in Jackal hands, starting from their end."

"So there really is a quartermaster sergeant tossing skimmers, air defense domes, and crates of plasma rifles out the back of a transport pod in exchange for more money than he'd make in ten years of honorable service."

"Something of the sort." Langton's tone told Zack he had said all we would say.

"Sorry if we screwed up your mission."

"I suppose it's just another example of the various branches not speaking to each other and ending up in a crossfire."

"As I said, Hal and I are on a personal mission. It would have been pretty difficult to coordinate with the CIB, at least not without my boss putting a stop on my furlough."

"Furlough?" Langton snorted in disbelief. "You're on furlough? I heard that some of you jarheads are strange, but this beats all."

"You've never had a nightmare that keeps coming back for years at a time, have you?"

"No." The CIB agent shook his head. "I suppose I haven't."

Silence, broken only by the soft sigh of waves coming to die at the base of the ramparts, fell between them.

"What do you think will happen next?" Langton finally asked.

"I don't know, but somehow, I think it'll involve Sister Anca's mind-meddling talents, though I don't know what Doctor Sakal's part in this really is."

"You never mentioned what they and Mazkow were doing when the reivers took them."

"No, I didn't."

This time, Langton heard the unmistakable tone of a man who had said all he intended.

"I guess I'd better finish my rounds," he said, leaving Zack to his thoughts.

The Marine stared up at the sky, wishing Hera was here. She would have known how to deal with Elyce Sakal and would have put the fear of eternal damnation into the fugitive Sister of the Void.

A soft laugh escaped his lips. He missed her, the woman who had forced him into intelligence work and who had saved his ass more than once. She was the only person with whom he could be himself, not the man of a thousand faces.

Decker glanced up at the blank window of Anca's apartment. No light escaped the polarized pane, but he sensed the Sister watching him and had to forcibly suppress the urge to make an obscene gesture.

*

A week passed without another chance encounter between Decker and Sakal where none could overhear their conversation, and he began to suspect that she was deliberately keeping all of their interactions on a purely professional level.

Anca hadn't made another attempt to sift through his mind, though she watched him with keen interest every time they came face to face. Whenever a small, private smile twisted her thin lips, he wondered whether she had made him as a Naval Intelligence officer and was merely biding her time.

The evening of the ninth day since they started guarding Anca and Sakal, Harad announced they would be leaving the next morning on a shuttle belonging to a starship about to enter Asgard orbit.

"Where are we going?" Decker asked, happy that something was about to change. His furlough had ended the previous day, and he would now be listed as absent without authority. When he saw the Star Wolf's expression, he shrugged. "We'll find out in due course."

Then, he noticed Sakal's reaction at the news. Though she tried to remain impassive, he could read trepidation, if not fear in her eyes. Anca, on the other hand, seemed elated.

The next morning, an unmarked shuttle of civilian design but with visible weapon pods landed in the middle of the courtyard to the echoing rumble of high-powered thrusters.

Decker's team, wearing battle armor, backpacks, and solemn expressions, formed a defensive perimeter around their charges in the tower's lobby while the Marine approached the spacecraft. A side hatch opened, creating a short ramp and a man in a nondescript naval type uniform stepped out.

"I'm here to pick up two VIPs and their protective detail," he said without preamble.

"The name's Lorenzo and I'll need to check the inside of your shuttle."

"Be my guest." He waved Decker up the ramp.

Zack found nothing more than an ordinary passenger compartment and a standard cockpit, both clean, if somewhat worn. The pilot obviously flew solo, which wasn't unusual in places where the standard transport regulations didn't apply.

Satisfied, he stepped back out into the courtyard and waved. Tarra led the group through the doorway and across to where he and the pilot waited.

"We're good to go," he said. "I hope you all have everything you're planning on bringing." He gave Sakal and Anca a significant look. "Because we're not coming back."

Sakal nodded. Anca merely glared at him.

"In that case," he continued, "please climb aboard, ladies."

A few minutes later, the hatch slammed shut, sealing them off from Asgard for what Decker hoped would be forever. Then, the small craft began to vibrate, and they felt a giant hand push down on their shoulders as it left the ground.

Without windows, he couldn't see their swift rise through the atmosphere. Only a feeling of weightlessness told him they had reached orbit. Soon enough, gravity returned, and he knew they were aboard a starship.

The hatch opened again, revealing a cramped hangar deck and two men wearing uniforms identical to that of their pilot. Decker climbed out of the shuttle and directed his attention on the one who seemed to be in charge.

"I'm Jack Lorenzo, the head of the protection detail. I have two principals and four troops with me."

"Captain Kesin Bailey. Welcome aboard *Morgana*."

Decker swallowed a guffaw with great difficulty upon hearing the name. He had used *Phoenix*'s guns to rough up an Avalon Corporation mercenary starship by that name in Garonne orbit the previous year. It seemed unbelievable that he would now be on the same vessel.

He put his index finger and thumb to his lips and whistled. Almost immediately, Tiny and Langton came down the short ramp, carbines at the low port, followed by their charges, with Miko and Hal exiting last.

Bailey gave the two women a quick bow. "Doctor Sakal, Sister Anca, welcome aboard *Morgana*. I hope we'll be able to make your journey as comfortable as possible."

"Very kind of you," Sakal replied with a smile that didn't quite reach her eyes.

"If you'll follow me, I'll take you to your quarters." He gestured to the other man. "Please take care of Mister Lorenzo and his team."

"Sorry, Captain," Decker said. "I'll be accompanying my charges and inspecting their cabin. After all, I don't know who you are, who your crew is, and who your ship belongs to."

A flash of irritation crossed Bailey's eyes, but he inclined his head. "Of course."

Zack pointed at Alex. "You and Tiny, check the rest of the passenger deck. Miko and Hal, you're with me."

"Do you really think it's necessary?" This time, Bailey didn't bother disguising his annoyance.

"We were hired to do a job, Captain. I understand that you're sole master after God aboard *Morgana*, but I'm entirely responsible for Doctor Sakal and Sister Anca's welfare. If my methods of doing so bother you, feel free to contact my employers and state your objections while we're still in orbit. By the way, we're keeping our weapons, if your order to take care of us meant disarming."

Decker's emotionless, almost bored tone seemed to irritate Bailey further, but after a moment, he responded with a quick shake of the head. "That won't be necessary. Please follow me."

The narrow passageway confirmed his suspicions that they were aboard a sloop, though proof of its ownership remained elusive. The passenger deck seemed relatively spacious for a ship of *Morgana*'s tonnage and afforded each of them a small, but private cabin, to Decker's relief.

The saloon, while barely big enough for all seven of them, turned out to be reasonably comfortable and well equipped. They lacked space for a gym, but Decker intended to fix that as soon as possible.

"Our kind hosts seem to believe we've contracted the Halterian Plague," Langton remarked once they had settled in and broken out of orbit. "This deck is completely sealed off from the rest of the ship."

Decker shrugged. "Secrecy, more like. Bailey's probably under orders to keep his crew from knowing who they're transporting."

"Cloak and dagger stuff, eh? That should be right up your alley."

"I'll tell you what's up my alley. Finding out whether the saloon is well stocked with fruit juice and coffee."

"Figures," Langton chuckled. "Well then, you paragon of sobriety, why don't we determine if what's on offer meets your standards."

Steiger emerged from her cabin, wearing only trousers, a tee shirt, and sandals, but still carrying her holstered blaster.

"Did I hear right. Is this ship called *Morgana*?" She asked.

"Yes." Decker locked eyes with her before touching his earlobe.

"Gotcha. I guess we're all headed to the same place?"

"There's nowhere else to go," Langton said. "Who has the watch?"

"That would be me." Tarra stepped out of his cabin, making the narrow passageway feel even tighter. In contrast to the others, he hadn't stripped off his battle armor, though he had replaced his plasma carbine with one of the scatterguns Harad had issued before their departure. "Try not to drink the ship dry on the first day. I doubt we'll be doing a quick hop to the next star."

"You're just worried that they won't leave you any of the good stuff," Decker replied, "if there's some to be had in the first place."

Tarra made an obscene gesture at his friend, but the good-natured grin on his face turned it into a joke.

"Make sure Tiny's sober when he comes to relieve me," he said.

"Tiny's in his bunk right now. He knows better than to take even a whiff of booze when he has the next shift." Then, with a final wave, Decker left Tarra standing by the door to Sakal's cabin.

*

The days dragged on in a monotonous routine that began to wear on all of them. Anca and Sakal stayed aloof most of the time, and apart from the daily inspection of the passenger deck by the first officer, they had no contact with the crew. And that meant they also had no information about their destination, but it soon became apparent that it wouldn't be Kilia Station as Decker had half expected.

He had been keeping track of the time they spent traveling FTL and knew they had gone much further than the semi-legal habitat on the edge of the Commonwealth Rim.

Then, after one more jump, many hours elapsed without a further warning to secure for FTL, and he figured that they had arrived, a fact confirmed the next morning when the first officer told them they had an hour to prepare for a shuttle flight.

"Where are we?" Decker asked him as he turned to leave the passenger deck again.

"Nowhere," the man replied over his shoulder before the door slammed shut behind him, "we're in the middle of sweet fuck-all."

Decker and Tarra exchanged glances.

"I guess we're doing a ship to ship transfer," the latter said. "There goes your theory that we were staying on the Rim."

"Next stop the Home Worlds," the other Marine replied. "Yee fucking haw."

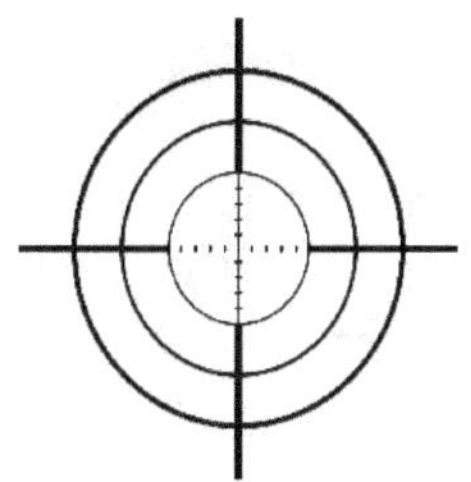

— THIRTY-FIVE —

They left *Morgana* at the appointed time, and when her shuttle approached the starship that would transport them on the next leg of their journey, Decker caught a fleeting glimpse of a name painted on the hull. His heart sank.

With a name like *Altair Nova*, it could only be a freighter of the Black Nova Line, a subsidiary of the Honorable Commonwealth Trading Corporation, ComCorp for short. His old enemies, the Amali family, one of the Coalitions most powerful backers, controlled the conglomerate.

Since the deaths of the two previous family heads were, if not directly at his hands, then through his actions, Major Zachary Thomas Decker remained high on their list of officers needing termination with extreme prejudice.

The moment their shuttle settled on the hangar deck, a red light strobed while the compartment was re-pressurized. As soon as the light stopped, an armored door slid aside, and a contingent of armed civilian spacers entered, their scatterguns held at the high port.

Zack counted ten in all before the pilot climbed out of his seat and blocked his view through the cockpit window. Then, the craft's side door opened to show the *Altair Nova* crew members lined up, firing squad style, a few meters away.

Their weapons still aimed upwards and to the side, but he sensed no welcome. Knowing they had no other choice than to play this hand to the end, Decker grabbed his pack and climbed out, followed by Tiny and Miko.

A lean, hard-faced man wearing the stripes of a merchant first officer stepped forward, his eyes on Zack.

"You're Jack Lorenzo?" He asked.

"Yes. I'm in charge of the protection detail for these ladies," Decker waved a hand over his shoulder to signify Sakal and Anca, who had emerged from the shuttle hard on Steiger's heels.

"Not anymore." The officer glanced over Decker's shoulder and then nodded slightly. He turned his head towards the hangar's inner door and made a come on gesture with his index finger.

Four men easily as large as the Marine entered and headed for the new arrivals.

"My bosun's mates will disarm you and your team, Mister Lorenzo," the first officer said, "then they will escort you to our brig. Your contract with Frontier Solutions has been terminated. If you don't cooperate, we will kill you where you stand."

Decker tried to look confused and angry, though, from the moment he'd seen the ship's name, he had a hunch that they might have reached the end of the line. No one's luck held forever. "What is the meaning of this?"

"The meaning, old chap," Alex Langton said, coming forward to stand beside the officer, "is that you're done. Your quest, infiltration, operation, whatever you wish to call it, is over. Yours too, Hal." A sad smile tugged at his lips. "Unfortunately, that means Miko and Tiny have had their run as well. Sorry about that, honey." He blew Steiger a kiss.

"You're not really a CIB investigator, are you?" Decker asked as a bosun's mate relieved him of his weapons.

"Actually, I am. But I also have another, more important employer."

"*Sécurité Spéciale.*"

Langton tapped the side of his nose with his index finger. "Got it in one. And now I'm going to find out who you really work for, Jack. Or is that really Zack, as in

Zachary Decker, well-known Fleet operative, assassin, and master of mayhem?"

The Marine shrugged. "I have no idea who you're talking about."

"I had a chat with Rika Kozlev while you were hatching your plan to destroy the Moria operation. Once I identified myself as an agent of the Confederacy's primary sponsor, she was more than happy to finger you as a serving Marine Corps chief warrant officer by that name."

"Kozlev was delusional."

"Let me verify," Anca said. "One peek inside his head, and we shall know."

As the words left her mouth, he felt Anca invade his consciousness with a savagery that stunned him for a fraction of a second. No Sister he had ever encountered would, or even could violate someone else's mind in such a manner.

Without conscious thought, he projected an image of unbelievable violence at her. He immediately heard a loud gasp. Her probing tendrils withdrew, and he slammed his mind shut.

"He's aware, he can project," she gasped. "And he shut me out!"

"Aware that you're a vicious bitch? Oh yeah, baby." Decker turned his head to leer at the Sister, whose face had turned ashen. "You thought my projection was bad? I have far worse for you if you ever try again."

"That'll be enough," the merchant officer said. "Now that you've been disarmed, you will remove your armor and place it on the deck." He turned to Sakal and Anca and then indicated the door, where a woman in merchant uniform wearing the stripes of a fifth officer waited. "Please follow her to your quarters. Your presence is no longer required here."

Anca, who had recovered her composure with admirable speed, said. "I wish to examine Lorenzo, or whatever his real name is. He's the first aware male I've come across, and I must determine whether or not the

Doctor and I can devise a way to detect those with his particular talent. That means you're not to harm him without my permission."

The merchant officer glanced at Langton, who replied, "I'd do as she says if I were you. There's plenty at stake."

"How about the others?"

Langton's eyes darted towards his former teammates. "Tarra and Steiger should be interrogated. I don't give a shit what you do with Tiktin. He doesn't know anything useful beyond the day of the week and which beer he likes best."

This time, Sakal gasped. "You're not going to simply kill him? He hasn't done anything."

"Try not to be sentimental, Doctor," Langton replied. "We are at war and these four are the enemy, spies wearing our uniforms. Perhaps it's not an open, declared war, but nonetheless. Now please follow the fifth officer."

"In charge, are you?" Decker asked, one eyebrow raised after they watched the two women leave.

"Only of your fate." A nauseating smile twisted the man's lips, and he turned to the merchant officer while pointing at Tiny. "Space him, then put the others in separate cells. I'll deal with them later."

Tiny needed a few seconds to understand, but when it finally dawned on him that he had been condemned to die, a roar of defiance escaped his throat, and he charged at Langton.

A scattergun coughed, its load catching Tiny in the middle of the chest. Although his battledress uniform didn't provide the same protection as armor, it stopped the pellets from penetrating his skin, though the force of the impact threw him backward. Within moments, the bosun's mates had him in shackles.

"How about you don't space Tiny and I'll answer some questions," Zack proposed in a reasonable tone. "I've been conditioned, and as you saw, your hired mind rapist can't do anything useful where I'm concerned, so all you have is my goodwill and cooperation."

Langton raised a hand, stopping the bosun's mates. "Really? Let's see how that works. Are you Chief Warrant Officer Zachary Thomas Decker, active duty member of the Commonwealth Marine Corps?"

"No." Decker shook his head.

"I'm actually sorry to hear that." Langton dropped his hand to signal that they should take Tiny to the airlock when Zack continued.

"The name's Zack Decker, but I'm not a chief warrant officer anymore."

"Please. I don't buy the nonsense that you're retired." Langton managed to sound disappointed.

"You *Sécurité Spéciale* gangsters need to keep the enemy order of battle up to date, Alex. They made me a major after Garonne. Yeah, I know. It's hard to believe the Commandant didn't commission me as a lieutenant colonel after I killed off so many of your kind."

"And your friend Tarra?"

"He's on active duty as well, so you'll have to think really carefully about what you're going to do. Torturing and killing two Marines isn't good for the continued health of your organization. My side tends to favor disproportionate retaliation." Decker paused to let his words sink in before asking, "How did you manage to set up this reception committee?"

Langton chuckled. "Captain Bailey was most cooperative once I reached out to him. It's amazing what can happen when you're the only one awake and on duty, though it saddened me to see your standards slip so badly."

"Fucking rat," Steiger snarled. "And I was beginning to like you."

"I've been called worse by better people." He turned his revolting smile back on. "You aren't an active duty anything, are you darling? If I have Anca sift through your feeble brain first, then put you to the question myself, I won't be annoying my military friends here, will I?"

"Sisters of the Void can't touch women's minds," Decker said.

"Perhaps this one can. Who knows what progress Doctor Sakal made in opening up her talents? But enough persiflage." He turned to the merchant officer. "Put them in the brig, including Tiny. I might have a use for him later."

"As you wish." Within moments, Decker, Tarra, and Steiger were shackled and led off to the brig. At least they had the consolation of Tiny following them under his own power.

They felt the universe shift shortly after that when *Altair Nova* went FTL.

*

A day passed before Decker, stretched out on the cell's only bunk, spied some motion out of the corner of his eyes, the first since the guards had shoved them in the brig with a few ration packs and some water. He turned his head to see Langton standing there, examining him.

"Bored already?" The Marine asked. "Coming to visit your private zoo?"

Langton shrugged. "Boredom's part of the job in our line of business, don't you think? I figured that while Anca and Sakal are setting up a lab in the sickbay to study you, we'd have a last chat, in case they do something that wipes your mind."

"Chat away. You know you'll never obtain anything classified from me. That's the way we play this game."

"I can always put Tiny in an airlock and start asking questions while it slowly depressurizes. Or Miko, or your friend Hal."

"You could, and you know that I wouldn't tell you anything useful. All three of them knew the risks when they signed up."

"True. Besides, Anca's claimed you, so I'll have to content myself with Tarra. I doubt your girlfriend has any information my superiors would find useful."

"Hal wouldn't have anything either. He actually did retire from the Corps at the beginning of the year — transferred to the inactive reserve as all of us do after finishing our hitch. I simply used my authority as the senior Marine officer on Naraka to recall him to active duty before we did our breakout number. It's legal, and he is a serving command sergeant right now."

"Perhaps." Langton gave a nonchalant half-shrug. "Of course, Sister Anca will do her thing with your friends as well, which is why we're chatting instead of me getting busy with proper interrogations."

Decker, tired of speaking over his shoulder, sat up. "That vicious bitch seems to have a lot of authority around here."

"The captain of this ship has made it abundantly clear that what Anca wants, Anca gets."

"No doubt. Someone who can fuck with another human being's mind is valuable to scum like your employers and their masters."

"Very true." Langton nodded agreeably. "Tell me, Major Decker, are you really on furlough and not working a mission?"

Zack snorted. "Actually, I'm absent without authority by now and will likely face a disciplinary board. Hal and I went into this looking for Doctor Sakal, whom he'd seen at Krommor. We couldn't save her from abduction six years ago and wanted to make good on that. I had no idea the Confederacy was setting up its own empire in the depths of the Protectorate Zone, presumably in connivance with your lot."

Langton raised his hand, palm down and waggled it from side-to-side. "Connivance? More or less, I suppose. More than the Confederacy would like and less than we actually want. But it doesn't matter. We still hold enough of their strings to ensure obedience when necessary."

"Then tell me, why did you enlist in Frontier Solutions?" Decker asked. "To check up on your wet work sub-contractors? You weren't really working your

CIB day job and tracking material stolen from the war stocks, were you?"

"I joined up because of you, my dear friend. The background check Gavin Bevaqua — you remember him, the Confederacy boss on Valeux Station — ran on you rang a few bells. Since I was already on Kilia, they sent me in to watch you. I was to determine whether or not you were a Fleet agent, and if so, why you were infiltrating Frontier Solutions. Your lot is slipping, Zack. You need to fire whoever's setting up the fake identities."

"Or, more likely, we have another mole. No worries, we'll find him or her when I'm back home."

A short burst of laughter escaped Langton's lips. "Please. You know I'm not letting you go back, not in this lifetime. You'll end up being listed as missing in action and eventually your heirs will receive a missive from the Commandant of the Marine Corps regretting to inform them that you gave your life for the Commonwealth."

"Keep thinking that way, Alex. But I warn you that the last few guys who tried to stop me from going home died a very messy death. Spare yourself the aggravation. Let me ask Doctor Sakal if she wants to be resurrected, so to speak. If yes, then let us leave, and that'll be the end of it. If she'd rather stay, then fair enough, have the captain drop the rest of us off at the next stop, no harm, no foul, no endless rounds of retribution between your organization and mine. As I said, I'm on a personal quest, so it's not worth your organization running the risk my bosses find out you killed us. They would have no choice but to strike back. Give it some thought. Stopping this here and now beats what'll happen if you don't release us."

"You know," the *Sécurité Spéciale* agent crossed his arms and nodded, "I think I may actually believe your story about not being on a mission for the Fleet. It sounds too damned stupid to be something hatched up by Naval Intelligence. Sadly, what I don't believe is that you'll let us continue to employ Sister Anca, which means the moment I let you go, the race to take her out of commission will be on, and that's something I cannot allow. Considering how important she could be to us, I know my superiors won't mind potentially annoying the Fleet. After all, no other Sister of the Void has so far volunteered her talents in service to the government. Of course, there's also the matter of still needing Doctor Sakal. She may have a few tricks up her sleeve to amplify Anca's talents and create more mind-meddlers, as you call them, meaning there's no way I would be allowed to release her either. So I'm sorry, but once we're done — or rather once the good sister is done, it'll be a shot in the back of the head and a quick burial in space."

"Don't blame me if everything goes to shit. I gave you fair warning and a way out."

Langton inclined his head. "That you did, and you have my regard as a fellow professional for trying." He abruptly glanced to his left and then smiled again. "Anca and Sakal must be ready. I see a trio of bosun's mates with shackles headed this way. Good luck, Zack. In case things don't work out for you, it's been a slice. Too bad we're not on the same side."

Decker stood and replied with a nasty smirk, "Remember this moment. I'll soon give you a reason to regret moonlighting for the wrong bunch."

"I love your bravado." Langton clapped his hands in a slow, ironic motion. "And believe or not, I'll feel a pinch of regret at killing you. Just a pinch, but that's more than I'll feel for the rest of your team."

Then, he stepped aside to let a pair of crewmen enter Zack's cell and shackle him, while the third held a large-bore scattergun aimed at the Marine.

As they led him down the passageway, Langton said, "Good luck. I think you scared Anca and she'll be anxious to return the favor. Oh, and by the way, your friends are already with the good sister. Well — not Tiny. I changed my mind. His body's awaiting disposal once we drop out of FTL."

"You'll get yours soon enough," Decker growled before his guards yanked him around a corner, pursued by Langton's derisive laughter.

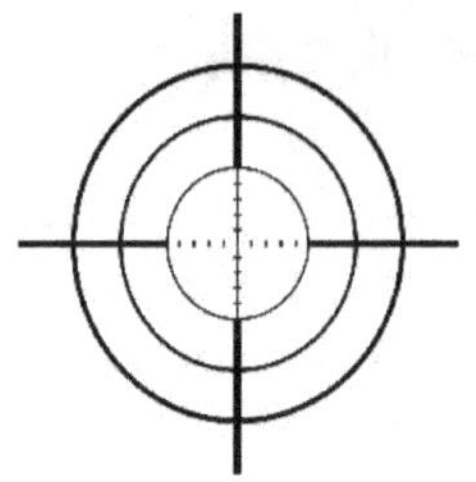

— THIRTY-SIX —

The sickbay door opened at their approach, and his escort shoved him inside. The compartment appeared more spacious than he had expected, and thoroughly modern. It had a row of diagnostic beds against the far bulkhead, two of which were occupied by Miko and Hal, both securely strapped down.

Sakal and Anca stood by a projection screen currently showing a three-dimensional rendering of a human brain.

Both turned when he stumbled into their presence, and a malicious smile appeared on the sister's stern face. "Finally — the test subject in person. Excellent timing. We were just wrapping up our examination of the control subjects. Put him on the bed next to the woman."

Sakal merely stared at Decker with expressionless eyes while the guards wrestled him into a horizontal position after removing his shackles.

"You may leave," Anca told the crewmen when they had strapped Zack down. "I'll call when it's time to take them back to their cells or," she smirked, "dispose of their bodies, depending on how things go."

Then she approached Decker's bed and looked down at him.

"Doctor Sakal has developed a means to detect the effects of an empath's mind touch on someone's brain by enhancing a conventional diagnostic scanner. Her research has shown that brain cells react to someone like me, even if the subject is not conscious of it. We've just calibrated this sickbay's machines by using your friends here, and it'll show how you react to my touch as well as reveal which parts of your brain generate the ability to project images at an empath and push her out. I know you're thinking that by blocking me, we'll not be able to study your awareness and ability to project. Therefore, I've taken steps to ensure your cooperation."

Anca raised her hand and said, "Elyce, the woman, if you please."

Sakal touched a screen at the foot of Steiger's bed, sending the mercenary into silent convulsions.

"That," the Sister continued, "was an outgrowth of Doctor Sakal's research — the ability to stimulate certain parts of the brain remotely. Your friend received a minimal dose. At higher outputs, the stimulator can induce violent spasms that might cause the subject to rupture parts of her body."

"I thought you mind-meddling nuns abhorred violence," Decker said. "How did they ever let a psychopath like you into the cloister?"

"They were under the mistaken belief that they could teach me to control my darker urges. Thankfully, by the time they realized the error of their ways, they had helped me unlock and manage the talent. Escaping from those stupid cows was easy after that. Finding an employer who valued my abilities wasn't all that more difficult."

Decker snorted in disbelief. "Don't tell me the Fleet wanted to enter the mind-meddling business."

A bark-like laugh escaped Anca's throat. "No, Mister Decker. The *Sécurité Spéciale*. Oh, Doctor Sakal belonged to your lot, but my employers wanted control of her research. One apostate sister wasn't enough for them. Your superiors already had a research program in operation and jumped at the chance to take me in, so they shipped me off to work with her. From there it wasn't terribly difficult to arrange a change of allegiance. Fortunately, your rescue attempt six years ago came too late, though it would have been better if fate hadn't decreed that your ship be close enough to allow you and the Doctor to speak at length. Yes, Alex Langton does like to talk, and he relished telling us about you at length, about your identity and your quest to free us from Confederacy bondage."

"So you arranged for the attack on Troy Station." Decker's even tone made it a statement rather than a question. He turned his eyes on Sakal. "And you, Doctor? Did you go along with Anca's plans to turn her into the strongest Sister of the Void ever seen? Are you creating more of her for an organization that serves a truly vile political faction?"

"My choices were limited, Major Decker," she replied without a shred of emotion in her voice. "Continue my work for different masters or die. I daresay you'd have opted for the same path."

"And, though she won't admit it, our dear Doctor is pleased to see said research finally bear fruit," Anca said. "Yes, I *can* touch females, not very well, yet still enough to taste a hint of her emotions. However, we're not here to rehash ancient history, nor am I interested in discussing the advances we've made. What interests me is how you are able to sense me, force me to see strong emotions you generate artificially and how you keep me out. We must know, and you will show us. Remember, your friends will suffer if you fail to cooperate. Perhaps a reminder would be appropriate. The male now, if you please, Elyce."

This time, Hal Tarra went into silent convulsions.

"I trust we understand each other?" The renegade sister asked.

"We do."

Sakal moved over to the projection screen and manipulated its controls. Another three-dimensional representation of the human brain appeared.

"This is yours, Major. Sister Anca will perform various experiments, and we shall see how they physically affect you. That way we might understand which parts of the male brain are sensitive to and in control of empathic stimuli."

Decker took a deep breath and forced himself to relax. Then, he felt Anca's touch, like invisible fingers, enter his skull and caress his thoughts. He felt a shiver of disgust run down his spine but refused to give her the satisfaction of seeing him squirm, though her amused cackle told him his efforts were in vain.

These strokes, each coaxing forth his emotions, went on for what seemed like an eternity, the stillness of the sickbay broken only by snippets of conversation between Anca and Sakal as they went through an extensive list of tests. Finally, her fingers withdrew, and he heard her sigh.

"Fascinating," Sakal said. "I might actually be the first researcher to map the male brain's reaction to an empath's touch. It's a shame I can't publish my results, at least not yet."

"You might be fascinated," Anca replied in a raspy voice, "but you didn't have to spend so much time in his mind. The things I've sensed... It's all been very tiring. I'd like to take a break before the next set of tests."

"As you wish. I'll recall the guards." Sakal reached for the comm panel.

"No need. I'd like to complete the full set today. A brief respite in my quarters will be sufficient." Anca looked down at Decker. "I don't think our subjects are going anywhere. Even the strongest man couldn't break through these restraints. You can stay here if you wish, Elyce."

Then, without waiting for an answer, she left. After a minute or so, Sakal wandered over to Zack's bed.

When her face entered his visual range, he said, "You realize Anca can't be allowed to use her talents in support of her employers. Imagine a secret police organization with the ability to enter its victims' minds and manipulate them. It would be the beginning of the end for what still passes as democracy in the Commonwealth. Surely you see that she's utterly amoral, and would have no qualms about participating in the overthrow of the political order. I know you're not at all like her, Doctor."

"I'm afraid I have no say in the matter," Sakal replied in the same flat tone as before. "Ever since we were taken, I've been a virtual slave."

"Any idea where you — we — are headed now?"

Sakal shook her head. "No. But it's for something that requires Anca's talents, and her lack of restraint."

"We have to ensure that she doesn't reach her destination."

She looked down at him with dead eyes. "You mean to kill her? How would you do that? You're a prisoner, and I understand that Alex Langton intends to have you and your friends spaced before we arrive."

"I mean take her out of circulation. Death is one way, but there are others. As to how — maybe you could help me. You're not like her. You have a conscience, I know that. Remember six years ago? You and I had a lot of time to get acquainted, and I can't believe that you've become someone like Anca since then."

Sakal seemed at a loss for words, so he continued. "Hal and I came out beyond the Rim to find you and bring you home. We'll still do that, if it's what you want, Doctor. You're a human with free will. Neither the Confederacy nor the *Sécurité Spéciale* can force you to do things that go against your deepest beliefs. Antoine Mazkow decided to stay on Naraka under his new identity, preferring to remain dead in the eyes of his family and friends, but that doesn't have to be your fate."

"Antoine is dying, Major. He surely must have told you so." She turned away from him, though he thought he heard a catch in her voice. "When the reivers attacked Troy, Mazkow's status as a doctor confused them, so they decided to hedge their bets and take him as well. When they discovered that he had no involvement in my experiments, being the station physician, they tortured him for entertainment before handing us to the Confederacy. He was — is a good man, who deserved better."

"So the Confederacy subcontracted the raid to some scummy clan of thugs," Tarra said in a raspy voice. "Nice way of staying at a remove from the crime. The *Sécurité*

Spéciale made a good choice when they hired the Jackals for their dirty work. But Zack's right, Doctor. If you help us, we can all escape and maybe stop something that might hurt many people. Besides, we came all this way, risking our lives, to bring you home. Surely that means something?"

"Doctor," Decker said in a gentle tone, "the fact that you didn't tell Anca about my awareness after I revealed it to you tells me you're not fully committed to life under the *Sécurité Spéciale*'s thumb. Help us, and we'll keep you safe. We'll take you away from people forcing you to violate your principles. That wasn't Elyce Sakal sending my friends into convulsions. That was a woman living in fear of an apostate, someone who had given in to despondency when there's still a chance to escape."

"Escape? We're on a starship in FTL. One doesn't just step off." A bitter laugh escaped her throat, but when she met Zack's eyes again, he thought he saw a spark of life. Something had penetrated the fog of her despair.

He smiled at her. "Actually, one does, if you're willing to take a few risks. Since my friends and I are condemned to a quick death and you to a slower one — a death that will destroy your spirit long before your body — any risk short of walking out an airlock without a pressure suit is worth taking. Trust me on this, the people Anca works for will kill you just as surely as Langton will kill us. Your death will simply take longer and be more agonizing as they replace your soul with unbearable darkness. You've already lost some of yourself. I can see it, hear it, and feel it. Perhaps you can feel it too." For a moment he thought he had laid it on too thick, but then he saw a faint glimmer of hope in her eyes. "There's still a chance for all of us. Help me, and you'll help yourself."

"Tell me what I can do," she whispered.

*

Anca returned two hours later, shortly after *Altair Nova* dropped out of FTL to retune the drives and adjust course. Walking into sickbay as if she owned the place, she asked Sakal, "Our test subjects have been quiet?"

"As the grave."

"We're not big on conversation," Decker quipped, anxious that Anca not detect any emotional changes in Sakal. "The military mind is just a tad dull."

"I find your mind rather interesting, Major Decker. And I'm anxious that we discover how you manage to project such clear emotions at me. Perhaps we can find a way to activate that part of my brain so I can do the same to others. Imagine the possibilities." Her raspy laugh held a distinct tone of menace. "Let's get to it. Remember what any lack of cooperation means for your friends."

"Do your worst." Then he hastily added, "To me that is."

The rogue sister turned to Sakal. "Are you ready?"

"I am." That flat, emotionless tone had returned, as had the dead eyes.

"Is something wrong, Elyce?"

"No. The system's on. You can proceed with the first test."

"The sooner the better," Decker interjected. "I'm tired of lying here like a sack of crap. My bladder's unhappy, and my stomach's about to take over as the whiniest organ in my body, and that'll screw up your readings for sure."

Anca smiled at him. "My, my. So impatient."

Those soft, invisible fingers touched his thoughts, but instead of sifting, they floated through his emotions.

"Project something sexual," she said, "the more depraved, the better."

Decker reached deep into his memory and pulled out an encounter that happened long ago, during his misspent youth, and embellished it with things he would never do in a million years, forcing himself to feel disgusted at the depravity.

Then, he projected the resulting thought at the fingers hovering over his consciousness. They vanished with breathtaking abruptness, and he heard her gasp.

"That," she said after taking several deep breaths, "was astounding. Do you have a reading, Elyce?"

"I do. Fascinating. It lit up parts of the brain I hadn't suspected — two in particular."

"Let's try something else." Anca looked down at him again. "I want a projection of loss, sorrow, regret."

The fingers returned, and he dredged up the memory of Raisa's death in the Hadley Kasbah, allowing himself to feel the same emotions he had experienced that night, years ago and parsecs away. He pushed the full force of his raw despair at the sister and once again, she gasped, withdrawing her touch.

"Elyce?" She asked.

"I have it. One of the parts that lit up is the same, but I also have a different one from the first try. Perhaps the one that remained constant is associated with the projection itself. We need further tests, of course."

"Indeed. Let's try a different emotion, Major, excitement this time, something nonsexual that arouses your passions in a positive way."

Once more, he felt her intrusion, then let her sense a Pathfinder drop from low orbit. He projected the thrill of jumping out of a shuttle, the long flight down as a human glider, then the rush of the kite-chute opening. This time, he heard no gasp, but an odd smile pulled up the corners of her lips.

"Interesting. What did you get, Elyce?" She asked.

"A pattern. We may be zeroing in on the part of his brain that controls projection. Try something more forceful this time."

Anca's smile broadened. "Why don't you scare me, Major Decker? Here. I'll give you some incentive."

A grasping hand violated his consciousness in a way he had never felt before and didn't believe possible. It sent a wave of pain through his skull, and he instinctively shoved back.   Hard.   Anca staggered against the bulkhead, her eyes widening in fear.

"Get the fuck out," Decker growled, "before I reach down your throat and rip your lungs out." He pictured himself holding a mass of bloody tissue and Anca dropped to her knees, paralyzed with terror.

It was the moment he had been waiting for. Still projecting raw horror with as much violence as he could, he freed his limbs from restraints Sakal had loosened earlier and jumped to his feet. Reaching down, he grabbed Anca's head with both hands and gave it a forceful twist to one side, snapping her neck. Sakal gasped as he dropped her body to the deck.

"Is she..."

"She won't meddle with anyone's mind again, ever." Decker released his friends, then said, "Doctor, please call in the guards.   We need their uniforms and weapons."

"Leaving her body where they can see it isn't a good idea," Steiger pointed out. "Give me a hand. We'll put her on a bed."

That done, Sakal touched the comm panel and summoned the three crewmen detailed to serve her. The sickbay door slid open moments later, and the leader entered, weapon slung, followed by his two mates, their eyes on Sakal who stood where she would attract the most attention.

Decker and his companions, who had been standing on either side of the opening, hidden from immediate view, pounced, taking the surprised spacers down with a few well-placed strokes. Once the door slid shut again, they stripped them of their coveralls and then bound them with their own shackles.

"Keep your battledress on," Decker said, stepping into the largest of the uniforms. "It may not be much, but it'll take a load from this at close range." He held up the leader's scattergun.

"You're sure it's going to work?" Tarra asked.

"I spent a few years on civilian freighters, buddy. I know how they run crews and what the general layout is.

We want to be in their engineering compartment before they can go FTL again. It's our only chance."

"What if someone challenges us along the way?" Steiger raised a scattergun and looked at it with a dubious expression. "This isn't a reiver ship, and the crew isn't made up of outlaws."

"Do you want to live?" Decker checked the charge on his weapon. "Besides, if things work the way I want them to, it'll be a moot point." He glanced at Sakal, who stared back with frightened eyes. "If we're ready, it's time to move out."

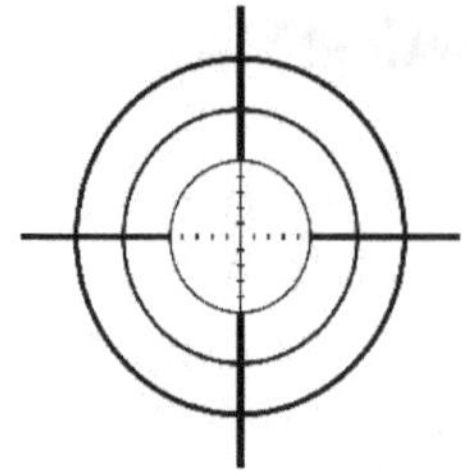

— THIRTY-SEVEN —

Zack took one last look at the deck schematic that had replaced the image of his brain on the sickbay projection screen, then touched the door controls. It slid open with a sigh, revealing an empty passageway.

If *Altair Nova* ran like any ordinary civilian ship of this tonnage, the crew would be small, no more than thirty or forty spacers, with most functions automated and monitored remotely from the bridge. He had no reason to think the Black Nova Line would be any different when it came to controlling costs.

They walked aft towards the spiral staircase that connected the decks in this part of the ship, without meeting anyone.

But as they approached the shaft, he could hear feet trudging up the metal treads and motioned at the others to stop. Seconds later, Alex Langton stepped out, coming to a sudden stop when he realized he was staring down the barrel of Zack's scattergun.

"What's this then?" He asked in disbelief. "An escape attempt in interstellar space? Have you all gone mad?"

"Better foolish than dead," Decker replied, swinging his weapon's butt forward and upward to strike Langton on the chin. "Ask Anca how dead feels."

The *Sécurité Spéciale* agent collapsed into a heap, out cold.

Tarra cursed vociferously before asking, "What the hell do we do with him?"

"Put him with the others."

"Just shoot him," Steiger suggested. "He's vermin."

"I might have said this before, but I don't kill in cold blood," Decker replied slinging his weapon before lifting Langton up by the shoulders.

"Anca might object to your characterization of her death."

"After what she did to my mind, that was in hot blood, sweetheart."

"He killed Tiny."

"That's still not a reason to execute him out of hand. Start down that road, and you'll end up like Langton and his ilk — an unfeeling excuse for a human being."

Between Zack and Hal Tarra, they had Langton lying on the deck beside the three crewmen in the space of a few moments.

"Miko didn't witness it because they brought me up before her," Tarra said while they were still out of the two women's earshot, "but Langton killed Tiny after he'd served as Anca's experimental subject. She did something to his brain that made him scream like a stuck pig for about a minute. After that, he turned into a drooling sack of potatoes. I figure she mind raped him into a vegetable."

"Then it's a good thing I snapped the witch's neck. Come on. The buggers could go FTL any moment."

The heavy doors sealing off the engineering compartment opened at Decker's touch, confirming his suspicion that they didn't bother with elaborate security measures. After all, the ship would normally have nothing more than trusted crew aboard, and any occasional passengers could be confined to a single deck.

It seemed empty at first, but then a thickset man in faded coveralls emerged from an office and froze when he saw the foursome. He opened his mouth to speak, but his words died stillborn when Zack and Tarra raised their weapons.

"Put your hands on top of your head, if you don't want to lose it."

Once the man had complied, Decker butt stroked him into unconsciousness.

"Hal, find the hatch that leads to the engineering compartment's escape pod. I'm going to see if I can screw with their reactors."

"Won't that alert them?" Steiger asked.

"We need a distraction big enough to make them ignore a pod leaving without authorization."

He entered the office from where the *Altair Nova's* engineer had emerged and found what he expected, a control board for all of the ship's propulsion and power systems. If necessary, the freighter could be helmed from here.

It didn't appear to be much different from the engineering controls on the ill-fated *Demetria*, which he had come to know very well before pirates turned her into a lifeless wreck, killing his partner Avril in the bargain.

An unexpected surge of fury rose up at the memory, unrestrained by his normal self-control thanks to the bruising inflicted via Anca's savage mental assault.

He took a few deep breaths and called up the schematics for the antimatter system. As he expected, it was thoroughly secured against tampering. The same proved to be true of the fusion reactor and the systems that depended on it. However, the designers hadn't counted on a Marine Master Gunner with ill intent breaking into the heart of their weapon systems.

Altair Nova, like all of its kind plying the star lanes along the Rim and in other frontier sectors, had been well equipped with defensive weaponry, and overloaded plasma gun capacitors could quickly become bombs. He pulled the engineer's limp body into the office and used his handprint to unlock the first layer of security.

On civilian vessels, cost and ease of maintenance were topmost in the minds of shipwrights. Therefore, the physical diodes that backed up the computer subroutines controlling power flow to the capacitors were in the engineering compartment rather than by the guns themselves.

He merely had to pull them and, after spoofing the main feed generator, send a power surge to one of the capacitors, then to another and then another. Once the first two or three began bleeding excess power to the others, the feedback loop would build up rapidly without anyone being the wiser. If the loop exceeded the capacitor's rating quickly enough, it would blow.

He found and disconnected the weapon system's link to the bridge, hoping no one would notice until it was too late, and then reconfigured the controls. When everything was ready, he hurried out of the office to where a hatch gave him access to the physical power conduits. Tarra intercepted him and pointed out the way to the escape pod.

"Found it. I'll wait to open her up until you say so. We wouldn't want the alarms to go off too soon."

"Good man." Decker clapped his friend on the shoulder and then started pulling diodes. He looked around for a disposal unit and when he found it, he dropped them inside. All that remained was to enter the last command, and the guns would power up without any of the safeguards in place.

As he was about to re-enter the engineer's office and set things in motion, the door to the compartment opened, and a trio of armed spacer ran in, weapons held high.

"Stop!" One of them shouted, pointing his gun at Zack as he skidded to a halt. "You're not authorized to be here."

The Marine glanced at them, then at the control panel inside the office, gauging whether or not he'd be able to find cover before the crewman pulled the trigger when Tarra emerged from a behind a massive block of machinery, scattergun at the shoulder.

"Drop it," he yelled, "drop it now, or I'm taking your head off."

The men, surprised by his sudden appearance, looked from Tarra to Decker and back again, unsure what to do next. Then, the leader turned his weapon on Zack's best friend and pulled the trigger at the same time as Tarra pulled his.

Two dense pellet blasts passed each other in the narrow space, one turning the crewman's face into a bloody mess, the other striking Tarra's upper chest. His battledress absorbed most of the tiny ball bearings, but enough slashed at his unprotected throat.

A geyser of blood erupted, splattering the bulkheads. He fired once more, taking down the second man, while Decker raised his own weapon and killed the third. Then Tarra dropped to his knees before falling to the deck.

After ensuring that the three spacers were out of action, Decker knelt by Tarra's side, trying to find the wound so he could staunch the flow of blood, but his friend shook his head in a weak motion.

"I'm done for," he rasped. "Carotid artery. Need an autodoc. Don't have one. Go. Take Elyce home."

Then, the light faded from his eyes.

A howl of fury erupted from Decker's throat, and he sprang to his feet with renewed energy. He had merely planned to disable *Altair Nova*, to spook her into ignoring the escape pod. Now, his plans would change.

Steiger ran up, alerted by the noise, and almost stumbled over the bodies. She skidded to a halt when Decker snarled, "Get back to the pod. When you hear me yell, open the hatch and climb in. We'll have maybe a minute before everything goes to shit on this ship."

She vanished back down the passage while Decker sat down at the console again. Fighting to keep the red veil of rage at bay, he tweaked the power flow governor, then entered the execute command. He waited for a few seconds to confirm that the feedback loop had started, then, with a last glance at the remains of his dead friend, he ran after Steiger, shouting, "Go, go, go!"

Decker piled in behind the two women and tapped the control panel beside the hatch to initiate the launch process. The hatch slammed shut, a red light began to strobe, and a voice counted down from ten.

Somewhere within *Altair Nova*'s hull, a plasma gun capacitor failed, and he felt a faint rumble before the docking bolts released them, ejecting the pod into space. Its thrusters fired, and he just had time to drop into a seat before the pressure of acceleration sent him careening into a bulkhead.

His eyes found a screen showing the rapidly shrinking shape of the freighter, just in time to see a bright flare of light erupt from its hull, followed by a gust of escaped gasses, then another and another as every single gun capacitor suffered catastrophic failure.

He knew that the number of hull breaches would quickly overwhelm the small crew's ability to deal with them and that meant *Altair Nova* wouldn't be able to go FTL. Right now, they must be in panic mode, unable to figure out what was happening and why.

When the pressure of acceleration eased, he looked for and found the pod's controls. He had to disable the beacon, at least for now, just in case they managed to get things under control and came looking for them.

"Zack!" Miko's urgent tone made him raise his head and turn around. "She's breaking up."

Before he had time to focus on the image of the dying starship, a massive flash of light blinded their video pick up. When it subsided, *Altair Nova* had vanished, the once proud freighter turned into a rapidly expanding cloud of wreckage.

"Wow." Steiger's eyebrows shot up. "Remind me to never piss you off again. How did you manage *that*?"

"I have no idea," he replied, slumping back into his seat. The beacon could stay on after all. "Removing the power regulators for a starship's guns is something I've only ever seen in theory on my Master Gunner's course, and then more as a way of teaching us what not to do. After they killed Hal, I removed all of the flow controls out of spite, but I never expected this. Maybe one of the weapon power conduits came too close to that of another system, and the feedback surge bridged the gap, setting off a whole new cascade."

"For a guy who doesn't kill in cold blood, you certainly did a job on that crew."

Decker looked at her with eyes that reflected a fury Steiger had never seen before. In a tightly controlled tone, he said, "They killed Hal."

Chastened, she nodded once.

Sakal, who hadn't said a word since they left sickbay, asked, "What happens now?"

"Now? We pray that a friendly starship picks up our distress signal and comes looking." The adrenaline that had been driving him since the moment he lashed back at Anca evaporated, and he felt the urge to yawn.

He examined the pod's interior closely for the first time since coming aboard. "We should have enough air, food, and water to last for a few weeks, provided the recyclers work properly." Then, he noticed the dozen human-sized protrusions along the pod's cylindrical bulkhead. "Or we might not need them. Those look like stasis chambers. If they are, you two will climb in. I'll stay awake and stand watch."

"We'll alternate," Steiger proposed, "to reduce the chances of suffering space madness all alone by yourself in zero gravity for weeks on end."

"Four days on, four days off?"

"That should work." She studied his face for what seemed like a long time. "Are you alright, Zack?"

"I'll live." He hiked his shoulders. "Damn assholes had to show up at the last minute. I probably fucked up somewhere and alerted them that something was going down in engineering."

"Do not," Steiger said, drawing out each word, "blame yourself for Hal's death. You want to do that, you're spending the entire time in stasis, and *I'll* risk space madness. Besides, he's the one who went off on this insane quest to find Doctor Sakal and drew you into it. At least you've found her and are fulfilling the promise you and Hal made to yourselves. No one left behind, remember?"

He shrugged again. "Sure. But now I've left him behind."

"No. You've left his body, no more than an empty shell behind. That which made him Hal is out there somewhere." She waved towards a porthole.

Decker speared her with his eyes, but she saw no anger in them.

"True," he said after more than a minute of silent contemplation. "And thanks for not saying he went to Valhalla. I would have strangled you for that." A faraway look replaced the fierce expression on his face. "I guess the Amalis and their *Sécurité Spéciale* lackeys owe me another life."

Steiger reached out to touch him on the arm with her fingertips. "I know you'll make them pay. But first, we need someone to rescue us, preferably while we're still sane. Why don't the doctor and I prepare for stasis while you figure out how this thing works?"

A few hours later, alone in the main compartment, Decker stared out at the stars through a thick porthole and had a silent conversation with Hal's ghost, telling him all the things he should have said while his friend was still alive. It seemed that everyone close to him wound up dying a violent death, except for Hera.

He missed his partner. She had a way of keeping his spirits up like no one else. Fortunately, whoever had stocked the escape pod had been kind enough to include a bottle of whiskey. Not the good stuff to be sure, but good enough for a toast to the dead. If there ever was a time to break his vow of abstinence from alcohol, this was it.

He raised the bottle to his lips and took a sip. Then he whispered a final farewell, releasing his friend's spirit to wherever Marines reported once their tour of duty in this life had ended.

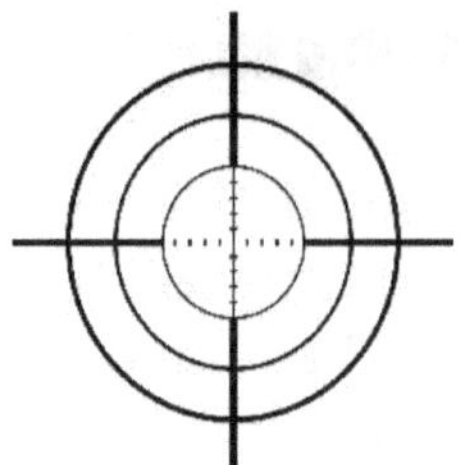

— THIRTY-EIGHT —

"Zack."

He felt a calloused hand on his cheek as Miko Steiger's face swam into focus.

"Wh-what?" His throat felt like sandpaper. "Is it my turn already."

It seemed like he had entered the stasis chamber only seconds ago, but if Miko had opened it to wake him, four days must have elapsed, meaning it was his turn to stand watch.

"No." He finally noticed the excitement in her voice. "It's not your turn, and it won't be your turn anymore. We're saved. We were just pinged by a starship. They picked up our beacon and are decelerating to pick us up."

"Tell me it doesn't have Lupus or Nova in its name."

Steiger chuckled. "Have no fear. It's the *Pallas Star*, Palladian Lines. They're Black Nova's biggest competitors."

He felt his fine muscle control return and pushed himself out the chamber, glad that his innards weren't protesting at the lack of gravity.

"Let's hope they're not some bad guys spoofing us so we won't turn off the beacon before they can lock on. How long have I been in, by the way?"

"Sixty-three hours, give or take a few minutes. Should I wake the doctor?"

"Not yet. Let's see what we have." He pulled his body towards the escape pod's rudimentary control panel and scrolled through the log, listening to the incoming message, Steiger's reply, and the starship's confirmation that they were on their way.

The short time lag between messages meant that *Pallas Star* would already be within civilian-grade sensor range of the escape pod.

"Seems legit," he said, "though I'd be happier if we had something that can reach out further than a few hundred kilometers. By the time we see the damned thing, it'll be on top of us."

Steiger laughed. "You have to be the only man in the galaxy who'd be suspicious of the one ship that managed to pick up our signal after we spent three weeks drifting through interstellar space. Talk about looking a gift horse in the mouth."

"Paranoia saves lives. You might wish to write that down somewhere for future reference." He shrugged. "Not that it matters at this point. Even if we turn off our transponder, they wouldn't have too many problems finding the pod, if they're sufficiently motivated. And if they're the enemy, they'll be motivated. But I hope they're the good guys. I don't think we'll be able to manage a second escape. Luck just doesn't work that way."

She patted him on the shoulder. "If we're about to be taken prisoner again, I'm sure you'll find a way. You always seem to find a way."

"Until the day I don't."

"You sure are a lot of fun right after a nap. Ever had sex in zero gravity?"

"I have. It's uncomfortable and if you're not careful, downright dangerous. I'll give it a pass if that was an invitation to lighten my mood."

"Suit yourself." She stuck out her tongue at him. "But you have no idea what you're missing."

"Actually, I do." He felt a rumble in his gut. "And right now, food is more important than scratching an itch. Why don't you break out the good stuff, since we're about to be rescued."

"There is no good stuff left."

"Right." He shook his head. "I guess I'm still suffering from stasis hallucinations. I could have sworn we had some food pouches in addition to those ugly ration bars."

"The food pouches ran out two waking periods ago, remember?"

"Apparently I don't. Damned stasis screws with my memory. If I have to go through a few more cycles, I probably won't even remember who you are."

"Considering how memorable I am, that's doubtful."

The radio came to life before Decker could reply.

"Hello people in *Altair Nova*'s escape pod, this is *Pallas Star*. We have a sensor lock on you and are matching velocities. I suggest you strap in. The tractor beam pickup might be a bit jerky."

Zack stroked the commo screen and said, "Understood." Then, he nodded at one of the padded seats. "Down you go, sweetheart. I'll hook myself up right here."

A few minutes later, the shape of a giant, boxy starship began to blot out the background stars, and the same voice said, "Deploying the tractor beam in one minute."

"We're ready for you," Decker replied.

Exactly sixty seconds later, the stars visible through the portholes began to shift, indicating a change in their apparent direction of travel, but it was so smoothly done that they didn't feel much by way of acceleration.

"Positive tractor beam lock confirmed," the *Pallas Star* officer said. "We'll have you dock on one of our port side airlocks. Unfortunately, we can't bring the pod itself aboard."

"As long as you bring us aboard."

Pallas Star seemed huge in comparison to the ship that had taken them out of the Protectorate and much larger than the now wrecked *Altair Nova*. Their escape pod would be nothing more than a pimple on its hull. Soon, their view of the universe shrank down to almost nothing, replaced by acres of scarred metal. Then, all motion stopped for a few minutes before resuming at a much slower rate, until they felt a nudge, followed by a loud thump.

Decker's control panel lit up with the joyful message that they had docked, and that there was an atmosphere on the other side of the hatch.

"You can open up now, escape pod."

"In a moment. We have to wake someone from stasis first."

"Alright. Don't take too long. We have to survey the pod before going FTL, to determine whether we can afford to keep it."

Steiger pulled herself to Elyce Sakal's stasis chamber and shut it down. After about a minute, she opened the cover to reveal a blinking and befuddled looking doctor.

"Have we..." she said in a raspy voice.

"We've been picked up by a ship, the *Pallas Star*." Decker gave her a warm, reassuring smile. "We're safe. Take a few deep breaths to get yourself going again. Just remember that there's artificial gravity on the other side, so hang on tight when you go through."

Sakal nodded, still uncertain, but said, "Whenever you want."

With a last glance at Steiger, he touched the controls and the clamshell hatch split open. He pushed himself towards it but before floating through he grabbed a handrail and positioned his body in the up position relative to the ship. Then he cautiously put his feet on the coaming and, hands on the sidewalls, crab-walked through until he crossed into the ship's artificial gravity envelope — right into a half-dozen spacers with scatterguns, all aimed at his chest.

An officer, pistol drawn, stood beside them. He raised his hand.

"You can stop right there, mister. Pirates have been known to infiltrate their victims via fake rescue operations, so we'll take this very slowly and carefully."

Decker nodded once. "Understood, sir. There are three of us, me, and two women. My name is Jack Lorenzo. I'm a retired Marine, and my companions are Miko Steiger, who retired from the Commonwealth Army, and Doctor Elyce Sakal, a former Fleet civilian employee."

"So you say. But you understand that we will proceed with all due caution."

"And you'll have our full cooperation, sir." He turned his head to glance back at the hatch. "Miko, Doctor, you can join me now. Our rescuers want to secure the pod, and they can't do that with you two still inside."

Moments later, a shaky Sakal stood beside him, followed by Steiger, who stumbled as she came out of the zero gee environment.

Decker gestured towards the hatch. "I believe that under the salvage laws, the pod's now yours, sir."

"You are correct." He pointed at one of his men and said, "You're with me. The rest of you, escort these people to sickbay."

"We're physically okay, sir."

"Are you a medic, Mister Lorenzo?"

"No."

"Then you're going to sickbay. Stasis doesn't agree with everyone and rescue protocols say you need a checkup first. After that, our first officer will interview you so he can begin the drafting the report for the authorities and *Altair Nova*'s owners."

"Whatever you say, sir."

*

"Let me recap, Mister Lorenzo," *Pallas Star*'s first officer said after listening to their story. "You were passengers aboard *Altair Nova*, headed for Pacifica when the crew discovered problems with one of their systems. As a precautionary measure, they bundled you into an escape pod which ejected soon afterward. Then, you saw the ship break up after witnessing a series of explosions breaking through her hull in several spots."

"That's pretty much it, sir."

"And you have no idea what the problem might have been? Starships, especially those belonging to an old and established shipping line like Black Nova don't just blow up."

"Not a clue." Decker shook his head. "I used to be a Marine, not a spacer, so when it comes to ship's systems, my knowledge is pretty limited."

"You say you saw several smaller explosions before the big one that broke it apart?"

"That's right."

"I wonder..." The man rubbed his chin, eyes staring sightlessly at his pad. "Black Nova ships, like ours, are well armed and it sounds to me like they might have had a problem with the gun capacitors that somehow spun out of control. Considering all the safeguards built into those systems, it must have been a cascading string of failures that fed on one another."

He shrugged. "I guess the investigators will have to figure that one out. We picked up *Altair*'s black box and with any luck, it'll have logged the last few seconds before the main reactor core went."

Decker's eyes widened for a fraction of a second. He hadn't considered that the flight recorder might point the finger at him.

"Did you find any other survivors?" He asked to mask his reaction.

"No. Yours appears to have been the only pod that ejected. Considering the state of the wreckage, no one could have survived three weeks in an airtight section of the ship. You and your companions were very fortunate, Mister Lorenzo, very fortunate indeed. *Altair*'s crew must have valued your lives highly to place you in the pod as a precautionary measure in the first instance."

It sounded like an invitation to elaborate, but Decker merely shrugged in reply.

"I'll take that kind of luck, sir."

"I'm sure you would. In any case, we can't access the black box and even if we could it would be against the law, so the full story of *Altair*'s last few minutes will have to wait. Our next port of call is Dordogne, where we'll put you ashore. The Constabulary, as well as representatives from Black Nova, will want to interview you, and they will be able to open the recorder. In the meantime, consider yourselves our guests, though you'll be confined to this deck for the duration."

"Thank you, sir."

The first officer eyed him with the expression of a man who felt that something was out of kilter but couldn't quite put his finger on what that might be.

"Yes." He nodded again as climbed to his feet and headed for the saloon door. "You were incredibly lucky. Enjoy the facilities, folks." With a final wave, he left them to their own devices.

"What will happen when we reach Dordogne?" Doctor Sakal asked in a small voice.

Zack glanced up at the deckhead, then at Sakal and touched his ear. "We'll see when we're there, won't we?"

Steiger leaned over and whispered into Sakal's ear. Understanding dawned in her eyes and she said, "We will."

*

A few hours after *Pallas Star* dropped out of FTL a few million kilometers from Dordogne, the first officer stuck his head into the saloon.

"I thought I'd let you know that we've radioed ahead, so there will be someone to greet you at the dock and make sure you don't wander off. The Black Nova representative is quite anxious to speak with you. They've never lost a ship in that way since the last Shrehari war."

I'll bet they're anxious, Decker thought. Black Nova knows who we are. He glanced at Steiger and saw the same thought reflected in her eyes.

"Thank you, sir. That will be most convenient."

Something in his tone must have struck a false note because the first officer stared at him for a few seconds.

"One might think that you're not keen on speaking with the authorities, Mister Lorenzo."

"I've never been a fan of the authorities, sir. That's why I retired from the Corps once my hitch was up and struck out on my own."

"I see. Well, this time, you'll have no choice. The loss of an expensive starship with all hands to a systems failure is a major event. We'll be docking tomorrow in the forenoon watch, so you have until then to think it over."

That night, Steiger climbed into Zack's bunk and put her lips to his ear.

"What are you going to do tomorrow? We can't fall into Black Nova's hands. They'll make us vanish before anyone notices we've arrived."

"Throw ourselves on the mercy of the Constabulary," he replied.

"And how is that going to help? Black Nova can accuse us of every crime under the stars, including that of destroying a starship and murdering its crew, which technically, comes under the piracy provisions of the criminal code."

"I may have a way of convincing the Constabulary that keeping us out of Black Nova's clutches might be in everyone's best interest."

"Let me guess. You won't tell me what that is, right?"

"Right. I have to take Doctor Sakal to Caledonia and put her under Fleet protection. We've come this far, and after what we've been through, I won't let Hal's death count for nothing."

"It would be nice if your regular partner and her ship were waiting for us, but I guess one miraculous escape is all we're going to get."

He grinned at her in the darkness. "I wouldn't be so sure of that."

*

The next day, shortly after *Pallas Star* docked at Dordogne's civilian orbital station, a pair of bosun's mates escorted them down the gangway tube and into the docking bay where a reception committee waited.

To Decker's relief, three of them wore the Constabulary's gray uniform, one with the twin four-pointed stars of an inspector on her collar.

The civilians with Black Nova logos on their jackets standing beside her had the annoyed look of people who'd been told they wouldn't be getting what they wanted.

"Jack Lorenzo, Miko Steiger and Elyce Sakal, I presume," the inspector said. "My name is Anna Lee. You'll be coming with me for the moment. You're not under arrest, but I am detaining you until I have your statements concerning the loss of the starship *Altair Nova*. Once that's done, these gentlemen from the company will have some questions for you."

"I still don't see," one of the Black Nova representatives said, "why we can't join forces and sit in on the interview. My superiors are gravely concerned at the loss of life resulting from the inexplicable destruction of a sound, well-maintained ship."

"I seem to recall that we had this discussion several times in the last day, Ser Charko," Lee replied in the tone of someone reaching the limit of her patience. "You will get a crack at them once I've collected the evidence I require under the Interstellar Transport Act, which is not necessarily the same evidence you need for corporate purposes."

Charko gave Zack a dirty look, as if to say their turn would come, confirming that the Black Nova folks likely had orders that didn't include letting him and his companions go on their merry way.

Lee led them to the Constabulary detachment's suite in the security zone, using corridors usually out of bounds to visitors. Once there, she had Steiger and Sakal escorted to a waiting room while she took Zack to her office.

"Please sit, Mister Lorenzo." She nodded towards the chairs arrayed in front of her desk. "Your arrival here poses something of a problem for me."

"Oh?" Decker cocked an eyebrow in question. "Why would that be, Inspector?"

"Several months ago, the Fleet issued a very quiet, very classified 'be on the lookout' bulletin with your name and particulars on it. And suddenly, you show up on my doorstep, one of three survivors of a Black Nova starship that mysteriously self-destructed. What intrigues me even more, is how keen the Black Nova folks are to get their hands on you and your two friends. If I hadn't brought a few constables with me, I do believe they might have resisted my taking you in. And that, in turn, makes me wonder what you've done to annoy one of the oldest and biggest shipping lines, owned by the mighty ComCorp no less."

"Did the BOLO come with any instructions if Jack Lorenzo were to appear in your jurisdiction?" He asked, knowing that Ulrich or Yang had issued it as a way to monitor his movements.

She nodded. "It did. We're to send a sighting report to a particular subspace address, which I have done, and then refrain from interfering with your movements unless you're in the process of breaking the law."

"Yet by detaining us, you're interfering with my movements." He smiled at her, to take the sting out of his words. "And for that, I'm very grateful."

"I beg your pardon?"

"It's a long story, Inspector and one that I can't fully share without clearing matters with my superiors first, but the Black Nova people aren't only interested in the loss of their ship and crew. They also want to take my friends and me back into their custody, something that would mean death for myself and Miko Steiger and a return to involuntary servitude for Doctor Sakal."

"Now I really want to know what's going on." She raised a hand, to forestall Zack's next words. "I know. You can't tell me. If I go through the motions of investigating *Altair Nova*'s destruction, will I find illegal acts?"

"That depends. If you're willing to accept my statement as is, then no."

She sighed. "I suppose I'll take your statement as is."

"That's probably a wise choice, Inspector. When the Fleet replies to your sighting message, I'm willing to bet that you'll be asked to expedite my return to Caledonia."

"The next thing you'll tell me is that you're involved in a matter of Commonwealth security."

He gave her a wry smile. "A cliché, I know, but it happens to be the case. If you have a contact inside the local Naval Intelligence Detachment, you can check my bona fides."

"As a matter of fact, I do."

"Have him or her verify the identity of Major Zachary Thomas Decker, code Rookie Trooper one nine five alpha."

"You're Major Decker? Of Naval Intelligence?"

"Yes."

"And I've just stumbled into an ongoing operation?"

"More or less. I have to take Doctor Sakal to Caledonia unharmed. She's an Armed Services employee who was abducted by people connected with Black Nova."

"And Steiger?"

"A freelancer working with me."

"I see." She tapped a manicured fingernail on the desk's hard surface while rubbing her chin with the other hand. Then, she seemed to come to a decision. "I've never liked that idiot Charko to begin with, and the way he pestered me since news of your rescue made the rounds yesterday does support your claim that they're anxious to get their hands on you."

Lee tapped her computer screen and established a link with the Navy's orbital station on the other side of Dordogne.

"Yann, it's Anna," she said to an unseen correspondent.

"Hey! How's my favorite cop? And why are you on the secure channel?"

"I'm fine, but I have someone here who's given me a code and told me to run it by you. He claims to be one of yours."

"Pass it on," a man's voice said. Once she'd done so, a minute passed in silence, then, "Major Zachary Thomas Decker, currently using the identity of Jack Lorenzo."

"So he says. Do you have any orders concerning him?"

"No, but then I wouldn't. Major Decker operates under direct orders from HQ. I assume you've already responded to the Lorenzo BOLO?"

"I have."

"If I may," Decker interrupted. "This is Zack Decker. You are?"

"Lieutenant Yann Marritt, sir."

"Can you do me a favor, Lieutenant Marritt?"

"Of course, sir."

"Send a message to Commander Manfred Yang at HQ and tell him that I'm on my way by the quickest means I can find. Tell him I'm bringing her home."

"Will do, sir. Was there anything else?"

"Yes," Lee said. "What am I supposed to do?"

"Help Major Decker in any way you can, Anna," Marritt replied. "Which is what the answer to your BOLO sighting report will probably say."

"Alright. Thanks, Yann."

"My pleasure. If there's anything else you need, Major, we can provide most of what's usually available at HQ."

"I'll probably need a few things, Lieutenant, beginning with new IDs," Zack replied. "Once I've figured out things with Inspector Lee, we'll call you again."

"No problems, sir. Until then."

"Bye, Yann." Lee cut the communication and sighed again. "I really hate getting involved in the Fleet's spy games, Major, but if Black Nova's gunning for you and your friends, my duty is clear. Shall we prepare Jack Lorenzo's official statement on *Altair Nova*'s loss before discussing Major Decker's next steps?"

"Sure."

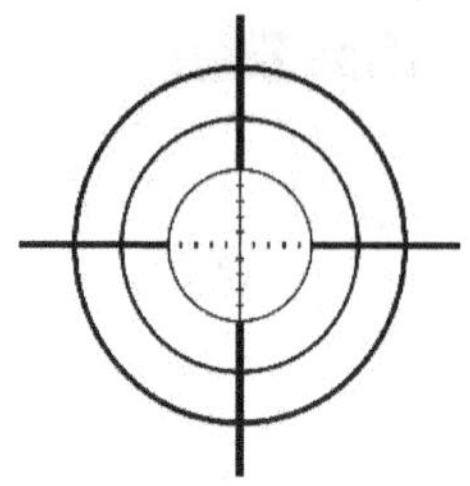

— THIRTY-NINE —

"You do realize that you're walking out of my life once again, don't you?" Steiger asked, watching Decker's gradual transformation as he removed the last traces of Jack Lorenzo from his appearance.

Inspector Lee had given them the duty officers' quarters within the Constabulary suite while they prepared for departure, claiming they were the safest place on the station.

Sakal occupied the adjacent room, resting, while the Constabulary officer fought off inquiries from Black Nova and searched for a safe berth aboard a commercial liner that didn't belong to ComCorp or any of its subsidiaries. Unfortunately, no Navy or Constabulary starship would be swinging by Dordogne on a route to Caledonia anytime soon.

Ever conscious of the irony, Decker had asked Yann Marritt to provide Doctor Sakal with a cover identity and him with a new ID chip under his real name.

"I think, this time, it's more like you're walking out of mine, honey," he replied. "You could come with me to Caledonia, but instead, you decided to go off on your own. It's enough to make a guy wonder what you're running from."

"I'm running from headquarters and all the annoying staff pricks they contain. Don't tell me you have a deep and abiding love for them."

"As a matter of fact, I don't." He hadn't revealed his status to Steiger, but he knew she had figured out long ago that he was an undercover operative. And if she hadn't before now, the ease with which he arranged for police protection would have confirmed it. "But that's where Elyce has to go, so that's where I'm going."

"And after you've handed her over to the Fleet?"

"I suppose I'll hook up with Hera and see what's next on the menu."

"Ah yes, that's right. I *am* the other woman." She smiled at his reflection in the mirror. "You missed her, didn't you? All the protestations that it's just a business arrangement is you lying to yourself."

"Let's just say that this was my first escapade without her, and it made me realize how much I depend on a stable partner." He paused, winked at her, and then said, "Thankfully I had you to watch my back on this one."

"Nice save, buster." Miko laughed. "Well, tell Hera I said hi. Better yet, tell her about how I so ably took her place for this one."

"How about I don't?"

"Coward." She swatted him on the arm. "Besides, I bet you'll get a thorough grilling when you next see her, and she has a way of bypassing your conditioning."

"What will you do now, not that I'm trying to change the subject?"

"You are, but I suppose we've exhausted that particular topic. I'm going to buy myself a berth on the next tramp out of here and ride it until I feel like jumping off." She glanced at her wrist. "And thanks to Inspector Lee, that should happen within the hour."

"So soon?"

"I'm not fond of long goodbyes."

"Says the woman who chided me for walking out on her."

"Irony's a bitch, isn't she?" Steiger leaned over and planted a kiss on Zack's lips. "Take care, big boy. The galaxy would be a boring place if you took a premature round to the head."

The door to the compartment opened, and a constable stuck his head inside.

"Sera Steiger, it's time."

"Thanks, and please call me Steiger or Miko or hey you. Sera Steiger's my mother and I can't say we're all that friendly with each other."

With a final wave and a blown kiss, Miko Steiger walked out of Zack's life. And he still had no idea who she really was, other than a soldier of fortune suffering from a severe case of wanderlust. A veteran who couldn't quite manage to shed the warrior's lifestyle.

A sleepy voice behind him asked, "Is Miko gone?"

Decker turned and smiled at Elyce Sakal. "She is and it's just as well. The Black Nova people want you, and by association me. They probably don't care all that much about Miko, other than her surviving the destruction of their ship."

"But now she's all alone."

"Something tells me Miko Steiger will be alright. She's the kind who travels light and has that rare ability to dance around raindrops without getting wet."

"That sounded almost like admiration, Mister Lorenzo, or rather, Mister Decker." Sakal finally returned his smile.

"I suppose I do admire her in a way." He shrugged, feeling slightly self-conscious at being so transparent in front of her.

"For what it's worth, I think she admires you as well."

"Is that the neuroscientist speaking?"

"No, merely the woman."

"Can we avoid mentioning Miko once we reach Caledonia?" He asked after a moment of outright embarrassment.

"Why?"

"My partner — work partner, you understand — doesn't much like Miko, so it'll be better if we didn't."

Sakal's delighted laughter caught him by surprise. "Oh dear, I can see that you're a man with a dilemma. Very well, I won't say a thing about the matter from this point on."

Lee's arrival saved Decker from having to answer.

"The Black Nova folks are becoming incredibly tiresome about you and Doctor Sakal," she said, settling on a chair with unfeigned weariness. "That asshole Charko has even threatened to have his head office contact Constabulary HQ and complain about my stonewalling their efforts to investigate *Altair Nova*'s loss."

"You don't sound terribly worried, Inspector."

"I'm not, though I'd like to choke the smarmy imbecile with my bare hands. No, the reason I'm here is not for a shoulder to cry on but to tell you that a ship headed for Caledonia is going to dock in two days. She's a liner belonging to White Star and left her last port of call with empty cabins. Since White Star's owned by a ComCorp competitor, you should be okay."

"In theory. Thank you, Inspector."

"De nada." She waved away his thanks. "I took the liberty of using the credit line Yann provided to make reservations in your name. The sooner you and Doctor Sakal get out of my hair, the better. No offense."

"None was taken." He gave her a wry smile. "I'm grateful for everything you've done."

"I'm sure your lot would do the same for one of us. Now if you'll excuse me, I'm going to process arrest warrants for Jack Lorenzo and Elyce Sakal, which I will share with my dear friend Phil Charko."

"Oh?" Decker cocked an amused eyebrow. "On what charges?"

"Suspicion of endangering space traffic. That shouldn't concern Zack Decker and Lydia Nerise, however."

"And what will happen with Lorenzo and Sakal once we're gone?"

Lee shrugged. "I'll figure something out. You'll have to stay here until it's time to board, but one of my people will make sure to bring you three meals a day."

"Can you let me know once Steiger's left? I kind of worry about her."

"Don't. We've taken her to the docking ring through the maintenance galleries, and she'll go aboard at the last minute. That'll keep Charko and his minions from interfering with her departure."

"Good. We really owe you, Inspector."

"I didn't have much choice, did I?"

"Perhaps, but your cooperation has been comprehensive and cheerful, and I'll be mentioning it in my report."

She gave him a wan smile. "Where would we be if the Fleet and the Constabulary can't work together?"

"Overrun by bad guys."

*

Two days later, a couple, man and woman, bearing only a very vague resemblance to Jack Lorenzo and Elyce Sakal walked down the gangway tube connecting the White Star passenger liner *Homeric* to the docking ring.

They had bypassed the usual exit controls, entering the secure area unnoticed via one of the station's maintenance corridors, thereby evading the surveillance Charko had put on all departing ships.

The purser at the head of the ramp took their identification chips and scanned them.

"Major Decker and Sera Nerise," he said, looking at each in turn. "Welcome aboard *Homeric*. I hope you'll have a pleasant journey with us. Your cabin is number twelve-twenty, two decks down. You can take the stairs to my left."

"Thank you," Zack replied with a smile.

Fortunately, the berth reserved by Inspector Lee had a pair of bunks instead of a single bed large enough for two. However, it would still be somewhat awkward sharing such a confined space with Sakal for the duration of the trip since, for some reason, Elyce Sakal triggered Zack's protective instincts rather than his inner Lothario.

Homeric undocked two hours later, leaving Dordogne and Phil Charko's Black Nova goons far behind. By the time they left their cabin for breakfast the next morning the liner had gone FTL on its first jump, headed towards the core.

*

"What will happen to me when we get there?"

Sakal twirled her empty coffee cup around with nervous fingers, eyes focused on something only her mind could see. Decker had been expecting the question for days, but it only came now, near the end of their trip, hours before *Homeric* dropped out of FTL on her final approach to Caledonia.

They were alone in a corner of the second-class lounge, most of their fellow passengers off to enjoy a last bit of entertainment before docking.

"You and I will be doing a lot of talking, Elyce. They'll want to know what happened on Troy since the last status report before the attack, and everything after that until the moment we left Dordogne. I'll be telling them about my actions since leaving Caledonia all these months ago."

"So I'll have to tell them that my research actually bore fruit?"

He nodded. "Yes, you will. They're going to be very curious about the late Sister Anca and her evolution."

"Will you be telling them about everything that happened aboard *Altair Nova*, about how you killed Anca and destroyed the ship?"

"I'll be telling them the truth, the whole truth and nothing but. It comes with the territory."

"And once I've told them everything? Will they expect me to resume my work under Fleet supervision?"

Decker shrugged. "Search me. They were quick to wipe out any trace of it six years ago. After hearing that some rather horrible people were about to use an enhanced Sister of the Void for a nefarious purpose that involved some sort of mind meddling, they might decide the risks are too high. Besides, finding another Anca might prove to be difficult. I'm sure her Order has become more vigilant since she fled the cloister."

"I was also close to developing a means of detecting wild talents who don't even know they have the gift, to eliminate our reliance on apostate sisters."

"Have you ever heard the tale of the sorcerer's apprentice?"

She nodded. "You're saying that we might not be ready for some things."

Decker tapped the side of his nose with a raised index finger. "Thinking about what Sister Anca might have done for those nasty people gives me the willies. Our minds are the last actual places of privacy left nowadays. Surrendering that privacy, be it to governments or private interests would be a step too far. Most people can't sense an empath's touch, but I'm here to tell you that it feels like a horrible violation, like a voyeur caressing your soul against your will."

"So you have no regrets about killing Anca?"

"None whatsoever." He drained the rest of his coffee. "If the Fleet asks you to take up your research again, tell them to jump into the nearest black hole."

Her eyes came up and met his. "That would probably be for the best, though part of me doesn't want to forget that I actually found the loci of the empathic talent and was able to help Anca enhance it. Not to mention that I mapped your reaction to Anca's touch, a first in human history. Some would say that makes me a contender for the Nobel Prize in neuroscience. Progressing the abilities of the human mind has been a holy grail for centuries."

"Some progress comes at too great a cost. Imagine a universe where some have the ability to directly influence the minds of others through extrasensory means. Imagine what kind of society that would lead to."

Sakal sighed. "I know. Still, it's a shame. Do you think the Fleet will pressure me to continue?"

"After I tell them my part of the story? I sure as hell hope not." He climbed to his feet. "Shall we take a stroll around the ship? I feel the urge to stretch my legs."

All too soon, the transition warning sounded, and they returned to their cabin. Once the emergence nausea had passed, Decker looked up the estimated time to Caledonia orbit, wondering whether he should send a message to warn Yang. The Black Gang's chief of staff would no doubt be keeping an eye on *Homeric*'s arrival, but it wouldn't hurt to confirm that he and Sakal were still aboard.

"I'm going to avail myself of their communications facilities," he told her, "and make sure we have someone waiting for us. Stay here while I'm gone, please."

He headed down to the passenger services center, where he could access the ship's radio for a fee, intending to send a brief text message to the anonymous address used by Naval Intelligence.

On the way back, he picked up a pair of tea bulbs and some pastries, figuring that Elyce wouldn't mind a snack. But when he entered their quarters, she had vanished.

He barely had time to put the food down when the cabin door opened without warning. Expecting Elyce, he turned to scold her for wandering off and came face-to-face with two men pointing needlers at his midriff.

Out of reflex, Decker reached for the gun provided by Lieutenant Marritt, to replace his lost Shrehari blaster, but the larger of the two shook his head.

"Don't. You're not fast enough."

"What do you want?"

"I thought that was obvious, Mister Lorenzo. We've come for you and Doctor Elyce Sakal."

"Then you have the wrong cabin. My name is not Lorenzo, and I don't know any Doctor Sakal."

"Please." The man chuckled. "We already have the doctor in our custody. Now it's your turn."

"My turn for what?"

"To decide whether you wish to live or die. Although our employers would rather have you alive, they won't be overly annoyed if we have to kill you, Mister Lorenzo."

Decker's eyes went from one to the other while he tried to calculate his odds in the confined space.

"For the last time," he said, "my name is not Lorenzo. I'm Major Zack Decker, Commonwealth Marine Corps.

And if you detained my wife Lydia under the absurd pretense that she's this Sakal person, you'd better release her before this gets out of hand. There's no place aboard for you to run and hide. Besides, Fleet officials are meeting us upon docking, so you can be sure our absence will be noted, and quickly traced back to you. The Corps doesn't screw around."

The men glanced at each other with a frown of uncertainty, put off balance by Zack's reaction, and the barrels of their weapons wavered. It was all he needed.

He rammed the nearest goon with his shoulder, sending him to slam his skull against the bulkhead while his hands sought out the second one's gun. He managed to push it away a fraction of a second before a hail of shards turned him into a pincushion, then clamped down hard on his wrist and yanked downward. His elbow connected with the man's nose, and he heard an audible crunch.

The goon staggered, then dropped to his knees, hands going to his face. Decker wrenched the needler away from him, and then struck his temple with a closed fist. He fell over, out cold. The other one tried to climb back to his feet but stopped when Decker shoved the gun's barrel into his mouth.

"Your turn, asshole. Do you want to live or die?"

"Live," he mumbled around the weapon.

Decker stepped back so he could cover both of them.

"Who are you morons? Black Nova? ComCorp? Freelancers hired by Phil Charko? Or better yet, *Sécurité Spéciale*?"

There was a spark of recognition in the man's eyes at the final name.

"*Sécurité Spéciale*, eh? Here's a piece of advice. Find another line of business. You stink on ice. Now, get this into your tiny brains, I am not Lorenzo and my wife is not Sakal. I am, however, prepared to kill you and claim legitimate self-defense. So to repeat my question, do you want to live or die?"

"Live."

"Then tell me where my wife is."

"She's in our cabin. Number ten-sixteen. We haven't harmed her."

Decker stepped over to the screen embedded in the bulkhead and touched the controls.

A voice came on seconds later. "This is passenger services, how may I help you, Major Decker?"

"I've detained two men who tried to assault me. Could you please send a security team to my cabin and take them in charge?"

Stunned silence followed Zack's declaration, then the voice stammered, "Immediately, Major."

"One more thing," he said. "These individuals tell me they've kidnapped my wife Lydia and are holding her in cabin ten-sixteen. Please send someone to fetch her."

"Of course, sir. Right away."

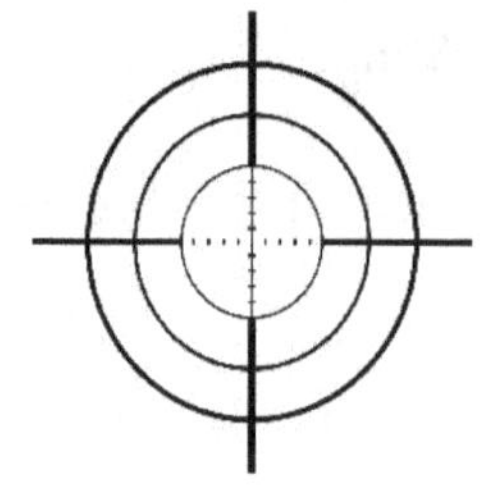

— FORTY —

Homeric's captain had tripped over himself with apologies once the two goons had been locked in the brig and Sakal freed. He readily accepted Decker's explanation of mistaken identity and radioed ahead to warn the orbital station's Constabulary detachment that they had a pair of would-be assassins to collect.

Decker and Sakal spent their last night on board as his guests and were invited to watch the docking maneuvers from the ship's bridge the next day. With a final apology still ringing in their ears, they walked down the gangway tube and straight into the arms of a one-woman reception committee.

"The prodigal son returns," Hera Talyn said, an unusually warm smile on her face.

Instead of replying, Decker took her in a bear hug and squeezed.

"Hey big boy," she protested, "not so hard. I'm a woman, not a feral Marine's chew toy."

He released Talyn but kept his eyes on hers. "I assume that you're not here to arrest me for being absent without authority?"

She shook her head. "Of course not." Then, turning to Sakal, she said, "I'd better introduce myself since Mister Lunkhead here seems to have forgotten he's a gentleman as well as an officer. I'm Hera Talyn, Zack's partner. I assume you're Elyce Sakal. Welcome back from the dead."

Sakal's face lit up with a shy smile. "Thank you."

"You have a ride to take us down, right?" Decker asked. "The boss will want to have us debriefed as soon as possible."

"I have a ride, and I'll be debriefing you," she winked at him, "in more ways than one."

Decker grinned. "It's good to be home. Any orders when it comes to the doctor?"

"The same as yours," Talyn replied, "but a different debriefer. You're both quarantined until we sort out exactly what happened."

She led them through maintenance corridors to an adjoining port that held not a massive starship but a shuttlecraft with naval markings. Two uniformed spacers stood on either side of the gangway tube's entrance.

"Hah!" Decker barked out a laugh. "I knew there would be an arrest somewhere along the way."

Talyn backhanded him on the arm. "Grow up. You know we always post sentries when we dock at civilian stations. What did you think? That I'd fly up here by myself? This is the HQ duty shuttle. The boss managed to snag it for us ahead of a bunch of pissed-off admirals by invoking Commonwealth security."

"Right. We need to be quarantined until the brass can figure out what to do next." Neither of the sentries tried to stop them when they entered the tube. Both merely followed in their footsteps. A few minutes later, the shuttle lit its thrusters and pulled away from the massive spindle shape, headed for the surface.

Upon landing, a pair of very polite but very firm noncoms wearing intelligence insignia led Elyce Sakal away. Hera took him down into the bowels of the HQ building, where the Special Operations Section had its offices. When he entered the bullpen, Commander Manfred Yang looked up from his desk and scowled.

"Major Decker. At last. Do you know how many weeks you've been absent without authority? And what the penalties can be?"

"It's good to see you too, Commander. And how have you been while I've single-handedly kept the Commonwealth safe from all enemies, alien and domestic?"

"I've been sweeping away the debris you always leave in your wake. I hope you have a good story to tell before I make my recommendations to the boss concerning your future."

"I have an excellent story to tell, and when I'm done, you're going to forget about laying charges and ensure the record shows I was on a mission all the time, meaning my furlough entitlement is restored and my expenses are reimbursed."

Yang raised a skeptical eyebrow. "Your story's that good, eh?" He turned to Talyn. "I don't know why the Captain chose you to debrief him, but you'd better be on it. He expects a preliminary report by close of business today."

"He chose me because I have ways of drawing things from Zack that no one else can." She winked at Yang. "Not that you'd know anything about it. Room three?"

"Room three. Everything's set up the way you asked."

Four hours later, with one coffee break, Decker wrapped up the tale and sat back, exhausted.

"I could murder a bottle of Shrehari Ale right now," he said. "Other than one little toast to the dead, it's been months since I touched booze, and even longer since I had some of the good stuff."

She gave him a startled look. "You've gone quasi-teetotal on me? Who are you and where's my Zack of the enormous appetites?"

"Remember the part I told you about having my ass kicked by that cage fighting monster on Kilia? It's the kind of thing that makes a middle-aged guy think carefully about his bad habits. It paid off aboard *Homeric*. Those two gorillas didn't know what hit 'em. But now that I'm home, it's time to break my fast, so to speak."

"I can help with that." She reached into the cabinet on her side of the table and pulled out a twisted greenish bottle. "Welcome home, honey."

Zack paused to admire the vintage inscribed on the label, then pulled off the cap before taking a long, appreciative sip.

"I missed you," he said.

"I missed you too," Talyn replied.

He snorted. "I was talking to the ale, but sure, I could have used your powers of evil to help out."

"Prick."

"What? You expected me to change?"

"No, but I'm glad you're back. Judging by the amount of havoc you created, you still need adult supervision. However, I think Captain Ulrich will forgive everything, even the destruction of the *Altair Nova*, which by the way has caused a bit of a stir. Black Nova Lines are looking for the three survivors who mysteriously vanished. Speaking of which, how is Miko Steiger?"

"Passable." He took another sip. "Not up to your standards, of course, but I made do."

"I'm sure you did," she replied with a dry tone. "You have a suite in the officers' accommodation block, and I've had your stuff taken out of storage. Why don't you get cleaned up while I prepare the preliminary report? Be back here at sixteen hundred, in uniform."

"Aye, aye, Commander, sir." He tossed off a mock salute. "What happens to Doctor Sakal?"

"I'm afraid that after the boss reads your report on her work, she'll vanish down the memory hole again."

"What?"

"They'll give her a new identity and a new life, something that doesn't involve turning sociopathic Sisters of the Void into super-empaths. Troy Station remains on the taboo list for the rest of eternity, and your romp through the Rim and the Protectorate will probably be just as highly classified. Keep in mind that the *Sécurité Spéciale* won't stop looking for her. The two specimens you beat up aboard the liner will eventually report back to their superiors."

"It makes sense, I guess. Provided no one gets the idea of resurrecting her research. What about Hal?"

"The boss will probably approve of your recalling him back to active service, and will have him listed as fallen in the line of duty, under classified circumstances. Which is pretty much how he would have dealt with your death, had you walked into a stray plasma round."

"Can we at least put Hal up for an award? I'll write the citation in the proper spook format myself."

"I don't see why not. Write it up. The boss owes you. We didn't know about half of what's occurring beyond the Rim. That alone is worth pestering the Chief for a signature on the submission to the awards committee."

A crooked grin appeared on Zack's face. "Damn right he owes me. After all, what would you fine intelligence people do without a guy like me to run the really hard missions?

"Hard missions, eh?" She cocked an eyebrow. "Keep that thought for after our chat with the Captain. I have one in mind for you. After all, it's been a while."

A knowing leer transformed his expression. "I'll have you howling in no time."

"And make me see stars? Promises, promises."

"Sweetheart, I always keep my promises."

About the Author

Eric Thomson is the pen name of a retired Canadian soldier with thirty-one years of service, both in the Regular Army and the Army Reserve. He spent his Regular Army career in the Infantry and his Reserve service in the Armoured Corps.

Eric has been a voracious reader of science fiction, military fiction, and history all his life. Several years ago, he put fingers to keyboard and started writing his own military sci-fi, with a definite space opera slant, using many of his own experiences as a soldier for inspiration.

When he's not writing fiction, Eric indulges in his other passions: photography, hiking, and scuba diving, all of which he shares with his wife.

Join Eric Thomson at http://www.thomsonfiction.ca/ Where you'll find news about upcoming books and more information about the universe in which his heroes fight for humanity's survival.

Read his blog at:
https://ericthomsonblog.wordpress.com

Or visit him on his Amazon Author's page.

If you enjoyed this book, please consider leaving a review on Goodreads, or with your favorite online retailer to help others discover it.

Also by Eric Thomson

Siobhan Dunmoore

No Honor in Death (Siobhan Dunmoore Book 1)
The Path of Duty (Siobhan Dunmoore Book 2)
Like Stars in Heaven (Siobhan Dunmoore Book 3)
Victory's Bright Dawn (Siobhan Dunmoore Book 4)
Without Mercy (Siobhan Dunmoore Book 5)

Decker's War

Death Comes But Once (Decker's War Book 1)
Cold Comfort (Decker's War Book 2)
Fatal Blade (Decker's War Book 3)
Howling Stars (Decker's War Book 4)
Black Sword (Decker's War Book 5)
No Remorse (Decker's War Book 6)
Hard Strike (Decker's War Book 7)

Quis Custodiet

The Warrior's Knife (Quis Custodiet No 1)

Ashes of Empire

Imperial Sunset (Ashes of Empire #1)